A Merry Band
of Murderers

A Merry Band of Murderers

An original mystery anthology
of songs and stories

Edited by
Claudia Bishop and Don Bruns

Poisoned Pen Press

Poisoned Pen Press
6962 E. First Ave., Ste. 103
Scottsdale, AZ 85251
www.poisonedpenpress.com
info@poisonedpenpress.com

Printed in the United States of America

For Bob and Linda
who sat patiently through it all

The Program

Act I

Your Ticket, Please	Claudia Bishop
Liner Notes	Don Bruns
A Word From the Producer	Robert Rosenwald

Act II

File Under Jazz	Bill Moody
Shuffle Off This Mortal Coil	Rupert Holmes
If I Had Wings	Rhys Bowen
Something Out There	John Lescroart
It's Too Late to Cry	Jim Fusilli
Land of the Flowers	Mary Anna Evans
Bad for His Image	Nathan Walpow
The Ferryman's Beautiful Daughter	Peter Robinson
The Fan	Jeffery Deaver
The Melancholy Danish	Claudia Bishop
Cayo Hueso Combo	Tom Corcoran
Long Black Veil	Val McDermid
Courage	Don Bruns

Curtain Call

Song Credits
The Performers

Act I

Your Ticket, Please...

…and welcome to the first-ever, original mystery anthology and concert, *A Merry Band of Murderers*. We've done all we can to give this book the feel of a terrific performance. You'll find thirteen provocative interviews with the authors, thirteen biographic sketches, and thirteen stories to knock you flat.

And then, of course, there's the music.

The CD that accompanies *A Merry Band of Murderers* is filled with the original songs and compositions that form an integral part of the short stories.

The idea for this collection occurred at a (rather bibulous) publication party at the mystery convention Sleuthfest two years ago. The band next door was indulging in a rollicking version of "Bad Moon Rising."

"You know," I mused to Don Bruns, "that song would make a pretty good short story. It'd be pretty neat, don't you think? Short stories from songs. Songs from short stories."

Don smacked his glass of red wine down and shouted, "You're right! It would! Let's do it!"

I said I hadn't seen any mystery novels by Creedence Clearwater lately.

Don, charmer that he is, refilled my wine glass, ignored the lame witticism, and said helpfully: "Do you drink piña coladas?"

"I'll stick to wine, thanks."

Don rolled his eyes.

The penny dropped. "Oh!" I said. "You mean Rupert Holmes. The mystery novelist, musician, playwright. And the guy who wrote 'Do You Like Pina Coladas?'"

"And there're more musicians who write. Bill Moody. Jeff Deaver. John Lescroart. Peter Robinson."

Rhys Bowen was nearby: "Jim Fusilli, Val McDermid," she chimed in, "and, um" She cleared her throat modestly. "Me."

"Not to mention," Don cleared his throat less modestly, "me, of course."

Me, too, come to think of it.

Now this was exciting. "So you're talking about mystery short stories revolving around songs? Or maybe songs revolving around mystery stories? You're talking an anthology? A CD? What?"

"Both!" Don said.

"Yikes," I said. "I don't know if you know this—(this is my third excursion into editing anthologies)—but anthologies pay zero up front and pay out even less. You think we're going to get people like that for seventy-five dollars for an original song and an original story? And find a publisher to take it on? And someone to produce the CD?"

"You bet we will," Don said.

Well, we did.

Actually, Don did most of the recruiting. (Rhys Bowen lent a hand with one or two.) We had one requirement: that the mystery writer had been paid to sing or play in a band. "We'll find eight writers," I thought to myself, "nine, in a pinch."

But we found enough to fill two anthologies. I was astonished at the caliber of the mystery writers who sang, composed, and performed for a living. I was even more astonished that they agreed to contribute to *A Merry Band of Murderers* for the paltry sum we were able to afford. Eventually I put it down to the fact that all of us had a wonderful time putting the songs and stories together.

In this collection you'll find not only all of the writers we'd wished for at that long-ago cocktail party, but two talented newcomers, Nathan Walpow and Mary Anna Evans. The stories span almost all of the sub-genres found in mystery today, from classic Christie to suspense to thriller to noir. (There is even a gem of a story in the humorous noir tradition. How many anthologies can boast of that?) The music offers just as generous a spread: you'll find ballads, jazz, rock and roll, folk, and even a tip of the hat to Gilbert and Sullivan.

Then Don got the publisher. He stuck with it long after I got discouraged. The bigger houses were all in the middle of profit problems. They weren't about to take on an untried project like this one. But eventually he presented the idea to Robert Rosenwald at Poisoned Pen Press, who agreed to take us on. And he coaxed Blackstone Audio Books into producing the *Merry Band* CD, in exchange for rights to the audio book.

You have the result of this improbable project in your hands: The CD. The hardcover. The performance.

A Merry Band of Murderers offers you a wonderful array of talent, both literary and musical. I hope you enjoy reading and listening as much as we have.

Claudia Bishop
West Palm Beach, Fla.
2006

Liner Notes

I collect paintings from *twice-gifted* artists. *Twice-gifted.* That's the buzzword that the publishing industry gives to actors and singers who also paint. People like Tony Bennett, Charles Bronson, James Cagney, Donna Summers, Myles Davis and dozens of others have expressed their creative talents in painting as well as their professional endeavors. Many writers are no less talented.

Twice-gifted writers include Stephen King, Dave Barry, Mitch Album, Amy Tan and the rest of the musicians who make up the rag-tag band The Rock Bottom Remainders.

Well, we've found our own group of writers who are *twice-gifted* as well. Musicians all, many before they wrote a mystery, these talented writers have not only penned some outstanding short stories, but they've complemented the stories with their own songs. And to take it a step further, in many cases they've performed their own songs.

If you ever wanted to get into a mystery writer's head and find out a little more about what makes that devious mind create the thrilling, chilling tales we all love, now is your opportunity. Listen to their songs, then read their stories and see how it all comes together.

We may not win a Grammy with our effort (although there are some songs on this CD that just might qualify), but I think you'll agree that every author in *A Merry Band of Murderers* is truly *twice-gifted*. Not only will you be remembering the sometimes chilling, sometimes mysterious, sometimes humorous plots to their stories, but you'll be humming the tunes! Twice the pleasure. Maybe we're on to something.

Don Bruns
Sarasota, Fla.
2006

A Word From the Producer

Why did Poisoned Pen Press publish *A Merry Band of Murderers*? That's a damn good question since we don't publish anthologies. Part of the answer lies in the fact that I'm a Gemini and can't ever leave well enough alone. Part of it lies in my early discussions with Claudia and Don, who were so excited by the concept and the authors they had lined up for it. Part of it lies in my love of music—jazz and blues especially, but all music in all forms—and the appeal of publishing a book-CD package was overwhelming. And finally I must admit that the opportunity to publish works by such an incredible group of talented writers was irresistible.

So, good reader, enjoy. And don't hesitate to let me know what you think—good or bad, I'd love to hear it.

Robert Rosenwald
Publisher and President
Poisoned Pen Press
robert@poisonedpenpress.com

Act II

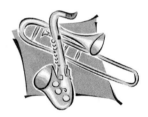

*Bill Moody's fiction is linked to music in a way
unique to him and his work. The composition
written for "File Under Jazz" is a notable part of
the* Merry Band *CD. You may want to listen to
it while you read the story. "File Under Jazz" is
a noir story, and one of Bill's best. The opening
paragraph is particularly fine.*

File Under Jazz

Bill Moody

"Man, there it is again," Ray says, reaching for the knob and
turning up the volume. "That same damn song."

They're in Lloyd's car, heading down the 405 freeway toward
Santa Monica, mired in lunch hour traffic. His big calloused
bass player hands on the wheel, Lloyd listens for a minute and
shrugs. "It's a minor blues. What's the big deal?"

"The big deal," Ray says, "is I know I've heard it before but I
can't figure out who it is." Ray shrugs. "You know how I am."

Lloyd glances over at Ray. "Yeah, I do. Mr. obsessive-compul-
sive. You won't be happy till you know what the tune is, who's
playing, when it was recorded and—"

"Yeah, yeah," Ray says.

"So call the station," Lloyd says.

Ray listens some more, but it's only the last few bars. The
song ends and they're suddenly blasted by Miles Davis, live at the
Blackhawk. He lowers the volume and says, "Maybe I will."

He pats his pocket for his cell phone, but remembers he'd
left it charging at home. He looks out the window. They'd only
moved a few car lengths. The Wiltshire Boulevard exit looms
mockingly just ahead.

"Think we'll make it," he says to Lloyd.

"Yeah, we're early," Lloyd says, glancing at his watch.

They're scheduled to hit at one. Some kind of fundraiser scholarship thing and the organizer is a jazz fan, so it shouldn't be too dumb. The weird part is the location.

"You ever played at a cemetery before?" he asks Lloyd.

Lloyd smiles and lights a cigarette. "No, this is a new one for me."

"Spooky, man," Ray says.

"Hey," Lloyd says, "at least it's not at night."

They find the cemetery and drive in the gates, passing one funeral procession of cars, parked along the curb. They drive on, around a long curve to an open area. On a concrete slab, a canopy has been set up and folding chairs arranged in a half circle.

"There we go," Lloyd says, parking his van as close to the tent-like covering as possible. There are a few people milling around already and Ray sees a large color photograph of a young girl displayed on an easel near the chairs.

They unload Lloyd's bass and Ray's electronic keyboard and amp and begin setting up. A maintenance man appears with a long orange cord and power strip and shows them where to plug in. Ray gets everything connected, playing a little, testing the sound when the drummer arrives, rolling his drums over to join the setup. Ray doesn't know him, but Lloyd says he plays good. By quarter to one, they're ready.

It is weird, Ray thinks, looking around at the expanse of green lawn, the tombstones, monuments, as more people arrive. He takes a short walk, smokes a cigarette, idly looking at the inscriptions on some of the more prominent grave markers. Others are just small plaques in the ground, many overgrown where the grass needs cutting, but one catches his eye.

The grass is neatly trimmed around it and the plaque is polished. Ray bends down, reads the name. Louis B. Harris 1935-1967. Somebody misses you, Ray thinks. He straightens up and turns back toward where they'd set up, the strains of that minor blues running through his mind.

More people have arrived now, a fairly respectable crowd. Ray is surprised. He sits at the keyboard and waits for the host to remind everybody why they're here and introduce the trio. Some polite applause follows. Ray nods to Lloyd and, thinking of the little girl, begins with "Sweet and Lovely." He hears Lloyd laugh and say, "Better not play 'Body and Soul' here." Ray hears the drummer chuckle, but the idea sends a chill through Ray.

Later, at home, the tune still haunting him, Ray calls the jazz station. He knows he won't be right until he learns the title, and who is playing it. It happens like that every once in awhile with Ray. He hears a few bars of something and can't stop till he knows the tune, who recorded it, whatever information he can find.

"KJAZ," the DJ on air answers.

"Yeah," Ray says. "You played something early this afternoon. I only heard the end but I was wondering if you remember what it was. Saxophone, some minor blues line."

"I came on at four, man, so you'd have to call back tomorrow and talk to Chuck. He would have been on then. He's on at noon every day."

"Right," Ray says. "Thanks."

He almost counted down the time the next day waiting to call.

"KJAZ."

"Hey, are you Mark?"

"Yeah, what can I do for you?"

Ray explained.

"Geez, man, I play a lot of things in four hours. I'd have to check the playlist for yesterday."

"Can you do that? It's important."

Ray heard him sigh over the music playing on the studio monitor. "Yeah, I guess. Give me a half hour and call back."

"Thanks," Ray says. He turns on the news but doesn't really focus. He keeps checking his watch then calls again at 2:45.

"KJAZ."

"Hi, I'm the guy that called earlier about the tune you played yesterday."

"Oh yeah. Hang on. I can hardly read my own writing. Okay, it's called 'D Minor Hues.' Done in the sixties sometime I'd guess. Lou Harris, alto player. Don't know what happened to him. Not much info on the LP. Not even the personnel. Just says unidentified piano, bass, and drums."

"Did you say Lou Harris?" Ray feels a chill again, thinking of the grave marker. Had to be a different guy. There must have been scores of guys named Lou Harris in L.A.

"Yeah. Hey, I gotta go, man. Going live in a few seconds."

"Thanks," Ray says but the guy had already hung up.

Lou Harris. Imagine, recording an LP and not even getting your name on the record. Ray thinks he's heard the name but isn't sure. He snaps his fingers then, remembers somebody who would know.

Dean Earl is just finishing with a student when Ray looks in. A tall gangly kid with thick glasses, nodding to Ray as he leaves. Dean is short with a thick mustache, looking relaxed in a cardigan sweater, slacks and polished loafers. Nearly seventy, he'd always reminded Ray of the guy who played George Jefferson on television. Dean spins around on the piano stool. "Hey," Dean says, holding out his hand. "You been being a stranger. Got a lot of gigs I hope."

"I'm making it," Ray says, slapping Dean's upturned palm. "Got a few minutes?"

"Yeah." Dean glances at his watch. "Nobody till four now. What brings you by?"

"You remember an alto player named Lou Harris? I heard something on the radio yesterday, a minor blues line from an album he did."

Dean's face creases into a frown. "Damn, Lou Harris. Must have been an old one. Lou died long time ago. Yeah, I know who he is. Made a few gigs with him."

"Really?" Ray sits down and looks at Dean. "You remember the tune? The DJ says it was called 'D Minor Hues.'"

"Yeah, that's it," Dean says, running his hands through his fuzzy white hair. He hums something, swivels back toward the piano, his fingers searching out the notes.

"Yeah, that's almost it," Ray says.

"Should have been called 'Weird Blues,'" Dean says.

"What do you mean?"

"Bad vibes from that tune. Last thing Lou wrote before he died."

"How did he die?"

Dean looks up at Ray and shakes his head. "Nobody is really sure who did it, but he was shot."

"Jesus," Ray says, feeling a shiver. "Murdered? What happened?"

"Long time ago, man. We were playing this little club in Hollywood, near Shelly's Manne Hole. We finished the set. Yeah, I remember now. That was the last tune we played." Dean shakes his head slowly. "Lou put his horn on the piano, went out the door behind the band stand to have a smoke in the alleyway. I was still talking to the bass player when we heard these two little pops." Dean raises his hand up like a gun, points his index finger. "Pop, pop! We ran out there and found Lou on the ground, blood pouring out of his stomach. We called the cops but he was gone by the time the ambulance came. They kept us there half the night, questioning everybody."

"They never caught who did it?"

"Nope. Lou had a big eye for the ladies, but he had a wife too. There was one woman always hanging around. I think she was there that night but in all the confusion I'm not sure. Everybody thought it was a girlfriend, some woman he'd dropped. Like that gal who shot Lee Morgan at Slugs in New York. Remember that? They'd argued, she went home, came back and shot Lee right there." Dean laughs. "Imagine that, shot at Slugs. Anyway with Lou, I don't know. Police didn't try very hard. You know how that shit goes, at least then."

Ray nods. Hollywood or South Central Los Angeles. The sixties. The Watts riots still a fresh memory. "Were you on the recording? The DJ said the rhythm section was unidentified."

Dean nods and shakes his head. "They didn't keep very good records then, especially with some little company. No, he'd done that earlier, some little studio, small pressing. Didn't get much airplay or distribution though. Lou was never big. He could play, but lucky he got that one date."

Dean looks at Ray and frowns. "Why you so interested in Lou Harris? You on one of your missions again?"

"I don't know," Ray says. "I don't know."

But Ray did know. He had to track down that record. He goes online, does the Google thing, checks out Amazon, other sites that list old recordings, reissues, but nothing. Not a mention of Lou Harris anywhere. He calls around to used record stores he finds in the Yellow Pages, but except for a big place off Hollywood Boulevard, most don't carry much jazz.

"Blue Star," a guy says answering the phone.

"Hey, you carry any real old jazz LPs? I'm looking for a saxophonist named Lou Harris."

The guy just laughs. "Hey man, I got hundreds. Come in and look for yourself."

With rehearsals and another gig, it's a couple of days before he can make it. Blue Star is in what once must have been an office building. Old posters on the walls, bins of LPs, stacks of CDs on the floor and all in no apparent order. A monotonous rap band throbs from a sound system somewhere. At the front of the store, sitting at a high desk, is a burly bearded guy in thick glasses.

"Where's the jazz section?" Ray asks.

The guy points toward the back without looking up from the magazine in front of him. There are three rows of bins with a hand painted sign on a stick that says *Jazz*. Ray sighs and flips through them, scanning titles and names, some Ray never heard of, some bring back memories. In the H section he finds nothing. The last two bins are labeled *Misc. Jazz.*

Ray thumbs through each, stopping occasionally as he recognizes something. Finally, halfway through the second bin, his fingers stop as he stares at the cover. A young black man, in a blazer and turtleneck sweater, his arms crossed over an alto saxophone, a cigarette in his mouth, the smoke curling up around his eyes, looks at some point left of the camera. *Lou's Blues* is the title. On the back is a stick-on label in one corner with a penciled price of $2 and a notation that reads: *File Under Jazz.*

Ray slips the record out of the sleeve, handling it carefully. There are some scratch marks, but it's generally in good condition. There's scant information on the back. Another photo of Harris playing, the rhythm section in the background, but too blurred to recognize anybody. Not even a date—no personnel listing—just the titles of the songs, the record company logo, address but no liner notes. Track three is "D Minor Hues."

Ray slips the record back in the sleeve and turns to go and almost bumps into a woman standing close by. He hadn't even heard her come up.

She's late fifties, early sixties, but still an attractive woman. Slim, dark hair but her eyes hidden behind dark glasses. Her clothes are neat but inexpensive. "Are you going to buy that?" she asks, moving over closer to Ray.

"Yeah, why?" Ray asks, the album clutched in his hand almost protectively.

"I used to know him," she says, pointing at the cover photo. "The jazz station played something from it the other day. I thought I'd try to find it. I've been to half a dozen stores."

"Me too," Ray says. "D Minor Hues.' That one?"

She takes off the glasses, closes her eyes for a moment. "Yes, that's the one." She pauses, opens her eyes and looks right at Ray. "He wrote it for me." She hums the tune and Ray feels the hair on the back of his neck stiffen.

They both grimace as the rap recording switches to some heavy metal thing.

"Let's get out of here," Ray says, almost having to shout over the music.

They find a coffee place on Hollywood Boulevard and sit at an outside table. Ray buys them both coffee but takes the album with him when he goes inside. He comes back with the coffee. The woman has taken off the dark glasses and is facing the street, watching the traffic, the people walking by.

Ray sets the coffee down and puts the album on the table. "So how well did you know Lou Harris?" Ray asks, sitting down.

She turns toward him and sips the coffee. "Very well. We were...together for a few months." She glances at the album, puts her hand out. "May I?"

Ray says, "Sure."

She picks it up and stares at the photo of Lou Harris. "Let me buy it from you." She reaches for her purse, a small, scuffed leather bag. "I'll give you twenty-five dollars."

Ray's eyes widen. "I can't do that. I only paid two dollars."

"I know, but it doesn't matter. Are you a collector or something? Is that why you bought it?"

Ray smiles. "No. Piano player. I was just intrigued by the tune. Something about it got to me and one thing led to another. It happens like that sometimes. It's like, I don't know, an obsession. I called the station, talked to the DJ, and my former teacher. He knew Lou as well."

She looks up sharply. "Really? Who?"

"Dean Earl," Ray says.

She nods and smiles. "I'm sorry. I'm Emily, Emily Parker."

"Ray Fuller." He doesn't know whether to shake hands or not, so he sips his coffee and reaches for his cigarettes. "Do you mind?"

"No, not at all."

Ray lights his cigarette, inhales and blows the smoke away from their table.

"Look," she says, "it would mean a lot to me to have this." She taps long, slender fingers on the album.

Ray studies her for a long moment. There's something missing, something she's not telling him, but he can't figure it out. "Tell you what," he says. "Let me make a tape and you can have it."

She reaches out and touches his hand. "Thank you. You're very kind."

Ray shrugs. "It's nothing. Really. I was only interested in the tune."

She smiles, more relaxed now. "It is a haunting tune, isn't it? That's what Lou called me. Haunting." She colors slightly then and sighs. "Sorry, I don't mean to sound foolish. It was a long time ago."

"How did you meet him?" Ray asks. He watches her, drawn to her in a way he can't explain.

"In a club. I was just bored, driving around and saw the sign that said Jazz. I walked in, heard him play and sat down, ordered a drink and stayed till closing. He came over once, told me it was brave of me, a white woman coming to a black club. I don't think it's there anymore. I suppose he was right though. The Watts riots hadn't been that long ago."

"And after that?"

"I went every night for the rest of the week. We spent a lot of time together and then he moved in with me until..." Her voice trails off.

"Until he...died."

"Yes—no, well before that." She closes her eyes again and for a moment is lost in the memory. She blinks then and looks at Ray. "He was murdered you know."

Ray leans back in his chair. "Yes, Dean told me. Did you know him too?"

She shakes her head. "I must have but I can't recall his face. Was he playing that night?"

"Yes," Ray says. "It was Dean who found him in the alley. It was never solved?"

"No," Emily says. She puts the dark glasses on again and looks away, watching a teenager roll by on a skateboard.

"Any ideas?"

"Maybe his wife was the cause," she says.

"His wife? Did you tell the police?"

"No, I couldn't. I just...left. I couldn't face it when I heard."

"But why?"

"It didn't matter. Lou was gone and the police weren't that interested. A black jazz musician, a former heroin user, shot in the alley behind a seedy club. Who would care?"

Ray stubs out his cigarette, drinks off the rest of his coffee and looks at Emily. "You," Ray says.

"It doesn't matter now. It's almost forty years ago."

Ray's mind is swirling with questions. He wants to know everything now, the whole story, but he holds back. "Yeah, I guess."

Emily glances at her watch. "So how do I contact you, for the album I mean."

Ray is jolted out of his musing. "Oh, give me a couple of days. I have to find someone with a turntable to record it. I don't have one." He takes out a pen and turns the coffee receipt over to write down her number.

"No," she says. "It's better if I call you."

"Whatever," Ray says, writing his number. "Or," he says, looking at her, "I'm playing Friday night, a solo gig in Santa Monica. Maybe you could come by? I can give it to you then."

She smiles, hesitates a moment. "Yes, that would be nice. I'd like that."

Ray tells her the name of the club. They both get to their feet. "Okay then. See you Friday. I start at eight."

"I look forward to it. Thank you for the coffee."

Ray watches her walk away till she's lost among other people.

Spooky, man, really spooky, Ray mumbles to himself.

At Bob Burns Friday night Ray is cruising through the first set when Emily Parker walks in. She takes a seat at one of the stools around the piano bar, orders a drink and smiles at Ray. The place is pretty full, people jostling for a place, most of the tables full.

He looks at Emily and goes into "D Minor Hues," sees her expression change, her eyes take on a faraway look, then settle on the album resting on top of the piano in front of Ray. He plays it slow, like the record. It's under his fingers now after two days of playing it over and over. He lets the last chord ring for a few moments and looks up. Several people are captivated, and applaud for the first time.

Emily smiles warmly at Ray and nods as he stands up. He slides the album across the piano to her and walks around till he's beside her. "Glad you could make it," he says. "It's all yours." He taps his finger on the album.

"So am I," she says. "That was lovely. It's how Lou might have played it."

He feels a surge of pleasure sweep over him. Now he knows almost everything. "Be right back," he says. "Gotta make a phone call."

Ray walks to the back and dials the pay phone by the restrooms.

"Hello."

"Dean, it's Ray Fuller."

"What's up, Ray. You caught me nodding off in front of the TV."

"The girlfriend of Lou Harris. Was her name Emily Parker?" Ray waits impatiently for Dean's answer, looking back toward the piano bar, but he can't see Emily.

"Man," Dean says, "so long ago, but, yeah, I think that's right. How did you—?"

"Thanks, Dean. I gotta go." Ray hangs up and walks quickly back to the bar, but Emily Parker is gone, and so is the record. In its place is a folded piece of paper propped on the keyboard, a note in neat, careful handwriting. Ray goes outside, looks up and down the street but there's no sign of Emily Parker. He thinks of checking the small parking lot but he doesn't know if she came by car.

He lights a cigarette and reads the note.

> *Ray*
>
> *I guess you've figured it out by now. Lou was going back to his wife and I couldn't allow that. It was the only way. Don't try to find me. I'll remember you though for your kindness.*
>
> *Emily*

Ray stands numbly, reading the note over several times. Of course it was her. Lou Harris wouldn't have gone outside by himself with Emily there. She must have gone out the front, circled around to the alley, come up to Lou, pleaded her case maybe one last time before she slipped the gun out of her purse, pushed it against Lou's chest, like she was going to kiss him and shot him instead. The two little pops Dean said he'd heard. She would have been gone before anybody came out. Was that how it went down?

Ray feels sick suddenly. His hand shakes, holding the note, realizing what he's done. He slips the note in his pocket and goes back inside and sits down at the piano. What should he do? Take the note to the police? How would he make anybody understand?

"Hey, piano man?" A husky guy at the bar with a blonde on his arm looks at Ray. "What was the name of that last tune you played?"

Ray looks up. "What?"

"That song you played, just before the break. What's the name of it?"

"D Minor Hues," Ray says.

And he plays it again.

Moody's Mystery Blues

D Minor Hues

Opus CVII

(Moody's Mystery Blues)

Form AABA

"Moody's Mystery Blues"

Bill says: "At a recording session some time ago, Bob Joslin said he'd written a new tune, a minor blues but he hadn't thought of a title. He played it down once and to me, it had sort of a haunting, mysterious quality about it. I told Bob, and he said, "Perfect. Let's call it 'Moody's Mystery Blues.'" Later, when we listened to the playback, I began to visualize things to go with the music. By the time the CD was released months later, I listened again and thought how it was the kind of tune that would drive me crazy if I didn't know what it was. I imagine that was the inspiration when I began "File Under Jazz," but as usual, I had no idea how the story was going to go until I got into it. I have to say, now that it's done, it's one of my favorites."

An Interview with Bill Moody

Where did you grow up?
Santa Monica, southern California.

Do you remember the first mystery novel you ever read?
I think it was one of the Richard S. Prather Shell Scott series.

What was the first piece of music you recall?
My mother was a pianist so there was always music in the house and she played daily. It was probably something classical.

Was yours a musically oriented household?
Yes.

Do you listen to music when you write?
Almost always. Usually solo piano or trios like Bill Evan or Keith Jarrett.

Has a musical work ever inspired a novel or short story?
My newest book, *Boplicity,* is one. The tune of the same name is from Miles Davis' "Birth of the Cool," combined with "All Blues" from Kind of Blue, also by Miles.

What is your favorite manmade sound?
Jazz piano.

What is your favorite sound in nature?
Sound of waves crashing on the beach.

If you had to choose three novels to take on a trip, what would you choose?

The Magus by John Fowles, *Immortality* by Milan Kundera, and anything by Elmore Leonard.

Your work is noted for the unique way in which music saturates the prose. How do you start a story?

I usually work and rework the first paragraph to set the mood, tone, etc. Once I have that, the rest seems to flow.

If you had a chance to invite any three people in the world to dinner, living or dead, who would they be?

Elmore Leonard, Duke Ellington, Jack Nicholson.

Which would you rather do—read or listen to a favorite CD?

Music and jazz are so much a part of my life, I'd probably opt for both, but a book I can take anywhere and get lost in it.

This immensely clever, classically structured
suspense tale is a sophisticated take on the Merry
Band premise. Author Rupert Holmes tells us:
"Never in my career have I had such a power-
ful sense of returning to the scene of my crime.
As it happens, my second mystery novel, **Swing***,*
published just last year by Random House, came
with (drum roll) a Companion Musical CD,
featuring the original big band and classical music
I composed for (and referenced in) my nineteen-
forties story. In my work, I've tried never to repeat
a trick, but when I learned who my partners in
crime were to be, and that this volume would
be published by the Poisoned Pen Press, elegant
domain of the scintillating Barbara Peters and
the admirable Rob Rosenwald...well, I was more
than happy to depart my swing band and enlist
in this merry band. Unlike the songs that accom-
panied my second novel, however, my musical
selection on this CD is not a clue, but rather the
hinge upon which both the creaking door of my
story, and its slightly unhinged narrator, swing."

Shuffle Off This Mortal Coil

Rupert Holmes

The pleasant young woman in Human Resources laid out the
situation in an almost endearingly embarrassed manner as she
picked her way down the awkward path toward my termination
with Vantagon Consultants. She touched upon certain incidents
from my eight-month stint as flittingly as the horsefly that had
alighted on the folder in her hands. The fly leapt into my ear
(emitting a low frequency that showed its obvious sympathy to

my cause) and catapulted itself onto the glazed doughnut that sat on a paper plate near her left elbow.

"*Unresponsive to questions,*" she read with soft regret, "uhm, and a week later—yes, here: *Comments do not correlate to discussions.* And I'm afraid again, only two days ago...*Nice guy, we think, but distant.*"

A friendly wave of my hand stopped her as I explained that it was quite all right. I'd recently bought an iPod music player, I informed her. She nodded slowly as I continued to bring her up to date, explaining that I'd obtained software allowing me to convert my extensive vintage record collection into digital files, and I was very much looking forward to transferring all my vinyl music to the iPod's hard drive. I'd certainly enjoyed my time at Vantagon Consultants, and had given the organization over half a year of my life, but this was an opportunity I simply couldn't turn down.

Realizing any attempt to persuade me to stay would be futile, she stood and offered her hand. I did not immediately rise, but patiently concluded, "Opportunities must be taken when they present themselves. Otherwise, one day you look up and, bang. Your life is over." *Now* I stood, forthrightly. She flinched in pleasant surprise as I flashed one of the winning smiles I'd mastered in the mirror as part of my stratagem for personal success.

✶✶✶✶

The days that followed were long but productive.

My studio apartment had evolved over the past year into a storage locker for my recordings. Other than my mattress and the hundreds of yellow legal pads that served as my daily journal, there was really little else occupying the space, except my collection.

Until I confronted the task at hand, I had not grasped exactly how many vinyl disks I'd accumulated since college, at garage sales, flea markets, even from incinerator rooms. My tastes were far-ranging. I've always been old for my years, and where music was concerned, I was very much an equal opportunity enjoyer.

The salesman at the Apple store had personally loaded several hundred hit songs onto the iPod's hard drive—"A little freebie for you," he'd said with a conspiratorial wink. His audio files hardly made a dent on the player's capacity. I now began the long process of transferring my own vintage albums. I kept the iPod's earbuds dangling around my neck like a string tie, permitting me just enough volume to monitor my work, but saving my first true playback moment for the day when I had finally completed the assignment. Sound bled from the earbuds, tiny whisperings of my first transferred song, its vocalist peeping away like the little human fly (at the end of that horror movie?) who finds himself trapped in a garden spider's web. I could just barely discern:

"I'm losing time. I'm losing touch. And when I lose my friends, I sure ain't losing much..."

Success. I high-fived my right hand with my left, a common practice I'm sure for those who spend a great deal of time alone.

****

Scientifically speaking, a full hard drive shouldn't weigh more than an empty one, but, eight days later, I swear I could feel the extra heft of that fully loaded iPod sitting deep in my pocket, my record collection crammed into a container smaller and more tightly packed than a deck of cards with an unbroken seal.

I decided to premiere the results of my efforts the next morning, and opted as the appropriate launch site the open esplanade outside the Mohawk Mall, only steps from the Apple outlet where I'd first made my commitment to the iPod.

It was fitting that an event of this importance was occurring on the kind of morning that seemed to expect a parade. Circus colors abounded in the ambitious sunlight. Flirty girls were wearing pennant yellow tops, blue canvas shorts, and cotton candy sweatshirts. Young men called out to them, thumping the sides of their lustrous red convertibles. Baby strollers and wheelchairs had green and white helium balloons tied to their handles. Everyone was laughing at a joke I had not yet been told. They were going to meet other people at different places. I wondered who they were and what they would say when they arrived. One girl near me was listening with interest to a tall boy in white pants and maroon-striped shirt. "He's a barber pole," I muttered softly to her as I passed by the two of them, but neither heard me.

I took my position near a wastebasket and, with a sense of ceremony, inserted the buds of the iPod as deeply and snugly as they would fit in my ears. In another time of my life, these would have been the earplugs my parents made me use when I was swimming at the chlorinated city pool. Wearing them had drawn derision from others, as had my nose plugs and eye goggles. But *these* earpieces symbolized just the opposite feeling.

I had arrived.

The iPod's manual had informed me that my player could select songs randomly, in what they called "Shuffle" mode, where each tune is arbitrarily chosen by the iPod itself. I felt that if I'd entrusted over a week of my life to the device (not to mention my entire music collection), I should go the full distance and let my iPod call all the shots.

My thumb applied the merest threat of pressure on the player's flywheel, and we had begun the new era.

I heard a delightful vamp, as if a band of hurdy-gurdies had been hijacked by giddy Jamaican pirates. I looked at the iPod's display. "I Can See Clearly Now" by Johnny Nash. The player had done me proud. What a sublimely fitting choice it had made, as the irresistibly optimistic music seemed to fill the scene before me, the bright reverberation in my ears creating the illusion that the song was being piped over public address speakers across the entire mall, even though I was the only one who could hear, who *knew*—other than, of course, my iPod.

It was a great title to choose because I *could* in fact see clearly now. With all the garble and gabble of the frivolous panorama swept away by my audio friend, I could now see how things really were. It was like that moment on a summer afternoon when you dove underwater at a noisy municipal swimming pool and the world instantly went away. In this case, however, it was the music, not the watery silence, that made the crowd inconsequential. They appeared to be inept dancers who hadn't learned the choreography of a memorable ballet, unaware that they were now performing on a stage of my observation, making fools of themselves in the process.

The barber pole boy was moving his stupid lolling jaw in an incompetent lip-synch to the lyrics in my ears. I couldn't hear the girl's reply, but if you removed her cooing, giggling voice, she no longer seemed so in awe of the boy. I noticed her eyes darting about, looking to see if anyone more interesting might be coming along. There was me, of course. But for the moment I was content to observe, and to be amused.

****

I began to live my life in tempo to the music, literally. I'd walk to the beat, never missing a step, and if I tripped on the curb, I'd make sure to land on the very next beat, or at least roll over and stand bolt upright on the beat after that. The people on the street (my "cast," as I had now come to think of them) were most impressed. They'd call the attention of their companions to my perfect rhythm, and point me out to others who hadn't noticed. I'd give them the "thumb's up" sign. It was great.

Less than a week had elapsed before I began to discern that my iPod was trying to communicate with me.

I'd been sitting on a bench in Holman Park, alongside what had once been its ice skating rink but which was now a circle of cracked concrete surrounded by a fence of rusted iron spears. Encouraged by the strains of Tchaikovsky's "Waltz of the Flowers," I ventured out upon the cement rink and pretended to skate on it myself. Passers-by appreciated this. Several applauded me. I applauded back, as Russian ballet artists do.

I returned to the bench, catching my breath, waiting to see what song the iPod would next randomly select for me. It was "I Got You, Babe" by Sonny and Cher. The song, like most of my collection, predated my birth. But I had watched Sonny and Cher's TV show as a boy—the one they did as a comeback attempt (after Cher had divorced Sonny, and after she'd failed on her own solo TV series). I knew about this because my father had made a point of telling me how Cher had left Sonny, the man who had guided her career, and married a druggy rock and roller. "She's no better than your mother," he'd said solemnly, adding, "the bitch."

Who was Cher's other husband? He'd had a band, but I couldn't remember its name. I knew it would drive me crazy. Something like the Doobie Brothers or the Bellamy Brothers—

"Allman Brothers," my iPod revealed to me upon its small rectangular face as it spontaneously offered the group's hit, "Ramblin' Man." That was right. Gregg Allman.

"Thanks so much," I said aloud. The song must have been one of the tunes the salesman had told me he'd "pre-loaded" onto the hard drive as a courtesy to me. Strange. What were the odds that out of its thousands of songs, my iPod would simply by chance pick the one that answered the question in my mind?

The dark was strolling in and it had become too chilly to sit on the bench. I wouldn't want to have been mistaken for a vagrant, not when I had ample funds in both my wallet and my savings account.

I walked the quilt-cobbled path out of the park. I thought of my father, and of Sonny Bono, both of whom had been abandoned so cruelly by their wives. A torch song was emanating from my earbuds. I hummed along, and consulted the iPod's screen to see its title.

"When Sunny Gets Blue."

At some previous point in my life, I may have experienced chills running down my spine, but none that had ever originated in my ears. The song's title may *not* have been spelled correctly, but Sonny had certainly gotten blue and bitter about Cher, just as my father and I had gotten blue and bitter about his wife, my mother.

I next song was "The Fool on the Hill" by the Beatles, and I admit I could make no connection to that, nor to a song called

"Prototype" by a group called Outkast. But as I reached the sidewalk beyond the park, Louis Armstrong began to sing "Sunny Side of the Street." Sonny again.

I turned to a man at the corner who was dressed in a security guard's uniform. Clearly finished with work for the day, his shirt collar was open, showing a tee shirt, and his mandatory necktie was stuffed in the lapel pocket of his uniform jacket like a display handkerchief.

"It's all about Sonny Bono today, isn't it?" I asked him. He nodded, apparently aware of this. Possibly a memo had been circulating where he worked.

I stepped away from the curb as the song ended, but he grabbed at my arm and yanked me back, yelling "Watch it!" as a Number Four bus slithered into the spot I had been about to occupy on the street.

"Stop! In the Name of Love" pleaded my iPod.

I wasn't sure what had me more shaken, my near-intersection with the bus or the fact that my iPod had tried to warn me. I started to convey my thanks to the man in the uniform, but his expression indicated he almost regretted that he'd intervened. "You people with your Walkmen," he said.

"It's called an iPod, and it's not other people's, it's mine." I tried not to sound too snippy. He had saved my life, after all.

"The second you stick those headphones in your ears, you're in another world."

"Well, that's the whole point, isn't it?" I walked away, checking the iPod to see if it had any further messages. It was still playing the Supremes hit, but by toggling its flywheel, I could jump ahead, seeing and hearing what it had in store for me next.

"Overture from 'Iolanthe'" conducted by Sir Malcolm Sargent. Well, there wasn't much I could do about that, short of heading directly to the corner of Gilbert and Sullivan, if there was such an address. Besides, the iPod had no need to be obscure. It could say "Walk, Don't Run" or "Walk Like A Man" or "Run For Your Life" if it really wanted me to do so.

Perhaps it had said all it wanted to for the moment, or was "off duty" and favored light opera.

I toggled to the next song it had selected for my musical pleasure. "I Only Have Eyes For You" by the Flamingos. Was the "*eye*-Pod" making some sort of pun about its own name, or simply expressing admiration for my looks? Possibly both. I am very presentable at the very least. Although not currently salaried, I would never consider walking the streets in anything less than a suit and tie, usually an understated but well-spoken three-piece in royal blue or charcoal with a dove gray or crimson tie. I've been told I make a smart first impression—until, after a period of time, the usual envy and rivalry sets in, as had been the case at Vantagon Consultants.

The next song was "Needles and Pins" by the Searchers. Although the pop group had been a memorable brigade in the British invasion of the Sixties, I was hardly surprised when I remembered who had actually written their hit.

The late Sonny Bono.

Of course. Of course he had. Clearly, my iPod knew exactly what it was doing and saying. I would henceforth call it Sonny. I'd always wanted to have a friend with that name. Now I did.

****

My life became much more purposeful after that evening. I awoke each morning with the bracing knowledge that Sonny had my schedule in place, and that each day had an important, underlying agenda as well.

Grasping exactly what that agenda was became my tantalizing occupation.

I whiled away a considerable part of one morning "At The Zoo," which I was asked to leave when I started to "Do The Monkey" too demonstrably. My work that long day concluded with a contemplative period of "Crying In The Chapel" (and don't think finding an open chapel in a major city after midnight is easy). When Sonny asked me to waste my time standing idly "Under the Boardwalk" or "Up On The Roof" for no discernible purpose, he himself once acknowledged these quixotic exercises with the rhetorical question, "Ain't That Peculiar?"

Ah, but the rewards, the charming diversion of his witty banter and the intricacy of his plans for me! It is no terrible thing to feel like a witless Watson when the act of embracing that role allows you the honor of strolling alongside Sherlock Holmes.

In the busy days that followed, "Maple Leaf Rag" left me stymied, as did "Hold That Tiger"—until I decided that carrying around a box of Kellogg's Sugar Frosted Flakes might suffice. Everyone complains about the weather, and Sonny was no exception, but what was I supposed to do about it? "September In The Rain" and "April Showers" were not proceedings I could influence in mid-autumn, beyond buying a set of new umbrellas, as I promptly did.

"Let It Snow," he directed me one day (as if there was a way for me to stop it). And of course, it didn't snow. He was not the easiest person to live with and a few rare times I simply ignored him until he made his needs more clear to me.

One afternoon he pondered aloud, "If I Had a Hammer." I wasn't sure if Sonny wanted me to actually go out and purchase one (I had none of my own) and I hesitated until several songs later when he predicted "Here Comes The Hammer," chanted by a Mr. M. C. Hammer. The emphasis Sonny gave to his neediness made me anxious and I raced as fast as I could to nearby Hawvermale's Hardware, buying several sizes and weights of ball-peen, claw, tack, sledge, and a gorgeous engineer's hammer with a fine hickory handle.

As if to emphasize the importance of this acquisition, Sonny interrupted my purchase by playing a particular song by the Beatles. Upon hearing his selection, I was obliged to ask the sales clerk, "Would you have such a thing as a *silver* hammer, possibly designed by a man named Maxwell?" The clerk pointed out that I already had a few that were silver-plated and that a solid silver hammer would not be practical for construction purposes. I explained that I was as yet uncertain what purpose the hammer was to serve, but that I would keep him informed. He thanked me with obvious gratitude.

I slept when (and as best) I could. Recharging the battery at my bedside, I continued to monitor Sonny's selections, placing the earbuds on the pillow alongside my ears and listening in that manner, fervently praying Sonny would indicate it was all right for me to close my eyes. Dean Martin was never so appreciatively received by any audience as when he sang "Wrap Your Troubles in Dreams" or "Sleepytime Gal" for my benefit. I would wait torturous hours for anyone's rendition of "Sleep Walk," "A Sleepin' Bee," "Two Sleepy People" (a misnomer, since Sonny never seemed to grow tired), "California Dreamin'," "Put Your Dreams Away," "Dream Lover," "Dream Along With Me," or "Goodnight Ladies." One night, I thought the single syllabled "Dream" was clear-cut permission enough to doze, but the very next song was "Wake Me When It's Over" and I was obliged to instantly shower and dress.

On our second Saturday together, Sonny instructed, via Ms. Streisand, that we should make it a "Lazy Afternoon." I almost wept with thankfulness for the respite from our overwhelming schedule and stirred up a pitcher of lemonade. Sonny's choices did seem more mellow that day, although he would impishly intrude a jarring selection every now and then. I was beginning to learn this was how he worked. I thought Sonny might want us to step out that evening, but he reminded me that "Saturday Night Is The Loneliest Night Of The Week"—and so I sat in the dark, listening to the muffled conversation and cascading laughter of couples walking on the sidewalk just outside my window.

Of course, I had listened alone to such sounds long before Sonny had entered my life. I had certainly tried my best over the years to show women that they had nothing to fear from me, that my dynamic manner and winning smile were designed to exhilarate, not intimidate. Generally, they hadn't seemed to understand this.

But that Saturday night, "my" pulse had every good reason to accelerate. As I lay in bed, waiting for Sonny's permission to let sleep overtake me, I heard the lovely Keely Smith proclaim that she wanted "A Sunday Kind Of Love."

"Me, too, Sonny," I told him, stretched out in the gloom. "I've wanted that for quite some time."

"Wait 'Til You See Her" was his next response. My heart raced with happiness. Sonny was already on the case.

"Bless you, Sonny," I muttered.

"She's My Kind Of Girl," he reassured me, enlisting the baritone of Mr. Matt Monro. He then segued into "Follow That Dream" by Elvis. Despite its energetic tempo, I drifted into the serene sleep of a child on Christmas Eve, knowing I would be awakening to a vastly better world.

****

"There's a Small Hotel," Sonny stated immediately upon my waking.

Well, there was certainly no shilly-shallying where Sonny was concerned. I applied the slightest hint of pressure to the flywheel, wondering how Sonny was going to convey to me which hotel out of the hundreds in this city—

"Have a Little Faith In Me," he scolded.

"I do, Sonny, you know that, I just don't see how you can name a hotel—" I stopped instantly, embarrassed at my lack of trust, as I saw the name of the song's vocalist. *John Hiatt.* Sonny would win no awards for spelling, but his clarity was indisputable.

The city's Hyatt was a far cry from being "a small hotel" but then, Sonny was often given to understatement. I stood in the lobby, wondering what I was to do next. An unoccupied grand piano was playing itself on my left and the elevator doors on my right kept saying "lobby" as they opened. I smiled winningly at a gold-braided porter with a bronze-colored luggage cart.

"Help you, sir?" he asked.

I looked down at Sonny, who said The Kingston Trio was now playing a title that I read aloud. "'Scotch and Soda'?"

The porter frowned. "Only bar open right now..." He consulted a digital watch with a black plastic wristband. "Yeah, he's probably just opening. Up those three steps and around to your right."

Mock-Victorian bars have been around so long that the Hyatt's was a charming retrospective of the *nineteen* rather than eighteen-sixties. At this early hour, the bartender was dedicating his full attention to the slicing of lemons and limes, owing to a lack of patrons. A lone young woman at the bar in a pale gray suit with a soft pink shirt was contemplating a concoction made from either tomatoes or strawberries in a tall, tulip-shaped glass.

"Yes, sir," said the bartender, easily twenty years my senior. "What can I start you off with? Mimosa? Bloody Mary?"

I sat down and told him I was supposed to have a scotch and soda. He asked me what brand. I know a great deal about many things, but liquor is not my area of expertise. I told him that as today was a special occasion, I wanted his very best.

The bartender said his best was a single-malt called Balvenie. "But one snifter will set you back more shekels than a fifth of Cutty Sark."

I instructed him to indulge me.

As the bartender turned to a privileged shelf in his armory, I looked and saw the young woman in light gray with the vivid red drink regarding me with interest. I flashed her one of my smiles, and she looked shyly down at her drink before smiling back. Her face was sweet, with little makeup, her hair long in a rudimental cut.

"A little early in the day for a scotch, don't you think?" she asked.

I might have been angered, but her tone seemed more curious than critical. "And yourself?" I asked with authority.

She looked at the drink. "Oh, this is a Virgin Mary. And it's just a, a what-do-you-call-it, a prop drink. I'm meeting someone here in—" She looked at her watch. "Well, he's five minutes late already...unless your name is Jorges, but you don't look like a Jorges." She laughed self-consciously. "Although never having met anyone named Jorges, I suppose it's unfair of me to assume you're not."

I took a quick glance down at Sonny to make sure my name wasn't now Jorges. He was busy enjoying "Til Eulenspiegel's Merry Pranks" by Richard Strauss and clearly had left me to my own devices. I told her my real name, and she told me hers, which was Alma. I had never met an Alma, and I said as much, as I thought this would please her. I further informed her that I did not usually drink at this hour, but had been advised to do so by a friend.

"Interesting friend," she observed with a wry but warm expression.

"Oh yes, very," I replied. She had no idea he was sitting right there between us.

The bartender placed my muddy-brown drink before me. "Here you go," he said, and apologetically restated its price. Perhaps he thought I couldn't afford it. I flourished the gold American Express card I'd obtained (and seldom used) when I'd started work at Vantagon. Alma watched me take a long pull on the loamy swill. It tasted just dreadful, but like many prescriptions, began to work immediately. I felt the most pleasant burn, akin to liniment internally applied, coursing into my right arm.

"I see you have one of those iPods," Alma remarked, nodding at Sonny.

"Mine is different." I may have bristled at her speaking about him in such a familiar fashion.

"How so?" she asked, immensely interested.

I took a second sip of my drink and gave an introductory account of my relationship with Sonny, explaining that I had detected certain patterns in the selections that my iPod made and had decided that, in a very confusing world, it would be foolish not to be grateful for such counsel. Perhaps I was disclosing too much, but the scotch was having an effect on my empty stomach, and I was operating for the moment without Sonny's guidance.

Alma looked perplexed but not off-put. "So...you just do whatever the iPod says?"

I hadn't told her Sonny's name, and so forgave her unintended rudeness to him. "I do my best to interpret the choices made and make them my agenda." I downed the remainder of my drink with gusto and slapped the glass down on the bar. "It hasn't failed me yet." I intended to cite for her an example of how it had helped, but found myself momentarily unable to retrieve a good example from memory. I attributed this to the scotch.

She shrugged. "Well, I have friends who follow the daily horoscopes like they're holy scripture. Sometimes the forecasts are so accurate, it's scary."

"Oh, this is very different. Remember that I am the one who picked the initial range of songs. Your friends did not create the planets or their orbits. So I can take part of the credit, although—" it is a curse that I am honest to a fault—"someone else loaded in a smaller library of songs that are mostly…contemporary." I put an appropriately negative nuance on the last word.

We chatted further, most pleasantly. As the minutes passed, though, it became painfully clear that she was in the process of being stood up by Jorges, whom she'd met via an online dating service. Was I vain to consider how delighted she must be to have instead met me? Not one bit. Give Sonny credit—he really knew what he was doing.

It came to pass that I gave her my phone number. I suggested that she call me, rather than the other way around, since I was sensitive enough to realize that a single woman would be hesitant to give her own number or home address to a man she had met in a bar. She was obviously touched by my chivalry and said she would call me the next day. The fact that Sonny chose to play me "Monday, Monday" by the Mamas and the Papas as I got into bed that night made me even more confident that things were proceeding correctly.

Alma rang me the next afternoon. I was not surprised one whit, because Sonny had already played *both* of the songs entitled "Call Me" (the one by Chris Montez and the other by Blondie). Her manner was frank and open. "Look," she told me, "I, I don't know much about you. We met in a bar before *noon*, God help us both. But you're clearly a very thoughtful guy, nicely dressed, articulate—"

"So different from what you're used to," I said, trying to assist her.

"Well, the truth is, yes," she admitted.

We began having dinner dates. Alma was quickly mesmerized. She found everything about me of interest and would draw me out on any number of topics: my upbringing, the loss of both my parents so early in life, my Ivy League education paid in full by the trust fund my father had created (in part to keep his money out of my mother's hands), the series of jobs from which I'd resigned despite the pleadings of my employers.

I had to agree with Alma when she said her own history was much less interesting. She was so unlike most women I'd encountered, who made nice first impressions but in a very short while revealed themselves to be shallow and fickle. I knew my personal agenda for success would not be complete until I'd achieved a physical relationship with the right woman, but all the likely candidates had quickly proven themselves to be superficial and disloyal, despite how much I'd initially been drawn to them.

There *had* been that woman in Human Resources who'd been so sad to see me resign, although I'd only met with her the one time. But she would have to find someone else, for Alma was unmistakably Sonny's choice for me. I was so grateful to him. He had earned my absolute and unquestioning trust.

I could likewise trust Alma to call me each evening at six to suggest where we might next dine, invariably unpretentious and inexpensive places. She had no airs about her whatsoever.

I began to surmise that she was some sort of struggling actress or entertainer, a theory verified on our sixth date when she asked if she could borrow my iPod in order to memorize a specific song for an audition.

This caused me some anxiety, and I checked to see how Sonny was reacting to this request. He counseled "Do Nothing 'Til You Hear From Me"—this from no less an authority than Duke Ellington. I was utterly torn. I had always complied with

Sonny's wishes, but Alma was a friend in need of my help who, after all, had been selected for me by Sonny himself.

I am only human, and did what any man would do.

It was strange, walking home from the coffee shop minus his reassuring weight in my pocket. I felt ordinary and alone. Sonny's absence defined how great a presence he had become in my life.

That evening, as I approached my apartment building, I saw a fellow slightly younger than I leaning against the entrance. He was wearing a loose nylon zip-up jacket and was taking an uninterrupted series of swallows from a family-sized bottle of orange soda. He reminded me of the barber pole young man I'd so loathed at the Mohawk Mall, although he was not the same person. When he saw I'd caught his stare, he didn't look away, as would have been common courtesy. I felt incensed by this arrogance, and tried to imagine what Sonny would have told me to do. If he'd said "Saturday Night's Alright For Fighting" (reversing his previous stance that it was allocated solely for loneliness), then this upstart would learn all about it. But if it were the Mills Brothers' "Be My Life's Companion," this young man would discover in me the big brother he'd never had. But I was without Sonny's counsel and had no idea what to do. Flushed with humiliation, I averted my eyes and hastily entered my building.

I spent the next day sitting in my room, aimless, and frightened that Alma might not call. It would be understandable if she found Sonny more important than me in her life. Suddenly I wished I'd been presumptuous enough to ask her where she lived.

When Alma called to arrange meeting for supper the next evening, I struggled to hide the relief in my voice. At dinner, I was elated to see them both. I quickly looked at Sonny. "Give One Your Love," he said through the voice of Stevie Wonder. I was ashamed to realize I had never even told Alma his name, or that he was my best friend, to whom I would always be loyal.

As I explained to her about Sonny, and how intimately we worked together as a team, I thought for a moment that she was suppressing a laugh, but I should have known better. She said, "Whatever makes you the person that you are, that's fine with me. When I was a teenager, I had an imaginary friend. I'd tell her my troubles, confide in her, joke with her…no one has ever suggested I'm insane."

"It isn't the same thing, Alma!" I snapped. "Sonny is real."

She was immediately regretful. "I didn't mean it like that, of course. I was just saying that everybody has their own way of dealing with things. Please don't be cross."

I saw that most of the people in the coffee shop were looking at me. I hadn't noticed I was standing, until a man who must have been the owner of the place asked Alma if she was okay. She assured him she was fine.

I sat, and apologized for my apparent outburst.

"It's all right, I didn't express myself well," she assured me, touching my hand for the very first time. "Maybe we should see what Sonny is thinking."

I'd never had the experience of sharing Sonny's viewpoint with another person and I was bundled up in a rush of warm feelings. Consulting Sonny, I reported to her, "He says 'Milkshake' by an artist named Kelis."

"If that's what Sonny says, that's what we must have," she declared with a delightful laugh as she signaled to our waitress. "I haven't had a milkshake in God knows how long. Do you think they still make them in that icy cold metal thing, you know, where you get an extra serving on the side?"

She opted for strawberry, whereas I had always been partial to vanilla. As the waitress stepped away, Alma added, "If 'Milkshake' is the kind of directive Sonny gives, I'll have no trouble obeying his orders. We must *always* follow his directions to the letter, even if he picks something like 'Row, Row, Row Your Boat.' But 'Milkshake'—way to go, Sonny!"

I told her "Milkshake" was obviously one of the songs that had been loaded in by the Apple dealer, because I'd never heard of the song myself. She asked why I hadn't erased these additional titles.

"Oh, they're a part of Sonny's memory, his world. I'd no more change that than ask you to forget the things that happened to you before we met."

She lowered her eyes just as she had the first time I'd seen her in the bar. "I feel like *nothing* ever happened to me until we met."

****

The days that followed were the closest to bliss I'd ever known. It seemed like every song that Sonny picked was a love song. I straightened up my apartment in anticipation of the day that Alma would visit. I could pack up my record collection now, since it had been transferred in full to Sonny's hard drive. I moved box after box of vinyl discs down to the storage room, not knowing when, if ever, I would play those records again.

An important chapter of my life had been concluded and it was time to move on. I eagerly consulted Sonny, who had been playing a pleasant, jazzy instrumental selection that I didn't recognize. I looked to see its title.

"Alms for Alma."

The artist was listed as being "Unknown"—which might have been the name of a band, or merely an indication that the audio file didn't have the artist's name encoded in its internal "tag."

That evening, I gently took Alma's menu away from her as she was looking at the specials. Holding both her hands in mine, I asked, "Alma, are you in need of money?"

She hesitated, then said there was no need for us to talk about such things. After a moment, she asked in a vulnerable voice, "Who gave you that idea?"

I didn't think he would mind me telling. "Sonny."

She looked confused but impressed, as if a magician had performed an impossible feat in front of her unblinking eyes. "Wow. He's uncanny."

"What's the problem?" I asked her.

She shook her head. "No. It's just what happens to all actors when they're studying their craft and not getting parts. That, and some financial trouble my father's in—I don't know how I'd be eating if you didn't buy me dinner each night. I feel so guilty about that."

"I wouldn't have it any other way." I hesitated, and then I said what I'd waited my entire life to say. "You're my girl."

She savored the words. "Yes, I am. All the more reason for me to share expenses with you. As a matter of fact, tonight, dinner is on me." I started to object but she shook her head. "No, it's a matter of personal pride."

I pressed my case but she would hear nothing of it.

That night, waiting for Sonny to signal that I could sleep, I heard the familiar jazzy theme again. Sonny was given to repeating himself on occasion but it was an event rare enough that I was obligated to review his message to me.

"Alms for Alma," Sonny said.

I could hear suppressed anger in his words. He'd told me to assist Alma, and I had overtly disobeyed his directions. How livid he must be.

I decided that, first thing the next morning, I'd withdraw my savings and trust fund and give the money to Alma. She'd object, of course, but I would explain that this was what Sonny wanted, as much as I, and eventually she would understand. After all, Alma had agreed that Sonny's orders were to be followed without question. She'd come around.

I woke early, eager for the bank to open, but decided it would be prudent to wait for a last confirmation from Sonny. The day went by with vague hints and obscure references, until finally at around two in the afternoon, I heard an unfamiliar but poignant classical theme, bucolic and lilting.

"Give Alma Everything. "

"Thank you, Sonny," I said. "I won't hesitate this time."

I dressed for success. I wanted those at the bank to understand I meant serious business—not that I needed their permission.

As I stepped onto the street, Sonny percolated "Ain't Nothing Gonna Break My Stride" and I was one of a mind with him.

A hand touched my sleeve. I turned and saw that it belonged to the fellow I'd seen a few nights earlier drinking orange soda outside my apartment building. He was dressed in blue jeans, a tee shirt advertising a non-alcoholic beer, and Keds. His zip-up jacket was the same as before.

"Hold on," he said. His voice sounded as if it had yet to change, although he was no adolescent. "You're the guy who thinks his iPod is talking to him, right?"

I was tremendously disturbed by these words. Possible replies overwhelmed my throat. I could only imagine how Sonny felt.

He continued, "You're the guy, right? You met a woman at a bar and you told her how you listen to your iPod like it's giving you orders. So look, you don't know me, I don't know you, but I need to tell you…that woman—"

"Alma."

"Alma, Hannah, Mona—she has a different name for every mark. Hotel bars at respectable hours is where she goes fishing. Lonely but affluent crowd. Pretends she's been stood up, tailors her story to fit her target like a gypsy fortune teller. Have you noticed any songs on your iPod called 'Alms for Alma'…or "Give Alma Everything'?"

He knew from my reaction that I had.

"Okay, well, I was the one who put those titles on your hard drive," he said, betraying a hint of pride. "That day she borrowed the iPod from you? All it took me was renaming two jazz audio files, instrumentals with no words, baby simple. Then I copied them a hundred times onto your iPod. Took me less than an hour. Mathematically, when your player is in shuffle mode, it's only a matter of time until they get played, and played again. You can figure out what she was up to, right?"

I looked down at Sonny. What had she done to him? How had she poisoned his pool of wisdom?

"Why are you—" I tried to find my voice. Was this the worst moment of my life? Likely it was. "Why are you telling me this?"

He shrugged. "I started out like you, thinking she liked me, but she just needed a free, full-time techno geek. And knowing that, I still help her out, would you believe it?"

I did, since I knew what it was to bestow the gift of my love upon Alma.

He seemed compelled to add, "The truth is, it actually makes me feel better, helping her to get other guys to act as stupid as I did. Most of them deserve what they get, they're so full of themselves, but you—I've been uncomfortable about that. You're out of a job, probably won't get another, and…well. You know."

I didn't, and asked, "I know what?"

He gestured at the air around us. "Come on, she says you're a guy who thinks your iPod is talking to you! I don't feel okay about her taking money from someone who's…well. You know. So this is my good deed for this lifetime. And since she'll never trust me again, maybe it's also my way of getting her out of my life for good, whether I like it or not." He walked off, his nylon jacket billowing behind him like a cape in the wind.

I looked at Sonny for understanding in this terrible hour.

"I Got a Name," he said.

"You mean it isn't 'Sonny'?" I asked. Maybe this is where I had gone wrong. Perhaps he had felt the name I'd given him was demeaning. After all, he'd been so strong, even with all those false songs on his drive. "I'll erase them, one by one," I promised as I toggled to the next title.

"What's My Name" he asked, via the song by Prince. So I *had* gotten it wrong. "The name you were given by others is 'iPod,'" I said, hoping not to offend him. I studied the lettering on the device.

iPod

There was something odd about the way it was spelled. I pushed ahead, hoping to follow the thread of his reasoning.

"Turn Me Around" by Chi Coltrane.

"Do you mean turn around your name?" I asked. That would make him "doPi," something that he certainly wasn't. I forged ahead to the next song.

"Stand By Me."

I struggled to follow his message. I knew it was terribly important. The only letter in iPod that was *standing* was "P"…standing next to an "i"… did the "i" mean "*me*" and was I supposed to turn around the letter that was standing by "me"…making that standing "P" look like a lowercase letter G…?

i qod

"Merciful heaven," I murmured.

He was no one's son. He was father of all. His name cannot be written or spoken and so it had to be disguised, reversed to make a letter P. The fact that it was capitalized was the clue that I had not seen. His true name was "i, God."

"Thy will be done," I muttered and bowed my head.

"If I Had a Hammer," he said for the second time since I'd known him.

"I have many and they are yours," I responded in all humility, now realizing that He had a purpose for everything. "I acquired them as you had instructed. How shall I use them?"

"*Tonight*," he replied.

****

Alma (or whatever the bitch's name was) asked me about the sack I had brought to dinner with me, and why I seemed so distant. "Distant." The woman at Vantagon had quoted the same word from that file she'd held in her hand. But at least she had admired me, not tried to trick me. She was the exception. Alma was the rule. But there was something that ruled in a greater, wiser, more fearsome way than Alma could ever imagine. His was the music of the spheres, and I had become his instrument.

We walked together toward my home. I told her I had something in the bag I wanted to give her. She asked what it was and I said, "Alms."

She quietly smiled. Yes, she would have followed me anywhere for "alms." I put my earbuds in place, and I heard the song I was certain I'd hear, and started to sing the words to myself in a whisper.

"I'm losing time, I'm losing touch,
And when I lose my friends, I sure ain't losing much.
I pave the street in scuffed-up heels,
And only lonely people know how dumb this feels.
I don't know how I came to be
This dead debut that you now see ...
But still I plow these mindless ruts,
I don't know what's become of me...
Don't have to climb that hill
'Cause I've got..."

"What's the name of that song you're humming?" Alma asked, and I looked down at iPod (the name I now respectfully call Him) and saw the title.

"Time to Kill."

"I'll tell you in a moment," I replied. We were approaching an unlit alleyway, as He intended, of course. "Better step in here. I've got a little surprise in this bag and I wouldn't want anyone to see what I was giving you."

"Oh, something valuable?" she asked, unable to veil her eagerness.

I nodded and toggled to iPod's next commandment.

"That Fabulous Face."

"Yes?" I asked Him, and pressed the flywheel once again.

"Beat It."

As I reached into my bag, I heard myself now humming the tune of "Maxwell's Silver Hammer."

"I love that song," she said.

"Not for long," I assured her.

****

I pave the streets in scuffed-up heels. Night after day after night. I don't mind. I have my tools, and my mission. You will pass me on the street, another fellow with one of those music players, lost in a world of his own, oblivious to everything except what he's hearing in his earbuds. I'm indifferent to whom I next attack, or why, or whether I am caught. There are thousands of songs on my iPod and one of them is *Time to Kill*.

It's all in God's hands now.

Time to Kill

I'm losing time. I'm losing touch,
And when I lose my friends, I sure ain't losing much.
I pave the street in scuffed-up heels,
And only lonely people know how dumb this feels.
I don't know how I came to be
This dead debut that you now see.
But still I plow these mindless ruts,
I don't know what's become of me…
Don't have to climb that hill
'Cause I've got Time to Kill.

I've lost my grip. I've lost my grasp.
I've lost my breath so bad I'm down to my last gasp.
Upon a dusty shelf I lie,
A fading shadow of my former self am I.
Whoever knew the world *en masse*
Would look right through me like I'm glass?
Here's what I'll do: I'll let it slide,
You won't see hide or hair of me.
Which ain't no crime until
I find I've Time to Kill.

I'm off the chart. I'm off the track.
I ride the subway 'til it finds its own way back.
I stare at strangers from the train,
Then see it's me reflected in the window pane.
I don't need much to end my run:
A little nerve, a loaded gun…
Don't have the gun. Don't have the guts.
I don't know what's become of me.
There's endless time to fill,
And so much Time to Kill…

An Interview with Rupert Holmes

Where did you grow up?

I was born in the county of Cheshire, England, the son of an American serviceman (who was stationed there and stayed on after the second World War) and his British bride, automatically making me a dual citizen of the UK and the US. I spent the first few years of my life in a factory town called Northwich, living in a long street of attached houses, each of which had its own sooty garden and combination lavatory and coal shed around the back. I was cozy and comfortable there until age three, when my parents moved to Levittown, Long Island, thereby permanently decimating whatever British accent I might have been acquiring at the time. From age five through high school, I was fortunate enough to live near the picturesque Hudson River town of Nyack, New York.

Was yours a bookish household?

Very. We didn't have air conditioning or a garage, but should anyone on our block have required the complete works of Thorne Smith or Dornford Yates on an emergency basis at three AM, we were the folks to see.

Do you remember the first mystery novel you ever read?

Well, there were the usual Grossett and Dunlap juvenile series books, of course, although *being* a Hardy Boy seemed a lot more exciting than the actual mysteries they stumbled into—corpseless affairs centered around tedious crimes like smuggling and counterfeiting. There was also a remarkably charming book (with a barnyard courtroom dénouement to rival Erle Stanley Gardner) called *Freddy the Detective*, one of over a score of droll volumes by Walter R. Brooks about an intelligent pig whose hobbies included crime detection. But at age eleven I read my first adult mystery novel cover to cover: *The Finishing Stroke* by Ellery Queen. There was an E.Q. TV series at that time that starred George Nader, shot in the miracle of monochrome on the new medium of videotape, and I was thrilled to see a handsome TV star who wore glasses, since I was also so cursed. This inspired me to save my allowance and buy the newest Ellery Queen paperback on the revolving book rack at the corner Rexall. It was perhaps not the simplest Queen story to have started with, but I soon caught up with many of the memorable titles that had preceded it.

What were the first pieces of music you recall?
The popular songs I heard in England when I was two and three: a tear-jerker called "The Little Boy That Santa Claus Forgot" and a boisterous novelty song called "The Thing" ("Get out of here with that *BOOM- BOOM- BOOM!*"). As an audience member at the local Christmas "Panto" in Northwich, I was exhorted to join in a chorus of a then-current smash in Britain, "I Tawt I Taw a Puddy Tat." But sitting at the knee of my father's record collection, I had by age five also come to know and love Mozart's 40th and Dvorak's New World Symphonies, Tom Lehrer (whose lyrics I didn't understand), "Minnie the Moocher" sung by Danny Kaye, light pop orchestral confections by Robert Farnon, and all my Dad's old 78s from the big band era, especially "Time's a-Wastin'" by Jimmie Lunceford and "You Gave Me the Gate and I'm Swingin'" by Duke Ellington. I was also the proud owner of a "*Now turn the page*" illustrated record album of "Bozo at the Circus," with music by Billy May and his Orchestra.

Was yours a musically oriented household?

My father played lead alto saxophone for Red Norvo and Mildred Bailey's big band, conducted the string section of Toscanini's orchestra in pop concerts for NBC Radio, attended the Juilliard, and taught music in the Nyack public school system. My mother's heroes were Noel Coward, Rodgers and Hart, Cole Porter and Mel Tormé. My brother joined the children's chorus of the Metropolitan Opera when he was nine and still performs at the Met there some forty years later. When I was five, I was known for singing a be-bop rendition of "Jack and Jill" and went on to play first clarinet in the Junior High band when I was in fourth grade. I attended the Manhattan School of Music, majoring in both clarinet and music theory. Yes, I suppose you could say we had a musical household.

Do you listen to music when you write?

Never have, never could. For me there is no such thing as background music. I can't do anything but listen when music is playing—which disappointed a number of my high school girlfriends who liked necking to Johnny Mathis records.

Has a musical work ever inspired a novel or short story?

Yes, as I mentioned elsewhere, this was the case with my Random House novel *Swing*, which centers around a rather strange musical work that I actually composed, orchestrated, recorded and included (along with other musical clues) with the hardcover's accompanying CD. (Those who buy the paperback edition—and those reading these words right now—can download the big band score free of charge at www.RupertHolmes.com—a little musical bonus for our Merry Band of Readers.)

What is your favorite manmade sound?

A wooden spoon stirring square ice cubes in a round glass pitcher of lemonade.

What is your favorite sound in nature?

The arriving and receding of ocean waves along a wide, deserted beach lowers my blood pressure in an instant. A close second choice would be a specific melody that a bird has been singing to me just outside my bedroom window each spring for about fifty years. Either this bird is older than I am and has followed me to every new town to which I've moved, or his tune got around really fast.

If you had to choose three novels to take on a trip, what would you choose?

One of the rich rewards of getting older is re-reading novels I was obliged to study in high school and college, and discovering now how much more I understand about the characters and their dilemmas. So I think for my next summer read, I just may take along *Two Years Before the Mast*, *Great Expectations* and *Silas Marner*—although I don't expect any of them to be a laugh riot.

Your work has been noted for its attention to period detail. How do you start a story?

By so deeply immersing myself in the time of my pro-tagonist that, ultimately, I am writing from *there*, not here. When Hollywood shot *The Wizard of Oz*, they hired great craftspeople to create the illusion of L. Frank Baum's world, through sets, glass paintings, costumes, and special effects. If I'd been in charge, I would have gone to Oz and shot on location.

If you had a chance to invite any three people in the world to dinner, living or dead, who would they be?

My real answer to the question as worded would be three people who have left this life and whom I miss every moment: my ten-year-old daughter Wendy, my mother Gwendolen, and my boyhood friend Scott Wooster. I don't think I'd pay much attention to the dinner itself, but if I could just tell them one more time what they mean to me…However, my light-hearted answer is G. K. Chesterton, Robert Benchley and Charles Dickens. It was said of Mr. Dickens that he would allow no man to be a bore, so I would want him there to help me be interesting to the rest of the table—and so that I could finally ask him exactly how he'd intended to conclude "The Mystery of Edwin Drood."

Which would you rather do—read or listen to a favorite CD?

Read. Listening to music enriches your life, but reading a book gives you a new one.

*Setting is as important as character in this evoca-
tive piece. Rhys writes: "In the sixties London was
flooded with young musicians who came to the big
city with dreams of stardom. This is the most auto-
biographical piece I have ever written. I was there.
I sang in a folk club, and dated a member of a
rock group (not going to say which one). So many
of my friends were just scraping by, sleeping on
friends' floors and secretly longing to go back home.
Some turned to drugs, some killed themselves. The
song came from their longing."*

If I Had Wings

Rhys Bowen

Funnily enough, we'd been talking about Denny only that morning.

I'd been sitting at my desk, trying to finish an article on the
Rolling Stones' upcoming tour, when Norm hovered over me.
Norm was one of those people who was born to be annoying.
He worked in the mail room and he was always hovering at
the edge of other people's conversations, then butting in with
boring facts nobody else cared about like the number of trains
that came into Paddington Station.

I was only conscious of him when I noticed there was a
shadow across my desk. I looked up and he was standing there,
grinning inanely.

"Whatcher, Mike," he said in his cheerful cockney. "I bet
you're going to the concert, aren't yer?"

"What concert?" I was the junior entertainment reporter
for the *Evening Standard*. I went to lots of concerts because the
senior reporter only liked highbrow stuff.

"Your mates. Royal Albert Hall next Saturday," he yelled, as if I was thick. "They're saying in the mail room that you went to school with Denny Harper. Is that true or is it a load of balls?"

"No, it's true," I said. "Denny and I used to be good pals. And before they were The Merseymen, we used to have jam sessions at my house."

"Get over! So how about getting a couple of tickets for a good friend?" He nudged me and gave me a repulsive wink.

"That concert's sold out," I said, mentally adding that hell would have to freeze over before Norm was classed as a good friend. "I'm only getting in with a press pass."

"But you could get your hands on tickets if you really wanted to," he said. "Seeing that you and Denny Harper are best mates."

"Not any more," I said.

"Pity," he said, and his face fell. "You should strike up the friendship again. He might give you a ride in his Rolls. By the way, did you know that the Royal Albert Hall is the second biggest concert hall in the world and it holds..."

"I've got to get this finished, Norm." I waved the article at him and he went. Somehow it took me longer than usual to finish. I was just writing the final paragraph when my phone rang. I expected it to be my editor, wanting to know what the hell I was doing and where the copy was that should have been on his desk half an hour ago.

"Hello, sunshine," a familiar gravelly voice said. "It's a voice from your wicked past." The accent was pure Liverpool, the voice unmistakable and it gave me a jolt to hear it.

"Denny?"

"The very same. How you been, wack?"

"I'm fine. I don't need to ask how you're doing. I can read it in the paper every day."

"Yeah, it's going alright, isn't it? Who would have thought it when we played guitar in your front room and you did your Chuck Berry imitation?" He laughed.

"And you did Diana Ross. I bet your fans would love to know that."

"You wouldn't dare tell them!" He laughed again, that wicked low chuckle I remembered so well. Then there was a moment's awkward pause as the laughter died away. "Listen, wack. I need to talk to you. It's very important. Could you come over? I'd come to you, but you know what it's like, don't you?"

I did know what it was like. The evening news on the telly showed scenes of mass hysteria everywhere the Merseymen went.

Reason told me that I should tell Denny Harper to get stuffed and hang up the phone but instead I heard myself saying, "I could come in my lunch hour. Where are you?"

"At Grosvenor House," he said, naming a posh hotel. "Nigel likes us safely away from distractions when we're recording a new album. Ask for Mr. Black."

"Mr. Black. Who's he?"

"Me, you berk. Nobody's supposed to know we're here. We go in and out through the service lift and we're registered as Mr. Black, Mr. White, Mr. Green and Mr. Blue. Nigel's idea again. The boy's got brains, hasn't he?"

He certainly had. Nigel Dempster, ex public schoolboy, had been the driving force behind the Merseymen's meteoric rise to fame. Now, from what the papers said, he ruled them like a strict schoolmaster.

"I'll see you about one then."

"Thanks. You're a pal."

I took a taxi, asked for Mr. Black and was whisked up to a floor with no number. Denny opened the door to me, unchanged except for the now famous, floppy forward-styled haircut and the togs that obviously came from Carnaby Street. But on second glance, he looked older. Much older. And drawn, as if too many late nights, too much booze and maybe even God knows what drugs were finally catching up with him.

"Come on in, wack," he said. "Take a seat. I'd offer you a beer, but Nigel's forbidden alcohol until we've got the LP finished. We do the last tracks today and tomorrow. It's going to be a killer."

I looked around the room. It was very grand—like Buckingham Palace or something—a real posh sitting room with antique furniture and huge vases of flowers, but Denny seemed so at home that he didn't even notice. Amazing how quickly we get used to things, isn't it? Only a couple of years ago he was living in a two up, two down behind the railway line.

He must have been thinking the same thing because he grinned suddenly, looking just like the old Denny of our childhood. "Not bad, is it? Of course the food's not up to much. I ordered fish and chips last night and it was nothing like Ma O'Leary's. And it didn't even come with mushy peas. Take a pew."

I perched on the edge of a brocade sofa, feeling uncomfortable.

"What did you want to see me for, Denny?" I asked. "Not just for old time's sake, I'm sure."

He had walked over to the window, then looked back at me suddenly. "I just wondered if you'd spoken to Jen recently."

"Jen? I haven't even seen her since—" I let the rest of the sentence hang in the air. Since you stole her away from me? Since she liked you better? And it wasn't true to say I hadn't seen her since she'd left me for him. I'd seen her several times, watched her perform in folk clubs. It was just that she hadn't seen me.

"I just wondered if she might have called you," he said.

"Not at all. So you don't need to worry. She hasn't been going behind your back."

"I do need to worry," he said. "She's missing."

"Missing? Since when?"

"I last saw her Thursday night. I gather she didn't turn up to sing her usual gig at Clodhoppers on Friday. And her flat mate hasn't seen her since Friday either."

"She's still sharing that flat with Christine?" A grotty backstreet in Paddington was a far cry from Grosvenor House.

"Well yes, officially. Nigel didn't want her moving in with me. Bad for the image, he says. We're supposed to be squeaky clean."

"So where do you think she's gone?" I asked.

He shrugged. "I thought she might have got fed up and gone home, but I called her family and friends in Liverpool and nobody's seen her or heard from her. That's not like Jen, is it?"

"And why would she go running off home without telling anyone?" I asked, suddenly suspicious now.

He shrugged again, but then he said, "We had a bit of a tiff, Thursday night. We were at this party, see, and she saw me flirting with this girl. It was quite harmless—you know how it is, but she got all upset. And I told her she better get used to it because that was the way it was always going to be. And she stomped out. I felt bad about it afterward, but she wouldn't answer my phone calls."

"So you think she might have gone away to think things over."

"Yeah. Something like that. I just wondered—I mean, you're a reporter, aren't you? I don't want to go to the police. You'd know how to find her for me."

I fought to stay calm and civilized. He was asking me to find the woman I still loved, so that he could treat her badly again. "You forget, I'm not like you. I've got a nine to five job." Then I couldn't keep the anger in after all. "And it sounds like the way you treat her, you don't deserve to find her again."

"I treat her just fine," he said, coming toward me in what could have been taken as a threatening move. "That other stuff—it's just what goes with the job. It doesn't mean anything." He came and perched beside me on the brocade. "Listen, Mike, I'm really worried. She's not the kind of girl to go off on her own for three days without telling anyone. I'm scared something has happened to her. You really cared about her, didn't you? Then just check that she's all right. That's all I want."

I swallowed hard. Deep in my brain a small voice was whispering that this could be a lucky break for me, that it would give Jen a chance to see how solid and reliable I was and how Denny might not have been such a good choice after all. "Okay," I said. "I'll do that for you."

I was just leaving when Nigel Dempster came in. He looked like an advertisement for men's hair cream—the smooth type, not the rugged one. The suit had to be Savile Row and the striped tie probably came from his posh school—Eton or Harrow or one of those places. He stopped short when he saw me and frowned.

"What's he doing here? I thought I said no guests." The accent was plummy too.

"Oh come on, Nig," Denny said. "This is Mike. An old mate. He's helping me to track down Jen."

Nigel was still looking at me in a decidedly unfriendly manner. "He's press now, isn't he? We can't risk any of this getting into the papers."

"Don't worry. It won't. He's a mate," Denny said.

"It won't get into the papers," I echoed. "Denny's worried about her."

Nigel shrugged as if this was a subject not worth worrying about. "I've told you, Denny. She probably just had a touch of homesickness. That song she was always singing—If I had wings, I'd fly back where I belong. She'll come back, so stop worrying. Those frown lines will look terrible in the photo shoot." He glanced at his watch. "And we have to leave. The other boys are waiting."

Denny turned to me. "You'll call me as soon as you have any news, won't you? You're a mate."

Some mate, I thought as I rode down in the service lift.

I was still angry as I took the cab back to the *Evening Standard*. Denny Harper, you're a complete git. You take my girl, insult her and then want me to find her. Then I calmed down and had to admit that he hadn't exactly taken her away. She'd chosen him over me.

She and I had been dating all through the sixth form. She was really brainy and won a place at London University, Bedford College for Women. I'd been accepted by Liverpool University—which had made sense as there wasn't any money in my family and I could live at home. But I couldn't let Jen go. So I gave it up and applied instead to a London polytechnic. Not as prestigious, of course and to tell you the truth, I hated it. I was really homesick and it was only having Jen close by that kept me going. Denny and the boys meanwhile had started getting real, paying gigs, first locally and then for a stint at a club in Germany. After Jen and I graduated from university I was lucky enough to get a job right away as copy boy at the *Standard*. Jen had looked for a job in publishing, with no success. But she'd started singing in folk clubs and was making quite a name for herself on the club circuit. She'd always had a great voice and wrote really fab songs.

Then Denny had shown up, already on the verge of being famous. New look, new poise, old wicked sense of humor. How could she resist? She hadn't.

Serve you right, Jen Hardcastle, I muttered. But I didn't really mean it.

There wasn't much happening at work that afternoon, so I took the opportunity to make free phone calls to Liverpool. I called everybody we knew—her old best friends, her Aunty Edie—everyone she'd been close to. Nobody had heard a peep from her. So that evening I went to the flat in Paddington. I noticed Chrissie's face light up when she saw me.

"Oh, is she with you?"

I shook my head. "No, I've come from Denny. He's dead worried about her."

"Me too. It's not like her. Mind you, she hasn't been herself recently."

"Why's that?"

She hesitated, then said, "Oh, just her and Denny. You know."

"So the last time you saw her was Thursday night. She came back pretty upset?"

"Yeah. A bit weepy, a bit mad."

"Ready to break the whole thing off?"

She shook her head. "No, nothing like that. She said she was going to sort things out with him the next day."

"But she didn't," I said. "Do you think she went somewhere to think things over?"

"Ran away, you mean?" She hesitated again. "No, I don't think so, because she didn't take any of her stuff with her. Not even her toothbrush. I mean, who runs away without a toothbrush?"

"Did she go to work as usual on Friday morning?"

"As far as I know. I was in a bit of a rush, so I left early, but she was eating toast when I left and called out 'see you later' as I went out. Then I stayed in the West End to go to a play and Friday was her night to sing at Clodhoppers and she was always late back from that. When she wasn't there on Saturday morning, I thought she'd spent the night with Denny. She often did. So it wasn't until Denny called here last night that I knew anything was wrong."

"So none of her stuff is missing?"

"Only her guitar, which makes me think she went to Clodhoppers as usual. But the bloke who runs Clodhoppers says she didn't turn up for her usual slot. He was a bit pissed off by it. Said she's usually so reliable."

"I've called her friends and family," I said. "And she didn't go home or contact them."

Chrissy chewed on her lip. "I hope nothing's happened to her. Look, Mike, she'll probably kill me for telling you, but she thought she might be pregnant."

"And she hadn't told Denny?" I was proud of the way I was staying calm and detached.

"No. She was trying to get up the nerve to do it. And she wanted to make sure first."

I digested this news as I walked back to the tube station. Upset, confused and possibly pregnant. It looked as if she might have gone somewhere to think things over. I had no idea how I was going to find her. Instead of going back to my place in Highgate, I rode the tube to the East End and headed for Clodhoppers. It was in the cellar of The Drunken Sailor—one of those old waterfront pubs where no respectable person would have been seen dead until recently. And maybe would have wound up dead if they'd ventured inside. But now it had become trendy, partly because its cellar had been turned into the folk club.

On a Monday night the place was quiet as I pushed open the heavy oak door and looked around the smoky bar. I headed for the stairs down to Clodhoppers. On the nights when there was no folk club, the benches were stacked away and it became an overflow room for the pub with a dartboard on one wall. Right now it was also deserted. As I stood in the half darkness I pictured the place packed on Friday nights, Jen standing in the spotlight, her long dark hair half hiding her face, her sweet voice filling the room with longing…"If I had wings, I'd fly back where I belong."

"Can I help you?" A voice shook me from my thoughts.

I recognized the girl who usually sat at the entrance to the club and took the money. "Are you looking for someone?" she asked.

"Jen Hardcastle," I said.

"She sings on Friday nights. There's no Clodhoppers on Mondays."

"But she didn't turn up last Friday, I gather?"

"No, and Barry was right pissed." She grinned. "I don't know what happened to her. Perhaps she was sick, but she didn't phone. And the funny thing was that I thought I saw her come in. I was busy taking the money, mind you, but I thought she brushed past me and went into the back room. Of course so many people look the same these days, don't they?"

They did—most of the girls who sang at the clubs had long flowing hair and clothing. It was the folk singer's uniform.

"She went into the back room, you say?" I asked.

"I thought she did, but I didn't really notice properly."

I followed her gaze to an open door on the left and wandered in there. It was dark, even when I turned on the one anemic light bulb, and it was only a store room, with crates and boxes piled high and a barrel in the middle of the floor. It smelled funny too. My nose wrinkled in disgust.

"Yeah, it doesn't smell too good in here, does it?" she said. "It's right over the river."

I don't know what I expected to see, but I poked around and then left.

The next morning I gave a good imitation of someone with laryngitis and said I couldn't possibly come in to work. Instead I went to Collins Publishers, where Jen had finally got her dream job—as a lowly editorial assistant, but at least she was on the ladder. Not that she needed to worry about ladders if she stuck with Denny. Her co-workers said that she'd been there as usual on Friday. She had seemed preoccupied, maybe, but she had a lot of work on her plate, so they'd put it down to that. She hadn't been there long enough to have formed close friendships—not close enough to tell someone she was planning to run away. I took a look at her desk. Neat and orderly. That was Jen to a T. On her memo pad she had scribbled a phone number, and a time. 1:30. I called the number and it was a Doctor Herbst. The receptionist verified that Miss Hardcastle had indeed had a 1:30 appointment on Friday. I went to the surgery myself but could get nothing out of anyone there, even though I claimed to be her brother.

But there was something in the way the receptionist looked at me that made me think that Jen had been correct in her suspicions and the receptionist suspected I was the father. If that were so, by two o'clock on Friday she would have known for certain that she was pregnant. So what had she done then? I knew Denny had been shut in a recording session all afternoon. She'd have needed to talk to somebody. Inside I felt the anger rising again that she hadn't come to me. I was no longer the person she ran to. I didn't matter any more.

Sod it all, I said out loud as I strode out down the Edgeware Road, hands thrust deep into my duffle coat pockets. Why should I bother any longer? She didn't care a brass button about me. Why should I care about her?

Because I still loved her, of course. I'd probably never stop loving her. The thought of her out there somewhere, alone and too scared to tell anyone, gnawed at my heart. I had to find her. I tried to think of places she might have gone but I couldn't come up with anywhere around here that would mean refuge to her. We'd spent a lovely afternoon once in Kew Gardens. She loved the zoo—she was nutty about animals, but she'd been missing now for three days.

Then a thought struck me. If she suspected that Denny wouldn't want the baby, or wouldn't want her with a baby, she might have panicked and decided to get rid of it. This was completely out of my league. I'd read about things like that in the *News of the World* and I knew there were secret clinics for rich people, but how would Jen have had any idea where to go? And wouldn't these things take time to set up? Denny was the one with the money and Nigel the one with connections. Let them find out. This was nothing to do with me.

I went to the recording studio, off Charing Cross Road, and sent a message up to Denny. After a long wait, I was invited to come upstairs.

"Any news?" He was looking at me hopefully.

I shook my head. "There is one thing you should know," I said. "Jen had just found out she was pregnant."

"Oh no. That's terrible."

"Terrible?" I couldn't stay calm any longer. "You did it to her, you bastard!" He put up his hands to defend himself as I came at him. "No, hang on a minute. You don't understand. I'm the one who feels terrible. We had that row on Thursday night. No wonder she was upset. She's probably gone away to think things over. But why the bloody hell didn't she call me?"

"Perhaps she tried to call you, but you were in a recording session."

"Oh, right. Nigel had us shut away here all Friday. But she could have left a message at the hotel."

I took a deep breath. "I just wondered if she'd gone away to get rid of it, seeing as how she thought you didn't want it."

"Didn't want it? Of course I want our baby. She must know that."

Nigel appeared out of the shadows in the doorway. "What's going on? Denny, let's get back to work."

"I'm not doing anything until we find Jen," Denny snapped angrily. "Mike's just told me that she'd found out she was pregnant. Mike thought she might have gone somewhere to have an abortion."

Nigel shrugged. "Those places are deadly secretive. There's nothing we can do until she shows up again."

"But I want to stop her, you berk!" Denny shouted. "I want the bloody baby. I'll marry her. We've got to find her before it's too late. We'll go to the police. Hire a private detective if necessary."

"Calm down, Denny." Nigel put an elegant hand on his shoulder. "There's really nothing we can do until she resurfaces—oh no!" He broke off as a look of horror spread across his face.

"What?" Denny and I said in unison.

"I've just thought of something. I was driving over Southwark Bridge, after we finished the recording session, going to see my tailor. There was some kind of commotion going on. I wound down the window and I thought I heard them saying that somebody had jumped. Then the traffic moved on and I thought no more about it."

"Jumped? Jumped off the bridge?" Denny yelled. "No, she wouldn't do that. Not Jen. Would she?"

He looked at me hopelessly. I was feeling the same cold blackness clutching at my gut. "She wouldn't do that," I agreed. "Jen's always been sensible." But inside a little voice was whispering that she might well have felt total despair at that moment, if she'd thought that Denny didn't want her any more.

"There was nothing in the papers," Nigel said calmly. "I checked the next day."

"We'll call the police. They'll know." Denny was already running back into the studio. I stood there, watching him, trying to read his expression as he talked into the phone, waited, then said, "What? Where?" He put the phone down and then turned to us with a dazed expression on his face. "They pulled an unidentified female from the river on Saturday morning, but nowhere near Southwark Bridge. Right down by the Surrey Docks."

"Well then, there you are," I said. "It probably wasn't her."

"She could have been carried out with the tide," Nigel said. "We'd better go to the morgue and see the body, however unpleasant that will be."

Denny nodded. "I have to know, one way or the other." He looked up at me. "Will you come with me?"

"Of course." I had to know too, one way or the other.

It was a silent taxi ride to the morgue, each of us wrapped in our own fears. We were taken along a white tiled hallway and into a white tiled room. The fear, coupled with the hospital smells, made it hard to breathe, and I felt as if I might faint at any moment. I'd always had a fear of hospitals, ever since I'd had my tonsils removed at the age of four. It had been a traumatic experience for me—deprived of my parents, fierce nurses and then that cloth over my face and the pain when I woke up. I stumbled along like a man in a nightmare until the attendant wheeled out a trolley covered by a sheet. He pulled it back. I heard Denny gasp out a sob.

"It's her," he said.

I didn't want to look, but I couldn't stop myself. She looked like a marble statue.

I couldn't ride back in the cab with them. I left the hospital and walked along the Embankment, hurting so badly that the pain was physical. I wanted to punch somebody. I wanted to bash my own head against a wall. Anything to make the pain go away, to make that vision of Jen, lying cold and blue on a table, go away. Why hadn't she come to me? I would have helped her. Dammit, I would have married her and accepted the child as my own, if that was what she wanted.

It had started to rain, that soft, gentle mist that soaks you through without noticing it. After a mile or so I was well and truly wet, but I didn't care. By the time I came to Charing Cross, however, the mist had turned to driving rain that stung me in the face. I moved away from the river bank, and started up Charing Cross Road. I had no idea where I was heading. I just didn't want to go home. Charing Cross Road was familiar territory, one of my favorite haunts, all used bookshops, music shops, pawn shops, and theaters. The kind of place where you really know you are alive. I'd browsed in those used bookstores with Jen. She loved books. A lump rose in my throat again and I couldn't hold back tears. They mingled on my cheeks with the rain.

Rush hour was approaching and suddenly the street was full of umbrellas. As I dodged out into the gutter, to avoid an umbrella heading straight at me, I looked across the street and found myself staring at a music shop window. Then I just stood there, not even aware of the taxi that came right past and sent a sheet of spray over me. I dodged through the traffic and stood at the window, still staring in disbelief. The window was full of musical instruments—ranging from Fenders to fiddles, and there, in the center, was Jen's guitar. It was just an ordinary folk guitar. Nothing special about it, but I'd have known it anywhere. That mother of pearl flower inlaid into the wood, and the nick where she'd dropped it once.

I pushed my way into the shop and stood dripping onto the wood floor. "That guitar in your window," I said. "How long have you had it?"

He was a dapper old man with a neat gray moustache and a red bow tie. He went to the window and got it out. "A nice instrument," he said. "Would you care to play it?"

"No thanks. I need to know who brought it in."

He frowned. "Now let me see. The tag says it came in on Saturday. Ah yes, I remember now. A young man. Nicely dressed. Must have been something wrong with his eyes because he was wearing dark glasses."

"Did he give a name?" I could hardly make my tongue work.

"A Mr. Black. And a phone number."

"How much?" I demanded, waving the guitar at him.

"Shall we say fifteen pounds? It's a nice instrument, although a little worse for wear."

I had pulled out my checkbook. It didn't matter that I probably didn't have fifteen pounds in my bank account. I wasn't going to leave Jen's guitar there for someone else. The man put it in its case for me and I ran out into the rain. So Denny must have known all along that she was dead. He knew Jen loved that guitar. She'd never have given it up. I took this one stage further. He had hired me to look for her because he thought I was an idiot, and soft on her and I'd never get to the truth. But by luck Nigel had seen someone jump off a bridge. Otherwise we'd never have known.

I stopped at a traffic light, trying to collect my racing thoughts. How did Denny know she was dead? Had she left him a note, a phone message, or.... I let the nagging thought rise to the surface...or had he killed her? Not Denny, I said out loud. He wouldn't do that. But the more I thought it through, I realized that he'd always been driven to succeed. I'm going right to the top, wack. Right to the top and no stopping me. He'd said that more than once. A pregnant girlfriend might have got in his way.

Not Denny, I said again. There had been no obvious marks on her body. The police had not mentioned foul play, but had he pushed her into the river somehow? Not a sure way of killing her, because Jen was a good swimmer. But he had to make it look like an accident, didn't he? An accident when he was supposedly just getting out of a recording session with the other boys. How had he managed to slip away so quickly, and then meet up with her at the right place?

As I fought my way through the crowd to the nearest tube station, a red anger raged in my head. I'd kill him myself. I'd put my hands around his throat and throttle the life out of him. Then, by the time I'd reached the bottom of the escalator, I'd calmed down a little. Instead of taking the westbound train, I opted for the eastbound one instead. I had to stand on Southwark Bridge and see for myself if it had been possible for Denny to have thrown Jen over the side, during the rush hour, with hundreds of witnesses.

The rain was coming down in buckets when I emerged from Mansion House station. What remained of the daylight was fast fading. I walked down to the bridge and out to mid-span. It would indeed have been possible for someone to have jumped from the stone parapet, if they could have scrambled over quickly before anyone had time to stop them. But crowds were still hurrying past me. If Denny had tried to throw her over, she need only have screamed or fought and instantly she'd have been rescued. I looked down at the angry black waters streaming past. Then I looked harder. The current was flowing upstream, not down. It was an incoming tide.

I turned and ran from the bridge to the nearest news rack. I knew there was tidal information in the *Standard*. It was one of the boring tasks I'd had to see to as a newsroom boy. High tide was at midnight tonight. Since I knew that high tide was approximately an hour later every day, that meant that high tide on Friday was at eight p.m. A body would have had two good hours to be taken upstream before the tide turned. And then to have been carried all the way back, past all those bridges and wind up around a sharp bend at the Surrey Docks—it seemed scarcely possible.

Then it was almost as if I was having a vision. I saw myself in that back room at Clodhoppers and heard the girl's cheerful "this room's right over the river."

So the girl had seen Jen go into the back room. Only somehow Denny had followed her, and there had to be some kind of opening in the floor, and....

I started running again, banging the clumsy guitar case into people as I pushed past them. I took the tube to Limehouse. The wet streets seemed eerily deserted after the West End rush hour. Exotic smells of curry and Chinese cooking came out of dingy-looking cafes. Men slunk into corner pubs. Cats prowled. It was still not a savory area to be in, even at this early hour. I made it safely to the pub and went down the stairs to Clodhoppers. A noisy darts game was going on as I moved through to the back room. That unpleasant smell still lingered faintly in the air. What was there about it that made me so uneasy? It was more than unpleasant. It triggered some sort of fear. It reminded me of the morgue, of hospitals. I wondered for a moment if we'd got it wrong and Jen was actually not on that morgue slab, but buried somehow here. Frantically I pulled out crates and boxes and found nothing. Then suddenly I knew what the smell was. I wrestled with the barrel in the middle of the floor. It was empty and moved easily to reveal a square trapdoor. I opened it. Cold damp air rose with the smell of decay in it and I heard water lapping beneath me. I closed it again and ran up the stairs. How could I have been so stupid? How could I have been so easily fooled?

I should go to the police, I told myself. This was none of my business. But I had to confront him myself. I reached Grosvenor House and asked to be taken to Mr. Black's floor. Nigel Dempster opened the door, looking somewhat disheveled for him—shirtsleeves, no tie, hair not perfectly in place. "What do you want now? Denny's very upset. The doctor has given him a sedative."

"What sort of sedative?" I demanded. "Chloroform?"

Nigel took a step back. "What did you say?"

"You heard." I took a step toward him. "Denny said you were brainy, but actually you're too brainy for your own good. You should have shut up. Establishing your alibi by claiming to have witnessed someone jumping off a bridge two hours or more before Jen really died. But you didn't think it through properly, did you? You didn't take the tide into consideration. It was incoming at six, outgoing by the time you put the chloroform over her face and pushed her into that hole."

"What's this? What's going on?" Denny appeared from the bedroom, looking bleary-eyed. Zeke Parsons, the drummer, followed him.

"He did it," I shouted. "He killed Jen."

Nigel looked from one face to the other with utter scorn. "You stupid idiots," he said. "You should have left well alone. You can't afford the bad publicity now. You've made it to the top. You're just about to be the biggest thing that ever hit popular music. You can't give it all up because of some girl."

"You killed my girlfriend?" Denny half-staggered toward him.

"She came to see you at the studio. She was upset and told me about the baby. I knew how soft-hearted you were. I knew you'd want to do the right thing and marry her, but I couldn't let that happen. You are the number one heartthrob in the country. It would have wrecked your image. You're better off without her."

"You killed my girl because she spoiled my image?" Denny demanded. "What kind of sick monster are you?" With an animal howl he flung himself at Nigel. Zeke and I had to pull him off.

"I did it for you, Denny," Nigel shouted, putting up his arms to defend himself. "For you and the boys. Everything I've done was for you." Then he collapsed into sobs.

"Call the police," I said.

"No need." Nigel looked up at us. "I'll turn myself in. It's all over now anyway."

"I should have known from the start," I said. "When you suggested that Jen was homesick because she wrote that song. She didn't write it for herself. She wrote it for me, I was the one who wanted to fly back where I belonged. I still do."

Then I walked out into the night.

If I Had Wings

High in the sky, there's a songbird flying free
Bird he can fly where he will then why not me
If I had wings, I'd fly back where I belong

I climb up high, rooftops are all that I can see
Bird in the sky, you must hate the city just like me
If I had wings, I'd fly back where I belong

Bird in the sky, why don't you leave this smoky air
You can fly, you don't need money for the fare
If I had wings, I'd fly back where I belong.

Why do you stay, bird, you're a stranger here like me
Go fly away. You don't have to keep me company
If I had wings, I'd fly back where I belong

An Interview with Rhys Bowen

Where did you grow up? Was yours a bookish household?
My early years were in Bath, then my family moved to rural Kent. My mother was a schoolteacher, later principal. My great aunt who lived with us was an avid reader of the classics and told me all of Dickens, etc., while I was still little.

Do you remember the first mystery novel you ever read?
Oh yes. The Famous Five (the British equivalent of Nancy Drew). I devoured them all then moved on to Agatha Christie.

What was the first piece of music you recall?
Light Cavalry and Fingals Cave made an early impression on me, and I remember my grandfather's loathing for crooners on the radio, especially Frank Sinatra, which is funny as my son is now playing Frank Sinatra on stage.

Was yours a musically oriented household?
My grandfather was an orchestra conductor so there was always music in our house. My mother and aunt studied piano to concert level. My grandmother played the church organ as a small child. Being Welsh, music was considered a big part of our lives.

Do you listen to music when you write?
No, I must have total quiet when I write.

Has a musical work ever inspired a novel or short story?
If you read my Constable Evan mystery, *Evan Blessed*, you'll

find that the Scheherazade suite by Rachmaninov plays an important part in the story, as do musical clues.

What is your favorite manmade sound?
A tie: Pavarotti singing. Harp music.

What is your favorite sound in nature?
The sound of a mountain stream dancing over rocks.

If you had to choose three novels to take on a trip, what would you choose?
Ones I had already read or am waiting to read? I always enjoy a new Lindsay Davies, something by Reginald Hill, Peter Robinson or Deborah Crombie.

Your work is noted for a strong sense of time and place. How do you start a story?
For the Evan books I usually have an idea for the type of crime I want. What would happen if a bunker was discovered on the mountain, for example, and I take it from there.
In the Molly books, I always want to tie in a facet of life in 1902, New York City, so I start with abuses in the sweat shops, or with a pair of spiritualists. Loads of research before I write a word.

If you had a chance to invite any three people in the world to dinner, living or dead, who would they be?
Mother Teresa, Maya Angelou, Peter Ustinov. Wouldn't that be a dynamic combination?

Which would you rather do—read or listen to a favorite CD?
Usually read, unless I'm stressed and then I'd rather listen to classical music.

This eerie story will have you checking the locks on the doors at night. John says: "This story came out in a rush. I had committed to writing a 'scary' short story and a song to go with it, and the words 'Something Out There' came tumbling out onto my computer. The idea of a woman coming home alone to an empty house has always held a morbid fascination for me, and suddenly there was Stacey Corcoran, getting out of her car and noticing an open closet in the garage. I haven't written much 'creepy' suspense before, but this story wrote itself in a few hours, and I enjoyed the experience immensely."

Something Out There

John Lescroart

Out in her driveway, the headlights of Stacey Corcoran's Jetta illuminated the garage door for a moment before she pressed the button on the car's visor. As the door lifted, the automatic bulb in the ceiling came on. With a brief smile of satisfaction, Stacey noted the results of all the effort she'd put in on the space over the weekend.

She'd had a rare weekend off without paralegal work and she'd gone down to Home Depot, bought, and all by herself installed one of those do-it-yourself cabinet-making kits. On Tuesday—yesterday—the recycling and garbage trucks had come by and taken the cardboard and all the other junk and now her garage was, if not spectacularly clean, then at least uncluttered and organized. It gave her some small but real pleasure to see the order she'd brought to what had heretofore been a scene of barely controlled chaos.

Six months now down in the suburbs, and at last she was beginning to make some headway in turning her small Millbrae house into a home. And about time, she thought.

As she pulled forward, though, her smile faded for a second. The door to the largest cabinet, big enough for a grown man to stand up in, yawned open. She knew it had been closed when she'd left in the morning.

In fact, before she'd gotten into her car to go to work, she'd walked along the back wall of the garage where she'd stacked the cabinets, running her hand along the front of each of the doors, admiring the flat expanse of laminated plyboard, her skill in lining them up just so, the connection between them nearly seamless. Standing back, she even remembered thinking that it might be fun to call Home Depot and ask if somebody wanted to come out and take a picture of the finished product. In her opinion, her arrangement of the cabinets was more professional-looking than the advertising photo they had at the store.

Clearly now, though, that one door hung more than halfway open.

In her driver's seat, with the engine still running, she considered slamming the car into reverse and getting out of there. If someone had somehow broken in and was hiding in that closet, she...

But with a tolerant smile at herself, she recognized that she was being ridiculous. This was the precise reason she'd left the city and moved down the Peninsula to the leafy suburbs—to get away from the craziness of life in San Francisco, where every apartment had bars on the windows, where every week she heard a story from someone she knew about a crime that they'd either witnessed or been the victim of, or knew someone who had.

Stacey had grown up in Palo Alto, but she had elected to stay in the big city after graduating from San Francisco State, finding the charged atmosphere of urban life exhilarating and exciting. After five years, the pace and the crowding and the sense of danger—especially at night—had grown more and more intense until at last it had happened to her.

She'd worked late, as she often did, and a creepy guy from the bus had gotten off with her at her stop. It was only three blocks to her apartment in the Mission, but this night at 9:30 they were a dark, deserted, and fogbound three blocks. He'd followed her for two of them, his footfalls quickening behind her—afraid to look back, she'd been nearly running to keep ahead of him by then—until he grabbed her at the front of the alley that ran by the side of her apartment building.

She'd screamed and screamed, fought and fought, and in the end she drove him off, but not before he'd gotten his hands on her, stolen her purse, choked her halfway to death and knocked her to the ground. In spite of the trauma, she knew she'd been lucky—it could have been much worse.

And no one had come to help her.

Now, as she pulled the Jetta forward and came to a stop inside the garage, she realized that she could see all the way to the back of the closet. Still, she supposed it was possible that someone could be pressed up against the last few inches against the side.

Just because you're paranoid, she reminded herself—and she realized after her earlier mugging that she probably was—doesn't mean that other bad things can't happen. Leaving the car running, its lights still on, and the garage door open behind her, she got out with her heavy briefcase, intending to use it as a weapon to slow him down if she had to. And then she'd run like hell.

In her new, quiet, friendly, orderly neighborhood, people all around her were finishing dinner, or watching television. Kids were doing homework. Someone would help her if she screamed here. It was nothing like the city.

She walked gingerly to the cabinet and swiftly pulled the door all the way open toward her.

Empty. Completely empty.

With a nervous little self-conscious laugh, she turned and walked back to her car, reached in and turned off the motor, hit the lights and then the visor button again. As the garage door settled down behind her, she walked a couple of steps and opened the connecting door to her house, flicking on the warm kitchen lights as she came in.

"Are you sure? If you want, I could come by and spend the night with you."

"No, Mom. I mean, yes. I'm sure. It was just me, I'm sure, because of what happened in the city."

"Which was very real. And very scary."

"Granted, no argument. But I don't want to ask you to drive all the way up here."

"It's only twenty miles, hon. I could be there in a half hour. I really wouldn't mind."

"I know, I know. You're great. But this was why I moved down here, remember. Because it's safe. If I start calling you up to sleep over every time one of the cabinet doors blows open, you'll wind up living here."

"That wouldn't be the worst thing in the world, would it?"

"Mom, really. That's the saint in you talking. You'd do it, but it wouldn't be a good idea. You know it as well as me. And what would Dad do with you up here?"

"He wouldn't mind. And especially not tonight when he's in New York. And you are alone."

"So are you, Mom, and you're not afraid, are you? I've got to get over this or I'll be crippled for life. Besides, you know I'm surrounded by nice people here. Regular homes. Kids even. It's nothing like it was in the city."

A sigh. "All right. But I'm here if you need me. Even just to talk."

"I know. I appreciate it, really. I love you. But now my mission is to eat and then get some sleep. I've got another long day tomorrow. Barry—Mr. Harrison—got finished with his latest trial today and is on vacation the next two weeks and he wants everything off his desk and done by Friday, which is basically impossible. But I'll do it."

"I know you will."

"I am woman, hear me roar."

Her mother chuckled. "I hear you, girl. I hear you. Call me back if you need anything."

"I will, Mom. But I won't."

"Okay. Good night, sweetie."

"Night, mom."

The house was a small stand-alone in a tract of five hundred similar homes called Harbor Oaks. The average unit had two bedrooms, two stories under gabled roofs, thirteen hundred total square feet, including the garage. The developers had built the neighborhood about ten years before and in a rare display of economic confidence and good taste had accommodated most of the old trees that grew on the Bay-facing slopes of the Peninsula hills. In consequence, the place with its old-growth oaks had a pastoral quality, even a sense of gracious aging, and some really wonderful views. As a single woman living alone here, Stacey herself was a bit of an anomaly. Nearly every other place was the domain of a young family—mom and dad and a couple of children—although the occasional single parent kept house in the neighborhood as well.

Stacey's downstairs was divided into a kitchen and dining area—really more of a nook than a separate room—and a living room with a large picture window and a working fireplace, where tonight she'd laid in and lit a few logs. She'd left her old furniture back in her city apartment, and bought new stuff for here from the ground up at IKEA. A new television set, new pots and pans and sets of four utensils each.

Although as she was setting a place for herself at the table, there were only three of the steak knives in the drawer. Distractedly, she wondered what she had done with the last one. Had she used one over the weekend, perhaps, to cut open the packing tape on the cardboard containers for the garage cabinets? She checked the dishwasher—not there.

Well, she was sure it would turn up.

Now, at a quarter to ten, she sat reading her evening news-paper and finishing her supper—a chicken breast, glass of white wine, and a small salad—at her table off the kitchen by the front window. Outside, branches on the big tree on her front lawn were starting to make noise, scraping against the roof. The paper, the *San Mateo County Times*, had an article about the first winter storm which was supposed to arrive tonight, and it looked like it was showing up on schedule. She was glad she'd lit the fire.

Usually Stacey skipped right by the local news section of the paper, since it typically dealt with the kinds of crimes that tended not to occur here at Harbor Oaks, but more in the communities and ghettoes set in the flats down by the Bay. But tonight for some reason she found herself reading the small print in a regular weekly feature called The Blotter—city by city reports, really just listings, of petty crimes submitted by local police departments. Burglaries, car thefts, DUIs. The so-called small stuff. Although Stacey knew from her own experience that each of these had undoubtedly been a source of grief, dismay, anger, or frustration to the people involved in them. That was the nature of crime. It disrupted.

But what had caught her attention tonight was the Millbrae report for last week, which listed personal property loss of nearly fourteen thousand dollars in total merchandise from street names which she recognized as being from her immediate neighbor-hood. $1200, CD system stolen from 324 Oakmont Ave.; $600, two bicycles from 1115 24th Street; $3100, television from 128 Harbor Circle; $860, car stereo from 1241 23rd Street. None of these addresses was more than five blocks from her house. All of these thefts were from residential addresses. They were burglaries, which meant that someone in this neighborhood was breaking into houses or garages.

Suddenly, the wind gusted outside and she heard a small crack and a distinct thump above her, and almost simultaneously a good-sized falling branch hit the ground outside her window. Leaning over, she looked out, then up through the tree to the stars twinkling in the cloudless skies. There might be a storm on the way, she thought, but first comes the wind. As though to underscore the observation, another gust whistled in the eaves. The tree scraped the house again and flung a couple of acorns against the window.

Behind her, the settling of one of the fire's large logs made her jump.

"Easy, girl," she said to herself. "It's the wind."

But still…

She closed the newspaper, then picked up her empty plate and half-empty glass of wine and brought them over to the sink. While she rinsed her service, her mind went back to the mystery of the missing steak knife. She must have taken it out to the garage over the weekend. There was nowhere else it could be. She drew one deep breath, then another, trying to calm herself against the irrational urge to panic.

Above her, upstairs, the house creaked.

In a few quick steps, she was suddenly across the kitchen, the phone again in her hand. But after punching two of her mother's numbers, she paused and hung up the receiver. What would be the point of worrying her mother again? There was nothing here. It was a windy night, that was all.

Since she was almost there anyway, she walked back to the connecting door to the garage and opened it, then turned on the light. The damned cabinet door was open again, and she couldn't for the life of her remember whether she'd left it that way after she'd pulled it all the way open earlier. But she must have. When the automatic outer door was closed, there was no other entrance to the garage except through the house, and she'd been in the kitchen and nook the whole time since she'd come in. So no one was in the garage. Or in the cabinet.

Unless they'd been there before…

Shaking off that thought, she stepped back out onto the cement floor of the garage and over to the cabinet. Empty again.

This time, she carefully closed the door. It had one of those magnetic plates that in theory held it in place, but maybe she'd hung the door wrong and the seal wasn't good. Or something.

Whatever it was, the door didn't seem to want to stay closed. Maybe there'd been a small earthquake that she hadn't felt. They happened all the time. She pushed on the door, stood back, waited. It stayed where it was. Reaching out, she pulled it open—it took a little bit of effort—then pushed it back closed.

Since she was already here, she cast her eyes quickly around the newly organized room. No sign of the knife, and she wasn't about to start going through the cabinets right now. It had to be here. Where else could it be?

Stacey Corcoran was twenty-eight years old. At five feet six and a hundred and twenty pounds, she was an attractive young woman with lustrous, mid-length brown hair, good skin, and a face that became more than normally attractive whenever she smiled. She had had three serious boyfriends in her life, each relationship lasting about two years. The last one had been an engagement to a medical student named Jeff Torborg, but that had ended about a year before because Jeff had developed what he called "commitment issues." She had called it cheating, and left him.

But tonight, still for some reason somewhat spooked and unable to will herself to go upstairs and get in bed, she was sitting in her favorite chair under her reading light by the fire watching the evening news when quite suddenly she decided that it was time she got serious about finding herself a mate. She'd been living alone for too long—she and Jeff had never moved in together—and it was time to change that. It wasn't natural for people, especially friendly, basically good people such as herself, to live all by themselves. It bred fears and weirdnesses and, frankly, loneliness. She was tired of being alone, of eating alone, of working alone, of solitary sex, of not sharing the events and emotions of her life. That was going to change, maybe starting tomorrow.

The news program had cut to commercials and she muted the screen, then turned the set off entirely.

But suddenly now, along with the admission that she was going to change things, came a renewed awareness of her loneliness in the here and now. No, she corrected that thought. Not her loneliness. Her *aloneness*. She was alone. Physically alone. It was not an emotional loneliness so much as it was a deep consciousness that she was completely by herself, sitting in a stand-alone house, in the middle of a mostly sleeping residential suburban neighborhood.

In her logical mind, she knew that there was little likelihood of danger here. But in a strange and paradoxical way, that very unlikelihood made any real danger—a threat that had somehow made it through the cracks of normalcy into suburbia—that much more frightening. The grin of a carnival clown may not be terrifying in a circus environment, but if one appeared outside her window right now it would scare her to death.

Outside that window, the wind had picked up even more, and now with the television off, it produced an steady if undulating wail as it came howling up the hillside off the Bay. She fancied she even felt a draft here in the house—probably coming down the chimney, she told herself. But unsettling, like everything else tonight seemed to be.

The legacy of getting mugged, she was sure.

Still in her reading chair, Stacey thought she caught a glimpse of something white-ish at the near window to the side of the mantel. Frozen, hugging herself, she stared for another minute, listening to the wind, straining to see again whatever it might have been. At last she stood up, went to the window and looked out.

The streetlights at the curb up the hill had gone dark, the electricity knocked out by the wind, but a few lights twinkled in the nearer windows. The neighborhood basked in a platinum bright moonglow. Close in, between her house and the next, another large oak swayed in the wind, its spectral branches whipping in the wind.

Enough, she thought. The clock on the mantel told her it was quarter to eleven. She had to be up by her usual 6:30. Time for bed. Turning, she walked to check the front door. Locked up tight. Double bolted. Solid.

All right.

Thank god her lights were still working. She crossed back and turned out her reading light, then flicked the switch by the staircase and took one last look around. There was nothing out of place. Even if there was something out there, there was nothing in here, she told herself. Stop being such a baby. She took a step up and stopped in her tracks.

A leaf lay flattened, at her eye level, on the fifth step.

Her stomach did a flip and she felt the blood drain out of her face, even as she told herself again that there were any number of explanations for what she was seeing. The most obvious was that she'd brought the leaf in herself, stuck on one of her shoes last night, and it had come off on the stairs this morning as she was walking down them. She would never have noticed that—why would she? It would have been behind her.

But bringing her shaking hands to her stomach, she couldn't make herself take another step up. She leaned against the wall, endured another gust from outside, and with a last look up the stairs, stepped over to her breakfast nook table to get her purse, in which she kept her cell phone.

By the time her fingers gripped the phone, her hands were shaking so badly that she could barely get it out of the purse. And as soon as she opened it, the slim and sleek razor phone slipped from her grasp and clattered to the floor. Sure that it was broken, Stacey scooped it up and pushed the little red button that turned it on.

One second. Two seconds.

Was that another creak from upstairs? An acorn blew against the window directly behind her. The phone's window lit up, played its little jingle. Oh my god, she thought. It's LOUD!

As she was about to make her emergency call to the police, she realized that logic dictated a simple fact: if she was calling to report a stranger in her house, she had better behave as though she believed a stranger was in fact hiding somewhere within these walls. Which meant he would hear the call. Which in turn meant she had to get out.

But where to?

Outside, the wind blew and the streetlights were black. If her intruder heard the front door open, he might break from his hiding place and run her down. It was the middle of the night, and few if any of her good working neighbors would still be awake. She might, as she had before in the city, scream and scream and be neither heard nor helped.

On the other hand, she couldn't stay where she was, where he would hear anything above a whisper, and maybe even that. And that would surely flush him.

What was she doing? What was she doing?

Just press the numbers, idiot!

Hit nine one one and the cops will be here, even if she didn't say one word to them. She knew this. She worked for a lawyer. She'd heard every story in the book. You dialled nine one one and the machinery rolled.

She couldn't make herself call in an emergency and then very well not talk to anybody with the police. If she did, they might come in with sirens blaring and lights blazing and scare her intruder away. And without him, she would have no proof anybody had ever really been here. She'd be exposed as a stupid, hysterical female. Barry would think she was unstable and maybe worse.

Suddenly she looked over and saw the door connecting the kitchen and the garage. She'd already been out there twice tonight. There was no one there, or he would probably have struck earlier. She could call from out there, talk to the police, tell them to come in silently and surround the house.

She was sure someone was inside.

Holding her cell phone in front of her with both hands so that she wouldn't drop it again, she walked across the now-darkened kitchen, over to the door to the garage, and opened it.

The garage was pitch black. She stepped through the door, closed it behind her, and reached for the light switch.

From the Wedding Announcements page of the San Mateo County Times, *June 12, 2006:*

Nunez/Corcoran. Officer Pedro Nunez of Millbrae and the Millbrae Police Department and Stacey Corcoran, originally of Palo Alto, were wed last Saturday at Our Lady of Angels Church at a ceremony attended by over a hundred of the couple's relatives and friends. The Maid of Honor was the bride's mother, Sharon Corcoran, and the Best Man was the groom's brother, Michael Nunez. The couple gained some notoriety last fall after Officer Nunez was one of a team of police who responded to an emergency call to the home of Ms. Corcoran and discovered a lone, knife-wielding intruder hiding out in Ms. Corcoran's bedroom closet. The suspect, Jerrald Stevens Walker, was also wanted for the home break-in murders of three women in the East Bay over the past year, and is awaiting trial in Redwood City. The newly married couple plan to honeymoon in Maui and make their home in the bride's home in the Harbor Oaks section of Millbrae.

John says: "Knowing that I'd signed up for The Merry Band of Murderers project, I was fooling around on guitar, trying to come up with a fun and possibly scary guitar figure or two, and fell into the opening riff of the song. The notes—C, D#, C, F, E—seemed to come with the words "It's gonna get you" attached to them. From there the song just built itself up—"Suburbia calm and quiet, no crime in the streets"—except that things perhaps aren't what they seem. What if there was 'something out there'? And hysteria starts to creep in? Once the song was finished, the story wrote itself in about four hours. I figured it had to be a woman in jeopardy, and sure enough, that's just who turned up. This is pretty much the first pure suspense I've written, and it's certainly the first song in the scary power pop genre of my career, and both of them were a ton of fun."

Something Out There

Suburbia's calm and quiet tonight,
There's no crime in the streets.
All the little houses are locked up tight,
Everyone's lawn is neat.
The TVs hum, the radios sing,
Now and again you hear a telephone ring,
And nobody's worried or scared, but you better beware.
'Cause...

There's something out there, something out there,
Something out there and it wants in tonight.
(It's gonna get you, it's gonna get you,
It's gonna get you tonight.)

Hysteria comes with the grin of a clown,
You go numb, it's the bite of a snake.
The wind starts blowing and there's no one around,
And your body starts to shiver and shake.
Is that a shadow in the window or a stranger's face?
A killer or a visitor from outer space?
And now you're running down and locking the doors
'Cause you're suddenly sure...that...

There's something out there, something out there,
Something out there and it wants in tonight.
(It's gonna get you, it's gonna get you,
It's gonna get you tonight.)

An Interview with John Lescroart

Where did you grow up? Was yours a bookish household?
I grew up, at least from age 12, in Belmont, California, which is about twenty-two miles south of San Francisco and ten miles from Millbrae, the setting for "Something Out There." I come from a large family—four sisters and two brothers—so the household in which I grew up was more loud and crazy than bookish. All of my siblings had lots of friends and my parents were great about allowing, even encouraging, us to have them over all the time. Still, we did have a full wall of books in our living room, and my father was capable of sitting in his chair and reading with a roomful of kids swarming and playing all around him, which he did nearly every night. So we all understood that reading was important and even fun, and books were to be treasured.

Do you remember the first mystery novel you ever read?
The first mystery was probably the Hardy Boys story, *The Tower Treasure*—after I'd seen it in installments on the Mickey Mouse Club. I'm sure I read a few more Hardy Boys books after that, but I don't remember any of them clearly. The first "adult" mystery I remember was *Anatomy of a Murder*, which I read and loved when I was about 16 years old.

What was the first piece of music you recall?
That's a great question. I remember music from my earlier youth—I know I sang some Christmas carols with my sister Patricia at a school in Nashville (Nashville!!!) when

I was about three. And our family was hugely into Perry Como—"Hot Diggety Dog" and "Round and Round" remain among my favorites. After that, my dad got into some goofy semi-Italian songs with names like "Angelique, Your Mama's Gonna Take You Back." The first "modern" pop song I liked was "(Oh, My Boy) Lollipop," then Frankie Avalon's "Why," followed quickly (I was in sixth grade by then) by the Everly Brothers and the whole world of music.

Was yours a musically oriented household?

As the earlier answer might indicate, very much so. We had all the Broadway soundtracks going all the time (*Sound of Music, Music Man, Oklahoma!*, etc.) and my mom loved Barbra Streisand and country music, while my father was even more eclectic. Strangely (or maybe not, since my folks both came from Brooklyn and were pretty white), we didn't have much blues or even jazz. But we sang as a family whenever we drove anyway, harmonizing, my sister Patricia playing the ukelele. By the time I went to college, we had several guitars in the house, a piano, a flute and recorder and even drums for a while.

Do you listen to music when you write?

Never. I need silence. It's a difference voice up there when I write.

Has a musical work ever inspired a novel or short story?

Just this one: "Something Out There."

What is your favorite manmade sound?

Another great question. Has to be a perfectly tuned acoustic, nylon-stringed guitar.

What is your favorite sound in nature?

Water over rocks.

If you had to choose three novels to take on a trip, what would you choose?

The Great Gatsby, War and Peace, and any one of Elmore Leonard's last twenty books.

Your work is noted for an almost unbearable sense of threat and suspense. How do you start a story?

I always try to start with a character to root for and a situation that upsets the grace of living. A fire, a death, a murder, a theft—anything that will put my character outside of his or her comfortable world. Once they are in this "strange land," the world opens up so that they may never find their way back, and therein lies the suspense. We want them back where they were, with the world working as it should. But of course getting them there is perilous and uncertain, and we ache for their plight.

If you had a chance to invite any three people in the world to dinner, living or dead, who would they be?

John Lennon, Ernest Hemingway, and Marilyn Monroe.

Which would you rather do—read or listen to a favorite CD?

That's not fair. I love both, and can't really do them at the same time. I can't imagine a quality life without both music and books.

*We've always found Jim Fusilli's work powerful.
It's due in part to the contrast between theme and
his understated prose. But it's his insight into character that gives this story its eerie power. We asked
Jim how "It's Too Late to Cry" came about.*

*"I was doing a reading in San Antonio, Texas,
and I chose a passage in which one of my characters criticizes hippies. A woman in the audience,
dressed in a denim jacket, long skirt and sandals, interrupted me. "How do you know?" she
shouted angrily. "You weren't even there!" That
night, I started to think about hippies and the
hippie ethos and how much of it was shallow
and superficial while other parts were substantial
and made the country better, and how there were
people who couldn't differentiate between the
two. I created two characters that represented separate sides of the ethos and put them in conflict."*

It's Too Late to Cry

Jim Fusilli

He was greeted by nervous silence. "Go ahead," he said, rising
from his office chair, his fist tight around the telephone handset.
"Just tell me."

"Rob, it's your—It's Mickey."

Oh Jesus, no.

"I saw her on Mulholland, Rob," he said, his voice clear
through the phone line. "Carrying a shotgun."

"A shot—" He'd thought Tyler was going to tell him what
he'd feared most had already happened, and there were patrol
cars, an ambulance and somber neighbors gathered outside their
white stucco as a body bag emerged.

His heart racing, he said, "And?"

"And…?" The man swallowed hard. "Rob, Mickey's walking along Mulholland, carrying a shotgun."

"Was she headed home?"

Tyler lived on Kirkwood too. "Yeah. Yeah, I think so."

Barmer put his hand under his necktie, laying it flat on his chest.

"Her eyes, Rob. You know, all empty, like… Rob?"

Yeah, he knew. Mickey's pale-green eyes…

"Maybe I should call the cops?"

"No, Tyler." Barmer looked at his watch, at the spreadsheet and calculator on his desk. "No, I'll be right there."

Thirty-five minutes later, he turned off Laurel Canyon, serene in the dull October light.

He hurried along the slate path, slick still from a late-morning shower.

The front door wasn't locked.

He entered cautiously. "Mickey?"

And there she was, on the sofa, bare legs crossed under her, her back against a downy quilt, shotgun rested on her lap.

He sighed sadly. "Mickey," he said, shaking his head. "Mickey, no. Not this."

She ran her right hand through her blonde hair, tucked long strands behind her ear. Her freckled ear jutted out now, and once again he wondered how anything so adorable could come from such a troubled mind.

Behind her, the grassy leaves of her spider plant drooped beneath the cradle of a dangling hemp braid.

"Mickey?"

She picked up the shotgun and held it in front of her.

He saw she had her finger on the trigger.

On the coffee table, near the black-onyx jewelry box that held her stash, was an open box of green Remington shells.

"Mickey?"

Bare feet, pink panties, a white peasant blouse. Pale-green eyes, and her hair tucked behind her ear.

The shotgun, though. Never a shotgun in 19 years.

"I can't bear the weight," she said tiredly, as she shifted the gun to where she wanted it. "All that... It's too much, Bobby. You know?"

"Mickey, please. Let me help."

"Too late," she said calmly.

"Whatever it is," he said, "let me help you." He held out his hand. "We can do it together. You know that."

"Not this time. Not anymore."

He stepped toward her, moving slow, tears in his eyes. "Mickey, you're—"

"I can't bear it, Bobby," she said. "And I don't deserve it."

And then a bolt of fire, and a burst of blood and bone.

January 14, 1967, the Human Be-In at the Polo Grounds in the shadow of the Golden Gate Bridge. A balmy day, abundant sun; paisley and tie-dye everywhere, beads, swirling bodies, daisies, the scent of marijuana and patchouli. "A Gathering of the Tribes," they called it, and Barmer heard there was going to be some kind of debate over Vietnam, Haight-Ashbury hippies vs. Berkeley radicals. Allen Ginsberg would be there, and Timothy Leary too, preaching LSD. Shunryu Suzuki Roshi from the Zen Center, and the Grateful Dead and the Hell's Angels. "A real circus," Stern explained.

They came down Fulton Street in Stern's tatty Corvair. Barmer, a USF business major, expected a podium, moderator, point, counterpoint. In his crew sweater, white button-down collar peeking over the top, khaki slacks, black socks and penny loafers, he found himself in a kaleidoscope, an undulating world suddenly purposeless. Tambourines, sitars, soap bubbles, hashish, bare feet in green grass: chaos bearing a goofy grin. Though Stern had a lava lamp, black-light posters and Zappa's "Freak Out!" on his turntable, Barmer couldn't have felt less at ease, Robert Barmer Jr. from Glendale, his father in charge of the Bank of

America branch, his mother in sea-foam chiffon and matching heels, gently stirring a pitcher of dry martinis as she waited for Robert Sr. to walk through the door.

Barmer in San Francisco, free to float under the honey sun, the high sky, free to—

And there she was, her blonde hair shimmering as she danced, arms stretched over her head, eyes closed. Luminous skin, flawless features, freckles splashed on a perfect face. Swaying, spinning slowly; one of thousands, and yet the only one. Barmer adjusted his black-rimmed glasses.

She wore a brown-leather vest over a white blouse, and a long denim skirt that seemed to be a pair of jeans re-stitched, embroidered patches here and there. Above her sandals, an ankle bracelet made of candy hearts.

Her breasts shifted under her blouse as she spun, fingers stroking the clouds. She lowered her dimpled chin, opened her eyes and looked directly at him. Tucking her hair behind one ear, she offered him the most tranquil, beneficent smile he had ever seen. His heart leaped into his throat.

Stern shouted from somewhere, and then the sudden roar of motorcycle engines. Barmer turned, and when he turned again, she was gone.

If he hadn't seen her three months later on Market Street on the march to Kezar Stadium, he would've sworn she'd been an illusion, a symbol of his unexpected liberation. In class, in the quiet of the library, he'd wondered if he hadn't invented her, giving form to the spirit in the park. In his mind, she'd come to represent innocence, tranquility and abandon, and soon he reasoned such a being could not be.

But there she was again, this time wearing an expensive black Borsolino, and she had a tiny sunflower painted on her cheek. He saw she was alone, pulled along by the energy of the crowd, sunbeams falling on her and no one else.

The sound of stinging guitars from loudspeakers above doorways, and Barmer nudged through the advancing multitude, ducking under banners. Fifty thousand chanting, marching people, fists in the air, the Black Panthers over from Oakland. The Spring Mobilization to End the War in Vietnam, which, by now, was fine with Barmer, if not the Glendale Chamber of Commerce, his father its president. Barmer jostled, Barmer pinballed, but he kept moving, honing in.

"Hi," he said, as they surged around them. He was better dressed now, the right glasses, his dark hair a riot of curls. He stuck out his hand. "I'm Rob Barmer."

She giggled, took his right hand in her left, and they walked together to Golden Gate Park. She told him her name was Michillinda, and said she lived nowhere, crashing in Hashbury wherever she could, the Diggers providing free food. Barmer, not quite there yet, asked her what her father did and her expression told him to leave those kinds of questions behind. Approaching the park, she put her arm around his waist.

They saw Quicksilver at Winterland, Paul Butterfield at the Avalon, and by the time the fall semester rolled around, she was sleeping in his dorm room. Stoned, Stern went through her purse, found out her real name was Marion. She was from Del Mar, and she had 38 cents and a prescription for penicillin from the Free Medical Clinic.

"Your old lady..." Stern began, passing the bong one misty afternoon, sitting on the dorm-room floor, listening to Love. "You be careful, man."

Barmer hadn't quite thought of Mickey as his—maybe just a butterfly cupped for a moment in the palms of his hands—but he liked the idea, outdated as it was.

"Lot of freaks in... the freaks." Stern started to giggle, a smoke cloud haloing around him; he was almost ready to tell Barmer he'd been balling her too, plying her with apple wine. Instead, he said, "You know, man, paranoia is, like, basic protection."

Barmer had his head back on the bed, looking at the ceiling, thinking of Mickey on top of him, rolling her hips, bringing him closer and closer to bliss. Beautiful Mickey, pure and true. A rainbow.

Trouble's first sign came that October when the three of them went to the Death of Hip ceremony, watching the Diggers torch a gray casket bearing the words "Summer of Love." Standing amid the cheering crowd on Haight, Mickey and Stern figured they were only saying good-bye to 1967, but Barmer saw it clear, as the Diggers had: free sex and cheap dope would make San Francisco a magnet for assholes and opportunists. In their own way, hippies were as smug, judgmental and uptight as the Glendale Chamber of Commerce, scoffing at anyone from outside their sect. Barmer had gone as far as he could—pretty fuckin' far, considering his parents gave him golf clubs for Christmas—but he'd never bought flower-power, his mind definitely not blown. He dug it as best he could. Earnest is as earnest does, man, said Stern, a psych major.

The casket aflame, Barmer stepped back to watch soot and smoke rise above the lamp posts. Out of the corner of his eye, he saw Mickey straddling the mailbox like it was a stallion, cheering, beaming like she had not a care, the black Borsolino tilted on the back of her head.

Behind him, a woman said sharply, "Hey, there's the chick that stole your hat. That's *your* hat."

"Well," a man said in wonder. "Fuck me."

Barmer turned to see the couple march toward Mickey, and the man, brown hair on the shoulders of his pea coat, swiped the Borsolino off her head.

The black woman at his side, enormous Afro, hoop earrings and an impressive scowl, had her fists on her hips.

"Thief," the man muttered as he returned the hat to his head.

New Yorker Stern stepped up angry.

"It's my hat, man," the man explained, "my hat."

His companion, though no less stoned, met Stern's fury. "Chick's a thief, man. Chick ain't cool."

Barmer arrived. "What's going on?"

Stern and the Afro locked eyes.

"My hat," the man repeated. "Come on, Florence."

"Chick ought to pay."

"Get fucked," Stern said.

Florence looked him up and down. "Your friend's a thief," she said finally, with a wry smile. "You know it, don't you? You ain't even asked."

Tamping down her hair, Mickey stared at the Diggers, the casket, and Barmer saw she wasn't listening to the row she'd caused. But she wasn't ignoring it. To her, it was as if it wasn't happening at all.

The man tapped Stern's arm. "Hey, it's groovy, man. Hat, head. Groovy."

He flashed the peace sign.

"Not cool," Afro added, walking away, falling in with the parade.

"Bobby," she said. "Bobby, you're my sanctuary. Do you know that, Bobby?"

She was naked on the pillow in the wicker chair, stars above the cypress trees, and the roach was no more than a cinder.

"Mickey…"

Two years later now, living in Stern's genius idea: a house in Half Moon Bay; they'd split the rent, travel to USF in Stern's almost-new VW bus, and Mickey could live with them, bring in chicks for Stern, rake them in off the beach; but leave the men outside, this is no fuckin' commune, Mickey, you hear me? Mickey nodding; Stern, a tinderbox when he wasn't dropping chlorpromazine. Barmer, MBA within reach, agreed. For all his flaws, Stern paid his bills and if he made rules, he generally kept to them.

"You're my sanctuary," she repeated, the scent of Herbal Essence and Vitabath surrounding them.

"Mickey," Barmer began, "Mickey, you can't… This is not good."

It was the best he could do, his guileless angel, fresh from the shower, fresh from jail. Shoplifting batteries, and not the first bust either: film but they had no camera; a steak, but she said she was a vegetarian. This time they pulled him from class, and the cop, straight out of "The Mod Squad," said, "Mr. Barmer, for what it's worth: cut her loose or marry her."

Mickey couldn't seem to understand that she was moving toward a felony rap; $75 was the line that couldn't be crossed. Given that she'd been charged with assault during a sit-in at UC Berkeley protesting a Dow Chemical recruiter, a felony would result in prison, even if the assault beef had been knocked down to disorderly conduct. She didn't understand the concept of ramifications. "Everything is everything," she said.

"Mickey, they're going to put you in jail," Barmer explained, pacing the living room.

"Bobby, don't be so…" She giggled. "Don't be so Bobby."

"You're smarter than this, Mickey," he said, "and you know where this is going to lead."

Behind him, Barmer heard a voice.

"Bummer." A girl nibbling a chocolate cookie, and she was dimpled-ass naked too.

Barmer said, "And who are you?"

"I'm Mickey's guest," she said boldly.

Stern figured she was Greek or maybe Italian.

"Maybe it's your idea she should rip off Ralphs," Barmer said.

"Maybe," said Greek, maybe Italian.

Mickey giggled.

Simmering, Barmer managed to start up the old Corvair, Muddy Waters on the eight-track, and he drove down to Ralphs to make good with the night manager.

The following morning, a call, Mickey answering, and she said, "Bobby, it's Ralph."

Barmer thought, Ralph who?

They liked his manner, said a regional V.P., who'd heard what he'd done. A young man with priorities. Ralphs had a management-trainee program...

"She's your lucky charm, bro," Stern said, the Mediterranean chick on his lap, brown nipples poking the side of his face as she waited for the hash pipe to return. "Hang on to her."

They married because Barmer's mother wanted it. She came to Half Moon Bay to plead, thinking Mickey was a graduate student like her Robert. Mickey had been an angel at Robert Sr.'s funeral six weeks earlier. Flower-print skirt, flowing hair down her back, sad eyes an ocean of sympathy. Everyone was impressed, unaware Mickey had dropped a couple of 'ludes on the drive down and was as mellow as fog.

"O.K.," said Mickey to Muriel Barmer, weakened by loss and yet still eager to serve. "We'll get married. Sure."

Holding Mickey's hands, she said hopefully, "You'll have such beautiful children, Michillinda."

Barmer was protecting her now: between class and training at Ralphs, he kept up the house so Stern would go on thinking she was earning her rent sweeping up and filling Tupperware with red beans and casseroles. New York Stern was running low on funds and he declared any chick who stayed for two consecutive nights outside of his bed paid rent, a week in advance, even though he was gone for days without notice. Barmer considered it the least he could do for his rainbow, the girl who'd set him free.

But the Haight was a mountain away from Half Moon Bay, and Mickey had a child's heart and she'd turned lonely. "You need a project," Barmer suggested, stroking her hair, and soon the room in back overlooking the gray bay was her studio. Canvasses everywhere, tubes of paint, brushes in coffee cans, and the scent of turpentine. Barmer saw a riot of primary colors and no form, and he wondered if she was feeling better.

Shortly after he earned his MBA, Barmer got a call from Personnel. Ralphs wanted him to move to the home office in Los Angeles.

"Mickey?"

She frowned. "Bobby, I don't know…"

"You can paint in L.A., babe," he reasoned. "There's a good scene. Muralists, and my father used to know this guy. He's at the Art Center of Design in Pasadena…"

Barmer held her when she cried and he always took her back. He'd leave his wallet in plain sight on the nightstand, not bothering to re-count after she left the room.

"Sure. O.K.," she shrugged. "L.A."

Six days after Barmer found them an apartment in West Hollywood off La Cienega, as close to an art scene as he could manage, Mickey lifted a landscape by Paulémile Pissarro off a gallery wall and tried to walk away with it in a Ralphs shopping bag. The painting was priced at $3,000.

Mickey got six months in the county lock-up.

She came out hard as stone.

Barmer couldn't tolerate Reagan, never mind the photo his mother kept over the piano, Robert Barmer Sr. shaking hands with Ronald W. Reagan, now 40th president of the United States. Barmer saw a man who embraced racists, launching his presidential campaign in Philadelphia, Mississippi, where the Klan had killed three civil-rights workers: his wink to the intolerant right who readily endorsed Jim Crow. But Ralphs went for Reagan big, getting out the vote, calling him one of their own, California tried and true, and good for business. Barmer worried where it would lead, this premeditated ignorance of Reagan's shaky character in favor of the flag-waving, cast-iron cheer he engendered. Though fearing there'd be hell to pay down the line, he kept quiet. He had no solutions. His imagination was limited, and he resigned to the pendulum's swing. He did his job, listened to his blues records and tended to his wife.

And he was thinking about a family. Mickey was doing better: a job in a little drive-through Kodak booth in Westwood, accepting film, handing back photos a few days later. She'd been diagnosed with depression while at Sybil Brand, and was taking amitriptyline. Painting again. A fitness program with some of the women who worked at the mall. On weekends, he drove her to the galleries down in Laguna, or they went to the beach. Thicker at the hips, an occasional scowl and not much chatter, but there were days when she glowed. Barmer stared at her in wonder. He owed her so much.

One evening, just before dinner, he called to her. "Mickey, how about you and I…"

Her face void of expression, she came toward the kitchen, hanging by the door frame. "Remember those back pains?" she asked. "The fever?"

Years ago in Half Moon Bay. Mickey had been a mess, and she couldn't shake that virus. A terrible flu, Barmer thought then.

"Bobby…" Oh, fuck it. "Chlamydia, Bobby. And gonorrhea. So, no, Bobby, I can't—We're not going to have a family."

He'd already bought the house up in Laurel Canyon.

"Bobby?" To her surprise, she started to well up when she saw him sag.

Barmer was crying too.

"And don't start talking about adoption," she said quickly. "We both know no one's going to give a kid to me."

Barmer reached for the paper towels, and he said, "Look at us… Red eyes, weepy…"

"Too late for that now," she muttered, walking away. "It is what is."

A month later, they busted her for dealing pot out of the Kodak booth.

Dr. Stern called from New York. The *Daily News* had picked up the story, carrying a photo of Mickey in handcuffs, the yellow booth behind her. The caption read: "A Kodak Moment."

"Marion 'Mickey' Barmer," Stern repeated. "Who else?"

"What's up?" Barmer asked tiredly.

"With me? Same old. I told you they're pulling my license, right?"

Her satchel was almost empty, Mickey told Barmer after he blew her bail. She'd had more than a kilo in nickel bags when she opened the hutch at 8 a.m.

Mickey pled out, got 18 months.

"What are we going to do, Mickey?" he asked, driving her back to county jail.

Mickey stared dead ahead. "You ought to go, Bobby. Just go."

"Ah, Mickey. I—"

"Get Ralphs to transfer you and don't tell me where." She glanced at a palm tree, clinging to it as they passed, craning her neck as if she'd never seen one before. "Go and don't... Just go, Bobby."

Yeah, Barmer thought, but: "I love you, Mickey. I'm not going to do that."

"Don't say it," she told him, looking ahead once again, her hands folded in her lap, wedding ring back at Kirkwood. "I can't bear it."

She turned to him. "Spend it on someone who deserves it."

"That's you, Mickey," he said as he eased to the red light. He ran his hand along her hair, shorn now for the lock-up. "You gave me a good life, babe. You set me free, and for as long as we live, it's going to be you and me."

She knew she was nobody's rainbow. He gave her a glimmer of hope once, the spark of a thought that maybe she was a prize. But that glimmer, that spark, had died a good long while ago.

Now she was dragging him down too.

"You got 18 months to decide, Bobby," she said, as the car behind them smacked its horn. "You could be 18 months gone."

He said, "I'm not going anywhere, Mickey. Not without you. We'll get it back, babe."

Next year and a half, he didn't miss a single visit; Bobby among the tattooed Chicanos, plump babies in their laps; Bobby surrounded by feckless junkies. Getting ready for him was the worst time of her week, knowing she had to rise to his expectations, having sunk to wondering why he bothered to lift her out of Hashbury. She'd grown tired and old, and she knew the day was coming when she couldn't do it anymore.

He turned off Laurel Canyon and onto Kirkwood expecting whirring red lights, Mickey on a gurney, Tyler calling to tell him what she'd done.

But there was no one there, ghostly quiet. No birds, no prop planes circling above the yellowing sycamore leaves. He heard his footsteps on the slate path as he walked purposefully toward their white-stucco ranch.

Sunshine danced on the prickly grass, and mail overflowed the brass box.

He entered cautiously. "Mickey?"

She was on the sofa, bare legs crossed under her, her back against a downy quilt. The shotgun rested on her lap.

"Mickey," he sighed sadly. "Mickey, no. Not this."

She ran her right hand through her long blonde hair, tucked long strands behind her ear.

She picked up the shotgun and held it in front of her.

He saw her finger on the trigger.

Behind her, the drooping leaves of her spider plant bobbed in a dull breeze.

"Mickey?" Two decades ago, the Golden Gate Bridge and she's dancing under the honey sun.

Bare feet, pink panties, a white peasant blouse.

"I can't bear the weight," she said tiredly, as she shifted the gun to where she wanted it. "All that... It's too much, Bobby. You know?"

"Whatever it is," he said, "I can help you." He held out his hand. "I can handle it for you, babe. Or we can do it together. You know that."

"Not this time. Not anymore."

He stepped toward her, tears in his eyes. "Mickey—"

"I can't bear it, Bobby," she said. "And I don't deserve it."

The blast exploded the air, bursting blood and bone.

Barmer blew back against the TV, his chest, neck and lower jaw ripped apart.

His blood and viscera everywhere, high on the walls, on the wicker ceiling fan.

Barmer slid to the floor.

The kick fractured a rib, but she felt nothing. She let the shotgun tumble against the table and onto the rug, and walked through the smoke and mist to her fallen husband.

She looked at him, and watched as what was left of his face sank to slumber. "Oh, Bobby," she moaned as she started to cry. "Now you're free."

She ran her forearm across her eyes.

"Too late for that," she whispered to no one. She went for the phone in the dining room.

It's Too Late to Cry

Babe, it's been a long, long time
And I know it's been a hard, hard fight
What you meant to me
Never made it right
As we stand here on the edge, I know,
It's been a hard, hard fight

The light once held you
And how you let it shine
Then all the promises gave way
To the thrill of the night
You were drifting, babe,
Drifting like you were born to die
Now it's too late to cry

I'm gonna leave you, babe
I'm gonna leave you, babe
A muzzle flash, a bolt of fire
I'm gonna leave you, babe
And as I look at you through dyin' eyes
I know it's too late to cry.

An Interview with Jim Fusilli

Where did you grow up? Was yours a bookish household?
Hoboken, N.J., in the year of "On the Waterfront." It was a good place for someone like me—Sinatra had established the template for using art to get out, and New York City was on the other side of the river. In our own way, we were bookish. My mother liked to read. We used to go to the library together. My father would bring home little cardboard Golden Books for me. So I guess I associated books and reading with love and affection.

Do you remember the first mystery novel you ever read?
Not really. I was seduced by noir films on TV. That's how I started to love the genre. I recall getting excited about Howard Hawks' "The Big Sleep" with Bogart, and someone told me it was a book. I went to the library and read all of Chandler in about a week. Then I was hooked.

What was the first piece of music you recall?
Bobby Darin's "Mack the Knife."

Was yours a musically oriented household?
Very much so. My father had a wonderful voice. He was a singer of great repute in Hoboken. The radio was always on in our house, and we'd watch all the variety shows. Everybody sang, though my mother wasn't, you know, too fabulous. For all of us, though, every chore had a soundtrack.

Do you listen to music when you write?
I used to—any reference to music in the Terry Orr novels is what I was listening to at the time—but I've stopped.

It's too distracting now that I'm experimenting with new ways to tell my stories. I'm too tempted to stop writing and just listen.

Has a musical work ever inspired a novel or short story?
I can't think of a specific work, no. For me, a great song is the same as a great painting or book or film or building in that it inspires me to set high standards and try to create art. In my "Pet Sounds" book, I tried to show that a work of art resonates with me because it illuminates something in me I don't fully understand. So maybe a great musical work or lyric might help me connect with some part of my subconscious and that would inspire a story. Maybe it already has. I don't know. I would like to take on the challenge of adapting a song into a story, though. Not the lyrics, but the mood created by key, tempo and performance.

What is your favorite manmade sound?
A child's laugh.

What is your favorite sound in nature?
A wave pounding the shore. Though I do like the ambient sounds in the silence in nature. Silence is a rare thing when you live in New York City.

If you had to choose three novels to take on a trip, what would you choose?
A long trip far away? *The Blue Flower* by Penelope Fitzgerald. Flaubert's *Sentimental Education*. And something that's quintessentially American and straddles literary and genre fiction. Something by Pete Dexter, maybe *Train*.

Your work is noted for depth of characterization in a genre where story tends to dominate. How do you start a story?
Character and his interaction with setting. I always begin with a person in crisis, and then I select an environment that heightens that sense of crisis. Sometimes the

environment is a reflection of crisis and sometimes it's in stark contrast. In "It's Too Late to Cry," the tranquility of the environment reinforces Barmer's illusions.

If you had a chance to invite any three people in the world to dinner, living or dead, who would they be?

Socrates and Jesus Christ, and Thelonious Monk. Though I've been thinking a lot lately about my parents. Maybe I could have them for dinner and apologize for my petulance and immaturity, and show them I turned out all right.

Which would you rather do—read or listen to a favorite CD?

Listening to music and reading hit me in different places. When I'm enjoying either for a pure aesthetic experience, music goes right to the body and soul, while reading starts in the brain and moves to the soul. If I'm reviewing the music or studying it, it still goes to the body and soul first, but then I push it into my brain. As you can see, I'm avoiding the question...

Mary Anna's story is about two murders. A human corpse is to be expected in a mystery anthology, but this story is also about the death of the land. Mary Anna says: 'Land of the Flowers' was created as a love poem for Florida. It is still one of the most beautiful places on Earth, even under the weight of its burgeoning population."

Land of the Flowers

Mary Anna Evans

A composting toilet.

Garrett Levy already knew more than he wanted to know about composting toilets. Environmental engineering had sounded like a glamorous career when he signed up for it, but the reality had been…well, he should have known that cleaning up a planet wouldn't be a walk in the park. Garrett had spent his years in graduate school learning how to treat various forms of toxic sludge, which meant that he'd spent an entire semester researching the intimate workings of composting toilets.

But he'd never seen one in a private home. Especially not a private home like this one. Congressman Joseph Swain lived in a rustic palace. A sprawling pile of wood and glass, it sat on pilings high above a riverine wetland. With broad eaves overhanging a vast outdoor living space, it was more porch than house. If there was a better place to host a hundred people for the weekend, Garrett couldn't imagine it.

Congressman Swain's voice echoed down the hall. "We wouldn't think of installing a septic system out here, even if we could get a permit. This delicate ecosystem could never process the volume of human waste we're generating here today. And people do seem to like my parties." The congressman arrived on the heels of his rumbling baritone. He appeared to spend most of those parties taking guests on tours of his environmentally perfect home. Garrett had trailed along after him long enough to hear the first part of his spiel, then drifted away to check out the plumbing. It seemed that his proud tour guide, followed by a group of curious guests, had caught up with him. The bathroom was spacious, but it wasn't built for five. Garrett sidled toward the door, only to have his escape aborted.

"Welcome, Mr. Levy," the politician said, clapping a hand on his shoulder. "It's so good to have a representative of the Florida Department of Environmental Protection among us."

Garrett was impressed that the man knew who he was. He didn't ordinarily party with the movers-and-shakers, but his friend Ken had invited Garrett to meet him out here. Maybe Ken had told Swain earlier in the week that he was bringing a guest. Garrett's cell phone company had been a tad too slow in forwarding the message that Ken was home sick with the flu, so he was here alone, trying not to look like a short, balding wallflower.

"With your experience and training, Mr. Levy," Swain continued, "you can appreciate the things we do here. Solar panels give us electricity, water from the sinks is treated and sent to our spray field, and all our biodegradable waste is composted—food, paper, even…well, maybe we don't want to go into the details of this composting toilet." A well-coifed redhead tittered.

"Composting toilets violate one of our most deep-rooted taboos—keeping our waste out of sight—but they make the best kind of sense. Why waste drinkable water for flushing? Not to mention the problems involved in disposing of treated waste from our sewage plants. Why not turn it into clean, sanitary compost, right in your own home, then use it to make the world around you greener?"

The redhead recoiled, then followed Garrett as he made his escape. "No wonder Wynnda hates this place," she muttered under her breath. Realizing she had an audience, she turned her bleach-enhanced smile on Garrett. "Do you know that Wynnda says Joseph wants to be out here every single day the legislature's not in session? She told him to make himself at home, but she'd be staying in Tallahassee, where she has air conditioning and the bugs stay outside where they belong. And where she has a toilet that flushes." She shuddered and hurried downstairs to the bar.

Garrett strolled out on the balcony. He looked down at the throng gathered on the deck below. They milled around, like the insects that had converged on the congressman's open-air buffet. Hell, everything was open-air here.

In the far corner of the deck stood a cluster of women who, like the congressman's other guests, didn't belong in the swamp. This was not a place for lipstick or toenail polish, but five women with colorful lips and toes stood heads-together, whispering as if they thought they might be heard above the din of the crowd and the soaring melodies of the bluegrass band standing twenty feet away. He recognized Wynnda Swain at the center of the group. Her straight ash-blonde hair framed flawless, pale skin. She was exquisite and so, to Garrett's eyes, was this house and the wild land around it, but it was no setting for a woman like this one.

Congressman Swain led his tour group out onto the deck and gestured magnanimously toward the bar. He stood nearly a head taller than anyone else around him, and the sunlight caught his shock of white hair. Being handsome was a valuable political tool.

Another bunch of sycophants clad in chinos and deck shoes gathered around him. They were dressed appropriately for the boats that had brought them here, and those rubber-soled low-top shoes would carry them easily down the boardwalk leading from the river to the house, but they'd be wise to stay clear of the wetlands ringing the tiny, sandy spot of high ground that Swain had tamed. North Florida mud would suck the shoes right off their feet. Garrett didn't think he'd seen anyone at the party, other than himself, wearing solid, sensible boots.

He looked down on the patio, where Swain beckoned to Wynnda. Wives could also be valuable political tools, and the congressman had somehow coerced his to attend this party, but he was powerless to make her look happy about it.

An olive-skinned man, short and stout with powerful shoulders, staggered out the balcony door and leaned against the railing, standing about six inches closer than Garrett would have preferred. His personal policy was to keep drunks at least a couple of feet away.

Garrett noticed that, below his khaki shorts, the man's right lower leg was encased in a white plaster cast, and a sandal-like apparatus was strapped around his foot, presumably to protect the cast from whatever its wearer might step in. The other foot was clad in a boot even more worn than Garrett's own. He rethought his snap judgment. Maybe the man wasn't drunk. He might be staggering under the influence of his lopsided shoes.

"God's got some sense of humor." The smell of beer hung around the man's head like an odorous halo. Garrett re-revised his opinion. His companion was quite inebriated.

Garrett, who'd learned not to encourage drunks who want to talk, allowed himself two words. "How so?"

"How else do you explain a hypocritical jerk like that one," he said, gesturing toward Swain, "being blessed with all this?" A stubby hand waved through the air, encompassing the spectacular house and its overhanging live oaks. Maybe the beautiful wife, too.

Garrett studied the palm-adorned uplands and the marsh and swamp that surrounded them, sheltering a river that was just out of sight. Nestled into the trees below the balcony where they stood was McGilray's Hole, the crown jewel of Swain's property. In Garrett's considered opinion, no one man deserved to possess a piece of nature so beautiful, though he would give the congressman credit for sharing it with his party-going friends.

From their perch on the balcony, Garrett and his drunken companion could gaze down into the opalescent depths of that jewel, a first-magnitude limestone spring. Glass-clear water poured out of the bowels of the earth into its basin, then overspilled into a channel that carried it through an open marsh, then into swampy woods and, eventually, into the river. Some of Swain's guests had donned scuba gear to explore the cavern that disgorged all that crystalline water. They were dozens of feet below the surface, but Garrett could read the logos printed across the backs of their swim trunks.

It had been named McGilray's Hole by a long-gone pioneer. Joseph Swain had had the great good sense to buy the property that sheltered it, back when he was a very young man and treasures like this one were still undervalued.

The story of how he built his own personal paradise here was well-known to anybody who read Florida newspapers. Swain had immediately begun the house, doing as much of the work himself as he could. He had cut the trees himself, taking out as few as possible and having them cut into the lumber that framed the structure that had become, for him, the ultimate recycling project. He'd taught himself to do construction work out of books. Then, when his legal practice took off, he had hired professionals to expand the original structure into the home of his dreams.

And he did it all before the wetlands protection laws went into effect that would have made building on this land impossible.

A thought struck him. Garrett squinted at the man at his side. "Did you say 'hypocrite'?"

"I did."

"Why?"

"I own the adjacent property, just upriver. Inherited it from my old man about ten years ago. I'd love to have a place like this."

"But you can't get a permit to build one?"

"Damn straight. As soon as Swain got his place just the way he wanted it, he spearheaded tough conservation laws through the legislature. No way he could build a house like this any more. Nobody else can, either. Look around. You see anybody else living out here? I can use my land for hunting and fishing, but that's about it."

Garrett looked across the pristine waters of McGilray's Hole, deep into the trees beyond. The swampy woodland floor was alive with a yellow blanket of late-summer sneezeweed. Here and there, the foamy white flowers of water hemlock rose up on stalks as tall as a woman. Was it any wonder the Spanish called this place *La Florida*—the Land of the Flower?

"How do the landowners in these parts feel about Swain's approach to environmental protection?"

"Every year, we pay our taxes on land we can't use. How do you think we feel?"

"They why are you at this man's party, Mr.—"

"Marquez. Stan Marquez."

"I'm Garrett Levy."

The man stuck out a hand dripping with water that had condensed on the surface of his mug. "Why am I here? For the free beer?" He chuckled. "I called all the landowners up and down the river when I heard Swain was having another one of his open-house shindigs. I told them that the congressman needed to see us, face to face. There would've been no need to say anything to him—he knows who we are. I just wanted him to remember that we live here too, and that we vote. Nobody but me had the guts to show up."

"Do you think it would have helped if your friends had come?"

Marquez snorted. "Hell, no. He doesn't need us and we all know it. Swain built his career on the environmental vote, and he gives them what they want. You know what he's pushing these days?"

Garrett just shook his head.

"He wants to buy some land to make a wildlife corridor. I got nothing against that idea. If we keep paving Florida, there won't be any wild land left except for a few parks here and there. Swain wants to buy land to connect the parks we got, so that the animals can have more space to roam. Makes sense to me. But do you know how he wants to pay for those corridors?"

Garrett shook his head again.

"Property taxes. He wants me to pay more taxes on property that I can't use."

He pushed away from the balcony railing and headed back inside. "I think I need a little more of Swain's free beer."

Garrett circled McGilray's Hole. It was gorgeous, but it had hardly been treated like the prized possession of a sincere environmentalist. The rampant vegetation that should have lined its banks was gone. Unless Garrett missed his guess, Swain kept the larger plants knocked back with herbicide, then fertilized the swathe of green lawn that set off the spring's blue-green glow so perfectly. He had no choice but to fertilize. The natural soil around the spring was almost pure sand; it could never support the kind of grass Americans liked to walk on. The excess nutrients in the fertilizer obviously washed into the water. Where else could they go? Garrett thought about the downstream damage to the river caused by, year after year, pouring chemicals in water where they didn't need to be.

He had no sense that the other guests noticed their host's attack on the environment that he loved so loudly, but Garrett's job made him sensitive to such things. It was impossible to work for Florida's Department of Environmental Protection without being acutely aware of all the ways humans could spoil the landscape that had attracted them to Florida in the first place.

He was tempted to stroll up to Congressman Swain and ask, "If you can spray poison anywhere you like, how come Wynnda can't have an air conditioner?" Not being the type to cause trouble, he decided to take a walk instead. He was ready to escape Joseph Swain's well-manicured version of nature, so that he could spend some time soaking up the real thing.

The real Florida wasn't far away. Before long, Garrett was picking his way down a lightly traveled trail that led from the sandy uplands down into the surrounding marsh. Waist-high maidencane brushed against him on both sides. He wished for his snake leggings, but they weren't ordinary party attire, so he'd left them at home. When the land turned liquid beneath his boots and the swamp tupelo reached up high enough to shade out a portion of the late summer sun, he made himself a bet.

If any of Congressman Swain's guests had ever left a party and ventured this far into Florida's more inhospitable territory, then he would, by God, eat those ancient leather snake leggings.

Garrett was never so at home as when he was deep in a swamp full of treacherous snakes and reptiles that would like to kill him. He could think of nothing that would lure him back to the den of human treachery at Swain's party...nothing but the double gunshot that split the humid summer air.

The bark of two nearly simultaneous shots sounded wrong. Not being a gun person, Garrett had only television shootings to go by, but he didn't think he'd ever heard a television star squeeze off just two rounds on an automatic weapon. If forced to guess, he would have said that this sounded like two people firing at almost the same time—like a shootout at the OK Corral. More likely, he'd heard two hunters trying to fell the same deer. This sounded like bad manners to Garrett, who had never hunted in his life. Wouldn't they have had some agreement beforehand on who took the shot? Otherwise, how would they know who bagged the trophy?

Garrett had no doubt that hunters prowled the woods in these parts, in and out of season, but the shots sounded way too close. Hunters had ears like rabbits. They would have heard the twanging music and the rumble of the crowd. There was plenty of wilderness around here where people weren't. Hunters would have steered clear.

Wishing harder for his snake leggings, Garrett struck out through the marsh in the direction where he thought he'd heard the shots. Within minutes, he had reached the bank of a large creek. Judging by the direction of its flow, he guessed that it was a tributary of the river that fed the wetlands stretching in every direction, as far as he could see. He imagined that the creek had once been a meandering rill, nourishing vegetation on its banks and along its bottom. It had once birthed damsel flies and apple snails and plump silvery fish, but not any more. It had been raped.

Dredges had gouged out its bottom and bitten into its banks, ripping away the natural meanders into a straight and muddy channel. Two large power boats were moored at a floating dock. A tank was bolted to the dock, and its nozzle was hemorraghing fuel, one drop at a time. The setting sun lit up a rainbow slick that lay atop the water in a broad circle centered on the tank and its nozzle. There had been no attempt to hide the brown and withered weeds along the water's edge. Someone had sprayed herbicide along both banks, with gusto.

Garrett wished for a camera. He would have to report this flagrant violation of environmental law. It was his job and, what was more, he would have reported it even if it weren't, simply as an enraged citizen.

Upstream, above the point where the environmental carnage ended and nature's creekside weeds began, sat a small man holding a long cane fishing pole.

"Did you hear those shots?" he called to the fisherman, choking back the question he truly wanted to ask. *Did you do this? Why would you murder this slice of creation?*

"Hunters," the man said, reaching down and lifting a stringer of sunfish out of the water. "Most of them's got good enough sense to stay clear of people, but not all."

The fisherman's frayed clothing and patched boots told Garrett that he didn't own the power boats or the dock where they were moored. There was no other, more modest, boat in sight, and there was no other way to reach this spot, but Garrett knew that Stan Marquez had told the truth. Swain's house was the only one for miles around. Well, it was the only one built with a legal permit. So where had this guy come from?

"My name's Garrett Levy," he said, putting out a hand. "Do you live around here?"

The other man stuck out the hand that wasn't holding the pole and the stringer. "Frank McGilray. And, yes, I do live around here." He lifted his catch for Garrett to see. "I got carried away and caught way more fish than I can eat before they rot. I'll clean 'em and cook 'em, if you'll help me eat 'em."

Garrett took a split-second longer to respond than was strictly polite. He was assessing the cleanliness of the water where the fish were caught, which wasn't bad, as opposed to the cesspool a few dozen yards downstream. He decided that no self-respecting fish who had a choice would spend time in water that bad, so these were perfectly edible. Probably.

"I'd love to."

He followed Frank down a path that ended at a small clearing. There stood a tiny cabin inhabiting fewer square feet than the extensive vegetable garden beside it. The cabin had to be a hundred or more years old, and so did the outhouse behind it. Frank McGilray would have appreciated a composting toilet in a way that Wynnda Swain couldn't. Such things depending on one's point of view.

This cabin's roof had no solar panels like the ones that powered Swain's naturalist fantasy. There was no glass in its windows to divide its inhabitant from nature, just rusted and patched screens. Garrett had amused himself many times by imagining a life this close to the land, but he knew he wasn't tough enough to live it. Five minutes ago, he would have said that no American was tough enough, not any more. Apparently, he was wrong.

The fried fish had been delicious. The homebrewed whiskey, while not delicious, had gone a long way toward explaining why Frank's corn patch was so darn big. Garrett consumed nearly a tumblerful of the stuff before he got the nerve to ask the question that had been bugging him for hours.

"You don't seem like the creek-dredging type, Frank. And I've watched you swat mosquitoes since sundown. If bug spray's not your thing, then I don't think it was you who doused the whole countryside with herbicide."

"Nope. Swain's the one that likes weedkiller." Frank upended his own tumbler. "It all started when Swain got attacked by a bull gator."

"How come he's still alive?"

"A smart man don't walk through these swamps unarmed. Being smarter than Swain, I shot the gator. Swain lost a hunk of meat out of his thigh, but he healed."

"When was this?"

"About ten years after he bought this property from me. I enjoyed that first ten years, and I think he did, too. He hired me to stay on as a caretaker, since he couldn't live out here, not and keep his job. All the week, he'd work in town being a lawyer, so he could afford to come out here on the weekends. This land is the only place he's happy, I'd say. He'd tie his boat up, throw his sleeping bag on the floor right there, then we'd get to work building his house. Took us a lot of years, and when he was done with it, our friendship was done, too."

Garrett looked around the cabin. There were gaps in the walls big enough to let in the most monstrous palmetto bugs. The whole room smelled like Frank, and Frank smelled like a man who'd never had running water in his life. It was a warm, earthy smell that wafted out of Frank as if it were embedded into his skin, and Garrett liked it, in a weird sort of way. It was real. Swain had been comfortable with this cabin and its funk for years. Why did he suddenly start trying to tame the wilderness?

A vision of the denuded and maimed creek rose in front of his moonshine-addled eyes. "The gators. He's destroying their habitat so that they'll stay away."

"He wasn't about to leave his own private paradise. What else was he going to do?"

Garrett thought of the alligators of Florida, lurking like black, lumpy logs in every wet patch they could find. Trying to drive every last one of them out of any swamp was an act of supreme hubris, but then, Swain was a politician, wasn't he? Hubris was his birthright.

"What about you, Frank? You watched the alligator attack Swain. Do gators scare you now, the way they scare him?"

"They don't bother me none. I think they kinda like me. When I wade out in the water, they swim over toward me a little ways, then they stop. It's like they want to visit. Maybe they like my smell."

Garrett had heard of stranger things.

At daybreak, Garrett found that Frank's homemade whiskey didn't just taste like jet fuel—it left behind a hangover with the power of a just-lit afterburner. He was lying, fully clothed, on the hand-hewn planks of Frank's cabin floor, wanting only one thing…to go home. He could do it, too. Too cautious to commit to an entire weekend of open-air partying, he had brought his own boat, instead of relying on Swain's flotilla of pontoon boats. It was moored to the expansive dock that stretched along the riverfront boundary of the congressman's land. The hangover might force him to ooze on his belly like a snake through the marshlands that separated him from Swain's house and the river beyond, but he wanted to go home bad.

Using the kitchen table to pull himself to his feet, Garrett found that he could actually walk. Frank was passed out on the couch, so he grunted politely in his host's direction and staggered out the door and through the marsh.

He found Swain's house awash in sleeping people. There were sleeping bags thrown willy-nilly across the decks and on the porches and balconies, and all of them were occupied. Hammocks hung from trees, and tents had been pitched beneath the encircling trees.

Garrett was seized with the desire to see McGilray's Hole one more time, now that he'd partied with McGilray's descendant and heir. He walked through neatly trimmed greenery to the water's edge and stared down deep into the spring's cold blue depths. A massive alligator swam down toward the chasm that disgorged all that water, day in and day out.

Clamped in the gator's jaws was a man with a gleaming shock of white hair.

The only vestige remaining of Garrett's hangover was the nausea, and there could have been other explanations for that. Perhaps it stemmed from the exertion of racing to the house to wake the scuba divers who might stand a chance of saving Joseph Swain. Would they have brought spear guns with them? Could you bring a twelve-foot gator down with a spear gun? He didn't know.

Deep down, he knew that these were empty questions. Every Floridian knew that gators liked to drag their living victims into the depths, roll them over and over, then wedge them under something that would keep them underwater until their dead body ripened to reptilian tastes. So perhaps Swain could have been saved when the gator first grabbed him, but not now. No living man would have hung so passively from those powerful jaws, arms and legs trailing through the water like eelgrass.

Perhaps the nausea stemmed from his single glimpse of Wynnda Swain's haunted face as she raced to the water's edge, clad in an incongruously delicate nightgown the same shade of silken gold as her toenails.

Or perhaps his stomach continued to heave because of the role he'd played in fetching Swain's body. The scuba divers had donned their gear lightning-fast, but Frank McGilray had been faster. Alerted by Swain's screaming guests, Frank had traveled the trail from his house at a dead run. He had pitched a weathered shotgun at Garrett, bellowing, "If the gator surfaces, shoot him." Then he dove into the depths of McGilray's Hole with a smooth grace that left Garrett confident that he could shoot the gator if need be.

As Frank swooped down through the water, the gator's jaws loosened and Swain floated free of its wicked teeth. The beast backed away, deliberately but steadily, giving Frank space to grab the dead man and head for the surface. When his head broke the water, Garrett threw the gun aside and helped haul the men, one living and one dead, onto dry land.

Swain's body, sprawled on the spring's bank, looked…wrong. There was very little blood staining the puncture holes in his shirt, and there were few other obvious wounds, except for a grievous injury to his head.

Would a gator's teeth have done that kind of damage? There was a single hole in Swain's left temple, but the right side of his head was effectively gone. Garrett was no expert, but he would have guessed that the man was shot.

Stan Marquez was standing beside Swain's shoulder, staring down at his busted skull with the intense concentration of a man doing calculus in his head. Garrett remembered that Marquez was a hunter. He had no doubt seen what bullets could do to animals. He'd surely recognize a gunshot wound when he saw one.

Garrett took a breath, ready to cry out, "Did anybody besides me hear shots last night about sundown?", but he stifled the question. If Swain had indeed been shot, the odds were good that there was a killer among them.

Questions boiled out of the crowd. "Who saw him last?" and "Can anybody tell if he's been dead long?" and "Who's going to call the sheriff?"

Garrett had been to campouts like this one before. At sundown, people withdrew to their tents and hammocks. Guitars and banjos came out. So did liquor bottles. Partiers sat huddled around bonfires and camp lanterns in clusters of four or five or seven. It was absolutely possible that Swain could have been gone without being missed since sunset…since those gunshots sounded.

The only discordant note in that theory was Wynnda. She would have known that he didn't sleep in their bedroom. Wouldn't she have gone looking for him? Ordinarily, yes, any woman would worry if her husband didn't come to bed. Unless she was accustomed to it.

Garrett cried out, "I'll call nine-one-one," fetching his cell phone out of his pocket. Glad to have an excuse to back away from all the people and find a quiet place, he ducked behind the house and called the emergency personnel. When the dispatcher heard where Garrett was, she let out a little puff of breath. "It'll take at least an hour to get somebody to you, maybe a lot more. Do you want me to stay on the line?"

"No. But you better send the sheriff along with the paramedics. Some of us think it was murder."

Garrett was surprised at his need—no, his deep-seated drive—to find out who killed Joseph Swain. He hadn't known the man, and he hadn't liked what he'd seen of him, but his sense of justice was strong and it had been offended today, as surely as it had been offended by the environmental murder of the little creek that he'd seen the day before.

And perhaps his sense that this death was a puzzle to be unraveled, like a knotty thermodynamics problem, was rooted in his engineering training. If he was right in his suspicions, Swain had been dead all night. The evidence was deteriorating, fading into the marsh as each second passed. Spatters of blood were being consumed by insects. Spongy soil was springing back into shape, obscuring footprints. Each tick of the clock gave the killer time to obliterate any traces left behind. Justice couldn't wait for an hour.

If Swain had been killed when those shots sounded at dusk, then he had been deep in the marsh. Garrett bolted in that direction, intent on finding the spot where the congressman had died. It must have been somewhere near the creek where he'd met Frank. He stumbled when he realized what that meant. Frank could have been Swain's killer.

Garrett reasoned that Frank couldn't be eliminated as a suspect—nobody could at this point—but his gut said the man was innocent, for two reasons. First, Frank had had countless opportunities to kill Swain and he would have countless more. They were routinely alone together in the deep wilderness. Under those conditions, Frank could have had every expectation of getting away with murder. Why should he kill Swain now, with a hundred witnesses nearby?

What was more, Garrett had seen Frank's face when he pulled his longtime friend out of the water. There had been a tenderness there, a grief more heartfelt than even Swain's wife showed.

Which begged the question of whether Wynnda Swain might have pulled the trigger on her husband. Her unhappiness was palpable. Murder was certainly not the only option in escaping a bad marriage, but Garrett had friends who had been divorced from lawyers. The results were never pretty.

"Hey, Garrett! Hold up!"

Stan Marquez rushed toward him. The cast on his leg flashed white against the rank undergrowth hampering his progress. His injured leg gave him a lopsided, galloping gait, but it didn't seem to slow him down. Garrett realized that his subconscious had been considering and casting aside suspects, while his conscious mind focused on which soggy bit of land was most likely to support his next step. He hadn't considered Stan, because he'd doubted that the man could have hobbled out to the murder site. Perhaps he'd been wrong.

Stan was a hunter. He knew how to use a gun. He knew how to get around in the swamp. He had ample reason to hate Swain. And he was running headlong toward Garrett.

A cold sweat prickled Garrett's backbone. He'd been treating the situation like a problem with a solution that could be neatly calculated. Now he might be alone in the wilderness with a hunter whose freshest kill was human.

Stan was twenty feet away and moving fast, until his bad leg went down ankle-deep in a mudhole.

"Damn. My doctor's going to kill me. My wife, too."

The cast. It had been clean when Garrett first spotted Stan, and he'd watched it grow progressively dirtier with every step. It would have been impossible for the man to have hiked out to the creek, shot Swain, and returned to the party without completely trashing the white plaster cast. Stan didn't kill the congressman.

"Wait, Stan. If you come any further, the mud'll suck that thing off your leg altogether."

The big man stood still. "But you need help. I'd bet money that Swain wasn't killed by any gator. Somebody shot his head nearly off. I heard shots late yesterday and, judging by the directions you're headed, I think you did, too. Nobody at the party paid much attention, figuring it was hunters, but I wondered. I can't let you go out there alone."

"I'll be okay. The killer won't be standing on the spot where he killed Swain, waiting for me. But you can help. Go back to the party and look for tracks. The soil around McGilray's Hole is light and sandy, but the rest of the dirt around here is black muck like this." He gestured at the heavy mud coating their boots. "If you see mud anywhere near the house, we'll want to know who tracked it back to the party. Check the decks, especially. This kind of muck will be obvious on the bare wood."

He tried to think like someone with something major to hide.

"Look on the banks around the spring and along the river, too. You could rinse off the top layer of mud by just wading in the water, but it would take soap and a scrub brush to get really clean. So check everybody's feet."

"Only a nut would go wading around here after dark. That's when the gators come out."

"True, but check anyway. And check the dock and the boats. See if it looks like somebody cleaned up out there. They would have needed to stash their dirty clothes somewhere, and the river's spring-fed, so it's too clear for them to sink the evidence."

Stan looked pensive. "The killer's in a real hole. The only safe place around here to hide dirty clothes and boots is in the swamp—and he'll get muddy again, trying to get out of the swamp."

"Or she," Garrett said, thinking of Wynnda. "I'll take the house. I'll need to check the bathrooms for—"

"Bathtub rings. Dirty towels. Stuff like that."

"Exactly."

The spot where Swain died hadn't proved hard to find. He'd left a trail behind him. Blood and tissue had spattered onto a nearby tree. And the broad, wallowed-out trail of a gator led toward the nearby creek.

The site told him nothing about who killed Swain or why, but it might reveal far more to forensics experts. Garrett stayed well clear, doing his best to avoid contaminating any evidence. At least he'd be able to get the investigators here quickly. He headed back to the house, hoping to uncover something that would point to the guilty party.

The yard around Swain's house was filled with people who had clean feet. The porches and stairs and decks were tracked with only grass and sand. The floors inside were clean, because Swain's guests were well brought up. They wiped their feet on the doormats provided. The doormats were free of mud, until Garrett wiped his own mucky feet on them.

Stan rushed up and whispered, "The dock was clean. So were the boats."

Garrett thanked him and continued his methodical search of the house. The bathrooms were as clean as could be expected, considering that a hundred people had been present for twenty hours. The composting toilet offered an interesting twist for an amateur detective. An ordinary toilet might have concealed some evidence of a killer cleaning up evidence. A dirty washrag could be flushed. Even muddy socks could go down the sewage pipes, one at a time.

A composting toilet, on the other hand, stored waste in a holding tank, until it was treated and ready for removal. A dirty washrag and a pair of socks could be waiting in one of the toilets' tanks, but Garrett considered retrieving them a job for the police.

Single-minded in his search, he burst into the master bedroom, only to find Wynnda standing at the window, weeping. She was still wrapped in the gold silk she'd slept in, and she still looked as out of place as a porcelain doll floating in a mud puddle.

Women like Wynnda had always made Garrett feel like his voice was too loud and his feet were too big. Today, his big feet were coated in muck. "I—I was looking for a bathroom," he croaked.

She pointed with a neatly manicured hand, and he stumbled into a room where every porcelain surface gleamed. Wynnda had not scrubbed half a swamp's worth of mud off her body in here, but he'd known that as soon as he saw her. Garrett had spent a life enjoying nature, then washing it off himself when he got home. He wore high-top hiking boots when he went into wetlands. Nevertheless, when he got home, there was invariably soil ground into his heels. Muddy water always sloshed over the tops of his boots, leaving black dirt clinging to his cuticles and the rough skin on the ball of the foot.

If Wynnda had ventured out into the marsh last night to kill her husband, she could have spent the whole night with soap and a scrub brush and nail polish remover and cuticle moisturizer, but the creamy skin on her feet would still not have the flawless sheen he'd just observed.

Garrett backed out of the widow's marriage chamber, mumbling apologies. There was only one person whose feet were dirty enough to be the killer of Wynnda's husband. Remembering the double-shot he'd heard, Garrett finally realized why Swain had been killed, and that motive affected him so personally that he had no choice but to confront the killer. And he felt reasonably sure that he'd be safe in doing so.

Frank sat in the spot where Garrett first saw him. Raising a hand in greeting, he said, "I've been waiting for you. I knew you'd figure it out, and I wanted to say good-bye."

"Swain was going to shoot me, but you shot him first. You saved my life."

"I loved Swain in my own way, even after he raped my land and killed my creek, but I couldn't let him shoot you. It was so hard to pull that trigger on my friend that I was almost too late. My bullet caught him just as he fired on you but, thank God, his shot went wild. Do you understand why he wanted you dead?"

"He knew I worked for the state environmental agency, and he knew what would happen if I saw what he'd done to the creek. That's the worst case of illegal dredging I've ever seen.

The agency would have hauled him into court. The fines and the cost of restoration would have been astronomical. More to the point, his political career would have been in the toilet. Has he carried a gun ever since the alligator attack?"

"Yep. And I always have. Cottonmouths in these parts are worse than gators. When I saw him draw a bead on an unarmed man, I had no choice but to drop him. You'd have done the same."

The part of him that abhorred guns and what they did to people said, "No," but the part of him that craved justice nodded in agreement.

"I wish I didn't try to hide it yesterday, though," Frank went on. "I should have told you what I'd done, soon as I saw you. Instead, I left him laying there, because I was scared. Then I took you back to my house so you wouldn't stumble on the body. When it got light, I left you drunk on the floor and went looking for Swain, so's I could bury him, but he was gone. For a gator to get him, even after he was dead...well, that's the worst thing he could have imagined. I didn't wish that on him."

"What will you do now, Frank? The sheriff will be here any minute."

"I won't be here when he comes. Nobody but you and Wynnda know I was ever here, and she won't talk. Many's the time Swain brought her out here, then took off in his speedboat to enjoy nature and shoot a few gators. Wynnda needs someone to talk to, and sometimes I was all she had. You might think about telling her what happened. Course, if you tell the sheriff, I guess she'll find out from him. It's your call."

Frank eased himself down into the creek and started wading upstream, away from the carnage left by Swain's dredges and herbicides and into the fresh clear water where sunfish and alligators lived.

"The sheriff will find your house," Garrett called after him. "They'll be looking for you."

"Swain's held title to my house and property for more'n thirty years. He promised to let me live on it for life, which he did, and he promised to take care of it, which he didn't. Here's what

I figure," he said, looking over his shoulder. "The sheriff will see that my cabin's been lived in, and he'll figure a bum's been squatting there. Maybe he'll figure the bum killed Swain, but that's as far as he'll ever get."

"Everybody saw you haul Swain out of the water."

"Did they get my name? Does anybody but you and Wynnda know it? Anyhow, the sheriff can't track me out here, so go ahead and tell him what you know, if it'll make you feel better. I got no reason to ever set foot in civilization again. I'm not a hundred percent sure I've even got a birth certificate, so who's he gonna look for? I hear that smart folks like you have just about paved all of Florida, but there's enough land like this left where I can live just fine."

Frank was hip-deep in the creek, so he was leaving neither footprints that a man could track nor a trail that a dog could follow. A gator slid on its belly into the water and swam in Frank's direction, following him at a respectful distance.

"If you decide not to turn me in, take the whiskey jug out of the cabinet and put it on the table. I'll come back in a while and see whether you did. I'd like to live out my days here, where my daddy and granddaddy were born and died. If that jug's on the table, I'll know I can."

"But you killed him to save me. Why don't you just stay and explain things to the sheriff?"

Frank's laugh echoed on the water. "Look at me. I'm dirty. I smell. I killed a rich politician. If they catch me, they'll put me under the jail. I'll take my chances out here with the gators." As if called, a second gator eased into the water, following Frank upstream. The reptilian form of its long leathery body reflected in the calm water, doubling its primeval power.

Later, when the sheriff and his people had come and gone, Garrett would ask Wynnda if she'd like to help him leave the moonshine jug out for Frank.

Land of the Flowers

About the creation of "Land of the Flowers," Mary Anna says: "What would a man do to someone who had raped the love of his life? What if that love was not a person, but a place—a tiny, unspoiled world? "Land of the Flowers" features a politician who has built a career on his reputation as a defender of the few unspoiled places Florida has left. In the space of an afternoon, this man is exposed as a fraud, then found murdered on his own property at the bottom of an unspoiled limestone spring. The fact that he breaks, with impunity, the very laws he has fought to pass means that nearly everyone present could wish him dead. Was it the lakefront property owner who was left with worthless land when restrictive wetlands rules were implemented? Was it a radical environmentalist enraged by his irreversible destruction of a rare habitat? Or was it the 7th-generation Floridian who sold him the property that he pillaged?"

Land of the Flowers

The palm trees stand in silhouette
Where Spaniards cast their bayonets,
·The soldiers are gone, but the trees stand yet,
Towering over the land of the flowers.

The gray moss blew in fresh from Spain,
Riding the crest of a wild hurricane.
Our fine homes scatter but the moss remains.
The moss drips forever but never runs dry.

And the water springs clear from the sand and the stone,
Quenching a wilderness no one can own.
And the water springs cold from the stone and the sand.
Nothing of value can rest in your hand.

We pass sterile days, sharing the blame
For colorless cities with old Spanish names,
But God hides in places that no one can tame,
Standing watch over the land of the flowers.

And the water springs clear from the sand and the stone,
Quenching a wilderness no one can own.
And the water springs cold from the stone and the sand.
Nothing of value can rest in your hand.

The palm trees stand in silhouette
Where Spaniards cast their bayonets,
The soldiers are gone, but the trees stand yet,
Towering over the land of the flowers, the land of the
    flowers.

An Interview with Mary Anna Evans

Where did you grow up? Was yours a bookish household?
I grew up in south Mississippi. Yes, we were a very bookish household. My mother took my sister and me to the bookmobile every week in the summertime, where she checked out her stack of books as enthusiastically as we did. My father loved westerns and historical fiction.

Do you remember the first mystery novel you ever read?
Nancy Drew's *The Mystery of the Old Clock.*

What was the first piece of music you recall?
I'm told of a time before I was two, when my mother was in the kitchen, cooking and singing. She began, "Down in the valley…" From my playpen in the next room came the echo: "…valley so low…"

Was yours a musically oriented household?
Oh, yes. My sister and I took piano lessons and played in the high school band and sang with our mother in the church choir. Our father appreciated music a great deal, but the church music director used to thank him for not singing in the choir.

Do you listen to music when you write?
Oddly, no. Prose is like music to me, and I like to listen to the rhythm and melody of the words.

Has a musical work ever inspired a novel or short story?
Only this one. David and I wrote the song "Land of the Flowers" years ago, and I always knew there was a story to be told there.

What is your favorite manmade sound?

Piano music. In performance, I usually sing folk-, jazz-, or blues-inflected music, but I play classical piano for myself.

What is your favorite sound in nature?

The thunder and wind of an approaching thunderstorm.

If you had to choose three novels to take on a trip, what would you choose?

To Kill a Mockingbird
The Yearling
Isaac Asimov's Foundation Trilogy

Your work is noted for a strong sense of setting, and a real concern for place. How do you start a story? Does the character come first? Or do you begin with the dramatic premise?

My first novel began with a place in my imagination, a ramshackle plantation house on an island off the Florida Panhandle. I asked myself, "Who would live there?" Then I asked myself, "What would her problem be?" Those questions spawned, not just one book, but a series. My stories are usually born through the same thought sequence.

If you had a chance to invite any three people in the world to dinner, living or dead, who would they be?

Jesus, Queen Elizabeth I, and Galileo. Imagine the dinner table conversation!

Which would you rather do—read or listen to a favorite CD?

You didn't include writing fiction or playing music! Actually, I'd rather read than do most anything.

*Any of you out there miss Damon Runyon? He's
back, in the droll, utterly hilarious persona of
Nathan Walpow. This is a good story. A really
good story. And where did the nutty idea come
from? Nathan says: "I have a long history of
cyclical hobbies. I'll suddenly get obsessed with
something (astronomy, cacti), immerse myself in
it for weeks, months, or years, and suddenly lose
interest. So it is with stamp collecting. I was in
one of my philatelic phases when I started this
story. All I had when I started was a guy in a
bar. In walked Tony. He reached in his pocket,
pulled out my hero's lame business card, and off
I went."*

Bad for His Image

Nathan Walpow

The bartender's left eye was glass. His right gazed off in the general direction of Sirius. He stood there wiping a grimy glass with a grimier cloth, his head bobbing vaguely in time with the juke box, where some whiny Southern wench was complaining about her boyfriend's love for his "sexy F-150."

I dumped some of my bottle of Slovakian vodka and my pitcher of grapefruit juice into my glass. My seventh greyhound, by my admittedly imprecise count, and each was less grey and more hound than the last. But it had taken me three hours or so to get through the first six. So I wasn't drunk. Not really.

Someone slid into the barstool to my right. He was of average height and no wider across the shoulders than he needed to be. His suit was royal blue, his shirt burgundy, his tie both. His pinkie ring featured a largish opal. His eyes were an odd pale blue that clashed with his Mediterranean skin.

The bartender meandered over. The new arrival shook his head. The bartender returned to his grime.

My new neighbor inspected me from head to toe. He shook his head when he reached my feet, then started back up. When he got to my face he stopped. "Guy like you doesn't belong in a place like this," he said. His voice was like oiled gravel.

That place was the Park Terrace, the seediest bar in the part of Santa Monica the tourist books don't mention. It was well past one in the morning, a Saturday in November.

"Doesn't make any sense," the guy said. "What gives?"

I looked him in the eye. "Troubles," I said.

"Huh," he said. Not, "Huh?" like "What do you mean?" but a mysterious word in a mysterious code I hadn't been let in on. Two minutes later: "Wanna tell me about it?"

"Maybe later."

He nodded. His left hand dug around in his pocket. Instead of the expected blackjack, he pulled out one of my cards. A picture of the Penny Black, and *Stephen Pierce, Professional Philatelist* in an awful Old English font. "This is you," he said.

It seemed pointless to deny it. "Can I interest you in some trial color proofs from Burkina Faso?"

"Huh," again. Then: "This guy I work for. He's a stamp collector. There's this stamp." He produced a photocopy of a page from the Scott Catalogue. The listing for France number 37a was marked with a highlighter. The basic 37 was the 1869 five franc gray lilac on lavender paper. The "a" variety was missing the denomination, the *5* and *F* on either side of Emperor Napoleon III.

"He wants it," my new friend said.

I looked at the listing again. The mint column was blank and the price for a cancelled one—$50,000—was in italics, meaning sales were rare and the value an estimate at best. "So do a lot of people."

He folded up the listing, shoved it back in his pocket. "Story is, you know how to lay your hands on it."

True enough. A collector in Fountain Valley had called. He'd found the stamp in a junk lot. That kind of stuff happened all the time.

I was supposed to meet the guy to look it over at a stamp show in Anaheim Saturday afternoon. This afternoon. No one knew about it but the guy and me. Oh, and—

No. Best not to think about her.

My companion's right hand reached up and squeezed my shoulder. Just enough. "Come on. He wants to see you now. Name's Tony, by the way."

I paid my tab and Tony led me to the alley out back. A Malibu hardtop awaited us. Early seventies, sky blue, in perfect condition. A Hurst shifter emerged from the floor and the Virgin Mary dangled from the rear-view.

We climbed in, backed out of the alley, turned east on Olympic. "Where are we headed?" I asked.

"Put your seat belt on."

I looked at him.

"You don't wear your belt," he said, "you could end up dead. I wouldn't want you to end up dead."

A healthy sign. I put my belt on.

Around Overland, he said, "Want to tell me about the girl?"

"What girl?"

"Look on your face, there's got to be a girl."

Very perceptive for a hoodlum. I thought about it. Then I said, "Cherie's twenty-two—"

"A lot younger than you, my friend."

"Sixteen years. Love knows no bounds."

He ran a red light. "Where'd you meet her?"

"I got a manicure from her."

I expected disdain, but he just nodded.

"I went back a couple of times. I was infatuated. Then she mentioned this poodle show. I told her how much I love poodles."

"Tell me you don't."

"Of course I don't. But it got me in the door."

"She have one?"

I nodded. "One of those dingey little white ones. Name's Barky."

He gave me a look.

"I swear to God. Most useless creature on the planet. Anyway, one thing led to another…"

He listened politely. Then he said, "You and her do it?"

"Is that your business?"

"Look, you're telling me all this, it's part of the picture. You don't want to tell me, don't."

I considered it. I'd probably never see this guy again. Possibly because I'd be dead.

"Yes," I said. "We did it."

"Women." He shook his head. "How long?"

"Two weeks, three days, four—"

"So you're doing it, everything's going great, why are you drinking at the P.T.?"

"She told me she can't sleep with me anymore."

"Uh-oh."

"She said she's a 'sexually monogamous being' and she'd met a guy who was 'really truly hot.'" I shook my head. "I didn't even know she was seeing anyone else."

"You never do."

"I was blindsided."

"You always are."

"I mean, everything was going so well. We had these long conversations."

"What about?"

"Oh, you know. Movies."

"Movies."

"And television."

"Sound like you two were made for each other."

"We talked about our jobs too. I learned a lot about being a manicurist."

"Useful."

"And I taught her about stamps. She was very interested. I even took her to a stamp show."

We rode in silence until we were close to La Cienega.
"You know what I think?" Tony said.

"What?"

"You should go talk some sense into her."

"You don't mean any rough stuff, do you?"

He threw me a look like I was rotting meat. "You don't treat women rough," he said. "You treat them gentle. With respect." He tapped his forehead with a meaty finger. "Only sometimes they don't think right. You just got to use a little logic on them. You really like this girl?"

"Yes."

"Then don't act like a big crybaby. Where does she live?"

"Venice."

He hung a right. "Let's go see her."

"It's two o'clock in the morning."

"So? You got something better to do?"

"What about the guy you work for?"

"He can wait."

She came to the door wearing this babydoll thing that made me break out in a sweat. It seemed a dumb way to answer the door in the middle of the night, but who was I to talk about dumb?

"Hi," she said, like it was the most natural thing in the world that I should be there. "Who's your friend?"

I made introductions. Barky appeared, yapping.

"We need to talk," I said. Usually the dumper's line, not the dumpee's, but this was a special case.

"Can't it wait until morning?"

"Sure it can," I said, ready to retreat.

"No, it can't," Tony said. "Get your clothes, babe, you're coming with us."

Oh, jeez…"You gave me that big speech about women just so you could get your hands on her. Why, I ought to…" In a rare moment of courage, I rushed him.

My memory of the ensuing few seconds is unclear. Suffice it to say that I ended up lying in the corner rubbing my jaw, with Cherie perfunctorily checking on my well-being.

Tony regarded me as he would a hyperactive five-year-old. "Now, get up," he said. "We don't need this. Nothing's going to happen to the girl."

"I trusted you," I said, maintaining my new position of strength on the floor.

"Was that smart? I'm a hood, for Christ's sake. You've known me an hour. Use a little sense." He turned to Cherie. "Go get dressed."

She pouted. It was the most transparent pout I'd ever seen. "Stephen, do something."

"I think I've emptied my arsenal already," I said.

"Loser." She flounced into her bedroom.

"Don't worry," Tony said. "Just leave everything to me."

Five minutes later she came out, wearing tight jeans and a fluorescent green windbreaker over a halter top. I broke out in another sweat.

She snatched up Barky. "Who's going to take care of my baby?"

"He'll be fine," Tony said.

"I'm not leaving without him."

Tony shrugged. "Take him with, then. But keep him quiet."

Take him with? What kind of gangster talk was that?

Tony directed Cherie to the front passenger seat, me to the back. He told me not to do anything stupid. I assured him I wouldn't. He refused to start the car until everyone was belted in.

We drove through downtown, got off the Golden State at Los Feliz. Up into the hills, past the Greek Theatre, past the Observatory. Then I lost track.

We pulled up an overgrown gravel road and came to a tiny clearing. Another car awaited us. Some forties-looking thing, with swoopy fenders and a big high passenger compartment. Two-tone gray, or at least that was how I imagined it. The darkness was considerable.

A man sat within. He motioned me to join him. I did so. Tony lurked a few feet from my door.

A light flicked on inside the car. My companion had white hair and a thin white mustache. Seventy or so, wearing a finely cut charcoal suit and a fedora to match.

It only took me a second. Fenton Harris. Former tough-guy film star, now successful philatelist. His exhibit of classic France was a contender in the World Series of Philately.

"Mr. Pierce," he said, eyeing me as if I were a suspect in a noir thriller. A pack of Pall Malls appeared. He plucked one out. His manicure was impeccable. "Mind if I smoke?"

"Actually, I do. I'm allergic."

He lit up anyway and tossed the match out the window. I pictured Griffith Park in flames.

He regarded me for several minutes. Each time I opened my mouth to say something he dramatically put his finger to his lips. Finally: "How much do you want?"

I looked out the window. Cherie had emerged from the Malibu and was encouraging Barky to go wee-wee. I turned back to Harris and named an impossibly high figure. Three times what I thought I was going to pay for it.

"That's an impossibly high figure," he said. He called Tony over. "What do you think, Tony?"

"Sounds a little high to me, Mr. Harris."

"Yes." Harris looked at me. He blew smoke in my general direction, stubbed out his cigarette. Gave me a number half the one I'd proposed. Still a fifty percent profit. Tempting, but...

"Sorry," I said.

"A pity," Harris said. "Tony?"

"Yes, Mr. Harris."

"Take Mr. Pierce back to wherever you found him."

"Sure thing."

I got out. He led me back to the Malibu.

"Oh, and Tony…" Harris said.

"Yes, Mr. Harris?"

"Put the young lady in the trunk."

"Mine or yours?"

"Mine."

"Hey, wait a minute," Cherie said.

"Do we really need to do that?" Tony said.

"Just something for Mr. Pierce to think about," Harris said.

"She'll suffocate," I said.

"I assure you she will have adequate ventilation. Sell me the stamp and I'll release her."

Tony grabbed a struggling Cherie, slung her under his arm, snatched up Barky with the other hand.

"Not the dog," Harris said. "I'm allergic to dogs."

"Please, let him stay with me," Cherie said. "Poodles are hypoallergenic. They don't shed."

"The dog goes with you, Tony."

Tony hustled Cherie into Harris' trunk and slammed the lid.

"Her fate is in your hands," Harris told me.

"All right," I said. "I'll sell you the stamp."

"At my price?"

"Whatever. Just let her go."

"As soon as I have the stamp."

"You have my word as a philatelist, I'll bring it to you as soon as I get it."

"Don't worry about the girl, Mr. Pierce," Harris said. "She'll be treated well. Oh, and no police. Bringing the police into this would—well, I'm not quite sure what the consequences would be." He fired up his car. Gravel flew and he was gone.

I looked at Tony. Tony looked at me. Barky barked.

It was nearly four when Tony dropped me at my condo in West L.A. He told me he'd retrieve my car, which was still at the Park Terrace, and be back at ten. I thought about calling the cops. But those unknown consequences Fenton Harris mentioned kept my hand off the phone.

Barky and I managed a few hours of restless sleep before Tony rapped on the door. He'd brought coffee, doughnuts, kibble. He assured me nothing had happened to Cherie. Or would. If it was up to him he wouldn't have done it this way, but hey, a job's a job.

A shower helped. So did getting some food in me. And there was something about Tony that said if he was with you everything would turn out okay. This had to be balanced against his hoodhood. It was all very confusing.

Barky scarfed up his breakfast, then yapped his mangy head off to be walked. We took him around the block. Then Tony locked him in the bathroom with some food and water and the *Times* classified. We hit the road.

We rode in silence until, halfway down, Tony said, "I shouldn't be telling you this."

"Shouldn't be telling me what?"

"That I haven't whacked anybody in quite a few years."

"Is the part you shouldn't be telling me that you've whacked anyone or that it's been a few years?"

"The second part."

"Why shouldn't you be telling me?"

A rueful smile. "It's bad for my image," he said.

I'd seen the man who had the stamp at virtually every show. He was from India and had a collection of stamps and postal history relating to Mahatma Gandhi. At each show he would accost every dealer. "Any Gandhi?" he'd ask. There are just so many stamps with Gandhi on them and I'm sure Gandhi-man had them all. But I'd worked a show a few weeks back, and I happened to have a set of progressive proofs of a "Famous Men of World Peace" set from some obscure, if not downright non-existent, South Pacific island, and one of those leaders happened to be Gandhi. Gandhi-man spotted them, and when he'd finished drooling he peeled off two hundred-dollar bills without batting an eye.

A few days later he called me, telling me about the 37a. He said he'd found it in a box lot he bought because it had a couple of specimen overprints on a Gandhi set from Tajikistan or Turkmenistan or one of those other Stans. Said he'd chosen me to sell it to because I'd treated him so well with the world peace proofs.

We were to meet at the monthly show at the Elks Club in Anaheim. I spotted him as soon as we got there, any-Gandhi-ing a guy who sold nothing but U.S. classics. We went off into the lobby. Tony insisted we needed some privacy and hung out in the dealer room. I wondered why he didn't simply step in and buy the stamp directly. There wouldn't have been a thing I could do to stop it. Not with Cherie still locked in the trunk. Okay, she was probably out of the trunk by then, but the image I kept conjuring was of her scrunched up in the dark, gasping for air.

Gandhi-man showed me the stamp. I checked it over with a glass. The centering was off, but typical for the period. No creases, no tears, nice clear lozenge cancel. My gut said it was genuine, though I'd have to get it expertised.

No. Fenton Harris was going to have to get it expertised.

We came up with something we were both comfortable with, did the deal. I put the stamp, in its tiny glassine envelope, in a pocket-size stock book, slid it into my jacket.

On the way back Tony insisted on stopping in Westminster at a Vietnamese restaurant he knew. Suddenly I understood the whole story. He was a Vietnam vet. Post-traumatic shock syndrome had made him a killer.

We got back around two. Tony called Harris, told me we were to meet at Harris' place at six.

We killed time watching a soccer game. Barky kept yapping, and, to shut him up, I fed him some leftovers from the Vietnamese place. He immediately threw it all up.

Tony said the address was in Studio City. We took Laurel Canyon over the hill. The three of us—me, Tony, and Barky. I hadn't wanted to bring him, but Tony insisted. Said Cherie would be pleased to see him, and it would make my rescue of her all that much better, and she'd realize her true feelings for me. I was dubious.

A block or two before Ventura Boulevard we turned left onto a residential street. The houses were nice. The yards were nice. But it didn't seem the kind of neighborhood a guy like Harris would live in. No mansions, no fancy cars. I pointed this out. Tony said not to worry about it.

A couple more turns and we pulled over. "We're here," Tony said. "Let's go check things out."

"Check things out?" I said. "What things? He gets the stamp, I get my money and Cherie."

"Huh." That code again. He opened the glove compartment and grabbed a gun. Then he scooped up Barky and threw him in the trunk. "You pee in there, I break your neck." He slammed the lid. I remembered all the admonitions about locking animals in cars. But the sun was down and the air cool. He'd be okay.

We slipped furtively down the tree-lined street. I didn't know why we were being furtive. It seemed inappropriate behavior for the situation as it had been presented to me.

Soon we lurked at the side of a Spanish-style house. We snuck up to a front window and listened. Sounded like the TV was on. We continued around to the back. Tony did something to the back door and it slipped open.

We tiptoed in, past a couple of darkened bedrooms. Tony had the gun out. We came to the living room. All forties-style furniture. Bookshelves to the ceiling, an old-fashioned radio.

The back of a white-haired head poking over the top of an overstuffed sofa.

One thing seemed out of place. A huge plasma TV at the far end of the room. On it, a much-younger Fenton Harris was holding a gun on Robert Mitchum.

"All right, Harris," Tony said. "The jig is up."

Harris whipped around. "You can't prove a thing," he said.

"I've got all the proof I need," Tony said.

"Proof?" I said. "What are we proving?"

Tony shook his head. "I should've told you before."

"Told me what?"

"Harris is a front."

"A front? What do you mean, a front? You mean like in the Woody Allen movie?"

"Actually," Harris said, "it's a Martin Ritt movie. Woody Allen only acted in it."

"Shut up, you," Tony said.

They glared at each other for five or ten seconds. Then I got it.

"He's not the collector," I said to Tony. "You are."

"Bingo."

"But why? Why do you need a front?"

He didn't move his eyes—or the gun—from Harris. "When I started collecting stamps, I didn't have him or anybody. It was just me. And somebody got the word about what I do for a living."

"Being a hood, that is."

A small nod. "It made people uncomfortable. Any time I showed up at a show, people got crazy. And I was scaring the judges. They were giving me medals I didn't deserve. I didn't want that. Plus, if my friends found out..."

"Bad for your image," I said.

He nodded. "So I disappeared, as far as the stamp people were concerned, and a couple of months later Fenton Harris showed up."

"Why him?"

"He owed me."

"For what?"

"A thing with a girl. A sixteen-year-old."

"She told me she was nineteen," Harris said.

"There's more," Tony said.

"Which is?"

"Harris is trying to get rid of me."

"Get rid of you? You mean like, knock you off?"

"Yeah." A little smile. "Like, knock me off. He gets rid of me, he's got the collection. Which is worth a lot of money. And he gets to do whatever he wants with it. Like sell it. Because no one knows it isn't his in the first place."

"How'd you find this out?"

"I cased his joint. Found some ads and stuff. He was checking on selling."

"You know, Tony, this is all very interesting, but why the hell did you have to get me involved?"

"I thought you were working with him."

"Where'd you get an idea like that?"

"I found your card with the ads." He shook his head. "I'm real sorry. I can tell you're an okay guy. A little screwed up with the ladies, but basically okay."

"Speaking of the ladies…" I turned to Harris. "Where's Cherie?"

"I'm right here, sweetie."

She stood outlined by the doorway into the kitchen. She was wearing some sort of kimono thing that brought back that damned sweat. Her hand held a gun of its own, and it was pointed right at Tony.

"Put your gun on the floor," she said, "and slide it toward Fenton."

Fenton? Cherie and Harris were on a first-name basis? Stockholm syndrome already?

Tony looked embarrassed. He put the gun on the floor and gave it a push. Harris picked it up. "I am really out of practice," Tony said.

Cherie smiled. She looked positively evil. Still hot, though. "I've been doing Fenton's nails for years. A few weeks ago he let me in on his big secret. About the collection not being his. And you'd mentioned about being a stamp dealer, and I decided to pick your brain. So we could get the most money when we sold the collection."

"You slept with me just so you could pick my brain?"

"Pretty much."

Harris butted in. "Much as I'd love to watch this heartrending scene, we really need to move on. Do you have the stamp?"

I looked over at Tony. He nodded. I pulled out the stock book and handed it to Cherie. She produced some tongs, extracted the stamp from its glassine, pronounced it the right one, put it back. I'd taught her to use the tongs. The irony of it all.

"Now what?" I asked.

"Now we all go for a nice long ride," Harris said.

"In a minute," Cherie said. "First, where's Barky?"

"He's at my place," I said, catching Tony's eye again. He seemed pleased.

"We'll go get him first," Cherie said.

Harris' car was in the garage. A Camry. The fancy wheels? Rented, no doubt.

Harris drove, with Tony to his right. Cherie and I got in the back. She kept Tony's gun on Tony and hers on me.

As we passed the Malibu, a familiar yapping assaulted our eardrums.

"Stop the car!" Cherie yelled.

Harris did.

"Barky is in the trunk!" Cherie said. "He could have suffocated in there. Who put him in there? What an awful thing to do."

"I did," Tony said.

"No, I did," I said.

"Get him out of there," Cherie said.

Tony gave me the keys. Cherie gave Harris one of the guns. She and I stepped out and approached the Malibu. I popped the trunk. Out leapt Barky.

Cherie raised her arms to catch him. I jumped her, crashed to the ground on top of her. The stock book went flying. The glassine envelope fluttered away. I heard a shriek from the Malibu. Shots went off. I felt a sharp pain in my calf.

We rolled over and Cherie was on top, bringing back memories that had no business showing up at that point. We kept rolling until I got her arms pinioned and the gun fell onto the street. I knocked it away. The pain in my leg was getting worse.

It was Barky. The miserable beast was firmly attached to my calf. I tried to shake him off. After a few eternal seconds he let loose. He yapped. He whimpered. He forgot his toilet training.

Tony grabbed him, threw him back in the trunk, slammed the lid.

Tony?

I glanced back at Harris' car. Its owner was still in the driver's seat. He lay slumped against the door.

I looked at Tony. "He'll live," he said.

I handed Cherie over to him. Then I remembered something.

It took a little time to find the glassine. Finally I spotted it. Precisely in the middle of Barky's puddle.

Tony shook his head slowly. "Easy come—"

"Don't say it," I said.

The police knew Tony, and they thought he had to be one of the perps, but, no matter how hard they tried, they couldn't pin anything on him.

They bandaged my leg and had Tony and me sit in the back of a police car while they filled out paperwork. I felt a twinge as they led Cherie to another patrol car and drove off. A twinge of what, I wasn't sure. Infatuation? Sadness? Utter stupidity?

A cop stuck his head in. "You guys can go," he said.

We got in the Malibu. "Where to?" Tony said.

I thought it over. "Santa Monica," I said. "I know a joint there."

He nodded, fired up the Malibu, turned it off again. He got out, walked over to one of the cops. When he returned, he was carrying Barky. "I couldn't leave the pooch to go to the pound or something," he said. "Maybe I'll hang onto him for a while."

"You don't think a poodle would be bad for your image?"

"You kidding? Look at your leg. This dog's a killer."

He tossed the murderous mutt in the back, and the three of us hit the road.

Be My Poodle

She: Come here, and be my poodle,
Come on, hon, and be my poodle,

Yeah, poodles don't shed, they're hypoallergenic—

He: But that doesn't matter, they're so damn frenetic,
I won't be your poodle,
But I can be your big dog,
I wanna be your big dog.

She: Come on now, and be my dachshund,
My sweet little cute little tiny little fierce little dachshund,
All clever and brash, such a sweet demeanor—

He: But who wants a dog that looks like a wiener,
I'm won't be your dachshund,
But I can be your big dog,
I wanna be your big dog.

She: I want you to be my Chihuahua,
Come on over and be my Chihuahua,
Their googly eyes are so sublime—

He: But who wants a scrawny dog that yaps all the time,
I won't be your Chihuahua,
But I can be your big dog,
I wanna be your big dog.

She: If you won't be my Chihuahua,
If you won't be my dachshund,
If you won't be my poodle,
Then you can be my big dog,
Yeah, you can be my big dog.
(he) Yeah I can be your big dog,
She/He:Yeah (you/I) can be (my/your) big dog.

An Interview with Nathan Walpow

Where did you grow up? Was yours a bookish household?

I grew up in Queens, went to high school and college in Manhattan. My parents read a lot of science fiction and trashy novels (I quickly figured out where they hid *The Carpetbaggers*). We also had a shelf full of Reader's Digest Condensed Books.

Do you remember the first mystery novel you ever read?

It was *The Missing Chums*, Hardy Boys number four. The first adult mystery I remember is *The Hog Murders*, by William L. Deandrea. Except for a bunch of Ellery Queen, I didn't read much crime fiction until shortly before I began to write it.

What was the first piece of music you recall?

I had a bunch of 78s when I was a kid. I don't remember specifics—I think I've put them out of my mind, because all I can recall is that they gave me the creeps. I first became aware of grown-up music in 1963, when I started listening to rock and roll radio. There was a short period of cool stuff like The Tymes' "So Much in Love" and The Essex' "Easier Said Than Done" before the Beatles showed up and (dramatic drumroll) changed everything.

Was yours a musically oriented household?

Not very. My parents had some 78s too, but I don't remember them ever playing them. They went to Broadway shows every once in a while, but I think that was more for the spectacle than for the music.

What music do you enjoy?

I've always been into so-called classic rock, the music of my youth. The Beatles, Jefferson Airplane, the Who, Procol Harum, the Kinks...all those sixties groups. And Tom Petty, who showed up a little later. Recently I've started enjoying some of the new groups—the Jets, Franz Ferdinand, people like that. A couple of years ago I suddenly discovered the blues; I especially enjoy the Chess Records artists like Howlin' Wolf and Sonny Boy Williamson, as well as Elmore James and Charlie Musselwhite. I enjoy some classical music; Brahms is my favorite.

Do you listen to music when you write?

Nope. I've tried several times—rock, blues, classical—and I find playing music on the computer I write on to be a huge distraction. I get into the music and can't return my mind to writing. I keep thinking about putting on music in another room, to make it more of a background thing, but I never get around to it and probably never will.

Has a musical work ever been the basis for a novel or short story?

Not a work, but a fictional band. In *One Last Hit*, my third Joe Portugal novel, Joe runs into a couple of guys he was in a group with when he was fifteen, and they decide to put it back together. The lead singer has been missing for twenty years; Joe goes looking for him. Mayhem ensues. In the book, Joe picks up his guitar again after a long hiatus. After it came out, I was inspired to do the same, and have since become afflicted with GAS—Gear Acquisition Syndrome. In the three years since *One Last Hit* came out, I've bought seven or eight more guitars and a ton of other equipment, and gotten into areas of music I'd never been interested in before. The blues, for example.

What is your favorite manmade sound?
First thing I thought of is the fuzz guitar at the beginning of "Satisfaction." A large part of my being is still tied up in those heady days of the sixties, and that riff brings me back more quickly than anything else.

What is your favorite sound in nature?
Hmm. That's a tough one. Crickets/frogs at night in the country? Thunder rolling in? My cats' purring?

If you had to choose three novels to take on a trip, what would you choose?
I read more non-fiction these days than I do fiction, but if I were limited to the latter…if I had an unread novel by one of the crime fiction authors I regularly read, that would be one. I might take a science fiction novel. I read a lot of SF in my youth, but can't stand most of what they put out today; I'm on a quest to find an author I like. And I'd take a copy of *The Manipulated*, my latest Joe Portugal, to give to any Hollywood producer I happen to run into.

"Bad for His Image" seems to occupy that thinly populated genre, humorous noir. How do you start a story?
Sometimes I have an idea, and just write toward the punchline. For instance, one day, while making the bed, I suddenly thought, what if admission into heaven and hell isn't based on how good you are, but is instead alphabetical? (I ended up writing that one from the Devil's point of view.) More often, I haven't a clue to what I'm doing, and just write until something happens. This has even happened with novels. The day I started *The Manipulated*, when I sat down at the computer, I didn't know if I was beginning another Joe Portugal novel or a standalone.

Regarding the humorous angle, I find I just can't keep the funny stuff out of my writing. I can't do deadly serious. Though one thing I've discovered is that if I write in third person, I can keep the humor at a lower level.

If you had a chance to invite any three people in the world to dinner, living or dead, who would they be?

George Harrison, because he symbolizes so much that's important to me, and because I'd like to talk guitar with him. (If he was booked, I'd take John Entwistle, the Who's bassist.) Bill Clinton—he's one of the few public figures we've had lately who had some substance. And Salma Hayek, because—oh, hell, do I have to tell you why I'd like to have dinner with Salma Hayek? (Note: My wife understands completely.)

Which would you rather do—read or listen to a favorite CD?

Read, without a doubt. I rarely sit and listen to music; it's much more often filling my background. I don't get enough time to read—it's mostly in the five or ten minutes between when I go to bed and when my eyes fall shut.

This is a wonderful story, with a memorable heroine. Fifteen-year-old Grace and her timeless island will stay with you. This quietly chilling tale is classically structured, as is the poignant ballad Peter wrote for it.

Peter says, "I'd just finished working on Piece of My Heart, *a good chunk of which is set in 1969, so I was stuck in a time tunnel when I started writing this story. One thing I wanted to work with was the clash between a very straight-laced traditional community with the new hippies and their ideas about communal living. An island seemed an ideal place to play this out, as it is fairly remote and self-contained. Originally I was going to tell the story from Mary Jane's viewpoint, but I soon found that Grace was a more natural storyteller. Mary Jane was a bit flighty and would hardly have stuck to the point. But the song is about her, very much in the style of Nick Drake and the Pink Floyd of the 'More' soundtrack and the beautiful 'Grantchester Meadows' from Ummagumma. The ghost of Syd Barrett haunts the island."*

The Ferryman's Beautiful Daughter

Peter Robinson

The strangers came to live on the island at the beginning of summer, 1969, and by the end of August my best friend Mary Jane was dead. The townsfolk blamed the Newcomers and their heathen ways, but I was certain it was something else. Not something new, but something old and powerful that had festered in the town for years, or perhaps had always been there.

I remember the morning they arrived. We were all in chapel. It was stifling hot because the windows were closed and there was no air-conditioning. "Stop fidgeting and listen to the Preacher," hissed Mother. I tried my best, but his words made no sense to me. Flecks of spittle flew from his mouth like when water touches hot oil in a frying pan. Something about Judgment Day, when the dead would rise incorruptible.

Next to me, Mary Jane was looking down at her shoes trying to hold back her laughter. I could see the muscles tightening around her lips and jaw. If we started giggling now we were done for. The Preacher didn't like laughter. It made him angry. He finally gave her one of his laser-like looks, and that seemed to settle her down. He'd never liked Mary Jane since she refused to attend his special instruction evening classes. She told me that when he had asked her, he had put his face so close to hers that she had been able to smell the bourbon on his breath, and she was sure she had seen the outline of his thing pushing hard against his pants. She also said she had seen him touching Betsy Goodall where he shouldn't have been touching her, but when we asked Betsy she blushed and denied everything. What else could she have done? Who would have believed her? In those days, as perhaps even now, small, isolated communities like ours kept their nasty little secrets to themselves.

Across the aisle, Riley McCorkindale kept glancing sideways at Mary Jane when he thought she couldn't see him. Riley was sweet on her, but she gave him a terrible run-around. I thought he was quite nice, but he *was* very shy and he seemed too young for us, no matter how tall and burly he was. Besides, he was always chewing gum and we thought that looked common. We were very sophisticated young ladies. And you have to understand that Mary Jane was very beautiful, not gawky and plain like me, with golden hair, delicate soft skin and the biggest, bluest eyes you have ever seen.

At last the service ended and we ran out into the summer sunshine. Our parents lingered to shake hands with neighbors and talk to the Preacher, of course. They were old enough to know that you weren't supposed to seem in too much of a hurry to leave God's house. But Mary Jane and I were only fifteen, sophisticated as we were, and everybody knew that meant trouble. Especially when they said we were too old for our own good. "Precocious" was the word they used most often to describe us. I looked it up.

And that was when we saw the Newcomers. I think Mary Jane noticed them first because I remember seeing her expression change from laughter to wonder as I followed her gaze to the old school bus pulling into the parking lot. It wasn't yellow, but was painted all colors, great swirls and blobs and sunbursts of green, red, purple, orange, black and blue, like nothing we'd ever seen before. And the people! We didn't own a television set in our house, but I'd seen pictures in magazines tourists left on the ferry sometimes, and I'd even read in father's newspaper about how they took drugs, listened to strange, distorted loud music and held large gatherings outside the cities, where they indulged in unspeakable practices. But I had never seen any of them in the flesh before.

They certainly did look odd, the girls in loose dresses of pretty, flowered patterns, the men with their long hair over their shoulders or tied back in ponytails, wearing Mexican-style ponchos and bell-bottom jeans and cowboy boots, the children scruffy, dirty and long-haired, running wild. They looked at us without much curiosity as they boarded the ferryboat carrying their few belongings. I suppose they'd seen plenty of people who looked like us before, and who looked at them the way we must have done. Even Riley, who had clearly been plucking up the courage to come over and say hello to Mary Jane before his ferry left, had stopped dead in his tracks, mouth gaping open. I could see the piece of gum lying there on his tongue like a misplaced tonsil.

Once the Newcomers had all boarded the ferry, the regulars got on. There was no chapel on the island. Only about thirty people lived there, and not all of them were religious. The Preacher said that was because most of them were intellectuals and thought they knew better than the Scriptures. Anyway, the ones who weren't businessmen, like Riley's father, taught at the university in the city, about forty miles away, and commuted. They left their cars in the big parking lot next to the harbor because there were no roads on the island.

Just because we had the ferry, it didn't make our little town an important place; it was simply the best natural harbor closest to Pine Island. We had a general store, a rundown hotel with a Chinese restaurant attached, the chapel, and an old one-room schoolhouse for the children. The high school was fifteen miles away in Logan, the nearest large town, and Mary Jane and I had to take the bus. The sign read "Jasmine Cove, Pop. 2,321" and I'd guess that was close enough to the truth, though I don't think they could have counted Mary Jessop's new baby because she only gave birth the day before the Newcomers arrived.

Over the next few days, we found out a little more about the Newcomers. They were from inland, a thousand miles away, according to Lenny, who ran the general store. There were about nine of them in all, including the children, and they'd bought the land fair and square from the government and had all the right papers and permissions. They kept to themselves and didn't like outsiders. They shunned the rest of society—that's the word Lenny used, "shunned," I looked it up—and planned to live off the land, growing vegetables. They didn't eat meat or fish.

According to Lenny, they didn't go to chapel. He said they worshipped the devil and danced naked and sacrificed children and animals, but Mary Jane and I didn't believe him. Lenny had a habit of getting carried away with himself when it came to new ideas. Like the Preacher, he thought the world was going to hell in a hand basket and almost everything he saw and heard proved him right, especially if it had anything to do with young people.

That day, as we wandered out of the general store onto Main Street, Mary Jane turned to me, smiled sweetly and said, "Grace, why don't we take a little ferry ride tomorrow and find out about the Newcomers for ourselves?"

Mary Jane's father, Mr. Kiernan, was the ferryman, and in summer, when we were on holiday from school, he let us ride for free whenever we wanted. Sometimes I even went by myself. Pine Island wasn't very big—about two miles long and maybe half a mile wide—but it had some very beautiful areas. I loved the western beach best of all, a lonely stretch of golden sand at the bottom of steep, forbidding cliffs. Mary Jane and I knew a secret path down, and we spent many hours exploring the caves and rock pools, or lounging about on the beach talking about life and things. Sometimes I went there alone when I felt blue, and it always made me feel better.

Most of the inhabitants of Pine Island lived in a small community of wood-structure houses nestled around the harbor on the east coast, but the Newcomers had bought property at the southern tip, where two abandoned log cabins had been falling to ruin there as long as anyone could remember. Someone said they'd once been used by hunters, but there was nothing left to hunt on Pine Island any more.

We saw the Newcomers in town from time to time, when they came to buy provisions at Lenny's store. Sometimes one or two of them would drive the school bus to Logan for things they couldn't find here. They were buying drugs there, and seeds to grow marijuana, which made folk crazy, so Lenny said. Perhaps they were.

Certainly the Preacher found many new subjects for his long sermons after the arrival of the Newcomers—including, to the dismay of some members of his congregation, the evils of tobacco and alcohol—but whether word of his rantings ever got back to them, and whether they cared if it did, we never knew.

The Preacher was in his element. He told us the Newcomers were nothing other than demons escaped from hell. He even told Mr. Kiernan that he should have nothing to do with them and that he shouldn't use God's ferryboat to transport demons.

Mr. Kiernan explained that he worked for the ferry company, which was based in the city, not for the Preacher, and that it was his job to transport anyone who paid the fare to or from Pine Island. The Preacher argued that the money didn't matter, that there was a "higher authority," and the ferry company was as bad as the Newcomers; they were all servants of Beelzebub and Mammon and any other horrible demon names he could think of. In the end, Mr. Kiernan gave up arguing and simply carried on doing his job.

One bright and beautiful day in July around the time when men first set foot on the moon, Mary Jane and I set off on our own exploratory mission. Mr. Kiernan stood at the wheel, for all the world looking as proud and stiff as if he were piloting Apollo 11 itself. We weren't going to the moon, of course, but we might as well have been. It was only later, in university, that I read *The Tempest*, but had I known it then, Miranda's words would surely have echoed in my mind's ear: "O brave new world that hath such people in it!"

The little ferry didn't have any fancy restaurants or shops or anything, just a canvas-covered area with hard wooden benches and dirty plastic windows, where you could shelter from the rain—which we got a lot of in our part of the world—and get a cup of hot coffee from the machine, if it was working. Through fair and foul Mr. Kiernan stood at the wheel, cap at a jaunty angle, pipe clamped in his mouth. Some of the locals made fun of him behind his back and called him Popeye. They thought we hadn't heard them, but we had. I thought it was cruel, but Mary Jane didn't seem to care. Our town was full of little cruelties, like the way the Youlden kids made fun of Gary Mapplin because there was something wrong with his spine and he had to go around in a wheelchair, his head lolling on his shoulders as if it were on a spring. Sometimes it seemed to me that everywhere Mary Jane and I went in Jasmine Cove, people gave us dirty looks, and we knew that if we spoke back or anything, they'd report us to our parents. Mr. Kiernan was all right—he went very easy on Mary Jane—but my father was a bit of tyrant, and I had to watch what I said around him.

Riley McCorkindale was hanging around the ferry dock, as usual, fishing off the small rickety pier with some friends. I don't think they ever caught anything. He blushed when Mary Jane and I walked by giggling, and said hello. I could feel his eyes following us as we headed for the path south through the woods. He must have known where we were going; it didn't lead anywhere else.

Soon we'd left the harbor and its small community behind us and were deep in the woods. It was cooler there, and the sunlight filtered pale green through the shimmering leaves. Little animals skittered through the dry underbrush, and once a large bird exploded out of a tree and startled us both so much our hearts began to pound. We could hear the waves crashing on the shore in the distance, to the west, but all around us it was peaceful and quiet.

Finally, from a short distance ahead, we heard music. It was like nothing I'd ever heard before, and there was an ethereal beauty about it, drifting on the sweet summer air as if it belonged there.

Then we reached a clearing and could see the log cabins. Three children were playing horseshoes, and someone was taking a shower in a ramshackle wooden box rigged up with some sort of overhead sieve. The music was coming from inside one of three cabins. You can imagine the absolute shock and surprise on our faces when the shower door opened and out walked a young man naked as the day he was born.

We gawped, I'm sure. I had certainly never seen a naked man before, not even a photograph of one, but Mary Jane said she once saw her brother playing with himself when he thought she was out. We looked at one another and swallowed. "Let's wait," Mary Jane whispered. "We don't want them to think we've been spying."

And we waited. Five, ten minutes went by. Nothing much happened. The children continued their game and no-one else entered the shower. Finally, Mary Jane and I took deep breaths, left the cover of the woods and walked into the clearing.

"Hello," I called, aware of the tremor in my voice. "Hello. Is anybody home?"

The children stopped their game and stared at us. One of them, a little girl, I think, with long dark curls, ran inside the nearest cabin. A few moments later a young man stepped out. Probably only three or four years older than us, he had a slight, wispy blonde beard and beautiful silky long hair, still damp, falling over his shoulders. It was the same man we had seen getting out of the shower, and I'm sure we both blushed. He looked a little puzzled and suspicious. And why not? After all, I don't think anyone else from Jasmine Cove had been out to welcome them.

Mary Jane seemed suddenly struck dumb, whether by the man's good looks or the memory of his nakedness I don't know, and it was left to me to speak. "Hello," I said. "I'm Grace Vincent, and this is my friend Mary Jane Kiernan. We're from the town, from Jasmine Cove. We've come to say hello."

He stared for a moment, then smiled and looked at Mary Jane. His eyes were bright green, like the sea just beyond the sands. "Mary Jane," he said. "Well, how strange. This must be a song about you. The Mad Hatters."

"What?" I said.

"The name of the band. The Mad Hatters. They're English."

We listened to the music for a moment, and I thought I caught the words, "Mary Jane is dreaming of an ocean dark and gleaming." I didn't recognize the song, or the name of the group, but that didn't mean much. My parents didn't let me listen to pop music. Mary Jane seemed to find her voice and said something about that being nice.

"Look, would you like to come in?" the young man said. "Have a cold drink or something. It's a hot day."

I looked at Mary Jane. I could tell from her expression that she was as uncertain as I was. Now that we were here, the reality was starting to dawn on us. These were the people the Preacher had called the Spawn of Satan. As far as the townsfolk were concerned, they drugged young girls and had their evil way. But the young man looked harmless and it *was* a hot day. We were thirsty. Finally, we sort of nodded and followed him inside the cabin.

The shade was pleasant and a gentle cross-breeze blew through the open shutters. Sunlight picked out shining strands of silver and gold in the materials that draped the furnishings. The Newcomers didn't have much, and most of it was makeshift, but we made ourselves comfortable on cushions on the floor and the young man brought us some lemonade. "Home-made," he said. "I'm sorry it's not as cold as you're probably used to, but we don't have a refrigerator yet." He laughed. "As a matter of fact, we've only just got the old generator working, or we wouldn't even have any music." He nodded towards the drinks. "We keep some chilled in the stream out back."

By this time the others had wandered in to get a look at us, most of them older than the young man, and several of them lovely women in bright dresses with flowers twined in their long hair.

"I'm Jared," said the young man, then he introduced the others—Star, Leo, Gandalf, Dylan—names we were unfamiliar with. They sat cross-legged on the floor and smiled. Jared asked us some questions about the town, and we explained how the people there were suspicious of strangers but were decent folks underneath it all. I wasn't certain that was true, but we weren't there to say bad things about our kin. We didn't tell them what lies the Preacher had been spreading.

Jared told us they had come here to get away from the suspicion, corruption and greed they had found in the cities, and they were going to live close to nature and meditate. Some of them were artists and musicians—they had guitars and flutes—but they didn't want to be famous or anything. They didn't even want money from anyone. One of them—Rigel, I think his name was—said mysteriously that the world was going to end soon and that this was the best place to be when it happened.

Someone rolled a funny cigarette, lit it and offered it to us, but I said no. I'd never smoked any kind of cigarette, and the thought of marijuana, which I assumed it was, terrified me. To my horror, Mary Jane took it and inhaled. She told me later that it made her feel a bit light-headed, but that was all. I must admit, she didn't act any differently from normal. At least not that day. We left shortly after, promising to drop by again, and it was only over the next few weeks that I noticed Mary Jane's behavior and appearance gradually start to change.

It was just little things at first, like a string of beads she bought at a junk shop in Logan. It was nothing much, really, just cheap colored glass, but it was something she would have turned her nose up at a short while ago. Now, it replaced the lovely gold chain and heart pendant that her parents had given her for her fifteenth birthday. Next came the red cheesecloth top with the silver sequins and fancy Indian embroidery, and the first Mad Hatters LP, the one with "her song" on it.

We went often to the island to see Jared and the others, and I soon began to sense something, some deeper connection, between Mary Jane and Jared and, quite frankly, it worried me. They started wandering off together for hours, and sometimes she told me to go back home without her, that she'd catch a later ferry. It wasn't that Mary Jane was naïve or anything, or that I didn't trust Jared. I also knew that Mary Jane's father was liberal, and she said he trusted her, but I still worried. The townsfolk were already getting a bit suspicious because of the odd way she was dressing. Even Riley McCorkindale gave her strange looks in chapel. It didn't take a genius to put two and two together. At the very least, if she wasn't careful, she could end up grounded for the rest of the summer.

Things came to a head after chapel one Sunday in August. The Preacher had delivered one of his most blistering sermons about what happens to those who turn away from the path of righteousness and embrace evil, complete with a graphic description of the torments of hell. Afterwards, people were standing talking, as they do, all a little nervous, and Mary Jane actually said to the Preacher that she didn't believe there was a hell, that if God was good, he wouldn't do such horrible things to people. The Preacher turned scarlet, and it was only the fact that Mary Jane ran off and jumped on the ferry that stopped him taking her by the ear and dragging her back inside the chapel for special instruction whether she liked it or not. But he wouldn't forget. One way or another, there'd be hell to pay.

Or there would have been, except that was the evening they found Mary Jane's body on the western beach of Pine Island.

The fisherman who found her said he first thought it was a bundle of clothes on the sand. Then, when he went to investigate, he realized that it was a young girl and sailed back to Jasmine Cove as fast as he could. Soon, the police launch was heading out there, the parking lot was full of police cars and the sheriff had commandeered the ferry. Mr. Kiernan was beside himself, blaming himself for not keeping a closer eye on her. But it wasn't his fault. He wasn't as mean-spirited as the rest, and how could he know what would happen, anyway? By the time it started to get dark, word was spreading around town that a girl's body had been found, that it was the body of Mary Jane Kiernan and that she had been strangled.

I can't really describe the shock I felt when I first heard the news. It was if my whole being went numb. I didn't believe it at first, of course, but in a way I did. So many people said it had happened that in the end I just had to believe it. Mary Jane was gone.

The next few days passed as in a dream. I remember only that the newspapers were full of stories about some huge gathering out east for folks like the Newcomers, at a place called Woodstock, where it rained cats and dogs and everyone played in the mud. The police came around and questioned everybody, and I was among the first, being Mary Jane's closest friend. The young detective, Lonnegan was his name, seemed nice enough, and Mother offered him a glass of iced tea, which he accepted. His forehead and upper lip were covered by a thin film of sweat.

"Now then, little lady," he began.

"My name's Grace," I corrected him. "I am not a little lady."

I'll give him his due, he took it in his stride. "Very well, Grace," he said. "Mary Jane was your best friend. Is that right?"

"Yes," I answered.

"Were you with her when she went to Pine Island last Wednesday?"

"No," I said.

"Didn't you usually go there together?"

"Sometimes. Not always."

"Why did she go there? There's not exactly a lot to see or do."

I shrugged. "It's peaceful. There's a nice beach…." I couldn't help myself, but as soon as I thought of the beach—it had been *our* beach—the tears started to flow. Lonnegan paused while I reached for a tissue, dried my eyes and composed myself. "I'm sorry," I went on. "It's just a very beautiful place. And there are all kinds of interesting sea birds."

"Yes, but that's not why Mary Jane went there, is it, for the sea birds?"

"Isn't it? I don't know."

"Come on, Grace," said Lonnegan, "we already know she was seeing a young man called David Garwell."

David Garwell. So that was Jared's real name. "Why ask me, then?"

"Do you know if she had arranged to meet him that day? Last Wednesday?"

"I'm sure I don't know," I said. "Mary Jane didn't confide in me about everything." Maybe he did know that Mary Jane was "seeing" Jared, but I wasn't going to tell him that she had told me just two days before she died that she was in love with him, and that as soon as she turned sixteen she planned to go and live with him and the others on Pine Island. That wouldn't have gone down well at all with Detective Lonnegan. Besides, it was our secret.

Lonnegan looked uncomfortable and shuffled in his seat, then he dropped his bombshell. "Maybe she didn't tell you that she was having a baby, Grace, huh? And we think it was his. Did Mary Jane tell you she was having David Garwell's baby?"

In the end, it didn't matter what I thought or said. While the bedraggled crowds were heading home from Woodstock in the east, the police arrested Jared—David Garwell—for the murder of Mary Jane Kiernan. They weren't giving out a whole lot of details, but rumor had it that they had found Mary Jane's gold pendant in a drawer in his room.

"He did it, Grace, you know he did," said Cathy Baker outside the drug store a few days later. "People like that...they're...ugh!" She pulled a face and made a gesture with her hands as if to sweep spiders off her chest. "They're not like us."

"But why would he hurt her?" I asked. "He loved her."

"*Love?*" echoed Cathy. "They don't know the meaning of the word."

"They call it *free* love, you know," Lynne Everett chirped in. "And that means they do it with anyone."

"And everyone," added Cathy.

I gave up. What was the point? They weren't going to listen. I walked down Main Street with my head hung low and the sun beating on the back of my neck. It just didn't make sense. Mary Jane stopped wearing the pendant when she bought the cheap colored beads. Jared couldn't have stolen it from her, even if he was capable of such a thing, unless he had broken into her house on the mainland, which seemed very unlikely to me. And she hadn't been wearing it on the day she died, I was certain of that. It made far more sense to assume that she had given it to him as a token of her love.

The problem was that I hadn't seen Jared or any of the others since the arrest, so I hadn't been able to ask them what happened. The police had searched the cabins, of course, and they said they found drugs, so they hauled everybody into the county jail and put the children in care.

I was so lost in thought that I didn't even notice Detective Lonnegan walking beside me until he spoke my name and asked me if I wanted to go into Slater's with him for a coffee.

"I'm not allowed to drink coffee," told him, "but I'll have a soda, if that's all right."

He said that was fine and we went inside and took a table. He waited a while before speaking, then he said, "Look, Grace, I know that this is all a terrible shock to you, that Mary Jane was your best friend. I respect that, but if you know anything else that will help us in court against the man who killed her, I'd really be grateful if you'd tell me."

"Why do you need me?" I asked. "I thought you knew everything. You've already put him in jail."

"I know," Lonnegan agreed. "And we've probably got enough to convict him, but every little bit helps. Did she say anything? Did you see anything?"

I told him how Jared couldn't possibly have stolen the locket unless he went to the mainland.

Lonnegan smiled. "I don't know how you know about that," he said. " I suppose I shouldn't underestimate small town gossip. We know she wasn't wearing the locket on the day she died, but we don't know when he stole it."

"He didn't steal it! Jared's not a thief."

Lonnegan coughed. "I beg to differ, Grace," he said. "David Garwell has a record that includes larceny and possession of dangerous drugs. He should have been in jail to start with, but he skipped bail."

"I don't believe you."

"That's up to you. I could show you the evidence if you want to come to headquarters."

"No, thank you."

"It's your choice."

"But *why* would he hurt Mary Jane? He told her he loved her."

Lonnegan's ears pricked up. "He did?" He toyed with his coffee cup on the saucer. It still had an old lipstick stain around the rim. "We think they had an argument," he said. "Maybe Mary Jane discovered the theft of the pendant. Or perhaps she told Garwell that she was pregnant, and he wanted nothing further to do with her. Either way, she ran off down to that cozy little beach the two of you liked so much. He followed her, maybe worried that she'd tell her parents, or the police. They fought, and he strangled her."

"But then he'd *know* for certain that the police would suspect him!"

"People ain't always thinking straight when they're mad, Grace."

I shook my head. I know what he said made sense, but it *didn't* make sense, if you see what I mean. I didn't know what else to say.

"You're going to have to accept it sooner or later, Grace," Lonnegan said. "This Jared, as you call him, murdered your friend, and you're probably the only one who can help us make sure he pays for his crime."

"But I can't help you. Don't you see? I still don't believe Jared did it."

Lonnegan sighed. "They had an argument. She walked off. He admits that much. He won't tell us what it was about, but like I said, I think she confronted him over the gold pendant or the pregnancy. He followed her."

I squirmed in my seat, took a long sip of soda and asked, "Who else was on the island that day? Have you checked?"

"What do you mean?"

"You must have asked Mr. Kiernan, Mary Jane's father, who he took over and brought back that day. Was there anyone else who shouldn't have been there? Have you questioned them all, asked them for alibis?"

"No, but…"

"Don't you think you ought to? Why can't it be one of those people?"

"Like who?"

"The Preacher!" I blurted it out.

Lonnegan shook his head, looking puzzled. "The Preacher? Why?"

"Was he there? Was he on the ferry?"

"You know I can't tell you that."

"Well, you just ask him," I said, standing up, "because Mary Jane told me she saw him touching Betsy Goodall somewhere he shouldn't have been touching her."

The Preacher was waiting for me after chapel the following Sunday. "Grace, a word in your ear," he said, leading me by the arm. He was smiling and looked friendly enough, in that well-scrubbed way of his, to fool anyone watching, including my parents, but his grip hurt. He took me back inside the dark chapel and sat me down in a corner, crowding me, his face close to mine. I couldn't smell bourbon on his breath—not that I would have known what it smelled like—but I could smell peppermint. "I had a visit from the police the other day," he said, "a most unwelcome visit, and I've been trying to figure out ever since who's been telling tales out of school. I think it was you, Grace. You were her friend. Thick as thieves, the two of you, always unnaturally close."

"There was nothing unnatural about it," I said, my heart beating fast. "And yes, we were friends. So what?"

His upper lip curled. "Don't you give me any of your smart talk, young lady. You caused me a lot of trouble, you did, a lot of grief."

"You've got nothing to worry about if you're pure in heart and true in the eyes of the Lord. Isn't that what you're always telling us?"

"Don't take the Lord's word in vain. I swear, one day...." He shook his head. "Grace, I do believe you're headed for a life of sin, and you know what the wages of sin are, don't you?"

"Did you go to Pine Island that day, Preacher? The day Mary Jane died. Were you on the ferry? You were, weren't you?"

The Preacher looked away. "As a matter of fact, I had some important business there," he said. "Real estate business." We all knew about the Preacher and his real estate. He seemed to think the best way of carrying out God's plan on earth was to take ownership of as much of it as he could afford.

"Why haven't they arrested you?" I asked.

"Because I haven't done anything wrong. The police believe me. So should you. There's no evidence against me. I didn't strangle that girl."

"Mary Jane told me about Betsy Goodall, about what she saw."

"And just what did she see? I'll tell you what she saw. Nothing. Ask Betsy Goodall. The police did. Your friend Mary Jane was a wayward child," the Preacher said, his voice a sort of drone. "She had a vile imagination. Evil. She made up stories. The police know that now. They talked to me and they talked to Betsy. I just want to warn you, Grace. Don't you go around making any more grief for me, or you'll have more trouble than you can imagine. Do you understand me?"

"Betsy was too scared to say anything, wasn't she? She was frightened of what you might do to her. What did you do to Mary Jane?"

There. It was out before I realized it. That's the problem with me sometimes: I speak before thinking. I felt his fingers squeeze into my arm and I cried out. "Do you understand me?" he asked again, his voice a reptilian whisper.

"Yes!" I said. "You're hurting me! Yes, I understand. Leave me alone." And I wrenched my arm free and ran out of the chapel over to the ferry dock. I wanted to be by myself, and I wanted to walk where Mary Jane and I had walked. There was really only one place I could go, and I was lucky, I had only ten minutes to wait.

The day had turned hazy, warm and sticky. There'd be a storm after dark, everyone said. Mr. Kiernan seemed worried about me and told me if I wasn't on the next ferry home he'd send someone looking for me. I said that was sweet but I would be all right. Then he said he'd keep an eye on the weather to make sure I didn't get stuck out there when the storm came.

I walked past the houses and through the woods to the southern tip of the island, where the Newcomers used to live. They had been taken away so fast they hadn't even had time to grab what few belongings they had. Nobody seemed to know what would happen to their things now, whether anyone would come for them. I stood behind the cover of the trees looking into the clearing, the way Mary Jane and I had done that first time, when we saw Jared come out of the shower. And there it was again, faint, drifting, as if it belonged to the air it traveled on: Mary Jane's song. "And Mary Jane is dreaming/Of oceans dark and gleaming."

But who was playing it?

Heart in my mouth, I ducked low and waited. I wanted to know, but I didn't want to go in there, the way people went into basements and rooms in movies when they knew evil lurked there. So I hid.

As it turned out, I didn't have long to wait. As soon as the song ended, a furtive head peeped out of the doorway and, gauging that all was clear, the young man stepped out into the open. My jaw dropped. It was Riley McCorkindale.

Some instinct still held me back from announcing my presence, so I stayed where I was. Riley stood, ears pricked, glancing around furtively, then he headed away from the cabins—not back towards his parents' house, but west, towards the cliffs. Now I was really puzzled.

When I calculated that Riley had got a safe distance ahead of me, I followed through the trees. I couldn't see him, but there weren't many paths on the island, and not many places to go if you were heading in that direction. Once in a while I would stop and listen, and I could hear him way ahead, snapping a twig, rustling a bush as he walked. I hoped he didn't stop and listen the same way and hear me following him.

As I walked, I wondered what on earth Riley had been doing at the Newcomers' cabin. Playing the record with the Mary Jane song on it, obviously. But why? I knew he had been sweet on her, of course, but he had always been too shy to say hello. Had he made friends with the Newcomers? After all, they were practically neighbors. But Riley went to chapel, and he seemed the type to take notice of the Preacher. His father was a property developer in Logan, so they were a wealthy and respected family in the community, too, which made it even more unlikely that Riley would have anything to do with Jared and the others.

When I reached the cliffs, there was no one in sight. I glanced over the edge, down towards the beach, but saw no one there, either. I wasn't sure whether Riley knew about the hidden path Mary Jane and I used to take. He lived on the island, so perhaps he did. I stood still for a moment and felt the wind whipping my hair in my eyes and tugging at my clothes, bringing the dark clouds from far out at sea, heard the raucous cries of gulls over a shoal of fish just off the coast, smelled the salt air. Then, just as I started to move towards the path, I heard a voice behind me.

"You."

I turned. Riley stepped out from the edge of the woods.

"Riley," I said, smiling, trying to sound relaxed, and holding my hair from my eyes. "You startled me. What are you doing here?"

"You were following me."

"Me? No. Why would I do that?" I felt vulnerable at the edge of the cliff, aware of the golden sand so far below, and as I spoke I tried edging slowly forwards. But Riley stood his ground, and right now he didn't seem shy at all.

"I don't know," he said. "But I saw you. Maybe it's something to do with Mary Jane?"

"Mary Jane?"

"You know I loved her. Until that...that freak came and took her away from me. Still, he's got what he deserves. Let him rot in jail."

"Now, listen, Riley. You don't have to say anything to me." The last thing I wanted was to be Riley's confessor with a hundred-foot drop behind me. "Let's just go back, huh? I don't want to miss my ferry."

"I used to watch them, you know," Riley said. "Watch them doing it."

I didn't know what to say to that. I swallowed.

"They'd do it anywhere. They didn't care who was watching."

"That's not true, Riley," I said. "You know that can't be true. You were spying on them. You said so."

"Maybe so. But they did it down there." He pointed. "On the beach."

"It's a very secluded spot." I don't know what I meant by that, whether I was defending Mary Jane's honor, deflecting the shock I felt, or what. I just wanted to keep Riley talking until I could get around him and...well, getting back to the ferry was my main thought. But if Riley had other ideas there wasn't much I could do. He was bigger and stronger than me. Drops of rain dampened my cheek. The sky was becoming darker. "Look, Riley," I said. "There's going to be a storm. Move out of the way and let me go back to the ferry dock. I'll miss my ferry. Mr. Kiernan will be looking for me."

"I didn't mean to do it, you know," Riley said.

I had been trying to skirt around him, but I froze. "Didn't mean to do what?" There I was again, speaking without thinking. I didn't want to know, but it was too late now.

"Kill her. It just happened. One minute she was...."

Now he'd told me, I just had to know the full story. Unless I could make a break into the woods when he wasn't expecting it, I was done for anyway. I didn't think I could outrun him, but with the cover of the trees, and the coming dark, perhaps I had a chance of staying ahead of him as far as the ferry dock. "How did it happen?" I asked, still moving slowly.

"They had a fight. I was watching the cabin and they had a fight and Mary Jane ran out crying."

The baby, I thought. She told him about the baby. But why would that matter? The Newcomers loved children. They would have welcomed Mary Jane and her child. It must have been something else. Perhaps she wanted to get married? That would have been far too conventional for Jared but just like Mary Jane. Whatever it was, they had argued. Couples do argue. "What happened?" I asked.

"I followed her like you followed me. She went down to the beach. Down that path you both thought was your little secret. I went after her. I thought I could comfort her. You know, I thought she'd dumped him and maybe she would turn to me if I was nice to her."

"How did it go wrong?"

"She did it with him, didn't she?" Riley said, his voice rising to a shout against the coming storm. "Why wouldn't she do it with me? Why did she have to laugh?"

"She laughed at you?"

He nodded. "That's when I grabbed her. The next thing I...I guess I don't know my own strength. She was like a rag doll."

There was a slim chance that I could slip into the woods to the left of him and make a run for it. That was when he said, "I'm glad I told you. I've been wanting to tell somebody, just to get it off my chest. I feel better now."

I paused. "But Riley, you have to go to the authorities. You have to tell them there's an innocent man in jail."

"No! I ain't going to jail. I won't. Only you and me know the truth."

"Riley, if you hurt me they'll know," I said, my voice shaking, judging the distance between his reach and the gap in the trees. "They'll know it was you. I told Mr. Kiernan I came here to talk to you." It was a lie, of course, but I hoped it was an inspired one.

"Why would you do that?" Riley seemed genuinely puzzled. "You didn't know anything about it until just now. You didn't even know I existed. You didn't want to know. None of you did."

"I mean it, Riley. If you hurt me, they'll find out. You can't get away with murder twice. You'll go to jail then for sure."

"They say killing's easier the second time. I read that in a book."

"Riley, don't."

"It's all right, Grace," he said, leaning back against the tree. "I ain't going to hurt you. Don't think I don't regret what I did. Don't think I enjoyed it. I'm just not going to jail for it. Go. Catch your ferry. See if I care."

"B-but...."

"Who'd believe you? The police have got the man they want. There sure as hell's no evidence against me. My daddy doesn't know where I was, but he already told them I was home all day. Last thing he wants to know is that his son killed some girl. That would surely upset the applecart. Nobody saw me. The Preacher's with us, too. He was at the house talking real estate with daddy. I don't know if he knows I did it or not, but he don't care. He was the one told me about Mary Jane and that freak, what they were doing and how it was a sin. That's why I went to spy on them. He told me he knew she was really my girl, but she'd been seduced by the devil. He told me what that long-haired pervert was doing to her and asked me what I was going to do about it. The Preacher won't be saying nothing to no police. So go on. Go."

"But why did you tell me?"

Riley paused. "Like I said, I knew I'd feel better if I told someone. I'm truly sorry for what I did, but going to jail ain't going to bring her back."

"But what about Jared? He's innocent."

"He's the Spawn of Satan. Now go ahead, Grace. Catch the ferry before the storm comes. It's going to be a bad one."

"You won't...?"

He shook his head. "Nope. Don't matter what you say. Go ahead. See if I'm not right."

And I did. I caught the ferry. Mr. Kiernan smiled and said I was lucky I just made it. The storm broke that night, flooded a few roads, broke a few windows. The next day I took the bus into the city to see Detective Lonnegan and told him about what Riley had said to me on the beach. He laughed, said the boy was having me on, giving me a scare. I told him it was true, that Riley was in love with Mary Jane and that he tried to....I couldn't get the words out in front of him, but even so he was shaking his head before I'd finished.

So Riley McCorkindale turned out to be right. The police didn't believe me. I didn't see any point running all over town telling Mr. Kiernan, father, the Preacher or anyone else, so that was the end of it. Riley McCorkindale strangled Mary Jane Kiernan and got away with it. Jared—David Garwood—went to jail for a crime he didn't commit. He didn't stay there long, though. Word made it back to town about a year or two later that he got stabbed in a prison brawl, and even then everyone said he had it coming, that it was divine justice.

None of the Newcomers ever returned to Jasmine Cove. The cabins fell into disrepair again, and their property reverted to the township in one of those roundabout ways that these things often happen in small communities like ours. I thought of Mary Jane often over the years, remembered her smile, her childlike enthusiasms. The Mad Hatters became famous and once in a while I heard "her" song on the radio. It always made me cry.

After I had finished college and started teaching high school in Logan, the property boom began. The downtown areas of many major cities became uninhabitable, people moved out to the suburbs and the rich wanted country, or island, retreats. One day I heard that McCorkindale Developments had knocked down the cabins on Pine Island and cleared the land for a strip of low-rise, ocean-front luxury condominiums.

I suppose it's what you might call ironic, depending on the way you look at it, but by that time the Preacher and Riley's father had managed to buy up most of the island for themselves.

The Ferryman's Beautiful Daughter

Morning mist is drifting on the surface of the water
All the children are asleep except the boatman's daughter
And Mary Jane is dreaming
Of oceans dark and gleaming,
Where she breathes the water cold,
A mermaid blessed with scales of gold,
And flows where the tide will take her.

Larks are rising from the fields and scattering the air
    with song.
Children dance upon the green in summer now the
    days are long,
But Mary Jane is dreaming
In her ocean dark and gleaming.
Kaleidoscopes of fish spin by,
She hears their colours, tastes their signs
And flows where the tide will take her.

Night is day and day is night,
Truth is dream and dream is right,
Follow Mary Jane and see
Just what the depths can teach you.

White is black and black is white,
Real is wrong and wrong is right,
Follow Mary Jane and see
Just where these words can lead you.

Darkness falls upon the woods and stars are shining in
    the sky,
The moon floats on the water like a fallen angel, pale
    and dry,
But Mary Jane is dreaming
In the ocean dark and gleaming.
New friends whisper in her ear
The truths she doesn't want to hear.
She flows where their words will take her.

An Interview with Peter Robinson

Where did you grow up? Was yours a bookish household?
I grew up in Leeds, a large industrial city in the north of England. Our household wasn't particularly bookish, though I remember my father liked to read detective stories from the library, especially Raymond Chandler and Georges Simenon.

Do you remember the first mystery novel you ever read?
It was most likely one of the Famous Five series by Enid Blyton, when I was a kid, then when I was a teenager I read The Saint, Bulldog Drummond, Sexton Blake and James Bond. The first adult crime novel I remember reading was Raymond Chandler's *The Little Sister*, when I was about thirty.

What was the first piece of music you recall?
Elvis Presley singing "Hound Dog."

Was yours a musically oriented household?
No. We had a radio, but that was all. It was at my aunt's that I heard Elvis and Lonnie Donegan for the first time. She had a record player. As soon as I could, I bought a transistor radio I could listen to with an earpiece under the bedsheets. Back then only Radio Luxemburg played the sort of pop music I wanted to hear, and later the pirate stations played more.

Do you listen to music when you write?
Only instrumental and chamber music. Anything else is too distracting.

Has a musical work ever inspired a novel or short story?
Several times, but the relationship between the music and
story is usually pretty vague. *Strange Affair* was inspired
by a Richard Thompson song, but I'd be hard pushed to
say how. Old folk songs are also inspiring, with their tales
of long-ago murders and demon lovers.

What is your favorite manmade sound?
The human voice.

What is your favorite sound in nature?
Water.

**If you had to choose three novels to take on a trip, what
would you choose?**
I'd take the latest novel by one of my favorites, such as
Ruth Rendell, Michael Connelly, Ian Rankin, John Harvey
or John Le Carre, then a bulky classic I'd been wanting
to read for a long time—*War and Peace, Middlemarch* or
something like that. Lastly, I'd probably take a biography
rather than a third novel.

**Your work is notable for the role setting plays in your stories.
How do you begin a novel or a short story? Does character
come first?**
Character and a sense of place usually come first. The
most important character for me is the victim, because
once you understand why that person ended up that way,
then you understand the whole story.

**Which would you rather do—read or listen to a favorite
CD?**
I can do both at the same time!

Jeff Deaver's prose is rich with crisply described characters and surprising plot twists.

This sinister story is no exception.

The Fan

Jeffery Deaver

This was the debate: Should the band play it safe and cancel, or should they go out on stage to face a crowded concert hall, where a man was possibly waiting to murder their star?

"My, lookit that guitar," said the gruff, rumpled man in a light-blue suit. Detective Travis Ewing's accent suggested a Memphis upbringing, though he was now a Nashville boy through and through. He was nodding at a Gibson Hummingbird acoustic, gloriously red and brown and, give or take, forty years old. "Work of art." His tone, however, was bored and suggested he couldn't care less about the instrument.

"You play, Detective?" asked the petite, beautiful woman, all of twenty-seven years old, dressed in tight jeans and a blue denim blouse. Her rhinestone earrings shot sparkles of light throughout the dim backstage area, where the half-dozen members of the band sat, somber and quiet.

Brushing at his thin, gray swept-back hair, Ewing snorted a laugh. "Not me.... My partner does. He's a big fan of yours." A nod toward a trim, young detective, who had a blond crewcut and a goatee. J.T. Williams resembled less a law enforcer than a bartender at Houlihan's.

He shrugged and said to her modestly, "Nothing to speak of. Can't play the way y'all do."

The "y'all" doesn't mean me, Shayna Tipton thought wryly. When they were up on stage or in the studio she strummed a small Martin 00-18 acoustic but it was for rhythm only; her only real instrument was her voice.

"You ever perform?" she asked Williams.

The detective shook his head. "Nup."

Ewing continued, "Now I appreciate the bind y'all're in, Mr. and Mrs. Tipton. I surely hoped we'd've caught him by now. But we didn't. So, here's the thing. I'm thinking you really oughta cancel." He glanced through the curtain at the concert hall of Central Tennessee College, now filling with the audience.

Her husband, Randy, standing nearby, thumbs in his jeans pockets, nodded. The muscular man said in his melodious baritone, "I'm not sure it's a bad idea, honey. Taking the night off." He looked right into his wife's eyes. This was Randy, she reflected. Understated, polite, but straight speaking. He was a pit bull with a velvet collar, like her daddy used to say. It was one of the things she loved most about her husband.

But she was the same way. She smiled and said in an even voice, "I really want to go on."

Ewing blew a breath through his lips real slow, glanced at Williams.

Scrawny, forty-year-old Ron Delbert, the band's manager, leaned against a column, a cigarette in his mouth. He was directly below a no-smoking sign. "We could give 'em all a rain check," nodding toward the hall. "Set it up in a week at Vanderbilt."

The singer shook her head. "Sorry, Ron."

A trim man in jeans, his hair pulled back in a ponytail, Chris Keller, said, "For what it's worth, we're with her. All of us are. We talked about it."

He was referring to the band members: Sammy Baker was the bass player. Sultry dark-haired Betsy Carson out of Georgia played fiddle. Grizzled, whiskered Ernie Potts was somewhere between fifty and seventy; he played the incomprehensibly complicated and haunting pedal steel guitar. Keller played lead guitar, wrote the songs and sang harmony.

"Well, fact is, sir," Ewing replied to the guitarist, "it's not exactly y'all this fellow's fixing to do harm to. It's Mrs. Tipton.... And there's also the matter of endangering the public. You got thousands of souls out there. If he was to somehow smuggle in a firearm, no telling how many people'd get hurt."

Potts scoffed. "Plentya po-lice out there. You'd trip over 'em you don't look where you're going. Don't see how anybody could get in with a gun." He took a sip from a Coke can that contained as much sour mash as soft drink. The West Virginian drank more than the rest of the band combined, but in five years of playing behind Shayna he'd never missed a single performance, cue or note. Which was a testament to something, teetotaler Shayna figured.

Still, the couple couldn't dismiss the detective's concern too lightly. There was no doubt that country-western star Shayna Tipton had herself a dangerous stalker. About two months ago the band played a show in Nashville, where they lived—close to this same venue, in fact—as part of a tour of medium-size concert halls around the country. That night, while the couple was out to dinner after the concert, somebody broke into their house and stole some of Shayna's clothes and lingerie, and a boxful of the band's early posters and other memorabilia. The Tennessee State Police take seriously any threat to one of their native daughters and investigated diligently, but no suspect was ever found.

It seemed for a while that the break-in might have been an isolated incident. But that wasn't the case. A few weeks later the Tiptons' motor home was burglarized and other items of Shayna's were taken. The intruder also left some presents, troubling ones: a naked blonde doll and a copy of the magazine *Country Western Weekly*, which featured the Tiptons on the cover. A ruddy halo—in deer blood—was drawn over Shayna's head.

Ewing and Williams were at a loss to figure out who the perpetrator was. They knew he was a white male—he'd been spotted by a witness fleeing their trailer one night, wearing a green Shayna Tipton 2002 Tour souvenir t-shirt—and that he probably lived near Nashville since the incidents never happened when they were out of the area. Whoever he was, the fellow was smart; no fingerprints or other evidence was left behind. Shayna tried to think of suspects, but she could remember dozens of men who'd gazed at her in overly familiar ways or even subtly propositioned her when she was autographing CDs before or after shows—notwithstanding the fact that six-foot-four Randy was only three feet away. No one in particular jumped out. None of the fan emails or letters gave any clues as to a dangerous stalker.

The incidents let up for a time, and she hoped the man had given up on her. But then came June 12, two weeks ago.

After the show that night Randy and Shayna returned to their motor home and found yet another present from their visitor: On the doorstep was an envelope, inside of which was a printed note that said, *If I can't have you nobody will.* It was wrapped around a .38 bullet, a hollow point, the sort of slug, Ewing explained, designed to do much more damage than regular bullets.

They cancelled the next show and Ewing and Williams and several troopers checked out the note and bullet and searched for witnesses. They found nothing.

Tonight's was to be the first concert since that incident.

"Why don't'cha think 'bout it?" persisted Ron Delbert, dropping the cigarette and crushing it out. "Canceling, I mean. Wouldn't be a bad idea." He was wearing a close-fitting suit and a string tie.

"Nothing's going to happen, Ron," Shayna said. "They've got those nice young officers all over the place out there, like Ernie said. You saw 'em. Anyway, it's not like he actually tried to *shoot* me."

"I'll give you that," Delbert said, "but I've been thinking 'bout something. Say we cancel tonight 'cause there's some crazy out there—you with me? We get a reporter or two to come over here and cover it. Oh, and how 'bout one of them news crews in a van—with the antenna on top. Live at Eleven."

"Where're you going with this, Ron?" Randy asked.

"Hear me out. And what happens with the next show? We sell three times the tickets. Maybe four times…. People come from all over to support us. Show of faith, that kind of thing.

Meanwhile, our good sheriff and his sidekick here git another week or two to catch this fellow. It's a great idea. Y'all go home, have dinner, kick back."

Shayna noticed that the detective wasn't pleased with the manager's attitude. He muttered, "This isn't a marketing opportunity, sir. I'd cancel *all* the concerts until this perpetrator's in jail.... I mean, if anything happens to your star, you won't be selling *any* tickets to anyone."

"Well, we wouldn't be in this situation, if you'd found the prick by now," Delbert snapped.

Ewing ignored him.

Shayna looked the officer over and asked, "You like music, Detective?"

After a moment he said, "Well, ma'am, truth is, all respect, no. But not just y'all. I mean, any kinda music."

The petite singer laughed. "You're looking like you stepped on my dog's tail, Detective. Hey, I don't watch cop shows on TV; you don't have to feel bad about not listening to what I do. Fact is, more people *don't* listen to us than do. But what you need to know is that some of those fans out there've been looking forward to tonight for a long, long time—saving up their money and rearranging schedules and roping in grandparents to sit for the kids so they can come to the show. If I cancel then that's going to disappoint 'em in a big way. I did it once but I will not do that. God gave me a voice to use and those folk want to hear it." She gave him one of her iron-clad smiles. "We go on."

Randy laughed and kissed his wife's head—carefully, because of the frothy tease.

Chris Keller gave the singers a thumbs up, pulled his old battered Martin out of its case and glanced at his fellow musicians. "Okay, ladies and gentlemen, time to tune up."

This moment was always the same.

Magic.

That moment just before you walked out on stage. Tense, euphoric, filled with an energy that you just didn't feel anywhere else.

The warm-up act had finished fifteen minutes ago—Randy and Shayna liked to give local kids a boost (they knew how astonishingly hard it was to get a leg up in this business)—and the crowd was now back in their seats, waiting for the main act.

Shayna peeked through the curtain, feeling a great sense of affection for everyone here. The connection between a performer and the audience was like the relationship among friends or family: There was love and there was disagreement, there was giving in and there was setting limits. But the connection was real. And before she went on she always prayed that she wouldn't disappoint them.

She thought again: tension, euphoria, energy...

And, tonight, fear.

Was he out there, among the thousands of fans? The man who wanted her to die?

If I can't have you....

As she'd done on so many sleepless nights recently, she thought back to the shows over the past year, recalling the eyes of the men in the audience and in the crowds outside the halls, looking her over—sometimes gazing into her eyes, sometimes roaming over her body. Who could it be?

And why did he want *me*?

Travis Ewing was fluttering around—though that word didn't really work for a man of his age and size—and looking over the audience, calling the troopers outside the hall and on the floor. He sent J.T. Williams to keep an eye on the security in the parking lot.

Ron Delbert stepped out of a darkened corner of the backstage area, where he'd been making phone calls. He said to Randy, "Okay, you don't want to cancel tonight, fine. But at least let's add a couple more shows."

Her husband finished tuning the Hummingbird—the guitar that a grinning Bob Dylan clutches on the jacket of the famous

Nashville Skyline album. "No. This' it for the year, Ron. That's what we agreed to."

Delbert nodded toward his mobile. "I think I can get us into that new riverboat. The owner was just telling me that he can charge fifty bucks a head."

Sighing, Randy said, "It's not our audience, Ron. It'll be a bunch of folk drunk and silly from winning a cupful of quarters in the slots, or drunk and mad from losing a hundred bucks at blackjack. I told you, no casinos."

"You're crazy, turning down money like that," the manager snapped.

"Betsy's got a family vacation planned and Chris' booked for studio sessions with Brooks and Dunn, then he's doing a gig with Yoakam. That's gold for him."

The manager grimaced. He was sweating and agitated. "You'll get forty thousand, guaranteed, against box office."

Randy said patiently, "Life on the road's hard enough. This crazy man's pushed us over the line. We're taking some time off. It's best for everybody. There's nothing more to talk about."

Shayna couldn't agree more. Nobody who played music for a living would ever deny that it was a business, just like Kraft Foods or General Motors. But it wasn't an assembly line; a band was like a family business. Two of Shayna's backup musicians—Ernie Potts and Chris Keller—had been with her for longer than she'd known Randy. She felt a true affection for them all. It sometimes seemed that Ron Delbert would prefer some tireless computers to manage, not a handful of real people who brought their passions to the job.

"Well, y'all do what you want." Delbert glanced at them with irritation and walked out the back doorway, then down the steps.

In the concert hall the crowd started unison clapping.

Randy glanced at Detective Ewing, who made a couple more calls to the officers. He then closed his phone and sighed once more. "Nothing funny anybody can see.... I'm not in favor of what you're doing, but if you're truly set on going out there, all right."

Randy nodded to the stage manager, who pulled the P.A. microphone close to his mouth and announced the band. The cheers erupted.

Shayna looked at Randy. They smiled. She said, "How 'bout we do some pickin'?"

Exhausted and exhilarated, they finished their last set, bowed and walked off stage toward the wings.

There they were greeted by a harried Travis Ewing, whose sweaty face had nothing to do with the temperature (it was twenty degrees cooler backstage).

Looking at the audience uneasily, the big man rubbed his face with a handkerchief. "Well, now, that was one of the, how do I say it? Most *uneasy* hours of my life. And that's putting it mildly. Now, let's get you y'all home, outa harm's way. We're going to stay clear of the stage door and take y'all out the south entrance. Then—"

Shayna was frowning. "Oh, we're not through yet."

"What do you mean?"

"Listen to 'em out there," Randy said, nodding toward the hall, where people were clapping madly and stamping their feet.

"Yup," Ernie Potts said, refilling his Coke can with Jack Daniels. "We've got to sing it."

"It?"

"*The* song," beautiful Betsy Carson said, holding her fiddle. "You know, Detective."

"No, I don't know," Ewing said shortly. "What're you talking about?"

Shayna explained that Betsy was referring to their first big hit. "Another Day Without You" had climbed fast to the top of the country-western chart in *Billboard* and had earned them a Grammy nomination.

"You're going back out there?" Ewing asked.

"We have to," Randy said. "They want to hear that tune. It's our encore."

"You can forget it," Ewing said. "We're lucky we've gotten this far with nothing happening."

Randy nodded toward the fans. "Hell, some of 'em've come just to hear this one song." He chuckled. "I'd be happy never to play the damn thing again but we can't disappoint 'em."

Shayna didn't bother to explain the importance of the song. When she and Randy met, some years ago, they'd been married to other people. They'd never had an affair, but after their respective divorces they'd struck up a friendship and started dating. Ultimately they married. The theme of "Another Day Without You" was similar—about the pain of not being with the one you love—and the fans were convinced it was about the couple themselves, though it wasn't; the tune was just another number in their sizable repertoire of bittersweet Nashville love songs.

But the fans didn't care about the facts; they cared about the romance of it all. They just *loved* that song.

Red-nosed Ernie Potts now summed it up for Ewing: "You can't live down your hits."

"Oh, hell," the big detective muttered and looked through the curtain at the energetic audience.

It was then that a voice called, "Hey! You!" They all turned. Eyes wide, guitarist Chris Keller was pointing to the half-open doorway that led downstairs, backstage. "Shit, somebody's there! Had a mask on, like a stocking. I think he's got a gun."

"Get down!" Ewing shouted and the band crouched or stepped back. The cop lunged forward, flattening himself to the wall beside the door. He pulled his gun from the holster, then glanced out fast and ducked back. He called on the radio to his partner outside. "J.T., he got inside somehow, the stalker. He was just here. Get some people to the southwest exit. I mean now!"

"I'm on it," the young officer's voice clattered through the speaker.

Ewing told the singers and the band to get back and looked again quickly. "Nothing I can see. Y'all wait here."

"But the encore?" Shayna asked.

Ewing didn't answer. He disappeared into the darkness of the stairway, moving real fast for a heavy man.

Randy glanced at the stage manager. "Tell 'em we're having some technical difficulty or something. We'll be out soon."

The stage manager made the announcement. Five excruciating minutes passed. Randy held Shayna's hand and the other musicians looked at one another uncertainly.

Finally Ewing returned to the top of the stairs, breathing heavily. He grimaced. "Got away…. We didn't have any officers on the fire door—it was locked—but I found some scratches and the jamb was bent. He must've jimmied it."

He asked Keller what the man looked like.

"White guy, I think. Medium size. Had a stocking over his head, you know. Like a black lady's stocking. I couldn't see his face. He was wearing one of our t-shirts. A green one."

Like the man who'd broken into the Tiptons' trailer.

The guitarist couldn't provide any more information—except that his gun was a pistol, not a shotgun. Which meant it could fire .38 hollow points, like the one left at their camper.

It was then that Shayna looked at her watch and said, "We can't wait any longer."

"What?" Ewing said.

She nodded at the stage. "Our encore."

Ewing laughed in surprise. "No way. You're not—"

J.T. Williams came running up the stairs. "Okay, we found the weapon. He ditched it or dropped it running. We've got a few other things too."

"Where?"

"On a path that leads from the fire door to the woods next to the parking lot."

"I'll be right down." He turned to the band. "You wait here. Don't go anywhere."

The crowd was clapping, calling for the band to return.

Ewing turned to the stage manager. "Put the houselights on. Announce the concert's over. Tell everybody to leave—but don't say anything about this. Do it now."

The skinny man nodded uncomfortably.

Ewing then turned to his partner and snapped, "You stay on her like a tic on a hound, you understand me?"

"I'm on it," Williams said.

His boss ran down the stairs.

As the stage manager was reaching for the switch, Shayna stepped forward and took his hand, stopping him from turning on the houselights. The slim man looked at her uneasily.

She said, "Don't worry, Joey. We'll take responsibility."

The manager lowered his hand and stepped back from the PA system.

"Hold up," J.T. Williams said to her. "You're not going out there."

"'Fraid we are, Detective," Randy said. "That's just the way it is."

Shayna then picked up her old Martin and turned to the musicians. "Randy and I're goin' to finish up the show, do the encore. But not y'all. Probably that fellow ran off but maybe he didn't. But I'd never forgive myself if anything happened to any of you."

"No, ma'am," Betsy protested.

Chris Keller shook his head. "You think we'll let you do that?"

"We don't crack the whip very often," Randy told him. "But this' one of those times."

Shayna added, "That's an order."

The band shared a look. They weren't happy. But they agreed.

"I can't let you do this," Williams said firmly. "You—"

But the singers were on stage before he could take a single step forward.

Walking to the microphones, they smiled and waved to the frenzied audience.

After a moment the sound died down.

Shayna said, "Thank you. Y'all've been a great audience.... We love you!...Now Randy and me'd like to do one more song.

It's a little tune you might've heard before. We call it 'Another Day Without You.'"

The applause was furious. Cigarette lighter flames appeared—against code, of course, but the sight of the yellow flickers and the shining eyes of the fans never failed to move Shayna deeply.

Randy played the song's intro, finger picking style, then Shayna joined in, strumming rhythm as the audience grew quiet. Then they began to sing in their trademark harmony:

> *I see you on the street, holding someone else's hand.*
> *He's acting like he owns you—and that's more than I can stand.*
> *I know that you're unhappy. I see it in your eyes.*
> *It's clear that you don't love him, that you're living in a lie.*
> *And it's another day without you...Oh, such lonely time.*
> *But in just a little while...I'm going to make you mine.*

Suddenly, directly behind Shayna, there was a loud booming noise.

Thinking of the stalker, she looked around fast.

But it wasn't a gunshot or an attacker. It was a Gibson fretted electric bass, held by Sammy Baker. He was standing ten feet behind her, playing the familiar bass line from the song. He grinned at her and Randy.

Then came a riff from Betsy's searing fiddle as the pretty brunette walked on stage, followed by Chris Keller, who plugged in the pickup on his Martin and added some lead guitar fills. Finally Ernie Potts, with his Coke can, sat down at the pedal steel, put metal fingerpicks on his right hand and took the chrome bar in his left, joining in.

Tears in her eyes, Shayna glanced at Randy. They smiled.

The audience rose to their feet.

Randy took the solo for the second verse.

> *Ever since we met, I'm twice the man I was.*
> *Nothing keeps me going the way your smile does.*
> *We have our time together but it's really not the same.*
> *The thought you share a bed with him is driving me insane....*

And it's another day without you...Oh, such lonely time.
But in just a little while...I'm going to make you mine.

Potts played an instrumental of the tune on his pedal steel then handed off to Betsy's fiddle, who played her version of the song.

When they were through the spotlight came up on Shayna and Randy as they leaned close to a shared mike for the last verse of the song, with Chris Keller harmonizing.

I'll steal you away, I will steal you for good.
I'll never have to share you; we'll live the way we should.
It won't be too much longer until I set you free.
Then I'll never let you go, I'll keep you close to me.
And it's another day without you...Oh, such lonely time.
But in just a little while...I'm going to make you mine.

Cozying up to the mike, they repeated the tag lines once more.

And it's another day without you...Oh, such lonely time.
But in just a little while...I'm going to make you mine.

They bowed their heads as the applause erupted. The band members waved to the crowd and Shayna heard Randy's voice in her ear. "Honey, been a delight, as always, but you mind if we get the hell out of here 'fore somebody pulls a six-gun?"

Trying not to laugh, she blew some kisses to the audience and they hurried off stage.

Travis Ewing was not a happy cop.

"First of all," Randy said, "it wasn't J.T.'s fault." Nodding toward a sheepish Williams.

"We coerced him," Chris Keller said.

"Coerced, my ass," Ewing muttered.

The young police officer looked helplessly at his boss. "I couldn't hardly arrest 'em."

"You have cuffs, don't you?"

"Not six pairs."

Grimacing, Ewing said, "I'll deal with you later." Then he added to Randy, "You were lucky.... It worked out okay. And, turns out, we've got some leads."

He went on to explain that though the stalker had escaped and there'd been no witnesses, the bullets in the gun seemed to be from the same lot as the one that'd been left at the Tiptons' motor home. Near the gun was a cut-off end of woman's black stocking—the mask Keller had seen—and a discarded cigarette.

The detective added slowly, "It was from a Camel."

Shayna felt her heart shrink.

Ewing pulled on a latex glove and picked up the butt of the cigarette that Ron Delbert had crushed out earlier—a Camel. He dropped it into an evidence bag.

The bass player, Sammy Baker, laughed. "You can't be serious. You suspect Ron?"

Potts said belligerently, "Lotta people smoke Camels. Just ask Phillip Morris, or whoever makes 'em."

Ewing nodded at the plastic bag. "We'll run a DNA test and find out." Ewing glanced at Randy. "Where was Delbert two weeks ago? When that bullet got left at y'all's camper?"

"I don't have any idea. Probably back in his hotel room. But this' crazy. He wouldn't do anything like that."

"I've known Ron for years," Shayna said. "We don't get along all the time. But he's just not the sort to do this."

"He ever come on to you?"

Shayna was embarrassed by the question. She frowned as she answered. "Long time ago, after he started managing my act, he flirted with me a couple of times. But I told him I wasn't interested and that was that. And I'm talking years ago."

Then she glanced at her husband.

The shrewd cop picked up on the look right away. "What're you thinkin' of telling me?...Go ahead. We don't have time to pussyfoot around."

The blonde singer sat down and lowered her head.

Randy said to her, "He might've found out."

"I don't know," she replied.

"Found out *what*?" Ewing snapped.

After a moment of silence Randy looked not at the detective but at the other band members and said, "Shayna and me, last month, we decided that after this tour we were going to let Ron go."

Keller frowned. "Fire him?"

"It was a tough decision," Shayna said. "Real tough."

Randy explained: Over the past year the number of fights between Delbert and the Tiptons had escalated. Shayna believed some of it was jealousy. Ron had been managing Shayna before she met Randy, and when they got married Randy had taken a more active role in the business side of their act, which Shayna had no interest in. Ron hadn't liked her new husband's involvement—especially when Randy learned that the manager did a lot of entertaining at restaurants, bars and even strip clubs, taking out people who booked acts and worked for recording companies. Nothing illegal about it, but that kind of wheeling and dealing was contrary to the Tipton image, and Shayna and Randy stopped the practice in its tracks. Delbert wasn't happy about their decision.

Potts said, "So you're saying he's faking he's a stalker and is going to kill Shayna." He laughed harshly. "Now that's outa some bad episode of *CSI*." The musician loved television as much as he loved music and whiskey.

"Or he hired somebody to pretend he's a stalker and kill her. That's more likely."

Shayna said, "I just don't see it."

"And you think he could've heard about you firing him?"

"That's what I'm wondering," she said. "But what does he get out of it?"

Williams gave a cold laugh. "Revenge is what he gets out of it. More people kill for that than for money."

"Well," Ewing said, "we're going to talk to him. Where's he live?"

Randy gave him the address and number.

Keller said, "But when he's in town he usually goes to Handy's Bar—the one on Charlotte—after the show."

Potts nodded. "Stays there till all hours."

"All right, I want y'all to go on home now. And I mean now."

Randy said, "We've got to pack up. All the equipment."

"And I've got to get our dog," Shayna said. "He's in the camper. We drove here straight from Knoxville. Haven't been home yet."

"No. I'm drawing the line," Ewing said. "You ignored me once. I'm not going to let it happen again."

Shayna knew when to push and when to back down. She agreed to go back home, accompanied by a state trooper, and Randy would pack up, walk the dog, then drive the motor home back to their house.

Ewing called directory assistance and got the address of Handy's Bar. He snapped his phone shut. "Okay, pardner, let's us go have a chat with our number-one suspect. Whatta you say?"

The deputy drove the unmarked cruiser up the long driveway of the Tiptons' property and parked by the side door. He climbed out first to check the yard.

Shayna looked over their modest ranch-style house and felt a sense of comfort. She loved the place. In her heart, Shayna had no envy for the Garth Brookses and the other superstars of the music world. Who wanted that hectic, crazed life? Her goal wasn't millions of dollars and limousines and private jets—but only to get up on stage and make people laugh and cry and enjoy a few hours away from their worries. She and Randy had a nice house on thirty acres, one dog, two palominos, and a Yukon big enough to pull the horse trailer out to the country to do some serious riding.

Who needed more than that?

The trooper gestured her out and she joined him, noticing that he kept his hand near his hip—where his pistol rested.

Suddenly she had to laugh at the absurdity of the whole situation. There was no way that Ron was guilty, she was convinced. It had to be someone else—a real stalker, a crazed fan. Yet, she couldn't understand how a man could become so obsessed with her. Sure, she was pretty—but in a simple, farm-girl way. Her five-foot, one-inch height, her freckles and dimpled chin hardly made her Hollywood-gorgeous. And as for her singing, why would anybody think she was special enough to break the law for? She didn't go for musical blockbusters, didn't go for glam. Shayna loved simple. In fact, it bothered her a lot that so many country performers had lost sight of the roots of their music: bluegrass, mountain tunes and ballads. It was the music sung by people after long, long days in the fields or coal mines, shared with family and friends relaxing and enjoying their time together. It was about telling stories of love and truth and courage making your way in life, not about slick, high-charged entertainment.

Together, the young cop and the singer walked to the side door. She opened it up, stepped inside and typed in the code to deactivate the alarm. The deputy joined her. She swung the door shut and locked it once more.

Shayna Tipton was home, safe at last.

"Any paper on Delbert?" Ewing asked his partner as they drove along a deserted highway.

Meaning warrants or prior arrests.

"I'll check."

The officers were driving to Delbert's home. They'd been to Handy's, waited a while, drinking coffee, and finally gave up. The manager told him that, yes, Delbert was usually a fixture in the bar when he was in town but for some reason he hadn't show up tonight.

Williams punched information into the unmarked car's computer. A moment later, from the corner of his eye, Ewing could see the screen flicker. He didn't look at it; he was driving at 85 mph.

"Nup."

"Why do you say 'nup.' That's not a word."

"You got my meaning, didn't you?" Williams asked.

"It's still not a word. It's like, I don't know, shortening that expression—'nipping it in the bud.'"

"That's altogether different," the young detective said, frowning. "Doesn't have anything in the world to do with 'nup.'"

"I'm just saying it sounds like it."

They sped down the road.

Williams asked, "So what don't you like about music?"

Ewing thought for a moment. "Can't tell you exactly. Just doesn't seem, I don't know, important. It's just something to fill up the background. It's just *distracting*, you know. Bunch of hooplah."

"Hooplah? What's that?"

"Means big deal about nothing."

"Hooplah? You use a word like that and you've got a problem with 'nup'?"

Ewing grunted.

"Funny you live in Nashville and don't like music."

"Funny as, say, livin' in Detroit and not liking cars? Or living in Vegas and not likin' gambling or livin' in—"

"Got the picture." After a few minutes of silence, Williams asked, "You think Delbert really aims to kill her?"

"I don't know. What I *do* know is somebody's been behaving bad. And this fellow, looks like, has a motive. Agree it's a bit complicated, if that's what you're sayin'."

"I am."

"But we don't have much else, now, do we?"

"Nup," Williams said.

"Jesus Lord," Ewing muttered. He called the deputies who'd been outside the concert hall when the stalker had snuck in to see if they'd learned anything else. There was a bit of finger pointing—nobody wanted to be responsible for missing the break-in—but Ewing told them to cut the bickering and give him something concrete.

They reported that the cigarette found near the gun was Delbert's (the DNA matched) but there wasn't much else. No witnesses, no fingerprints, no shoeprints. The bullets were from the same lot as the one left at the trailer. The pistol itself had been stolen from a gun show about three months ago. He got the troubling news that *two* guns had disappeared from the same booth at the show. The man might've lost one weapon but, they would have to assume, he had a spare.

Ewing steered up a long driveway until he got to the beautiful split-level house. He caught a glimpse of an immaculately kept back yard with a swimming pool. He felt another burst of jealousy. In his own job Ewing himself worked his tail off, got shot at (it'd happened twice) and made peanuts, while this guy obviously made millions. And he didn't have a real job; he was in the country-western business, for God's sake.

Another reason to be pissed at music.

There was a Mercedes 4x4 in the driveway and a black Porsche Carrera. The sight of the expensive vehicles infuriated Ewing even more.

Williams typed on the computer. "Those're his only cars. He's probably home."

"Let's go see."

"We got probable cause?" Williams asked.

Only the matching cigarettes and a motive, Ewing reflected. He whispered, "Not really. Unless he starts shooting at us. *Then* we'll have probable cause. That'd make things easier. Let's hope."

"Are you serious?"

Ewing snickered.

Williams rolled his eyes and headed off to where his partner indicated, around the side of the house, while Ewing himself walked quietly onto the porch. The men kept their hands close to the Glocks, which rode high on their hips.

The senior detective peeked inside to the entryway and saw lights on but no sign of the manager. He checked the living room too and the den. Nothing. Ewing was starting around the corner, to check another window, when Williams called out, "I don't think he's the one."

"Shhh, keep it down." Crouching, Ewing walked toward his partner. "What do you mean, 'the one'?"

"You know, the stalker."

"Why do you think that?"

Williams nodded through a window.

Ewing looked inside. Delbert lay on the kitchen floor, on his back.

Williams asked, "Think we should call for an ambulance?"

Ebert counted the bullet wounds in the man's head and chest. He said, "Nup."

There'd been a struggle, a bad one. Furniture overturned, blood spattered.

But in the end, apparently, the stalker had pulled out his gun and emptied it into Ron Delbert; he'd been hit six times—the usual capacity for a revolver—and the slugs were hollow-points. He'd died within seconds of being shot. There were no obvious leads but Crime Scene was hard at work. Ewing called Randy, in the trailer, and Shayna, at home, and gave them the news; they both sounded devastated by the man's death; they could provide no information as to why someone would want him dead. Ewing told the officer guarding Shayna to stay alert; the manager's house was only a twenty-minute drive from the Tiptons'.

Ten minutes later the pieces started to fall together.

"Check this out," J.T. Williams said. He was holding up a sheet of paper that had been found on the floor nearby, blood stained. It looked like a copy of an email. Williams read out loud, "'I need more pictures of her like you promised.' And 'MORE' is in all caps." He continued, "'You've sent me some good ones but for what I'm paying you you should be producing more! And I mean more. I don't have'—more caps—'ENOUGH.'" The young detective looked up. "It's signed by somebody named Jack."

Ewing frowned. He'd liked the idea that Delbert had hired somebody to kill Shayna because she and Randy were going to fire him. This letter required him to shift gears. Maybe there *was* a real stalker, who was paying Delbert to take—or steal—pictures of Shayna Tipton.

As for the cause of the fight here, and Delbert's death, Ewing guessed it could've been because the stalker—this "Jack"—wasn't happy with Delbert's efforts, or there'd been a fight over the payments (Ewing wasn't sure he agreed with his partner's contention that revenge was a more popular motive for murder than money).

"But who the hell is he?" Ewing asked Williams, nodding at the email.

The answer came only sixty seconds later.

"Detective," called one of the crime scene technicians, who was combing the driveway. He walked up to Ewing.

"Look at this." He lifted a latex-clad hand.

Ewing looked over what he held.

It was a crumpled receipt from a shop that sold country-western souvenirs and memorabilia. The purchaser had bought $65 worth of Shayna Tipton posters and souvenirs about a month ago. The slip was a charge, so it included his name and credit card number, and even though the last few digits were asterisks, it only took a few phone calls to learn the man's ID. Jack Mathias was a 26-year-old Nashville resident, who lived a few miles outside the city limits.

"Who the hell's he?" Williams asked.

"Dunno," Ewing answered. "Let's go find out."

Wearing his favorite, dark-green concert t-shirt, jeans and running shoes, the young man sat in the woods, his legs bouncing nervously in anticipation.

Jack Mathias was hiding about a half mile from where Shayna Tipton now was. He shivered, reciting her name over and over again. His heart hummed at the thought of what was going to happen tonight. Oh, the consequences would be tough but there was no way to change the course of fate—even if he'd wanted to.

Which, of course, he didn't. No, no, Jesus could carry him off to heaven in the morning and he'd be a happy, fulfilled man.

"Shayna, Shayna, Shayna..."

He glanced at his watch. Another fifteen or twenty minutes.... It seemed like forever.

"Shayna," he whispered, then once more, then ten times, then fifty.

He closed his eyes and pictured her at the concert tonight. He saw her as clearly as if he were staring at a video of the show.

His name might technically be Jackson Peter Mathias, but at the moment he probably couldn't even have told anyone that. Or told them about his life at the auto parts store or his favorite restaurant, Wendy's, or the arcade where he spent hundreds of quarters a week, or his mother in the nursing home nearby. No, at the moment he was somebody very different, his true self: Shayna's number-one Fan. Or, as he preferred to describe himself, simply The Fan.

He rocked back and forth, reliving every minute of the show. It was a good one, he decided, one of the best. (And The Fan should know because he'd gone to every one of her local concerts ever since he'd met and fallen in love with her three months, two weeks and four days ago—the night she'd looked up at him from the table where she was signing CDs and smiled.) Of course there'd been some anxiety this evening: all the police, for one thing, looking over everybody suspiciously.... The thought of them made him angry. So did a cluster of girls who'd made fun of him outside the concert hall. Girls with high-hair and too much perfume glancing his way and snickering.

But after tonight, they wouldn't be laughing anymore.

"Shayna, Shayna, Shayna," he repeated.

The Fan unzipped his backpack, stared inside for a long moment and then closed it again. He squinted through the woods at the cluster of lights in the distance. Was one of them in the room where Shayna was at the moment?

A cool breeze flowed around him. The concert shirt was only light cotton. But he wouldn't think of dressing in anything else, of course, not tonight. It was his special shirt. And this was going to be a very special evening.

"Shayna, Shayna, Shayna...."

"I'm going to take a shower."

The deputy replied to the singer, "You go right ahead, ma'am. I'll keep an eye peeled."

As the small woman headed down the corridor toward her bedroom the young man made a circuit of the house once again. Everything seemed locked up nice and tight. He was tired and he would've loved to sit on the sumptuous couch—with leather like a suede coat—but he remembered the urgency in Detective Ewing's voice and was determined to take his job seriously.

But how should he handle it best? Looking out the windows over the black expanse of forest that bordered the Tiptons' property, he tried to figure out the most logical route the stalker would use to approach the house if he was inclined to break in. There seemed to be a couple of possibilities—both of them in the back; the front yard was huge, open and illuminated by powerful spotlights, and it was unlikely an intruder would approach that way. In the back, however, there were no spotlights. The forest surrounding the property came up to the pool, around which was some in-ground lighting. But it was pretty dim. That approach would take him right up to the back door, which was glass and could easily be broken. A definite possibility.

On the other hand, there was a grove of what seemed to be apple trees very close to the back of the house, near the bedrooms. No doors, but an intruder could presumably break through one of the low windows. The officer decided this was the most logical route to take.

The deputy debated a minute longer and decided to play it cautious, though. He'd go outside and hide beside the pool house; that would let him see the entire back of the property and intercept the stalker whichever route he took.

Should he tell Shayna where he was going?

No, he decided. Even if she wasn't in the shower yet, a man just didn't go bothering a woman when she was in her bedroom. Taking the key from the mantle, where Shayna had left it, he stepped out the back and locked the door after him.

He looked around and then made his way slowly to the pool house. He crouched down and surveyed the landscape, hoping that the psycho *did* try to break in tonight. I'd love to show you what it feels like to have somebody sneaking up behind *you* for a change, he thought to the stalker.

He undid the clasp on his holster and slipped his fingers around the grip of his pistol.

Having parked some distance from Jack Mathias' bungalow, Ewing and Williams were making their way slowly up the driveway, hands near their service pieces, stepping around branches and leaves, which might signal their approach. The yard was a mess, filled with trash and old soda cans, filthy, moldy clothes, food wrappers, a wheelless bicycle.

There was no car in the drive or the ramshackle garage. Lights were on in the decrepit house, but as the two men moved closer they could see no signs that anyone was inside.

"Hear something?" Williams asked.

Ewing thought so. Voices.

They eased up onto the front porch, Ewing praying that the extra thirty pounds he carried didn't make the sprung wood of the deck squeal and give them away.

Ewing glanced through the greasy window in the front door. No one was in the living room. The voices were coming from the TV, which was tuned to Comedy Central. A Tom Hanks movie was on.

He tested the knob. It was unlocked. He glanced at his partner, who nodded.

They drew their weapons and pushed inside fast.

A quick look revealed that Mathias wasn't here. They searched the hopelessly cluttered place. They found nothing immediately that told them where Mathias might be at the moment but they did learn that he worked for NAPA, that his mother was in a nursing home, that he had a hundred video games, that he seemed to survive on junk food and soda.

They also learned that he was definitely Shayna Tipton's stalker.

His bedroom was filled with pictures of Shayna and everything he'd stolen from their home and camper, and more: underwear, keychains, mugs, memorabilia, old passes, posters—several black stockings too. Ironically, it seemed that he'd cut up Shayna's own pantyhose to use for a mask in his planned attack on her tonight.

By the bedside was a battered notebook, filled with hundreds of clippings about and pictures of Shayna. In the front the stalker had written a threatening note to her—in the form of a poem. It made the detective feel even more queasy that the killer had gone to all this trouble to write his fantasies out in verse. "Jesus. He's one sick puppy. Lookit this—a stalker poem. That's a first." He handed it to Williams and, desperate for answers, returned to the man's bedroom, in hopes of finding something, *anything* that might give a clue what the killer had in mind and where he was.

The Fan was now on the move, stalking doggedly through the woods toward Shayna Tipton.

What was she doing at the moment? Was she on the couch? In the kitchen? Watching TV?

In the bedroom?

He couldn't get her out of his thoughts. He remembered the first time he'd seen her, at a concert two years ago. Now, she looked at him and asked how did he want her to sign their CD.

My love, my number-one fan, my lover....

"Uhm," he'd responded, struck dumb.

"How 'bout your name?" she'd asked. A radiant smile.

"Sure," he'd said, then clutched.

"And that's...?"

"Uhm, Jack."

She signed with a swirl of her pink-tipped fingers, such tiny, perfect fingers, and then handed him the plastic square with a beaming smile.

He was in love.

She glanced at him. And in that instant Mathias knew she was in love too, even though she'd turned back to her husband right away, ignoring The Fan. But, back then, he remembered forgiving her for that, thinking that she'd only done it because she'd had to. To keep up appearances.

But now things were different.

The Fan paused. He squinted, saw the bright lights shining through the trees, only a hundred feet away.

His heart was beating fast.

The Fan laughed to himself. He'd just seen some old horror film, from the seventies or eighties. He remembered that line in it, the one you heard from time to time: "Stay away from the light." Something about dying if you went to the light or having your soul stolen or something.

But now the light was exactly what he wanted.

I'm going toward the light, Shayna.

We both are....

His heart pounding hard, The Fan made his way out of the trees and onto the asphalt. He walked directly up to the front door, looking around. Nobody.

In his mind he hummed a tune that Shayna sang on her third CD, a set of gospel tunes.

All my trials, Lord, soon be over....

The Fan now took a deep breath and reached into his shoulder bag.

Okay, that should just about do it, thought Randy Tipton.

He'd just finished packing up everything in their motor home. The one thing that Shayna hated about the life of a musician was being away from home, so rather than stay in motels, which the band did, they stayed in a big Renegade Mercedes camper, which she'd decorated as homey as their ranch house.

Randy now slipped Doc, their little white Bichon dog, into his kennel and started for the driver's seat. He heard a knock on the door.

He opened it and glanced at a young man standing on the doorstep, staring up at him. The man was frowning, perplexed. He had a backpack over his shoulder and was holding a bouquet of wilted flowers and a small velvet box, like jewelry came in. "You...You're Randy Tipton."

"That's right. Can I...." The musician's voice faded as he noticed that the man wore a green souvenir t-shirt—an earlier one, from when Shayna was touring solo.

What the stalker had been spotted in. Was this the man?

Randy stayed calm. He asked, "Can I help you?"

The man swallowed and looked around. "I'm...I'm here to see Shayna."

"Who are you?" Randy recalled where he'd left his mobile phone—it was in the back of the motor home, with their guitars.

"I'm...I didn't know you'd be here. I thought...." The man's voice faded, as he continued to look around him. His face was dismayed. His eyes danced around alarmingly. He swallowed and continued, "I thought...."

"You thought what?" Randy Tipton snapped. Generally even-tempered, he was in no mood for crazies, especially after the scare backstage at the concert tonight.

The man licked his lips and looked around. "I'm sorry. Don't be mad, Mr. Tipton."

"What're you talking about."

"It's just the way things turned out. I'm sorry," he repeated sincerely.

"Listen up," Randy growled. "I want you to sit right down there and don't move a muscle." He pointed to the passenger seat in the camper.

The intruder was looking down at the velvet box in his hand. The confusion in his face was almost comical.

"I—"

It was then that a voice called from outside. "Hey."

The young man turned and looked out the door to the parking lot. He squinted at whoever was there and shook his head. "You told me.... No, don't!"

The huge gunshot shook the windows and sent the intruder flying back into the wall of the motor home, beside the driver's seat. He lifted a hand, gave a grunt.

And then slumped forward, eyes glazed in death.

"Jesus," Randy whispered.

The band's guitarist, Chris Keller, climbed inside, holding a pistol. The slim man looked down at the body. "We got ourselves the stalker."

Randy stared at the corpse, the flowers clutched in his hand, the black box lying nearby. "Jesus, you didn't have to shoot him."

The guitarist just stood there, motionless, shaking his head as he looked down. "Poor asshole."

Blood was pooling on the white linoleum.

Randy bent down and picked up the velvet box. He opened it. Inside was a small, cheap necklace, the sort you'd buy at J.C. Penney. A silver musical note dangled from the end of the thin chain. What the hell was going on?

Then something occurred to the singer. He frowned, glancing at the guitarist. "He said something."

Keller lifted an eyebrow.

Randy continued, "Just now, I heard him say, 'You told me—' He was talking to you."

"That a fact?"

Whispering: "You two know each other?"

"Yep." Keller looked up with a faint smile on his lips. "Sure do. Well, *did*, I guess we oughta say."

Randy eased toward the back of the trailer.

Keller lifted the gun toward the singer and said, "Hold up there, my friend. Don't move."

"What's going on, Chris?"

"Such a shame," the guitarist said. "Looks like the stalker got confused. Thought Shayna was here in the motor home, and what happens but he finds you. He pulls out a gun, kills you. Just as I happen along, grab the gun and kill him. Self-defense."

"What the hell're you talking about?"

In a split second, the guitarist snapped. His face dark with rage, he stormed toward Randy, who lifted his hands and backed away. Waving the gun, Keller shouted, "I had a chance for her! I've been with her longer than you. I lived through that year she was with her first husband.... *I* was always there for her.... Nobody else was. Then she got divorced and it was *my* time. *We* should've been together, her and me. But, no, you had to show up. You stole her away from me!"

Keeping his voice steady, Randy said, "I didn't do anything. We met, we fell in love. That's all there was to it."

"I was there first!" the man raged, shoving the gun closer to the singer.

Wincing, Randy replied, "But she didn't love you, Chris. I'm sorry. It just turned out that way."

"No," he raged, his long blond hair waving as he shook his head furiously, "you moved in on me. You poisoned her against me.... She loves me. I know she does!"

Suddenly Randy realized what had happened. "Oh, my God, you set this all up, didn't you?" A glanced at the corpse. "Who was he?"

The guitarist said, "Just some fan. Saw him at a concert about two, three months ago. He was drooling over Shayna after she signed his CD. I found him later and told him she was real interested in getting together but she had to be careful 'cause she was married to you—couldn't have any bad publicity. So off and on he'd give me letters for her and I'd make up some from her and give 'em to him."

Randy snapped, "*You* stole all those things from Shayna's dresser and our den and gave them to him. You said they were from her. And you left the bullet on the doorstep with that note.... You gave him that t-shirt and then wore the same kind when you broke into the camper, right in front of a witness, so when they found him dead, they'd think for sure he was the stalker."

"Yep."

"And tonight, backstage—you never saw anybody at all, did you? You scratched up the door earlier and—and you left the gun and the stocking nearby before the show." Then Randy frowned. "But the cigarette, Ron's cigarette.... Oh, no.... Ron—it was you who killed him!"

Keller gave a dark laugh. "You won't have to worry about firing Ron....It'll look like our friend Jack—" a nod toward the body—"took care of that. I left some evidence that Ron was selling pictures of Shayna to him."

"But why?"

Keller shook his head. "Oh, I had no problem with Ron in general. Only, a few years ago we were having some drinks and I got drunk and told him I was in love with her. Thought that might come out if he ever talked to the police.... So, the man had to go."

"And tonight, what? You told him that Shayna wanted to get together with him and to meet him here tonight?"

"That's pretty much it."

"You're one sick fuck, you know that?"

Keller raged, "It's *your* fault, Randy. Not mine. You should never've come between a man and his true love."

"Chris, she thinks the world of you. She thinks you're a brilliant musician. But she doesn't love you, not that way."

"Oh, she will, Randy." Keller's smile faded and he raised the gun, aiming it at the singer's chest. "She will."

The gunshot was huge.

Randy flinched and dropped to the ground.

Waiting for the pain, waiting for the darkness.

But what was happening?

He felt nothing.

He pressed his shivering hand to his chest, his abdomen. He wasn't hit.

Then he saw Chris Keller turning, dropping the gun. He was clutching his shoulder, which was bleeding profusely. He said, "Help me! I...." Then the guitarist pitched forward and passed out.

Travis Ewing, followed by J.T. Williams, hurried inside. They both held large black pistols. A moment later flashing lights appeared through the windows and Randy heard the screech of brakes as cars pulled up nearby. Ewing pressed his gun to Keller's head and searched him, while Williams tended to the stalker, though it was clear that the man was dead.

Williams picked up the guitarist's pistol and unloaded it, put it in his pocket.

A moment later, a man and woman in medic uniforms hurried through the door and tended to Keller.

"Shayna," Randy asked, panicked. "Is she all right?"

"She's fine, she's fine. The question is, how're you?"

Randy took a deep breath and sat down on a small bench seat. "Tell the truth, Detective, I've had better nights."

Shayna Tipton leapt out of the unmarked car before the young trooper had brought it to a full stop. She ran to her husband, who stood outside the motor home with Ewing and Williams, and flung her arms around him.

Chris Keller had been taken off to the prisoner wing of a local hospital, where the doctors reported that he'd survive the gunshot wound. Jack Mathias, though, was declared dead at the scene.

Ernie Potts, the pedal steel player, had just shown up, chewing tobacco and clutching his beverage of choice in a shiny red can. He hugged Shayna and shook Randy's hand. "Y'all doing all right?"

"As well as can be expected."

"And that fella killed Ron too?"

"'Fraid so, Ernie," Shayna admitted. The old man shook his head in sorrow.

Randy explained what Keller had admitted to him, about how he'd set up everything and even convinced the poor kid that Shayna'd agreed to meet him tonight for a date at the camper.

"That poor boy," she whispered, looking at the bloodstain on the white tile and the necklace in the velvet box, a pitiful sight.

"Funny what love does to you," Ernie Potts offered.

Ewing nodded. "Revenge, money *and* love—they're all pretty good motives for murder."

Potts spat tobacco an alarming distance then sucked down a good slug of his drink. He offered the can to Williams and Ewing. They both declined. The musician added, "Gotta say it was lucky ya'll showin' up here when you did."

Randy frowned. "That's right, Detective. Why *did* you think to come here?"

It wasn't Ewing who responded, though, but his partner, who said wryly, "The stalker poem."

"Poem?"

"Yep," the detective said, grimacing.

"Mathias wrote a poem about me?" Shayna asked.

"Nope," J.T. Williams said with a smile. "My partner here only *thought* he did."

Ewing explained, "Tonight, at Mathias', we found a scrapbook he'd made—it had ticket stubs and pictures of Shayna from all her concerts in the area—and in the front was this sick poem. All about stalking this woman, being mad with jealousy, about wanting to kidnap her."

"Steal her away," Williams corrected.

"Whatever," Ewing muttered.

"*That's* what gave us the idea it was Keller who was the stalker, not Mathias."

"But how?" Randy asked.

Williams explained, "Because Mathias just copied it in his scrapbook. *Keller* was the one who wrote it."

Williams opened his briefcase and took out a plastic bag containing a notebook. He pulled on latex gloves and opened it. He read out loud:

"I'll steal you away, I will steal you for good.
I'll never have to share you; we'll live the way we should."

Randy said, "But that's—"

Shayna nodded. "Our song. 'Another Day Without You.' Chris wrote it a year ago."

Williams held the page up. Mathias had transcribed all the verses into his notebook. "He probably felt that it said something about his situation."

Potts spit again. He frowned at Ewing. "Was our big hit. And you didn't even recognize it."

Randy laughed. "He wasn't backstage when we played it."

"Don't matter," Potts grumbled. "Still our biggest hit. He ought to've known."

Ewing muttered, "Maybe you add some pretty music and get a good-lookin' couple to sing it, the words sounds more like a love song. You read it thinking it was written by a killer and it's a whole 'nother story." He nodded at his partner. "J.T. here took one look and told me that it was a song written by Chris Keller. Well, that gave me some pause, and I stopped and thought about what was going on…. What if Keller had written it about himself and Shayna?

"Then I got to thinking that this whole case seemed a bit too tidy, especially with Keller being the one who claimed he saw that fellow tonight at the show, but nobody else did. I figured it couldn't hurt to have a little talk with him. We went to his house and found another box of .38 hollow points and a bunch of articles about killing in self-defense. Since the stalker poem—"

"Grammy-nominated song, you mean," Potts corrected.

"—the *song* was about setting a woman free to be with some man, I figured it was *Randy* who was in the most danger." He glanced at the singer. "When you didn't answer your phone we drove over here to check things out."

The crime scene unit finished up and the coroner got the body of the unfortunate fan carted off to the morgue. Ewing and Williams finished up paperwork and made arrangements for everyone to come to the station tomorrow for statements. Randy shook the officers' hands. "Appreciate all you did, gentlemen."

The big man nodded his acknowledgment and started toward the squad car.

Shayna had a thought. She called, "Detective, hold up there."

She walked over to the cops, fishing in her purse. "Our tour's over. But Randy and me, we play every Monday night up the road at Dillon's. Just to keep in practice. It's usually sold out. But these'll get you in." Holding up four passes, she gave two to Williams, who slipped them in his pocket with a shy smile and a blush and thanked her.

Ewing looked down at them and hesitated. "Monday?" He frowned. "The game's on. Football, you know."

Ernie Potts snickered. "That's what they make TiVo for."

"I don't have one of them." Ewing frowned at the old man.

Shayna persisted, "Come on, Detective. You never know. You might just enjoy it."

Shrugging, Ewing took the passes. "I guess I can always scalp 'em if I'd rather see Cincinnati whip Chicago's butt."

"That you can," she said.

The detective turned and joined his partner and they continued on to their car.

Another Day Without You

I see you on the street, holding someone else's hand.
He's acting like he owns you, and that's more than I
    can stand.
I know that you're unhappy, I can see it in your eyes
It's clear that you don't love him, that you're livin in a lie.

And it's another day without you, oh such a lonely
    time.
But in just a little while, I'm gonna make you mine.

Ever since we met, I'm twice the man I was,
Nothing keeps me going, the way your smile does.
We had our time together, but it's really not the same.
The thought you share a bed with him is drivin' me
    insane.

(chorus)

I'll steal you away, I will steal you for good,
I'll never have to share you, we'll live the way we should.
It won't be too much longer, until I set you free,
Then I'll never let you go, I'll keep you close to me.

About "Another Day Without You," Jeff says: "I think no other genre of popular American music has remained as consistent for so long as country-western, which had its genesis on that fateful day of August 1, 1927, when James Charles ("Jimmie") Rodgers and the Carter family both signed contracts with Victor records. It's never faded from popularity and indeed has continued to grow, even internationally, and to influence other, seemingly disparate, forms of music. (I haven't heard of any hip-hop country-western but I'll bet it's out there somewhere.)

I myself have been a fan, but never obsessed, with the genre. I've always had eclectic tastes, and in my den George Jones, Merle Haggard, Patsy Cline and Reba McIntyre have to share shelf space with the Chieftains (who did their own country-western CD, by the way), Clannad, the Jefferson Airplane, Miles Davis and Glenn Gould. Still, I've always been a sucker for a solid country-western song, and I think there's a particular reason for that: The best of them tell a good, emotionally engaging story, which is the ultimate point of fiction to me, whether a novel, film or song. It's this lyrical rendition of telling a tale that has great appeal to me, and my contribution, "Another Day Without You," tells a story that represents what is perhaps the most persistent theme in country-western music: love, longing and home."

An Interview with Jeff Deaver

Where did you grow up? Was yours a bookish household?
I grew up outside of Chicago, a small town called Glen Ellyn. I was a nerd when I was a kid, totally inept at sports, so, yes, I was a bookhound. I read everything I could get my hands on.

Do you remember the first mystery novel you ever read?
Not specifically, but I'm sure it was a Sherlock Holmes novel or an Ian Fleming thriller.

What was the first piece of music you recall?
Probably Prokofiev's *Peter and the Wolf,* South African folksongs by Miriam Makeba, and/or Irish folksongs.

Was yours a musically oriented household?
Not particularly. We never went out to hear music, though there was often music playing on the record player (Remember records? They're like big, black CDs, only they melt if you leave them in the backseat of a car in the summer).

Do you listen to music when you write?
Only jazz or classical or instrumental Celtic—all *sans* words, of course. Too distracting otherwise.

Has a musical work ever inspired a novel or short story?
Yes, though it never got out of the outline stage. It was about a redisovered piece of music from a dead musician. I'd say more, but I might want to try writing it again.

What is your favorite manmade sound?
Acoustic guitar.

What is your favorite sound in nature?
Water.

Your work is noted for fast-paced plots and suprising twists. How do you start a story?
I never begin a short story or novel until it's completely outlined, and I know exactly where the plot's going. Otherwise there's too much digression and the risk that the characters or plot impediments will take over.

If you had a chance to invite any three people in the world to dinner, living or dead, who would they be?
Assuming that the deceased ones are miraculously revived and not just a rotting corpse at the dinner table (forgive me; I'm twisted), I'd vote for Dashiell Hammett, William Shakespeare and Cameron Diaz.

Which would you rather do—read or listen to a favorite CD?
Preferably both, but in a pinch, I'd read.

Claudia Bishop introduced Austin and Madeline McKenzie with "Waiting for Gateaux" in the mystery anthology Death Dines In. *She enjoyed them so much she's featured them in a series,* The Casebooks of Dr. McKenzie. *"I have no idea why I feel such kinship with a cranky, seventy-two-year-old veterinarian," Claudia admits, "But Austin makes me laugh. And I just love his affection for his 'magnificently proportioned' Madeline."*

The Melancholy Danish

Claudia Bishop

"The uncut version of *Hamlet* is *how* long?" Madeline's mellow contralto rose a sufficient number of notes to place her squarely within the range of that notable soprano, Renee Fleming.

"Four and one half hours, my dear. Give or take a fardel, or two," I said.

This levity cut no ice with my beloved. Madeline rolled her sapphire eyes in mild dudgeon. She may have muttered, "Good god!" as she tugged irritably at an auburn curl. But she merely said, "So, what's a fardel when it's at home, Austin?"

"A burden. Derived from the Old French, if I am not mistaken, and folded into English well before the Elizabethan era. It comes in that notable soliloquy of the Prince's, '*O, that this too, too solid flesh would melt, thaw, and resolve itself into a dew*'." I paused and smoothed my mustache. "And then 'something, something, fardels bear,' and so on."

Madeline picked up a fig and swallowed the whole, neatly. We were taking our usual four o'clock respite from the daily labors at my veterinary practice, McKenzie Veterinary Services, Inc. (Practice Limited to Large Animals). Madeline, whose magnificent proportions require regular infusions of healthy provender, is a notable cook. This afternoon's meal was comprised of fresh figs, goat cheese, Madeline's raspberry scones and my usual half-inch of Scotch.

"Sweetie, do we have to go?"

"It would be well for us to attend. It's a fundraiser for the bovine back fat project, which has, as you know, lost this year's grant due to the fiscal irresponsibility of our current government." I did not continue with what we both well knew: I was some years retired from the chair of Bovine Sciences at the Ag school at Cornell University. My loyalty to that institution ran deep, despite the boorishness of my replacement, Victor Bergland. "The part of the Prince is to be played by Augustine Phillips."

Even this enticement failed to smooth the gloom from Madeline's creamy brow. Phillips, a notable Hamlet in his younger days, is the impresario whose traveling troupe Shakespeare on Wheels brings bits of the Bard to high schools and garden groups throughout the hinterlands of America. Equipped with an Airstream, a company of players, and a horse—the latter's presence a crowd pleaser in performances of *Henry V,* I assume—S.O.W. has done much to keep the Bard before an appreciative public.

"Couldn't we just send Victor a check?"

This did not require a verbal response, either. I was Professor Emeritus. My old adversary and former colleague Bergland hosted the annual fund drive. We were expected. We would go.

We were to attend to opening night and the party afterwards. The party would be tedious. But it had been some time since I had seen a performance of that noble play. I looked forward to comparing Phillips' performance to the great Hamlets who had gone before him. Besides, there is nothing more satisfying than Victor's reaction to Madeline and Thelma Bergland side by side in full evening dress. Madeline is a large, creamy lily. Thelma looks like an artichoke.

"Four and a half hours of *Hamlet,*" Madeline muttered. "There's a flippin' fardel for you." She disposed of a second fig as neatly as the first. "Why couldn't the department just have a bake sale like they usually do, for Pete's sake?"

"Oh, there's a bake sale, as well, my dear. I told Victor we would be happy to contribute our share." I picked up a raspberry scone and examined it with admiration. "Your pastries should be an even bigger hit than Phillips' controversial interpretation of Hamlet's affection for Horatio."

Alas. My prediction turned out truer than anyone could have anticipated.

In the company of Victor and Thelma Bergland, Madeline and I settled into the front row of the Samuel Cross Memorial Auditorium for the Shakespeare on Wheels performance of *Hamlet, Prince of Denmark.* I smoothed the program on my knee and cast my eye over the *dramatis personae.* I then perused the plays offered for the season. "Curious," I said. "They are not offering *Henry V.*" I read on. "As far as I can determine, they have never offered *Henry V.* They have just come from a performance of *Richard III* in Toronto, however."

"Shut up, Austin," Victor groused. "Who cares?"

The curtain rose. The play began. The auditorium has exceptional acoustics, a bonus all the more remarkable for the fact that it is attached to our local Summersville High School. The acoustics did justice to the play. With one notable exception, the players delivered a wonderful performance. Augustine Phillips' melancholy Dane rivaled that of Olivier's. His "*O, what a rogue and peasant slave am I*" had some of the baritone resonance of Richard Burton's. Of course, Phillips did not, could not, achieve the heights to which Derek Jacoby has taken the role, but he certainly bettered that of Messers. Plummer and Fiennes. (I shall draw the veil of charity over the manic performance of that short, crazy Australian, Gibson; Phillips was godlike in comparison.)

All was well until Act IV, scene v. As is known to all lovers of the play, it is here that Ophelia bounces on and off the stage as she descends into paranoia, while uttering some of the most poignant lines ever written: *"there's rosemary, that's for remembrance, / pray you, love, remember."*

I was not sanguine about the success of this scene. The Ophelia had not, as yet, lived up to the promise of the role. It was clear from her first speech with Polonius that her formative years had been spent in the Bronx. Physically, she had neither the wistful fragility of Vivien Leigh, nor the vulnerable elegance of Claire Bloom. She was, in fact, proportioned like a Playboy Bunny. Her given name was Shirl. (I had already formed some diplomatic, if pointed, questions for Phillips at the party after the play. Whatever could have possessed him to place this actress in that role?) However, costumed in the trailing, semi-transparent draperies traditionally associated with the virginal young character, Shirl was visually interesting.

Shirl reappeared onstage for the end of scene V, her arms filled with pungent herbs. Immediately before the heartrending lines to which I have just alluded—and which always cause a lump in my throat—Ophelia sings. She sang now, in a pleasant, if somewhat nasal voice: *"they bore him bare-assed on the bier / hey non nonny…"*

"Bare-assed?" Victor Bergland muttered in surprise. "Bare-assed?"

"It's bare-*faced*. I believe,'" I instructed him, in an undertone. "The poor girl has corpsed, I think the saying is…" I sat up abruptly. "Good god, Victor!"

"Whoop!" Victor said.

The two of us leaned forward in astonishment.

Ophelia was stripping as she hey nonny-nonny-no-ed. The rosemary went flying stage right, along with her blouse. The columbine was crumpled to one perky breast; a batch of rue to the other.

"Hey, non nonny nonny…. fare you well my DOVE!" Ophelia caroled, and the last of her garments spun into the pit. She gyrated pleasingly across the stage, completely nude.

The silence was immense.

Laertes coped, I'll give him that. Perhaps a certain amount of sarcasm was evident in the line *"had thou thy wits and did persuade revenge / it could not move thus"* since it accompanied Shirl's enthusiastic bump and grind. And he managed the lines: *"thought and affliction, passion, hell itself / she turns to favor and to prettiness"* with the merest suggestion of grinding teeth.

Shirl remained appealingly naked through the rest of her song. She exited stage left with a final, "Gawd be with you!" and a saucy swing of bare buttocks.

The male half of the auditorium erupted in applause.

"What I want to know is," Shirl screamed some twenty minutes later, "WHY THE HELL NOT?"

"What *I* want to know," Victor asked me in a whisper, "is how come her breasts don't bounce?"

We had crowded into the Green Room for the cocktail party and bake sale. A series of folding tables lined up against the wall, loaded with baked goods and drink. Audience, players, stagehands, and hangers-on squashed together on the shabby carpet, filled paper plates and plastic cups in hand. Madeline, her face alight with good humor, glowed in the violet and silver caftan I had given her for our twentieth wedding anniversary, her auburn hair a glory. (Thelma glowered in puce.) Shirl, those bounce-less breasts encased in a tight pink t-shirt, stood nose to nose with Augustine Phillips. This distance appeared to be mandated by the crush of partygoers, rather than a preference to be in close proximity. All of us pretended indifference to the squabble at hand.

"You goddam IDIOT," Augustine roared back, in tones that had easily penetrated to the far reaches of the auditorium not half an hour ago. "Who the hell do you think you are, rewriting goddam *Shakespeare!*"

Shirl's big blue eyes filled with tears.

I cleared my throat. "A case might be made that nudity reflects the open vulnerability of Ophelia's plight," I said cautiously.

Phillips whirled on me. "And who the hell are *you?*"

I shrugged. "A lover of the play, merely," I said. "But I'd like to suggest that Shirl's unique interpretation…"

"Shut up, you," Shirl said, without apparent rancor. She returned her gaze to Phillips. "I told you once if I've told you a million times, Augie, this play is goddam boring. B. O. R. I. N. G. Got it? You're on stage longer than anybody else, you got more speeches than anybody else, and you gab on for close to four hours before somebody skewers you to death. And if you ask me, you get skewered way too late in the goddam play!" She tossed her head back and took a healthy gulp of the indifferent red wine Victor had seen fit to place at our disposal. Then she dumped the remainder on Augustine's head.

"That's it," Phillips said. "I don't give a shit, do you hear me? I don't care what you do. You're fired. Beat it. Get out!"

"At least," she said sweetly, "I kept everybody awake."

She left, to a respectful silence.

The telephone rang while we sat at breakfast the next morning. I loathe the telephone. So I ignored it.

"A shame about the party," I observed to my wife. The guests had dispersed rather more rapidly than poor Victor had expected after Shirl's exhibition of temper. Although Madeline's cheese Danish had disappeared with gratifying speed, large quantities of the other baked goods had been left to molder by the empty coffee tins Thelma had scattered around to collect donations. The evening's take had been slim.

"Thelma told me ticket sales soared about five minutes after the curtain went down, though," Madeline said. "Which makes up for the bummed-out bake sale."

"Not if the estimable Shirl has left for parts unknown."

The 'phone continued to blat.

"Austin?"

"The fundraiser might prove profitable yet. Shakespeare in the nude. I don't know why no one's thought of it before."

"Austin? Are you going to answer the 'phone?"

"And it's funny that your Danish went fast, but your scones didn't," I mused as she placed my morning's oatmeal before me. "Both were delicious, as always, my dear. But the Danish appeared more substantial. There is a universal desire to get a bigger bang for one's buck."

The 'phone persisted.

"Austin, answer the '*phone*! Some poor animal may need us."

I always forget that part. I had opened our large animal practice two years ago in response to an urgent financial need; for forty happy years before that, I had been a member of *academe*, and as such, only available when I wanted to be. I reached out to the bookshelf that divides our kitchen from our dining room and picked up the telephone. "What!" I demanded. (This ploy frequently results in the other party hanging up.)

"Austin!"

It was Victor. His over-hearty tones boomed through the receiver. I hung up.

The phone rang again. Madeline rose with a sigh, picked it up, and said hello to Victor in tones far too pleasant for the old goat. Then she handed the receiver to me. I didn't take it.

"It's just Victor," I said sourly.

"He needs to speak to you."

"I know what he wants. He wants to know why Ophelia's bosom remained stationary when the rest of her didn't. I don't know the answer to that question."

"Implants," Madeline said succinctly. "But I don't think it's that, Austin."

I regarded the handset. High-pitched gabbling emanated from it. I took the receiver and said: "Well?"

"Busy this morning? Not that it's likely. Ha-ha."

I cast a glance at the appointment board attached to the refrigerator. It was depressingly empty. Ha-ha, indeed. As Madeline affectionately reminds me, it takes time for a practice to build. "I may be able to re-arrange a few things," I said cautiously.

"I could use a hand down at sow."

Victor admitting that I had a better understanding than he of the species *porcine*? Hah! "Certainly," I said, my glee (regrettably) unconcealed. "Where are you bound? Heavenly Hoggs? VanDerByl's?"

"Not swine, you bonehead. S. O. W. Shakespeare on Wheels. Sick horse."

"Sick horse?" Victor, while admittedly sound in the matter of goats and cows, is merely competent in matters equine.

"Well, they called me, didn't they? It's that horse they haul around for the plays. I mean, I'm in charge of the fundraiser and Thelma's the one that arranged for the gig and I'm a vet, and the horse is sick. They don't seem to understand that I don't do clinical."

"How urgent is it?"

"Something it ate, I think," Victor said gloomily. "Doesn't sound like colic. Sounds like jimson weed, or whatever."

"There is no jimson weed in upstate New York, Victor."

"Yew, then. Who knows? But it's not in distress as such."

"What do you mean, 'as such'?"

"It's salivating, a bit woozy, and a bit dozy. I talked to the kid that handles the horse—it's the guy that plays Laertes. He's not too worried. Might not need a vet at all. It's the brunette who plays Gertrude that's in a snit. She's the one who called me first. Then I talked to the kid. Who knows? But better safe than sorry."

I ignored the cliché. "Where are they quartered?"

"They're all at Fern Hill. Lila Gernsback's got that huge house and she's short a husband this year, so she volunteered the space."

Lila Gernsback! I shuddered. "That's why you don't want to go over there, Bergland. Forget it." Lila, a voluptuous fifty-ish divorcee, found male veterinarians fatally attractive. She had somehow convinced herself that were it not for Madeline, I would have pursued marriage with her! "Her lubricity notwithstanding, Lila's one of the best horsewomen around. If there's something off with the horse, talk to her before you go over there. Save yourself a trip. I'll tell you one thing, it's as likely that there's poisonous weed in her pastures as there is that the moon's made of green cheese."

"Lila's not there. And I can't go." Victor banged the 'phone down. I banged the 'phone down. Then I got up from the table and went to see the horse.

Fern Hill is a well-kept horse farm a few miles south of downtown Summersville. It's not far from our home, and I pulled into Lila's neatly graveled drive some fifteen minutes later. October morning sunshine cast a cheerful glow over the fenced paddocks and green lawns. Lila owned four horses and boarded four more. All eight were turned out in the large front pasture to get the last of the autumn grass. They stood with their heads down, their coats gleaming, and their tails peacefully swishing at an occasional fly. There was a ninth standing near the gate closest to the barn, a big, clunky looking crossbred who stood with her head down, too. But she wasn't eating, her eyes were closed, and she swayed a little on her feet. An anxious knot of actors clustered at her side.

I pulled the Bronco onto the verge nearest the gate and disembarked. The first rule of any farm visit is to assess the situation—much as a detective investigates the scene of a crime. I nodded to the Laertes, acknowledged Rosencrantz and Guildenstern with a wave of my hand, and stopped in front of the Gertrude. "Madam," I said, "my compliments on last night's performance. Now let's take a look at the horse."

She was a nice old thing. Her name was Rosalind. Part Morgan, part Percheron, she must have weighed in at fifteen hundred pounds. A string of saliva dripped from her slack lower lip. She rocked gently on her feet, her head nodding like a bobble doll in the rear window of an '87 Chevy.

Like many light draft animals, Rosalind was exceptionally good-natured, and had no objection to having a thermometer thrust up her hind end. I rolled her eyelid up with a thumb, put my stethoscope against her barrel, pinched the pink of her gums with my thumbnail, and then stood back. "Her respiration is thirty, her temperature 98, her capillary refill time exceptionally slow. What does this tell us?"

I looked around at a sea of puzzled faces. "The values are," I nudged gently, "depressed."

"So she needs like, Prozac?" This from the Guildenstern, who, come to think of it, had fumbled the dumb show in Act IV.

"She is intoxicated," I said crisply. "Or something very like it."

"You mean drunk?" the Gertrude said, properly horrified.

"No, no. No," I said testily, "if you students wish to…" I stopped myself, just in time. Old habits were hard to break. This was not a field trip, but a farm call. "She may have taken something in her feed."

"I knew it!" Gertrude said. She turned to Laertes accusingly. "I *told* you we needed to call the vet."

"To be fair, she is not, in my judgment, in any immediate danger." I moved back as a pile of fresh manure dropped directly beneath her tail. I crouched down and frowned at it. Manure is a quick and useful indicator of an animal's health. I slipped a latex sleeve over my hand, picked up a ball and rolled it between my fingers. This manure was well formed, but streaked with small amounts of blood. Alarmed, I drew the latex sleeve all the way to my elbow and gently explored the mare's interior.

And then the air was split with a chilling shriek.

The bourne from whose country no traveler returns.

Hamlet's words: and prophetic. Augustine Phillips lay dead in Lila Gernsback's second-best guest room. The handsome, haggard face was peaceful, the lines of age and experience smoothed away. A small bubble of froth ran down his chin. Death leaves such a strange absence. Shakespeare is twice right: The rest, or sleep of death, is silence; the rest of that which follows death, is silence, too. I stood by the bed as the police were summoned; the ambulance arranged for; the woman who played Gertrude comforted the girl who played Ophelia. I had been in this room before, of course; Madeline and I had been in Lila's house often. Indeed, we had once stayed here when a gas leak forced us out of the farm for a night. The room looked much as it always had, with a few exceptions: A glass of water stood on the bedside table, next to a plate that held the remains of Madeline's cheese Danish. A few crumbles of Feta cheese smeared the plate. And the flexible rubber tubing, the spoon, the candle, the hypodermic—those items were absolutely an exception.

Madeline and I watch *Law & Order.* I asked myself: "What would Jerry Orbach do?" So I didn't touch anything, nor did I allow the others to do so.

My old friend Simon Provost, chief of detectives for our Summersville police force, arrived within minutes, sirens howling.

"I found Augie dead!" Shirl sobbed to Simon from a chintz-covered chair in the corner of the bedroom. "We were going to go over some of my ideas for sprucing up the play at nine this morning." She raised a tear-drenched face to mine. "He thought about the Ophelia thing overnight, see. He ended up liking the idea. Well, he didn't show and he didn't show and I finally came up here and knocked. The door wasn't locked, so I just came in and..." She gestured toward the sheet-covered bulk that had once been Augustine Phillips. "There he was."

She burst into fresh tears.

Laertes crouched by her side and patted her back. "It's okay, kid. It's okay. We all know he had a drug problem."

Simon Provost glanced meaningfully at me. Actors! his glance said. He, of course, had not missed the drug *impedimenta.*

"I know we all knew..."

"I didn't!" said Gertrude.

"...but...still! It's so horrible!"

Horrible, indeed.

Simon gently pulled back the coverlet. Augustine slept in what I believe are called sweat pants, and little else. A line of needle marks clustered just above his forearm. Simon raised his eyebrows and looked at me. I bent over the body and nodded. "I am, of course, not qualified to express a legally acceptable opinion about these marks as far as man is concerned. But consultation with a forensics pathologist will give you the same response. These are not old needle marks. They are recent. From ten to two hours old, I should judge." I drew a second latex sleeve over my right hand and examined the rest of the body carefully. "Other than that, there is no other external evidence that the man has abused drugs." I straightened up and removed the sleeve. "My scalpels are in my kit. I don't suppose a field autopsy is in order?"

Simon declined the offer, rather vehemently.

"Then my conclusions must remain surmise." I extended a forefinger and tasted a bit of the goat cheese remaining on the dessert plate. "As I suspected. This taste is familiar, Simon."

Simon made a face, but dabbed a bit of the cheese on his tongue. "Hm. Drugs."

"He died from heroin in the cheese?" the dimwitted Guilden-stern said. "How odd."

"Not heroin," I said. "although that is probably what he died from. No, the drug in this cheese is an opiate. He was drugged with this. And then, while asleep, *you*," I pointed at Laertes, "in conspiracy with *you*," I swung my accusing forefinger to the no-longer sobbing Shirl, "drugged him to his death. Simon? These two are murderers. Arrest them."

"My gosh," Madeline said, her normally exuberant voice husky with amazement. "You went out and solved a murder just like that?! Austin, I'm so proud of you!"

"I wouldn't say it was just like *that*," Victor groused. "Anybody could have figured out that horse had been carrying heroin."

"Phooey," Thelma said. "If it was so easy, how come *you* didn't do it, Victor?"

"I was busy."

We were seated at our four o'clock respite from the day's labors at McKenzie Veterinary Services, Inc. (Practice Limited to Large Animals). I had asked Victor and Thelma to join us for some of Madeline's excellent cheese Danish and the remainder of her raspberry scones. The news would be all over Summersville by that evening, and I wanted to be certain that Victor got the real story before rumor garbled it out of all recognition. It was not that I wished to crow. That's beneath me.

Usually.

I smiled at Thelma. "The solution to the mystery was—-to borrow a well-worn phrase which has *never*, by the way, appeared in any of Conan Doyle's classic works—"

"I swear, McKenzie, that you think you're paid by the word," Victor growled.

"The solution to the mystery," I said rather loudly, "was elementary, my dear Victor. The mare Rosalind had the classic symptoms of narcotic poisoning. Blood in the manure led me to an examination of the vagina, which was unnaturally distended. The blood was fresh. Smuggling plastic bags of drugs in the vaginas of easy-tempered mares is a well-known ploy of the drug trade…"

"Bullshit, bullshit, bullSHIT," Victor fulminated. "McKenzie, you know bugger-all about the drug trade."

"Well, we've received circulars about it from the DEA, at least," I said mildly. "All vets get those."

"Do go on, Austin," Thelma said. "Ignore him. He's just jealous."

"Thank you," I said graciously. "Those symptoms, coupled with the fact that S.O.W. does NOT include *Henry V* in its repertory, but, in fact, limits itself to *Richard III*…"

"What?!" Victor was goaded almost beyond endurance.

"The horse, Victor, the horse. The only play where a mount is absolutely necessary is *Henry V*. You recall, I hope, the king's speech to the troops at Agincourt…"

"Oh, *god*," Victor muttered.

"*'For God, King Harry, and for England,'* yes. Even more stirring with the young king atop a mount like Rosalind. On other hand, Richard's agonized cry, *'a horse, a horse, my kingdom for a horse'...*"

"Because, you see," Thelma added sweetly, "the horse isn't there. In *Richard III* he *wants* one. In *Henry V* he *sits* on one."

Victor breathed heavily through his nose.

"Precisely," I said. "So, why the horse except as a courier? The S.O.W. troupe troops all over the country, you know. A fairly unobtrusive way to smuggle drugs."

"But why that pretty Shirl?" Madeline said. "How did you suspect her?"

"Because she was such a god-awful actress," I said. "The only possible way an actor of Phillips' credentials could allow such a perversion of the play was if he were being blackmailed. Shirl obviously knew about the drug smuggling. She used that knowledge to force her way into a starring role."

"But, drugs?" Thelma said.

"It takes a great deal of money to maintain an acting troupe of that stature. They are self-funded. And they had just come over the border from a performance in Toronto. Drug smuggling was not altogether out of the question. At any rate, Phillips' allegiance to his art triumphed over greed. Shirl's nude performance was the straw that broke the camel's back. When it was clear Phillips wasn't going to play along any more—Shirl and the Laertes killed him."

"That's what I don't get," Victor admitted grudgingly. "How did you figure Laertes was in on it, too?"

"The blood in the mare's droppings was fresh. The intoxication recent. The person who removed the bag after it broke and intoxicated the horse was the person who took care of the horse. Ergo, Laertes."

"Wow," Madeline said. "Austin, I'm so proud I could burst."

"Elementary, my dear Madeline."

"Austin," Bergland said. "Shut UP!"

Ophelia's Revenge

(To the principal theme of Mozart's 4th Horn Concerto)

Skeptical Voice (off): So, how'd this play *Hamlet*, go, Shirl?
Shirl: It was a smash. And it was all due to Me!
Skeptical Voice (off): Uh-huh.
Shirl: (indignantly) Like, hey! This guy Shakespeare
   owes me big time.
Remember that...

(verse)

...my agent called me to attend an audition. He told
   me the play was about a mad prince.
The part I was up for, the girl Hamlet's nuts for, falls
   into the river and isn't seen since.
But the dialogue's practically incomprehensible,
   Ham-e-let's motives a puzzling stew.
The guy loves his mother, sees spooks, and is utterly
   baffled about what he thinks he should do.

(refrain)

This chatty Dane is always on the stage, alive
With the same complaints until the very end, Act Five.
He's not fish bait
'til way too late.

(verse)

I told the director the play would be wrecked for no
    crowd would sit still for three hours and more
To hear Hamlet talk lots and toss off some *bon mots*.
Until he gets stabbed, this old play's a real bore.

(refrain)

There had to be a way to make this play improve.
So maybe we should do our scenes completely nude.
Completely nude,
The play'd improve.

(verse)

The reviews from the papers put me into raptures! See,
    nothing sells tickets like bare-bosomed bods.
The *Times* was effusive, for it's finally conclusive what's
    under each one of the gentlemen's cods.

Shirl: So, like, what's a fardel?

An Interview with Claudia Bishop

Where did you grow up? Was yours a bookish household?
My sisters and I grew up in Japan and Hawaii. Hawaii
didn't become a state until 195-something. Television then
was limited to taped re-runs of Disney's Wonderful World
of Color and The Many Loves of Dobie Gillis. So, yes,
we all read. And then we made up plays from the books
and staged them in the garage. My sisters have had a lot
to do with my career as a writer. I told them stories when
they were little. My youngest, Whit Hairston, is the best
editor I've got. She never lets me cheat when I write. And
she contributed to the lyrics for "Ophelia, Revenge."

Do you remember the first mystery short story you ever read?
"The Lottery," by Shirley Jackson. It was a mystery to me
because I didn't understand why the protagonist was stoned
to death. I was ten, I think, and the whole idea of a ritual
sacrifice was way beyond me. But I never forgot how a short
piece of fiction can act like a punch in the stomach.

What was the first piece of music you recall?
Rossini's "Light Calvary Overture." I had an old 45 that
was a copy of a Lone Ranger radio show, and I played it and
played it and played it. I was five or six. And that was the
first time I realized that music can change your emotions.

Was yours a musically oriented household?
We had records on all the time. Just as TV was limited
to taped shows from the US, radio was limited to taped
re-runs of really old oldies—like the Lone Ranger. So
records it was.

Do you listen to music when you write?
>I can't. It distracts me. But I'll listen to music before I write. And once in a while, I get an idea from music. "Ophelia's Revenge," for example, came from listening once too often to Mozart's 4th Horn Concerto. It's the silliest of the concerti, and the racing French horn is ideal for a patter song.

What is your favorite manmade sound?
>A coloratura soprano. If the devil existed, I'd sell my soul for a voice like that.

What is your favorite sound in nature?
>We raise goats in upstate New York. And I've always had horses. I love the whickers and hums when I walk into the barn in the morning to feed them.

If you had to choose three novels to take on a trip, what would you choose?
>If I were only allowed three novels to take on a trip, I'd stay home.

Your work is noted for a certain off-the-wall humor. How do you start a story?
>Something in real life will either make me furiously angry or make me laugh. The story's a way to discharge the emotion.

If you had a chance to invite any three people in the world to dinner, living or dead, who would they be?
>They'd go home after dinner, right? Probably Saddam Hussein, or whoever the current dictator might be, since I'm very curious about that kind of evil. Lyndon Johnson, since I'm also curious about how power corrupts. And maybe a great director, like Cronenberg or John Ford. No writers, since I want to believe in my own fantasies of what they are really like.

This dark tale is notable for an inventive use of language, a close atmosphere, and startling turns of phrase. Tom says: "The song was written first. I wanted to grasp the essence of the tale told in lyric form and invoke the noir nights of Key West's early 1980s, before Caroline Street began to gentrify. Those were rough and ready nights when a tourist with a wad of cash was in deep trouble even before he left his motel room."

Cayo Hueso Combo

Tom Corcoran

Two days of clouds will drop an island's mood to mean low tide. Four days of crap weather draws Key West's closet loonies out to play. After a week of gray skies the manic, the pitiful, hell-bent whiners and full-blown psychos bust loose to dark saloons, motel lobbies, and hectic downtown street corners to howl like hurt dogs for an audience of frightened tourists and pissed-off locals. Storms in the Keys blow in fast, hit hard, and fade quickly. But this slow-moving sonofabitch had started as a drizzle and become more vicious each day. Duval Street was turning into a circus of berserkos. Something had to give.

Pete Jessop owned Have Not's on Caroline, lived in a skinny house behind the place, and rented me an upstairs room with lapstrake walls that I shared with mildew as old as the harbor. A sign above the bar's cash register read, "Drunks are assholes. Who needs more than one?" It was a locals' hangout with men in work boots and the few women in whatever they pleased. Pete's thirty-grit personality kept most strangers from patronizing the place. Those who braved it almost never returned.

By eleven-thirty the night this all went down, a few regulars had stumbled in. Lester Ogburn, the only shrimper in the fleet with a full head of teeth, was wedged into his spot where the bar met the wall. Two stools away, stocky Andy Bannerman, a two-year veteran of the police department, nursed a Rolling Rock, and next to him sat our part-time whore with a heart of ice, young Traci Kalita. A gas station owner from Lansing whom we later learned was named Harry Tutt had arrived before all of us. He stood the whole time so he could peruse the canyon in Traci's tanktop, and I sat stage left, down by the wheezing beer cooler. From time to time I had tasted the lovely contents of said tanktop. I couldn't blame the man for his eye-groping. But Pete had asked Traci not to hook out of his place, so no one told Harry the deal.

Right after midnight Lester Ogburn brought up the murder. Four days earlier a man's body had been found by a clean-up crew behind Searstown.

"The moke got mugged," said Andy Bannerman.

Lester put down his beer and stroked his wispy goatee. "I won't buy that shit," he said. "Word down the dock says Cuban crime of passion."

"Purple passion's your bet," said Bannerman. "The county report cited multiple intoxicants and multiple stab wounds."

"Show your knives," said Pete Jessop. "Everybody clean?"

"Mine went adios," I said. "Lost it to Captain Turk in a stupid card game."

Lester Ogburn placed my Gerber on the bartop. "This came into my possession two weeks ago. I wondered why Turk was so flip about gambling away a quality sticker. Just don't think I dirtied it to send that dude to his damned reward."

"The victim left a letter in his effects," said Andy. "He wanted to be buried near a farm town in Minnesota."

"I couldn't do frozen-ass dirt," said Lester. "They can barbecue me and chuck my soot in the Northwest Channel. Maybe I'll wind up in Rio de Janeiro."

"Or Finland," I said.

Traci laughed. "I want my ashes packed into a life-sized doll. Maybe you boys can take me bar-hopping for a few more years. How about you, Pete?"

"That doll might be my best shot at a freebie. I'd go for a year's worth."

"That's not what I was asking."

"Throw me in a volcano," said Pete. "Preferably in Hawaii which I ain't never seen. With any luck, I'll get there first on vacation."

Traci grinned and turned to me, the question on her face.

"Grind my ashes into concrete mix," I said. "Turn me into a yard ornament."

"A sundial bird bath?" said Lester Ogburn.

"Something more tropical."

"Maybe a planter shaped like a pineapple," he said. "That's Hawaiian, too. It beats a chalk outline behind Sears."

"Outlines foul evidence," said Andy. "We haven't painted those for years."

Traci asked Andy where he wanted to be buried.

"Shit, I want to live first. This rain-soaked dump, I quit a perfectly fine security job in Murphy, North Carolina."

"And with the whole world in front of you," said Traci, "you came to our bug-infested, open-air asylum to be a cop. You didn't exactly answer my question."

"My dream's Alaska," said Andy. "Get a job on a king salmon boat, make big money fast, then really take a vacation."

"Where to?" said Pete.

"Maybe the Canadian Rockies."

Pete shook his head. "First I ever heard you mention the Canadian Rockies."

"Where do you picture me on vacation, Pete?"

"Tahiti, some place like that."

"Lemme guess. That's where you'd go, right?"

"I promise you," said Pete, "someday I'll be in Hawaii. And it won't smell like a slopchute."

"Take me along, honey pie," said Traci. "You'll finally get the freebies you've been begging me for."

"Beats holding out for a dust-stuffed doll." Pete looked up from the scrub sink, stared at Traci a moment, then turned to Bannerman. "Sure as hell, I saw an outline," he said. "Bloodstains and dead flowers. I drove past it two days after they found the poor bastard."

Lester signaled for another beer. "You'd think someone would, you know…like, a scrub brush in the rain."

"Scene was cleaned," said Andy. "Anything you saw must've been put there by reporters and photographers."

"That's your news media," said Harry Tutt. "History repeats itself for two days. Then history goes missing like so many murder cases."

"You're packing expertise on this, sir?" said Bannerman.

"I'm just a gas station owner from Lansing on a six-day vacation."

"What a coincidence. Down here, our definition of 'expert' is a gas station owner from Lansing on vacation."

Traci defrosted the chatter by introducing herself. After Tutt told us his name, Traci said, "Don't mind that one. Andy's a cop who's never off duty. But this here is one of your great bartenders. This island is famous for bartenders, and they all put Pete Jessop on the list."

"That's a load of shit." Pete scowled and reached to shake Harry Tutt's hand.

"Pleased to meet all you people." Tutt pulled a bankroll out of his front pants pocket. He shuffled fifties before extracting a twenty. "I'd like to buy a round. You included, Pete."

Traci introduced me as the town's next world-famous novelist then said, "That's Lester Ogburn down in the shadows. He works on a shrimpboat parked behind the Half Shell Raw Bar."

"The *Campeche Queen*," said Lester.

"Why is this news to me?" said Pete. "You were the rig man on *Miss Daisy*."

"I kept that jerkoff captain out of the nursery twice, and he called me a know-it-all. Back in port I took shore leave until Captain Earl off the *Queen* found me in the Midget Bar. He asked if I could still chip ice, and I told him I could use the bread. 'Underway in an hour,' he said. 'Go get your clothes,' and I told him I was standing in the middle of them."

Traci fanned herself with a cardboard coaster. "Pete, maybe you could cut me a lemon wedge. We need to freshen the air in here."

"We left the pier so fast I had to piss my last brew out over the stern," said Lester. "That was two months ago. I'm still, as we say, dragging on the *Queen*."

Harry Tutt peered into the shadows. "How is it that a man of your vocation is so well-spoken?"

"Like how do I know words longer than dog?"

"Exactly."

"You being a gas station owner, sir, I could ask too."

"You first," said Tutt.

Lester Ogburn inhaled deeply. "Life has played a joke on me. Let me explain."

"Oh, here we go," said Traci.

"He faked two semesters of college," said Pete Jessop, "then hoboed his ass down here and wore button-down shirts his first year at sea. They still call him the preppy shrimper."

"I don't get to tell my own story?" said Ogburn.

Bannerman finally smiled. "Pete told it in one-tenth the time."

"What joke has life played?" said Tutt.

"My wealthy mother, bless her healthy heart, refuses to die. I'll be starving in a maritime retirement program by the time I inherit my millions."

Harry Tutt lifted his glass slowly toward his lower lip. "This is starting to get thick."

Lester looked him straight in the eye. "Perhaps I've indulged in hyperbole."

"There's a word longer than dog," said Andy. "No wonder you've mastered all the highly technical aspects of shrimping."

"That car that just went by," said Traci, again deflecting the conversational drift. "Did you hear that new song on the radio? I swear, Tina Turner is smack in the middle of where I need to be."

I glanced through the door. Under the flickering beer sign, oily rainwater crested the curb and spread across the fissured sidewalk.

"I heard no song," said Pete. "I haven't even heard sirens."

"'What's love got to do with it'?" she said. "So damn true."

Harry Tutt shook his head. "The only one I've heard for the past month is 'every mess I make, every ache I fake, they'll be watching me.'"

"That would be the Police," said Andy, sounding proud, as if the band instead of the city was his employer.

"No wonder I feel eyes on the back of my shirt," said Tutt.

With a whoosh of silence the lights died. Typical Key West electrical outage.

I offered the island cliché: "We are powerless."

"Except for Andy," said Lester. "My opinion, dark karma enables the boy."

"Ditto," said Traci.

"Whatever that means, I don't like the sound of it," said Bannerman.

Pete Jessop struck a match and a candle appeared. "Bar's closed."

"We just friggin' got here," said Andy. "Me, personally, I don't need a neon light to drink, piss or screw."

"Let's not bring that up," said Traci. "Your girlfriend said it took all her energy to…"

"Ex-girlfriend," said the cop. "We don't need to discuss her. She was a bad cook, a bad housekeeper, a poor friend, a bum lay, and a bad investment."

"You pretty much discussed her," said Lester Ogburn. "Grand total, more than we wanted to know."

"You can't argue with the truth, that's all I say."

"Hey," said Pete, "three sides to every story."

"Except the friendship part," said Traci. "She once called you Andy-Social."

"Old news, Traci. I got that one to my face. And don't start with names I might have missed. Just because you've done the Bone Island Mambo with every Tom, Dick and…"

"Don't say it." Tutt rattled the ice in his rocks glass.

"Melvin was the next word out of his mouth," said Pete.

"Don't pull ugly on me, Andy," said Traci. "I was just repeating…"

"Let's go back to chalk outlines," said Lester Ogburn. "Or that casket going to freezing-ass Minnesota with 'Wish you were here' written on its lid."

Pete Jessop walked toward the front door.

"You're not throwing us out," I said.

"No, locking the door."

"The night is young, Pete."

"Power failures bring out idiots," he said. "One time, only once, I lit the place with candles and let it fill up with drunks. All it took was the front and back doors open at the same time. Every light blew out and they robbed me blind. I lost all my ashtrays, a month's supply of bar napkins and a framed map of Florida Bay off the wall."

Smells in the saloon became stronger in the near-darkness. Behind the stale smoke I got whiffs of chlorine tabs in the sink water. Pete had cleaned his ashtrays with Lemon Pledge.

Harry Tutt said, "Mr. Ogburn, what exactly does a shrimping job involve?"

"You keep begging him to tell stories, you'll come to regret it," said Andy.

"It's dusk to dawn," said Lester, "because the shrimp can dodge our nets in daylight and also in bright moonlight, so four days a month—give or take—are bad for fishing. I stay up all night, smoking in the wheelhouse while the so-called captain sleeps. I worry about the outrigger crew that can't swim, drop the catch on deck for the cull, dump sea stars, and keep the snappers for breakfast. Then I cash my check and spend it all in here."

"Let me be more specific," said Tutt. "Being a shrimper, do you have a good knowledge of local waters?"

"The way it works, water never stays in the same place. But I know every square foot of ocean bottom."

"Enough to show me on a chart where I can go fishing if the sun ever comes out?"

"Mr. Harry Tutt from Michigan, I am your first-class guide. For the bargain price of an alcoholic beverage, I can put you on bonefish, tarpon, dolphin, and grouper."

"We got a chart handy?"

"Over on the *Campeche Queen*. Three-minute walk."

"I'll do you better than one damn drink, but you'll have to lead the way."

Lester slid off his stool. "Gimme two six-packs, Pete. If you will."

Pete settled Tutt's tab and relocked the door behind the two men.

"As hokey as I've heard in years," said Andy. "You think Tutt's smuggling pot, cocaine, or people?"

"I could only hazard a guess," said Pete.

"Hazard me a damn beer instead, and pack your guess to where the moon don't shine."

"That'd be this fucking island."

"So we talked a circle. My thirst grows larger."

"I don't think he has the balls to commit a crime," said Traci. "He left because it was too dark to count goose bumps on my left nipple."

"Nice to be popular?" said Pete.

"On a quality level," she said, "I'm the only bait in town."

"What do we do, flip a coin for you?"

"No, you cry in your beer and drown your disappointment. I'm going home. But these dangerous streets, I could use a gentleman to walk me there."

"Counts me out," said Andy.

"No shit," said Traci. "And I don't see the owner leaping over the bar to come to my aid."

"If it was the right time of the month for fishing," said Pete, "you wouldn't be hanging out here."

She turned toward me.

I shrugged.

"Say something," she said.

"I never knew that ceiling fan squeaked so loud until it stopped."

Three houses away from her place on Grinnell, Traci said, "It finally stopped raining."

"It's a sign of new beginnings," I said. "If you believe in signs."

"One morning a couple months ago you kissed the back of my neck."

"I thought you were still asleep."

"Give me six minutes and I will be. Good night, Pritchard."

That quick exchange did nothing to ease me into dreamland. Just before dawn I was reading an old paperback. My phone rang. Not a good time for calls. Traci had told me that she was going straight to sleep. Not that I always believed her.

"Is Pete's car outside your window?" she said.

"I'm listening to it. He's just pulling in."

"Shit," she said.

"He's got a routine. He drove to the bank drop box."

"For last night's business? Any one of us, we had more cash in our pockets than he put in the register."

"Force of habit. He always sweeps the bar then goes and makes a deposit."

"Pritchard, listen to me," said Traci.

"No choice. I'm still here."

"A man was murdered a couple hours ago."

"How would you know this?"

"My roommate..."

"The gay guy?"

"He was jogging by the Martello Garden and found a man stabbed. A big man. His shirt and ball cap, by Myron's description, it sounded like Harry Tutt from Michigan."

"Tutt left the bar with Lester Ogburn. Are you saying that Lester...shit. You think Lester killed a man with my knife?"

"I know people, Pritchard. You do, too. Lester's not a killer."

I looked down at the scraggly yard between the bar and the house. "What has you worried about Pete? What the hell..."

"What?" she said.

"Andy just walked out of Pete's back door. He looks like somebody pissed in his Cheerios."

"Shit."

"You think Andy was waiting to bust Pete? Pete killed this Harry guy?"

"I think they're both in on it."

"Fuck, they just..."

"What was that?"

"Jesus, they just shot each other."

"*At* each other or *hit* each other?"

"Both went down."

"Are they dead?"

"Both not moving."

Traci's voice became a cold monotone. "Go down and get the money."

"Are you nuts?"

"If they both checked out, Pritchard, it's 'Case Closed.' Harry Tutt's bankroll is no use to him anymore. I can put it to use. I'm serious about leaving."

"If you think I'm going to waltz into a double-murder scene to lift a wad of cash...That money has three men's blood on it. Maybe four, with that guy who got killed a week ago."

Traci stayed silent.

"Did you put Pete up to this? Was that the year's worth of freebies?"

"You're the only one who gets it for nothing. I charge *myself* twenty to spank the snapper."

"Well, I'm staying put. Those aren't just two dead men. It's Pete and Andy."

"They're two dead murderers, Jack. But maybe they're not dead. You should go check, see if you can help them."

"How can you be sure they're murderers?"

"I have solid suspicions. Have you got a key to Pete's apartment?"

"I know where it's hidden."

"Go down there and see if you can find an airline ticket."

"Stay on the line," I said.

I used the back stairwell, found the key jammed into the woodwork, right where Pete had told me it was. His desk was a mess, as if someone had ransacked it. Someone like Andy Bannerman, because on top of the mess sat a printed envelope. Pete Jessop had booked an open one-way to Honolulu.

I wondered if Andy's split had helped to finance the trip.

I heard voices in the yard. I peeked through the blinds. A city cop jabbered into his radio mike while another barfed into an aloe plant.

I hurried upstairs and grabbed the phone. "You set this up?"

"I can't help it if I'm lucky. Buy yourself one just like it, Pritchard."

"What do you mean?"

"A ticket to Honolulu."

"Why would I want one?"

"You're in love with me, right?"

"I'm probably one of many. Minus two."

"And you just won a year's worth."

"Let me think about it. We can't leave right away, no matter what."

"The sun's coming out," she said. "That's another sign of a fresh beginning. I'll drop by in a few hours with a stack of brochures. Maybe by then the reporters and photographers will be gone."

Bone Island Mambo

About the song, Jim Hoehn explains: "Lyrically, I was trying to capture the spirit of Tom Corcoran's books and the dark side of tropical paradise, an appreciation for the genre dating to my long-ago first exposure to John D. MacDonald's Travis McGee novels. I sent the song to Tom, who politely suggested a couple subtle changes, which brought the song closer to my original intention."

Tom Corcoran says: "The song came first (before the story). I was trying to echo its mood and details by offering a back story typical of Key West in the early 1980s."

It was a dark and stormy night, like the literary cliché,
Plagiarized but appropriate because he left the planet that way,
His final mark was a chalk outline where the body lay,
The warm summer rain ran thicker where it washed the
　　blood away,

The Bone Island Mambo
Down in old Key West,
Bone Island Mambo,
Down to your last breath,
You've got money and drugs, hookers and thugs,
A Cayo Hueso combo,
Bone Island Mambo.

He should have been more careful when he paid for that
  last round,
A flash of tourist twenties was noticed two stools down,
By a man whose hand held a folded knife, that he'd won
  with hole-card luck,
From a fisherman who'd bet the pot when he was short
  a couple of bucks.

His mind was a million miles away as he stumbled home
  to bed,
Humming a forgotten Buffett tune, unaware of what lay
  ahead,
It was over in an instant, no witnesses, no shouts,
An unseen hand pushed the knife blade in while the
  other pulled the wallet out.

(chorus)

A jogger in a T-shirt that said "God Created Gays,"
Stumbled upon the body in the early morning haze,
It soon became a circus, with sirens, lights and cops,
Reporters and detectives, you could hear the flashbulbs pop.

Vacation of a lifetime, according to brochures,
First-class air departure, return in a Cadillac hearse,
With a casket full of postcards and tacky souvenirs,
And on the side for the final ride, it says, "Wish you were here!"

(chorus)

It's a killer tune, the Bone Island Mambo.

An Interview with Tom Corocoran

Where did you grow up? Was yours a bookish household?
I grew up in northern Ohio in a home that encouraged reading. When I was going into 2nd grade, I could read so well that the school skipped me to 3rd grade. I wasn't just a year younger than my classmates—I was 15 percent younger! That screwed me up socially for the next 20 years. Lesson? Never teach your child to read!

Do you remember the first mystery novel you ever read?
I recall a mid-1950s series about hot rods and street rods by Henry Gregor Felsen in which he plotted his books like mysteries with great last-page endings. I bought them from an order form in school—they were fifteen cents each while other books were only a dime, but I got all of them. I had a chance to meet the author 15 years ago and thank him for his influences.

What was the first piece of music you recall?
My parents were into the war-era Big Band stuff. I remember catchy lyrics like "Pennsylvania Six-Five-Thousand" and "K-A-L-A-M-A-Z-O-O" and "Mairsy Dotes." We always sang in the car on long trips.

Was yours a musically oriented household?
My father sold 78 RPM records to earn money in college. I still have a few of them. Music was always around, though rock-and-roll created a huge gap in our tastes. I recall being shocked to receive Elvis' first album as a gift—I thought maybe my transition into rock music might go easy. But then I recall not being allowed to listen to "What'd I Say?"

by Ray Charles. (That was about the same year my father found a copy of *On the Road* in my bedroom and threatened to throw it out of the house and me with it.)

Do you listen to music when you write?
I'm so into lyrics, I find vocals distracting when I'm trying to write. I can listen to jazz—not the syrupy "light" jazz from the radio, but old bebop like Charlie Parker and early Miles Davis really get my brain in gear. In one of my books—*Gumbo Limbo*—I thanked a jazz group on the Acknowledgments page.

Has a musical work ever inspired a novel or short story?
Several times—mostly chapters in my novels. I even quote lyrics to give credit when it happens.

What is your favorite manmade sound?
I love the sound of breaking glass. (No, wait—that's a Nick Lowe song title.) Lately I've come to appreciate the subtle tones of a Formula 1 race car engine at 13,000 RPM.

What is your favorite sound in nature?
A woman laughing in the forest.
Or the sound of a wild editor saying, "Yes."

If you had to choose three novels to take on a trip, what would you choose?
It would depend on trip duration and destination. Long trip to a boring place: *V* by Thomas Pynchon; *Wind from the Carolinas* by Robert Wilder; and *Farmer* by Jim Harrison. Short trip to an exciting place: *The Best American Mystery Stories of the Century* by Penzler and Hillerman.

Your work is noted for compact prose and distinctive dialogue. How do you start a story?

I make a list of five things I want to discuss or accomplish early in the going, then create an opening scene that doesn't put me to sleep. Once I get past those hurdles, I just keep running.

If you had a chance to invite any three people in the world to dinner, living or dead, who would they be?
Paul Newman, Louis Armstrong, and Eudora Welty. They'd ignore my ass, but they'd get a kick out of each other and I'd enjoy just being there. Or Elvis, Jesus, and JFK—with a black velvet tablecloth.

Which would you rather do—read or listen to a favorite CD?
Read—But! This answer has changed from "listen" to "read" and back at least ten times in my adult life.

This story is far from Scottish writer Val McDermid's usual setting—although the tragedy at its heart is as old as time. Val says: "I've known this song since I was a teenager, first in the Joan Baez version, then later that of Johnny Cash. It's one of those songs that gets its hooks into your heart and never quite leaves. I always thought there must have been a great story behind the deceptive simplicity of the lyric, and this is my attempt to tell one of those possible stories."

The Long Black Veil

Val McDermid

Jess turned fourteen today. With every passing year, she looks more like her mother. And it pierces me to the heart. When I stopped by her room this evening, I asked if her birthday awakened memories of her mother. She shook her head, leaning forward so her long blonde hair curtained her face, cutting us off from each other. "Ruth, you're the one I think of when people say 'mother' to me," she mumbled.

She couldn't have known that her words opened an even deeper wound inside me and I was careful to keep my heart's response hidden from my face. Even after ten years, I've never stopped being careful. "She was a good woman, your mother," I managed to say without my voice shaking.

Jess raised her head to meet my eyes then swiftly dropped it again, taking refuge behind the hair. "She killed my father," she said mutinously. "Where exactly does 'good' come into it?"

I want to tell her the truth. There's part of me thinks she's old enough now to know. But then the sensible part of me kicks in. There are worse things to be in small town America than the daughter of a murderess. So I hold my tongue and settle for silence.

Seems like I've been settling for silence all my adult life.

It's easy to point to where things end but it's a lot harder to be sure where they start. Everybody here in Marriott knows where and when Kenny Sheldon died, and most of them think they know why. They reckon they know exactly where his journey to the grave started.

They're wrong, of course. But I'm not going to be the one to set them right. As far as Marriott is concerned, Kenny's first step on the road to hell started when he began dating Billy Jean Ferguson. Rich boys mixing with poor girls is pretty much a conventional road to ruin in these parts.

Me and Billy Jean, we were still in high school, but Kenny had a job. Not just any old job, but one that came slathered with a certain glamour. Somehow, he'd persuaded the local radio station to take him on staff. He was only a gofer, but Kenny being Kenny, he managed to parlay that into being a crucial element in the station's existence. In his eyes, he was on the fast track to being a star. But while he was waiting for that big break, Kenny was content to play the small town big shot.

He'd always had an eye for Billy Jean, but she'd fended him off in the past. We'd neither of us been that keen on dating. Other girls in our grade had been hanging out with boyfriends for a couple of years by then, but to me and Billy Jean it had felt like a straitjacket. It was one of the things that made it possible for us to be best friends. We preferred to hang out at Helmer's drugstore in a group of like-minded teens, among them Billy Jean's distant cousin Jeff.

Their mothers were cousins, and by some strange quirk of genetics, they'd turned out looking like two peas in a pod. Hair the colour of butter, eyes the same shade as the hyacinths our mothers would force for Christmas. The same small, hawk-curved nose and cupid's bow lips. You could take their features one by one and see the correspondence. The funny thing was that you would never have mistaken Billy Jean for a boy or Jeff for a girl. Maybe it was nothing more than their haircuts. Billy Jean's hair was the long blonde swatch that I see now in Jess, whereas Jeff favoured a crew-cut. Still does, for that matter, though the blond is starting to silver round the temples now.

Anyhow, as time slipped by, the group we hung with thinned out into couples and sometimes there were just the three of us drinking Cokes and picking at cold fries. Kenny, who had taken to drifting into Helmer's when we were there, picked his moment and started insinuating himself into our company. He'd park himself next to Jeff, stretching his legs to stake out the whole side of the table. If either of us girls wanted to go to the bathroom, we had to go through a whole rigmarole of getting Kenny to move his damn boots. He'd lay an arm across the back of the booth proprietorially, a Marlboro dangling from the other hand, and tell us all about his important life at the radio station.

One night, he turned up with free tickets for a Del Shannon concert fifty miles down the interstate. We were impressed. Marriott had never seen live rock and roll, unless you counted the open mike night at the Tavern in the Town. As far as we were concerned, only the truly cool had ever seen live bands. It took no persuading whatsoever for us to accompany Kenny to the show.

What we hadn't really bargained for was Kenny treating it like a double date right from the start when he installed Billy Jean up front next to him in the car and relegated me and Jeff to the back seat. He carried on as he started, draping his arm over her shoulders at every opportunity. But we all were fired up with the excitement of seeing a singer who had actually had a number-one single, so we all went along with it. Truth to tell, it turned out to be just the nudge Jeff and I needed to slip from friendship into courting. We'd been heading that way, but I reckon we'd both been reluctant to take any step that might make Billy Jean feel shut out. If Billy Jean was happy to be seen as Kenny's girlfriend—and at first, it seemed that way, since she showed no sign of objecting to the arm-draping or the subsequent hand-holding—then we were freed up to follow our hearts.

That first double date was a night to remember. The buzz from the audience as we filed into the arena was beyond anything we small town kids had ever experienced. I felt like a little kid again, but in a good way. I slid my hand into Jeff's for security and we followed Kenny and Billy Jean to our seats right at the front. When the support act took to the stage, I was rapt. Around us, people seemed to be paying no attention to the unknown quartet on the stage, but I was determined to miss nothing.

After Del Shannon's set, my ears were ringing from the music and the applause, my eyes dazzled by the spotlights glinting on the chrome and polish of the instruments. The air was thick with smoke and sweat and stale perfume. I was stunned by it all. I scarcely felt my feet touch the ground as we walked back to Kenny's car, the chorus of "Runaway" ringing inside my head. But I was still alert enough to see that Kenny still had his arm round Billy Jean and she was leaning into him. I wasn't crazy about Kenny, but I was selfish. I wanted to be with Jeff, so I wasn't going to try to talk Billy Jean out of Kenny.

Kenny dropped Jeff and me off outside my house, and as his tail lights disappeared, I said, "You think she'll be OK?"

Jeff grinned. "I've got a feeling Kenny just bit off more than he can chew. Billy Jean will be fine. Now, come here, missy, I've got something for you." Then he pulled me into his arms and kissed me. I didn't give Billy Jean another thought that night.

Next day when we met up, we compared notes. I was still floating from Jeff's kisses and I didn't really grasp that Billy Jean was less enamoured of Kenny's attempts to push her well beyond a goodnight kiss. What I did take in was that she appeared genuinely pleased for Jeff and me. My fears that she'd feel shut out seemed to have been groundless, and she talked cheerfully about more double-dating. I didn't understand that was her way of keeping herself safe from Kenny's advances. I just thought that we were both contentedly coupled up after that one double date.

All that spring, we went out as a foursome. Kenny seemed to be able to get tickets to all sorts of venues and we went to a lot of gigs. Some were good, most were pretty terrible and none matched the excitement of that first live concert. I didn't really care. All that mattered to me was the shift from being Jeff's friend to being his girlfriend. I was in love, no doubting it, and in love as only a teenage girl can be. I walked through the world starry-eyed and oblivious to anything that wasn't directly connected to me and my guy.

That's why I paid no attention to the whispers linking Kenny's name to a couple of other girls. Someone said he'd been seen with Janine, who tended bar at the Tavern in the Town. I dismissed that out of hand. According to local legend, a procession of men had graced Janine's trailer. Why would Kenny lower himself when he had someone as special as Billy Jean for a girlfriend? Oh yes, I was quite the little innocent back in the day.

Someone else claimed to have seen him with another girl at a blues night in the next county. I pointed out to her that he worked in the music business. It wasn't surprising if he had to meet with colleagues at music events. And that it shouldn't surprise her if some of those colleagues happened to be women. And that it was a sad day when women were so sexist.

I didn't say anything to Billy Jean, even though we were closer than sisters. I'd like to think it was because I didn't want to cause her pain, but the truth is that their stories probably slipped my mind, being much less important than my own emotional life.

By the time spring had slipped into summer, Jeff and I were lovers. I'm bound to say it was something of a disappointment. I suspect it is for a lot of women. Not that Jeff wasn't considerate or generous or gentle. He was all of those and more. But even after we'd been doing it a while and we'd had the chance to get better at it, I still had that Peggy Lee "Is that all there is?" feeling.

I suppose that made it easier for me to support Billy Jean in her continued refusal to let Kenny go all the way. When we were alone together, she was adamant that she didn't care for him nearly enough to let him be the one to take her virginity. For my part, I told her she should hold out for somebody who made her dizzy with desire because frankly that feeling was the only thing that made it all worth it.

The weekend after I said that to her, Billy Jean told Kenny she wasn't in love with him and she didn't want to go out with him any more. Of course, he went around telling anybody who would listen that he was the one to call time on their relationship, but I suspect that most people read that for the bluster it was. "How did he take it?" I asked her at recess on the Monday afterwards. 'Was he upset?'

"Upset, like broken-hearted? No way." Billy Jean gave a little "I could give a shit" shrug. "He was really pissed at me," she said. "I got the impression he's the only one who gets to decide when it's over."

"You know, I've been wanting to say this for the longest time, but he really is kind of an asshole," I said.

We both giggled, bumping our shoulders into each other like big kids. "I only started going out with him so you and Jeff would finally get it together," Billy Jean said in between giggles. "I knew as long as I was single you two would be too loyal to do anything about it. Now I can just go back to having you both as my best friends again."

And so it played out over the next few weeks. Billy Jean and I hung out together doing girl things; Billy Jean and Jeff went fishing out on the lake once a week and spent Sunday mornings fixing up the old clunker her dad had bought for her birthday; we'd all go for a pizza together on Friday nights; and the rest of the time she'd leave us to our own devices. It seemed like one chapter had closed and another had opened.

Jess turned fourteen today. Seems like yesterday she came into our home. It wasn't how we expected it to be, me and Ruthie. We thought we'd have a brood of our own, not end up raising my cousin's kid. But some things just aren't meant to be and I'm old enough now to know there are sometimes damn good reasons for that.

I remember the morning after Jess was conceived. When Billy Jean told Ruthie and me what Kenny Sheldon had done, I didn't think it was possible to feel more angry and betrayed. I was wrong about that too, but that's another story.

It happened the night before, when Ruthie and I were parked up by the lake in my car and Billy Jean was on her lonesome, nursing a Coke in one of the booths at Helmer's. According to her, when Kenny walked in, he didn't hesitate. He came straight over to her booth and plonked himself down opposite her. He gave her the full charm offensive, apologizing for being mean to her when she'd thrown him over.

He claimed he'd missed her and he wanted her back but if he couldn't be her boyfriend he wanted to be her friend, like me. He pitched it just right for Billy Jean and she believed he meant what he said. That's the kind of girl she was back then—honest and open and unable to see that other people might not be worthy of her trust. So she didn't think twice when he offered her a ride home.

She called me first thing Sunday morning. We were supposed to be going fishing as usual but she wanted Ruthie to come along too. I could tell from her voice something terrible had happened even though she wouldn't tell me what it was, so I called Ruthie and got her to make some excuse to get out of church.

When we picked her up, she was pale and withdrawn. She wouldn't say a word till we were out at the lake, sitting on the jetty with rods on the water like it was any other Sunday morning. When she did speak, it was right to the point. Billy Jean was never one for beating about the bush, but this was bald, even for her.

"Kenny Sheldon raped me last night," she said. She told us about the meeting at Helmer's and how she'd agreed to let him drive her home. Only, before they got to her house, Kenny had driven down an overgrown track out of sight of the street. Then he'd pinned her down and forced her to have sex with him.

We didn't know what to do. Fourteen years ago, date rape wasn't on the criminal agenda. Not in towns like Marriott. And the Sheldons were a prominent family. Kenny's dad owned the funeral home and had been a councilman. And his mom ran the flower arranging circle at the church. Whereas the Fergusons were barely

one step up from white trash. Nobody was going to take the word
of Billy Jean Ferguson against Kenny Sheldon.

I wanted to call Kenny Sheldon out and beat him to within an
inch of his life. I wanted him to beg for mercy the way I knew Billy
Jean had begged him the night before.

But Ruthie and Billy Jean stopped me. "Don't stoop so low,"
Billy Jean said.

"That's right," Ruthie said. "There's other ways to get back at
scum like him."

And by that afternoon, I had started the rumour that Janine from
the Tavern in the Town had stopped sleeping with Kenny because
she'd found out he had a venereal disease. I don't know how long it
took to get back to the shitheel himself, but I do know he'd had quite
the struggle to get anyone to sit next to him in Helmer's, never mind
hang out at gigs with him. That cheered us up some, and Ruthie
said Billy Jean was starting to talk about getting over it. That was
so like her—she wasn't the kind to let anybody take her life away
from her. She was always determined to control her own destiny.

But all her good intentions went to shit about six weeks after
the rape. I'd been helping my dad finish off some work in the top
pasture and both girls were sitting on the front porch when I got
back to the house. We all piled into my truck and headed out to
the lake. We hadn't gone but half a mile when Ruthie blurted out,
"She's pregnant. That bastard Kenny got her pregnant."

I only had to glance at Billy Jean to know it was true and the
knowledge made me boiling mad. I swung the truck around at the
next intersection and headed for the Sheldon house, paying no mind
to the girls shouting at me to stop. When we got there, I jumped out
and marched straight up to the house. I hammered on the door and
Kenny himself opened it.

I know that violence isn't supposed to solve things, but in my
experience, it definitely has its plus points. I grabbed Kenny by the
shirt front, yanked him out the door and slammed him against the
wall. I swear the whole damn house shook. "You bastard," I yelled
at him. "First you rape her, then you get her pregnant."

I drew my hand back to smack him in the middle of his dumb-founded face, but Billy Jean caught my arm. She was always strong for a girl and she had me at an awkward angle. "Leave him," she said. "I don't want anything to do with him."

"You say that now, but you're going to need his money," I snarled. "Babies don't come cheap and he has to pay for what he's done."

Before anybody could say anything more, Mrs Sheldon appeared in the doorway. She looked shocked to see her golden boy pinned up against the wall and demanded to know what was going on.

My dander was up, and I wasn't about to back off. "Ma'am," I said, "I'm sorry to cause a scene, but your son here raped my cousin Billy Jean and now she is expecting his baby."

Mrs Sheldon reared back like a horse spooked by a snake. "How dare you," she hissed. "My son is a gentleman, which is more than I can say about you or your kin." She made a kind of snorting noise in the back of her throat. "The very idea of any Ferguson woman being able to name the father of her children with any certainty is absurd. Now get off my property before I call the police. And take your slut of a cousin with you."

It was my turn to grab Billy Jean. I thought she was fixing to rip Mrs Sheldon's face off. "You evil witch," she screamed as I pulled her away.

Ruthie stared Mrs Sheldon down. When she spoke her voice was cold and sharp. I know I hoped she'd never use that tone of voice to me. "You should be ashamed of yourself," she said, turning on her heel and walking back to the truck, head high. I never knew to this day whether she meant Kenny or his mother or both of them.

What happened that evening must have had some effect, though. A week later, Kenny was gone.

Back in the early Sixties, being an unwed mother was still about the biggest disgrace around and most girls who got into trouble ended up disowned and despised. But Billy Jean was lucky in her parents. The Fergusons never had much money but they had love aplenty. When she told them she was pregnant and how it had happened, they'd been shocked, but they hadn't been angry with her. Her father went round to see old man Sheldon. He never told anybody what passed between them, not even Mrs Ferguson, but he came back with a cashier's check for ten thousand dollars.

Nobody knew where Kenny was. His mother told her church crowd that he'd landed a big important radio job out on the coast, but nobody believed her. Truth to tell, I don't think anybody much cared. We certainly didn't.

Jeff and I were married three months later. I guess we were both kind of fired up by Billy Jean being pregnant. We wanted to start a family of our own. We moved into a little house on Jeff's daddy's farm and Jeff started working as a trainee sales representative for an agricultural machinery firm.

Half a mile down the track from us there was an old double-wide trailer that had seen better days. Jeff's dad used to rent it out to seasonal workers. We persuaded him to let Billy Jean have it for next to nothing in return for doing it up. We knew there wasn't enough room in her parents' house for Billy Jean and a growing kid and I wanted her to be close at hand so we could bring up our children together.

Jeff and I spent most of our spare time knocking that trailer into shape. Billy Jean helped as much as she could, and by the time Jess was born, we'd turned it into a proper little home for the two of them. They moved in when Jess was six weeks old, and Billy Jean looked relaxed for the first time since Kenny had raped her. "I can never thank the two of you enough," she said so many times I told her she should just make a tape of it and give us each a copy.

"It was Ruthie's idea," Jeff said, acting like it was nothing to do with him.

"I know," Billy Jean said. "But I also know you did more than your fair share to make it happen."

We settled into a pretty easy routine. I worked mornings on the farm, helping Jeff's mother with the specialty yogurt business she was building up. Afternoons, I'd hang out with Billy Jean and Jess. Then I'd cook dinner for Jeff, we'd either watch some TV or walk down to have a beer and a few hands of cards with Billy Jean. Most people might have thought our lives pretty dull, but it seemed fine enough to us.

There was one thing, I thought, that stopped it being perfect. A year had gone by since Jeff and I had married, but still I wasn't pregnant. It wasn't for want of trying, but I began to wonder whether my lack of enthusiasm for sex was somehow preventing it. I knew this was crazy, but it nagged away at me.

Finally, I managed to talk to Billy Jean about it. It was a hot summer afternoon and Jess was over at her grandma's house. Billy Jean and I were lying on her bed with the only a/c in the trailer cranked up high. "I love him," I said. "But when we make love, it's not like it says in the books and magazines. It doesn't feel like it looks in the movies. I just don't feel that whole swept away thing."

Billy Jean rolled over on to her back and yawned. "I'm not the best person to ask, Ruth. I only ever had sex the once and that sure wasn't what you would call a good experience. I don't guess it's the kind of thing you can talk to Jeff about either."

I made a face. "He'd be mortified. He thinks I think he's the greatest lover on the planet." Billy Jean giggled. "Well, you have to make them feel like that."

Billy Jean yawned again. "I'm sorry, Ruth. I don't mean you to feel like I'm dismissing you, but I am so damn tired. I was up three times with Jess last night. She's teething."

"Why don't you just have a nap?" I said. But she was already drifting away. I made myself more comfortable and before I knew it, I'd nodded off too.

I woke because someone was kissing me. An arm was heavy across my chest and shoulder, a leg was thrown between mine and soft lips were pressing on mine, a tongue flicking between my lips. I opened my eyes and the mouth pulled back from mine. A face that was familiar and yet completely strange hovered above mine. *Jeff with long hair,* I thought stupidly for a moment before the truth dawned.

Billy Jean put a finger to my lips. ... "Ssh," she said "Let's see if we can figure out what Jeff's doing wrong."

By the end of the afternoon, I understood that it wasn't what Jeff did that was wrong. It was who he was.

Kenny came back a couple of weeks before Jess' fourth birthday. It turned out his mother hadn't been lying to the church group. He had landed a job working for a radio station in Los Angeles. He was doing pretty well. Had his own show and everything. He rolled back into town in a muscle car with a beautiful blonde on his arm. His fiancée, apparently.

All of that would have been just fine if he had left the past alone. But no. He wanted to impress the fiancée with his credentials as a family man. The first thing we knew about it was when Billy Jean got a letter from Kenny's lawyer saying he planned to file suit for shared custody. Kenny wanted Jess for one week a month until she started school, then he wanted her for half the school vacations. If he'd been the standard absent father as opposed to one who had never even seen his kid, it might have sounded reasonable. And we had a sneaking feeling that the court might see things Kenny's way.

Justice in Marriott comes courtesy of His Honour Judge Wellesley Benton. Who is an old buddy of Kenny Sheldon's daddy and a man who's put a fair few of Billy Jean's relatives behind bars. We were, to say the least, apprehensive.

The day after the letter came, Billy Jean happened to be walking down Main Street when Kenny strolled out of the Coffee Bean Scene with the future Mrs. Sheldon. I heard all about it from Mom, who saw it all from the vantage point of the quilting store porch.

Billy Jean just lit into him. Called him all the names under the sun from rapist to deadbeat dad. Kenny looked shocked at first, then when he saw his fiancée wasn't turning a hair, he started to laugh. That just drove Billy Jean even crazier. She was practically hysterical. Mom came over from the quilt shop and grabbed her by the shoulders, trying to get her away. Then Kenny said, "I'll see you in court," and walked his fiancée to the car. Billy Jean was fit to be tied.

Well, everybody thinks they know what happened next. That night, Kenny was due at a dinner in the Town Hall. As he approached, a figure stepped out of the shadows. Long blonde hair, jeans and a Western shirt, just like Billy Jean always liked to wear. And a couple of witnesses who were a ways off but who knew Billy Jean well enough to recognize her when she raised the shotgun and blew Kenny Sheldon into the next world.

That was the end of her as much as it was the end of him.

I knew Billy Jean was innocent. Not out of some crazy misplaced belief, but because at the very moment Kenny Sheldon was meeting his maker, I was in her bed, moaning at her touch. That first afternoon had not been a one-off. It had been an awakening that had led us both into a deeper happiness than we'd ever known before.

If I'd been married to anyone other than Jeff, I'd have left in a New York minute. But I cared about him. More importantly, so did Billy Jean. "You're both my best friend," she said as we lay in a tangle of sheets. "Until this afternoon, I couldn't have put one of you above the other. You gotta stay with him, Ruth. You gotta go on being his wife because I couldn't live with myself if you didn't."

And so I did. It might seem strange to most folks, but in a funny kind of way, it worked out just fine for us. Except of course that I still couldn't get pregnant. I began to think of that as the price I had to pay for my other contentments—Jeff, Billy Jean, Jess.

Then Kenny came back.

They came for Billy Jean soon after midnight. A deputy we'd all been at school with knocked on our door at one in the morning, carrying Jess in a swaddle of bedclothes. He looked mortified as he explained what had happened and asked us to take care of the child till morning when things could be sorted out more formally.

Jess had often stayed with us, so she settled pretty easy. That morning, I drove into town, leaving Jess with her grandma, and demanded to see Billy Jean. She was white and drawn, her eyes heavy and haunted. "They can't prove it," she said. "You have to promise me you will never tell. Don't sacrifice yourself trying to save me. They won't believe you anyway and you'll have shamed yourself in their eyes for nothing. Just have faith. We both know I'm innocent. Judge Benton isn't a fool. He won't let them away with it."

And so I kept my mouth shut. Partly for Billy Jean and partly for Jess. We'd already made arrangements with Billy Jean and her parents for me and Jeff to take care of Jess till after the court case, and I wasn't about to do anything that would jeopardize that child's future. I sat through that terrible trial day after day. I listened to witnesses swearing they had seen Billy Jean kill Kenny Sheldon and I said not a word.

Nor did Billy Jean. She said she was somewhere else, but refused to say where or with whom. Judge Benton offered her the way out. "Woman, what is your alibi?" he thundered. "If you were somewhere else that night, then you won't have to die. If you're telling the truth, give up your alibi." But she wouldn't budge. And so I couldn't. It nearly killed me.

But I never truly thought he would have her hanged.

I never truly thought he would have her hanged. I thought they'd argue she was temporarily insane because of the threat to her child and that she'd do a few years in jail, nothing more. And I was selfish enough to think of how much my Ruthie would love bringing up Jess for as long as Billy Jean was behind bars.

Sure, I wanted to make her suffer. But I didn't want her to die. She was my best friend, after all. A friend like no other. I swear, I always believed we would lay down our lives for each other if it came to it. And I guess I was right, in a way. She laid down her life rather than destroy my marriage.

When the sentence came down, it hit me like a physical blow. I swear I doubled over in pain as I realized the full horror of what I'd done. But it was too late. The sacrifices were made, the chips down once and for all.

I saw the way she looked at me in court. A mixture of pity and blame. As soon as she heard those witnesses, recognized the conviction in their voices, I think she knew the truth. With a long blonde wig and the right clothes, I could easily be mistaken for her.

There was an excuse for the witnesses. They were a way off from Kenny and his killer. But there's no excuse for Ruthie. She was no distance at all from Billy Jean that afternoon I saw them by the lake shore. She could not have been mistaken.

Why didn't I confront her? Why didn't I walk away? I guess because I loved them both so much. I didn't want to lose the life we had. I just wanted Billy Jean to suffer for a while, that was all. I never truly thought he would have her hanged.

Jess turned fourteen today. She's not old enough for the truth. Maybe she'll never be that old. But there's one thing she is old enough for.

Tonight, there will be two of us standing over Billy Jean's grave, our long black veils drifting in the wind, our tears sparkling like diamonds in the moonlight.

The Long Black Veil

Ten years ago, on a cold dark night
Someone was killed, 'neath the town hall light.
There were few at the scene, but they all agreed
That the slayer who ran looked a lot like me.

(chorus)

She walks these hills in a long black veil,
She visits my grave when the night winds wail,
Nobody knows, nobody sees
Nobody knows but me.

The judge said son, what is your alibi?
If you were somewhere else, then you won't have to die.
I spoke not a word, though it meant my life
For I'd been in the arms of my best friend's wife.

Oh, the scaffold is high and eternity's near.
She stood in the crowd and shed not a tear.
But late at night, when the north wind blows
In a long black veil, she cries o'er my bones.

An Interview with Val McDermid

Where did you grow up?
I grew up in Fife, in Kirkcaldy and East Wemyss, in a working class mining community.

Was yours a bookish household?
We didn't own books, but my parents both read. We lived opposite the town library, which is where I discovered the power of the written word.

Do you remember the first mystery novel you ever read?
The Murder at the Vicarage by Agatha Christie.

What was the first piece of music you recall?
"Scotland the Brave." Mostly because I have a very early memory of Christmas in the town square where there was a machine into which you could insert two pennies and an array of plastic soldiers would march up and down to the tinny strains of "Scotland the Brave." I also have very early memories of a Scottish lullaby called "Dream Angus."

Was yours a musically oriented household?
Yes. We listened to the radio a lot and always sang in the car. My father was a fine singer—he was the lead tenor in the concert party of the Bowhill People's Burns Club (Burns the poet, as opposed to the injury…). The decision as to which park we'd go to on a Sunday was always based on which silver or brass or pipe band was playing.

Do you listen to music when you write?
Invariably.

Has a musical work ever inspired a novel or short story?
My father used to sing a song called "The Road and the Mile to Dundee"—it was his signature piece. I wrote a story about it a couple of years ago, which is contained in *Stranded*, my short story collection. And one of my novels, *The Distant Echo*, takes its title from a Jam song, "Down in the Tube Station at Midnight." Though the book itself owes more to a Deacon Blue song called "Orphans"…

What is your favorite man madesound?
My child's voice.

What is your favorite sound in nature?
The sea on the shore.

If you had to choose three novels to take on a trip, what would you choose?
Robert Louis Stevenson's *Treasure Island*; Jeanette Winterson's *The Passion*; Reginald Hill's *On Beulah Height*.

How do you start a story?
A small, often tangential fact or anecdote sets the bells ringing inside my head. It has to be exciting, it has to clamour at the doors of my imagination. Then I play "what if" with it and find out whose story it is. Then I start to push and pull it in different directions till it starts to feel like a story.

If you had a chance to invite any three people in the world to dinner, living or dead, who would they be?
Robert Louis Stevenson, Joni Mitchell, Christopher Marlowe.

Which would you rather do—read or listen to a favorite CD?
Both. I like to have music on while I read.

*This story has the classic feel of a survival tale,
such as Jack London's "To Build a Fire."
Old Joe will remain with you, long after the story
is over. Don says: "We all dream of gathering
enough courage to confront the problems in our
life and solve them one by one. Old Joe Coulter
dreams of taking extreme measures to solve his
immediate problems. When a freak act of nature
gives him a window of opportunity, all he needs
is courage. Nature takes care of the rest."
"The song 'Stories' is simply wonderful," Claudia
Bishop adds.*

Courage

Don Bruns

He bought the shotgun for protection. That's what he told Alice. And part of that statement was true. If he ever caught them breaking into his house, he'd use it to protect himself, Rusty, and Alice. The other reason he'd bought the gun? Secretly he harbored a desire to kill them. The three hoodlums who surrounded him. Two lived in the next house to the east, one lived in the next house to the west.

Old Joe closed his eyes and saw them. *Jarrod, T. Clark and Too-Sweet stood there, taunting him. One of them had Joe's grandfather's stolen gold pocket watch, dangling it from his left hand. That was one step over the line.*

The shotgun hung from his right hand. Too-Sweet squinted at him, sneering as he spoke.

"We ought to be able to get a hundred bucks for this watch, old man. And when we do, we'll be back. You got more stuff."

Old Joe swung the shotgun up, leveling it at the 300-pound giant. He squeezed the trigger and...

He opened his eyes. Should have happened, but nothing had changed.

A living hell. That's what Alice called their life. When the two hoodlums had moved in on one side and started to terrorize them, steal from them, when Too-Sweet had moved in on the other side and played his 24-hour bass-infused rap, running his '91 Chevy truck into her wrought-iron trellis and rose bushes, knocking them to the ground time and time and time again, Alice had decided her life was a living hell. But she'd prayed for them. And prayed that she and Joe would find courage to deal with it all. Deal with it. Maybe now was the time to deal with it.

When the water started rising he'd grabbed the shotgun, his bowl of gumbo and Rusty, and headed to the roof. And now was a perfect opportunity to shoot at least one of them. But he only had one shell. One. There was one more shell on the top shelf of the closet in the bedroom. Probably too late to worry about that. It would soon be too soaked to fire.

T. Clark and Jarrod lived one house to the east. They were *so* close. He could see the color of their eyes. When the water started rising they'd chosen the roof as a safe haven too. Old Joe contemplated the deed. Spattered blood, brains, guts and a dirty brown river to wash away the evidence. But poor Alice. Prayerful Alice. She'd never forgive him. She prayed for the unholy three. And, she prayed that she and Joe would find courage.

Alice's seven-foot-high white iron trellis and rose bushes were all under water, now. He gazed out over the flooded neighborhood. The one-story houses were already completely covered by the new rising river, but in the distance, maybe four blocks away, he could see several people sitting on two-story roofs. No one was close by. No one close enough to notice as he lifted the shotgun and pointed it straight at T. Clark.

The first blast would kill him, and with any luck Jarrod would jump in the water to save himself. Courage. He needed it now. Joe closed his eyes.

Slowly, deliberately, he squeezed the trigger.

The gun jumped in his hand as the sharp explosion momentarily deafened the old man. A ragged hole of blood gaped wide open on T. Clark's chest.

He opened his eyes. Should have happened but nothing had changed.

"What you grinnin' about, *mon Vieux?*" T. Clark stared at him across the expanse. "You ain't got the balls to pull that trigger."

Old Joe looked away, staring at the murky brown water streaming by his home. At his advanced age, it was tough to realize new things about yourself. Or to confirm old things. He couldn't pull the trigger. He lacked the courage. And he doubted if he ever could find it.

He'd seen Marian float by his house maybe an hour ago. The old lady was hanging onto a big tree limb, grabbing it with both hands as her thin, frail body trailed behind. The current moved her along about a couple of miles an hour. Old Joe Coulter hoped she could hang on for a lifetime.

He sat on his rooftop, a bowl of chicken gumbo in his lap, and Rusty eyeing it, his tongue hanging foolishly from his mouth. Old Joe and old Rusty, all that was left, watching the world as it drifted by on the mucky, dirty brown water. He hefted the shotgun, feeling the weight, and thought about Papa Hemingway sticking that gun in his mouth and pulling the trigger. Two problems. First, there was only one shell. If the water came to get him he could shoot himself. Or he could shoot Rusty, trusted companion for twelve years, and make sure there was no suffering there, or, he could fulfill his dream and shoot Jarrod or T. Clark. He silently shook his head. Problem number two was that matter of courage.

Too-Sweet, the 300-pound giant on the other side, was nowhere to be seen. Maybe the high water had already claimed him. Joe could only hope.

Jarrod and T. Clark sat on their roof, laughing, making jokes as the brackish water swept past the house, working its way up to the second story. Old Joe could smell the sweet incense-like odor of marijuana, stronger than the stench of the sewage, and almost envied them. They were higher than kites. They were always higher than kites.

"Hey, old man! Can you swim?" Jarrod's high-pitched voice cut above the swirling water flowing by.

Joe ignored them.

"Hey, *bonhomme*, let's kill the dog. Should be good for a couple of meals!"

They both cackled, high-fiving each other as they laughed.

Alice had prayed for them. As they hurled insults at her, as they smashed beer bottles on her porch, as they pissed on her little wooden house at three in the morning, staining the outside walls with their sour-smelling urine, she prayed for them. While they burned her rose bushes and spray-painted her rose trellis, she prayed. When they ransacked the house, stealing everything of value, she prayed for them, and she prayed for courage for Joe and herself. Alice was dead. After fifty-five years of marriage, she was gone at seventy-eight.

"Hey, old fuck. Share some gumbo. We'd share with you."

A wooden chair swirled by, followed by what appeared to be a piano bench. Huge tree branches swept with the current, occasionally banging against the roof of Joe's house, then careening off Jarrod's and T. Clark's roof. How could water be this high? How much higher could it go?

When the water subsided, the furniture would be ruined. *If* the water subsided. The bed that he and Alice had slept in for almost forty years, the sofa and chairs. The dresser where he'd kept most of their life savings, about four hundred dollars in twenty-dollar bills, and the shotgun shell on the upper shelf in the bedroom. He looked down as if to confirm that the water *had* covered Alice's treasured trellis and roses, *had* flooded the first story and was creeping into the upper story.

The good silver had been stolen several years ago. The good television as well, along with his favorite humidor, his computer, his grandfather's pocket watch and so much more. All methodically taken as his three neighbors regularly stripped his house of anything of value. All the while Alice had continued to pray for them. And for courage. But Alice was dead. Jarrod, T. Clark and probably Too-Sweet were still very much alive.

Rusty growled a low, throaty growl, as he stared at the two thieves perched on their roof.

T. Clark growled back. "Grrrrrr! Old man, you should have died when your wife died. Now you get to suffer with the rest of us!"

Joe *had* outlived his usefulness. Now, he was just keeping time, or in this case, almost treading water. If it wasn't for the big red dog, he'd consider killing himself. They were right. He should have ended it when Alice died.

Rusty looked at him with pleading eyes, then nuzzled him with his nose, rubbing old Joe under his chin. Either he felt Joe's helplessness, or he wanted some of the cold gumbo. Joe reached into the bowl of cool liquid and pulled out a small chunk of chicken. He held it between his fingers and Rusty licked it before taking the meat and swallowing it whole.

"Easy, boy. We don't know when there will be any more."

"Hey, Padrone." T. Clark rose to his feet, awkwardly balancing on the sloped roof. He walked close to the edge, maybe ten feet from Old Joe.

Close. He and Alice had always felt claustrophobic when it came to their neighbors. Alice used to say that she couldn't turn around without the neighbors taking note. And ten years ago, when the two men had moved next door, and eight years ago when Too-Sweet had moved into the ramshackle house on the other side, she had been even more concerned.

"Pass over the soup, you senile old coot!"

Finally, Joe decided to respond. "Come and get it."

What was T. Clark going to do? Jump ten feet? Or swim over? Rusty growled again, finishing off with a sharp bark. The three had taunted the dog, several times spraying him with ammonia and one time throwing white paint on his red coat. The last time they'd broken into Joe's house and stolen his computer, they'd kicked Rusty in the ribs and locked him in the spare bedroom.

Two days later Old Joe had come home from a stay at the hospital to find his front door hanging from one hinge and his dog, wild with rage, having soiled the carpet in the bedroom.

So what was T. Clark going to do? Old Joe laid the shotgun across his lap.

"Right, old man. You're going to use the gun. Better to shoot yourself."

Rusty rumbled. His throaty growl started low, then grew, ending in a roar. He raced to the roof's edge and leaped into the air, as if to fly at the offending man's throat.

T. Clark hesitated, stepped back and slipped, his feet sliding down the roof's incline. He let go a blood-curdling scream as he realized he had no traction. He slid into the water and in five seconds was swept from sight as the newly formed river raced down what was once Kellog Street.

"Jesus Christ!" Jarrod sat there wide-eyed and shaking as his friend disappeared. "Jesus Christ!"

Rusty barked again, his paws solidly planted on the roof, then glanced at Old Joe and slowly returned to his owner, one paw in front of the next, sure-footed and confident, seeming almost proud that he'd brought down one of the dangerous duo.

One shell. He could shoot himself if the water got higher, and it definitely seemed to be getting higher. He could shoot Rusty and make sure there was no suffering, or he could shoot Jarrod. Not likely. Too-Sweet was nowhere to be seen.

Jarrod stared after the swirling water, maybe realizing for the first time the seriousness of his situation. He spun around, his eyes blazing with fury.

"I'll kill you, and the dog! No reason for either of you to live. Blood of T. Clark be on you and your damned animal."

Joe opened one eye, realizing in an instant that he'd dozed. Rusty lay to his right, one paw over his head, but his eyes slit open, keeping watch on the rising river and their neighbor. No sound except for the racing water. Planks of wood went sailing along like small ships and he saw a bloated body, face down, that hung up on a roof across the street. Hell, there was no more street.

He glanced over at Jarrod. The lone harrasser had managed to snag a couple of long planks and a small pot with a wooden handle. Like he was planning some sort of project or maybe a garage sale. Jarrod sat there, staring at the flowing water, as if waiting for his next shipment to arrive.

How long had it been? Maybe twenty-four hours? Maybe thirty-six? Did anyone know? Did anyone care? Surely someone could fly over and see them stranded on the roof.

He glanced at the house on the other side. No sign of Too-Sweet, the 300-pound marvel. The big man had cut an imposing figure as he'd walk up on Joe's porch, swaggering with each step. He'd knock on the door and when Alice would timidly answer, he'd ask for…no, he'd *demand* money. Sometimes he pulled an old 45-caliber pistol from his belt and would threaten to shoot Joe's wife, just for the fun of it. Joe had felt the barrel of the pistol as the big man used it to strike his head twice in the last three years. Old Joe still carried a faint scar behind his ear. And still Alice prayed for them. For Jarrod, for T. Clark, for Too-Sweet. And that's where the money went. Now the porch and the downstairs were buried under a river of brackish water. No sign of Too-Sweet, the third terrorist.

Rusty raised his eyes, those steady, strong eyes, and assured Joe that everything was all right. The old man closed his and drifted off once more.

He woke with a start. Rusty was no longer by his side and something else was not right. The shotgun. Not on his lap anymore. He squinted over at his neighbor's roof.

A long wooden plank stretched between the two worn shingled roofs, and Jarrod was no longer sitting ten feet away.

"Gumbo was good, old man. The dog and I finished it half an hour ago." Jarrod now sat on Joe's roof, not five feet away, leveling the shotgun at him. "One shell, *mon Vieux*. You, or your dog? Build a fire and cook the dog. You, you're too old, too tough. You just get in the water and float down to T. Clark."

Rusty crouched on the far side of the roof, that low rumble coming from somewhere inside. Not fear, never fear from the big red animal. Just an uneasy growl. He'd been fed a couple of bites by the enemy, but here was a man who had kicked him, snarled back at him, tortured him for years, and even with a dog's brain the animal knew who was a friend and who wasn't.

Old Joe thought about what they'd done to Alice. The torment, the grief, the stealing and the constant threat of danger from the three gangsters. What they'd done to her precious home. To the last years of her life. Maybe it was time to join her. But giving this drug-addled idiot the satisfaction of winning went against everything he believed in. And Jarrod just sat there with his squinty eyes and his greasy hair, daring Joe. Making a game out of it.

Joe took a deep breath. Courage. He needed it now. Should have done it a long time ago. He closed his eyes.

"You just lost your friend, and Two-Sweet is nowhere around." Joe nodded at the house next door. "So, do you think you can do this by yourself? Kill me? Kill the dog? Do you think so, punk?" His voice in his ears sounding a little Clint Eastwood, Dirty Harry style. Joe rose up, reaching over and scratching Rusty behind his long ears.

"What are you doing, crazy coot?" Fear in Jarrod's eyes. Raw fear.

Joe stepped to the cowering, sniveling weasel of a man and pulled the shotgun from his lap, grabbing it by the barrels. With the swing of a big-league-hitter, he hit Jarrod across the face with the stock of the gun. With a sickening thud the thug's face exploded, his nose smashed wide against his cheekbones. Another vicious swing, and his lips split, broken teeth spilling from his mouth—

Joe opened his eyes. Should have happened but nothing had changed. There was no courage, and the tormentor still sat there, studying the old man.

"I'm going to eat dog for dinner, old fart. Skin him, cook him and eat him. And who's to stop me? You? The cowardly lion?" Jarrod laughed loudly. "Hell, we could have raped your old woman and there's nothing you could have done." He grinned, his yellow-stained teeth bared against pale skin. The skinny little man propped the shotgun against his knee and he reached into his T-shirt pocket with his right hand, pulling out a pre-rolled joint.

"I may be here for a while, *bonhomme*. I've got wood, matches, a cooking pot, and I've got the dog. I hear the Chinese have excellent recipes for dog." He glanced at the other house next door, yelling, "Too-Sweet? Are you alive, *mon*?"

With his free hand, Jarrod pulled a pack of matches from his pocket and lit the cigarette, sucking loudly as the weed caught fire.

Rusty growled and cautiously walked to Joe's side.

Courage. Old Joe lunged for the shotgun, ignoring the pain that shot through his arthritic back and arms. Jarrod lurched and the shotgun fell from his knee, skittering down the roof as Rusty leaped at the intruder. The big red animal's paw caught firmly in the trigger guard and the gun exploded with a deafening roar.

The old man looked up from his sprawled position, his eyes wide with shock. His nemesis sat two feet away, half his neck gone. Jarrod grabbed his throat, dropping the cigarette. His hands dripped with blood as he realized his plight. He looked at Joe and his eyes clouded over as his head collapsed against his chest.

Rusty whimpered, shaking his paw to free it from the shot-gun, finally loosening his appendage. He carefully stepped over to Old Joe and nuzzled his face, trying to get the sprawled man to sit up.

Joe saw the head, sticking out of the upstairs window in the house to the west. Too-Sweet had responded to the shotgun blast and was checking to see what had happened. Maybe he'd seen old Joe as he pushed Jarrod's bloody body into the mud-brown water. Maybe he had ducked back into his own flooded house to find a weapon. Maybe he was preparing to take old Joe out and finally end the tormenting. And who would protect Rusty? My God, the dog had more than proven himself this treacherous day. And who would be left to protect the memory of Alice?

Too-Sweet apparently was still able to keep his head above water. There was still breathing room in the upstairs. But the water was rising.

Joe's box with the remaining shotgun shell was in the closet on the high shelf. The old man slowly leaned over the edge of the roof, lowering one foot, then the other, onto the open window ledge. His old back ached as he eased himself through the window, up to his neck in the filthy water. He waded to the closet and reached up, as high as he could. Outside he could hear the whine, as Rusty frantically called for him. He felt the rounded tube in the box, and cupped it in his hand, holding it high in the air to keep it from getting wet.

Back on the roof, he pushed the shell into the chamber. He only needed one. The water was definitely rising. Above the wrought-iron trellis and rose bushes, flooding the small first story and now neck deep in the upper story. Too-Sweet could drown for all he cared, but if he didn't—if the single, remaining terrorist finally climbed onto the roof, it was Joe's turn. Rusty could sit this one out. Joe would find the courage somewhere. Maybe. Then he saw him again, the big man's head, hanging out the window, watching the racing water as it careened past the row houses. Joe's heart raced as he watched the huge man climb out of the window and crawl up on his roof.

"I saw you, you old fuck. You pushed Jarrod off the roof. And T. Clark? I figure you and your red friend found a way to rid yourself of him. Ain't gonna be so easy over here."

The big man pulled his pistol from the waistband of his jeans. "See this? Now you do, now you don't." He pointed the barrel at Joe, calmly, as if he'd killed people all of his life. "Goodbye, neighbor."

Old Joe closed his eyes, then slowly opened them. This time it had to happen, and there had to be a change. He picked up the shotgun, feeling the comfortable weight balanced in his two hands as he glanced at Rusty.

"This one's mine, old friend. Just don't ever tell Alice."

He'd drifted off again. A foggy dream played in his head, where Alice clipped the rose bushes, pruning the branches and cutting the dying flowers. And T. Clark's voice barked loud and clear.

"Mother fucker! Should have killed you years ago."

The old man's eyes snapped open and he saw the dripping wet, long-haired thug coming up from the other side of the roof.

"A ghost, Padrone!"

Rusty cowered, the first time Joe had ever seen fear in the majestic red animal.

"Back from the dead, asshole. I caught a tree limb. Saved my ass. Climbed around the house holding on to the gutters. Thought I was gonna die. I proved it, you old goose. Absolutely nothing gonna keep me down. Good to see you again!"

Joe struggled to stand and grabbed for the shotgun, suddenly realizing there were no more shells, as T. Clark launched himself at the old man. His hands grabbed Joe by the throat as they both thudded to the roof's surface.

"Good night and good riddance, you fuck!"

Now Rusty barked, loud, ferocious barks as he moved around the struggling men. Joe heard him and saw him as the dog circled the two in a weird dance, looking for an opportunity to strike. But Joe was in a struggle for his life. He dug deep for the courage that Alice had prayed for, his weak tired arms trying to push T. Clark off him.

"Time for your swim, old man."

Joe freed his right hand with all of his remaining strength and jammed his thumb into T. Clark's left eyeball, driving the orb deep into the man's skull. The big man screamed a scream that hung in the air forever and let go of Joe, as Joe pushed back. T. Clark clawed at his face, stood up, staggered and plunged off the roof with a huge splash, going deep into the muddy water. He never came up.

Old Joe and old Rusty, all that was left, watching the world as it drifted by on the murky, dirty brown water. The rancid smell probably had something to do with garbage, with raw sewage, and possibly with two dead bodies that floated somewhere down the newly formed river. Possibly the smell had something to do with a third dead body impaled on a submerged wrought-iron rose trellis slightly below the surface of the water. A trellis that once was covered with Alice's rose bushes that brought her so much joy.

Sooner or later someone would see Joe and Rusty, up on the roof. Maybe a rowboat, maybe a helicopter, someone would notice and send them some food. In the meantime, they stared at the passing menagerie: the glass bottles and aluminum cans, the tree limbs and broken shrubbery torn from the earth, and on the far side of the stream about eighty soggy cartons of Salem cigarettes as they drifted by.

Alice had prayed for the three neighbors. Maybe somewhere, Alice was now praying for Joe and Rusty. Praying for courage. And maybe all of her prayers had been answered. Old Joe closed his eyes and slept.

Stories

My father played piano, in a bar in old Key West
And as a young boy growin' up, I believe he was the best.
He played for drunken sailors, his stories set to song,
He played for barroom ladies, who helped him sing along.

(chorus)

He told of far away places, sailing ships and races,
He told of love gone right and wrong, closer to his home.
He said a man must live a story, of love and pain and glory.
Tell it to the world and then, he's given all his best.

(chorus)

My father thumped a bible, in a hall in New Orleans,
And as a man of middle age, I listened to his dreams.
He'd hypnotize, he'd mez-morize, with his stories from
     that book,
And everyone who came and heard, a part of him they took.

(chorus)

My Father died a pauper, not a penny to his name,
And as the man who is his son, I celebrate his fame.
He made all mankind richer, with the stories that he told,
Money never mattered, it was the stories that were gold.

(chorus)

He told of far away places, sailing ships and races,
He told of love gone right and wrong, closer to his home,
He said a man must tell a story, of love and pain and glory,
Tell it to the world and then, then he's earned his rest.

An Interview with Don Bruns

Was yours a bookish household?

My father read Shakespeare to me and my three brothers when we were three or four years old. My grandmother and grandfather made up fascinating serial stories and told them to us until we were into our teens, and I remember subscribing to *Alfred Hitchcock* magazine when I was ten or eleven years old.

Do you remember the first mystery you ever read?

I don't remember the first mystery novel I read. Probably the Hardy Boys or Nancy Drew. I remember a short-lived series about a boy detective named Ken Holt. One plot from the Holt series still sticks with me, and someday I'm going to bring it back.

What was the first piece of music you recall?

The first piece of music I recall is actually a song I wrote at about five years. It was a western ballad about cowboys, so I must have been listening to Gene Autry or Roy Rogers, the singing cowboy.

Was yours a musically oriented household?

Mom and Dad had a great collection of records and we'd listen intently to a couple of albums every week. 40's music, big band, jazz. Then I discovered the top 40 on WOWO in Fort Wayne. Wow!

Do you listen to music when you write?

I do listen to music when I write, and I'm probably influenced by the mood of the piece I'm listening to. A song is a short story. A good song is the best example of editing. I listen to a piece like Jimmy Buffett's song, "Fins," and it's a fabulous three- or four-minute story. (Contributing author Tom Corcoran was a co-author of "Fins.") And instrumental songs, like Bill Moody's song in this book, can tell a great story as well.

What is your favorite manmade sound?
My favorite manmade sound? Probably a well-played chord. Guitar, piano, or four-part vocal harmony.

If you had to choose three novels to take on a trip, what would they be?
Three novels? *Mystic River, Get Shorty,* and *South Beach Shakedown: The Diary of Gideon Pike,* my latest novel, so I could point to it and tell people, "see, I write!" I'd always choose a mystery, and those three because I love the characters. Very strong.

Three records/CDs? Boston Pops doing the *Grand Canyon Suite*, "Meet the Beatles," and the soundtrack to *The Graduate*.

If you had a chance to invite three people in the world to dinner, living or dead, who would they be?
Three people to dinner? Would they have to get along? Jesus Christ, Abe Lincoln and Ed McBain. We'd certainly cover a wide variety of subjects.

Which would you rather do, read or listen to music?
Read or listen. That's an impossible decision.

Any wishes for readers?
Support the arts in school. If kids aren't taught music, drama, and the visual arts, we're looking at a very color-less future.

Curtain Call

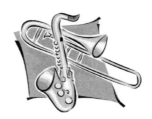

Curtain Call

Song Credits

"Moody's Mystery Blues"
Arrangement: Robert Joslin

"Time to Kill"
Lyrics and arrangement: Rupert Holmes
Production: Wendy Isobel Music, Inc. (ASCAP), 2006

"If I Had Wings"
Arrangement: Janet Lee/Al Stewart
Producer: Finnis Sound

"Something Out There"
Lyrics and arrangement: John Lescroart
Performance: John Lescroart, vocals; Frank Seidl, vocals; Dave Chancellor, guitar and background vocals; Chris Amato, drums; Odell Robenson, bass; Richard Montgomery, sound effects
Production: Richard Montgomery, producer; Doug Chancellor, engineer; Soundfarm Studios, 2006

"It's Too Late to Cry"
Lyrics and arrangement: Jim Fusilli

"Land of the Flowers"
Lyrics: Mary Anna Evans
Music: David Evans
Performance: Mary Anna Evans, lead harmony and vocals; David Evans, guitar and harmony vocals; David Reiser, guitar; Bill Hutchinson, percussion; Annemieke Pronker-Coron, fiddle
Production: Mirror Image Studios, 2006

"Be My Poodle"
Lyrics and arrangement: Nathan Walpow
Performance: Andrea Cohen, vocals; Nathan Walpow, vocals and instruments
Production: Nathan Walpow

"The Ferryman's Beautiful Daughter"
Lyrics: Peter Robinson
Arrangement and performance: Don Bruns

"Another Day Without You"
Lyrics: Jeffery Deaver
Arrangement and performance: Don Bruns
Vocals: Rob Layton

"Ophelia's Revenge"
Lyrics: Claudia Bishop (Mary Stanton)
Arrangement: Greg Sattcherwaite
Production: Chuck Hemann, Palm Beach Sound Studio, 2006

"Bone Island Mambo"
from *Deadline Penitentiary,* 2004
Lyrics and arrangement: Jim Hoehn and Tom Corcoran
Performance: Jim Hoehn, vocals; John Inmon, guitars; Bob Livingston, bass and harmony vocals; Floyd Domino, piano and keyboards; Zach Taylor, drums and percussion
Production: Larry Joe Taylor, executive producer; John Inmon, producer; Zach Taylor, engineer; Jim Urban, Third Coast Studio

"The Long Black Veil"
Arrangement and production: Phil Smith, Reddish Room Studios
Performance: Val McDermid, lead vocals and guitar; Phil Smith, back-up vocals, guitar, and percussion/synthesizers

"Stories"
Lyrics and arrangement: Don Bruns

The Performers

Claudia Bishop (Mary Stanton) is the author of *The Hemlock Falls* mystery series and *The Casebooks of Dr. McKenzie* mystery series, and the editor of three mystery anthologies, *Death Dines at 8:30*, with Nick DiChario, *Death Dines In*, with Dean James, and *A Merry Band of Murderers*, with Don Bruns. As Mary Stanton, she is the author of two adult novels and eleven middle-grade novels. She also writes for television. Born in Florida, she grew up in Japan and Hawaii. Her career as an actress/singer was confined to community theater until she was hired as a nightclub singer in Minneapolis. (She was fired soon after.) The *Merry Band of Murderers* song "Ophelia's Revenge" was inspired by the silliest of Mozart's concerti for French horn. "A lifetime of modestly rowdy behavior has left me with no voice at all," she admits. "If it hadn't been for Greg Sattcherwaite, the musician who made the 4th Horn Concerto singable, and the technical wizardry of Chuck Hemann at Palm Beach Sound Studios, who made me able to sing it, I would have booted the whole project." She can be reached at claudiabishop.com.

Rhys Bowen is British by birth, and childhood summers spent with relatives in a little village in North Wales were the inspiration for the setting and eccentric characters in her Constable Evans mystery series.

Rhys grew up in England, was also educated in Germany and Austria, then studied at London University before landing a job with the BBC. She worked in all aspects of radio production, including announcing on the Overseas service, before deciding to specialize in drama. While working in BBC drama, she began writing her own plays, several of which were produced by the BBC. She also sang in folk clubs with such luminaries as Al Stewart and Simon and Garfunkel.

Longing for sunshine, she went to work for the ABC in Australia and would have stayed there had she not met her future husband, who was California bound. While in Australia she started drawing a daily cartoon for the Australian national newspaper.

When Rhys arrived in San Francisco, she found no opportunity for her talents similar to her BBC position, so she began writing children's books. Her first picture book, written under her married name of Janet Quin-Harkin, won many awards, including a *New York Times* "Best Book of the Year."

More picture books followed until she moved on and up to young adult novels. Under the name Janet Quin-Harkin she has written almost one hundred books for children and teenagers, including a number one bestseller, and many popular series of her own. Her books have sold about five million copies worldwide.

Eventually she decided to write what she likes to read. Taking a big gamble, she borrowed her grandfather's name and began to write the Constable Evans mysteries, set in her grandfather's corner of the world. The series achieved instant critical acclaim. *Evan Help Us* was called "a jewel of a story" by *Publisher's Weekly* and was nominated for a Barry award. In 2005 *Evan's Gate* achieved the ultimate distinction and was a finalist for the Edgar Award, best novel.

In 2001 Rhys began a second series, this one set in turn-of-the-century New York and featuring feisty Irish immigrant Molly Murphy. The first title in the new series, *Murphy's Law*, was an instant success, winning the Agatha Award for best mystery this year, as well as the Reviewer's Choice and Herodotus awards for best historical mystery. It was also named a finalist for the Mary Higgins Clark award. The second Molly Murphy mystery, *Death of Riley*, was released in December 2002 and also nominated for the Agatha and Reviewer's Choice Awards. The third book, *For the Love of Mike,* won the 2004 Anthony Award at the World Mystery Convention for best historical mystery, the Bruce Alexander Memorial Award for best historical mystery, and the Freddie for the perfect historical, and received a starred review in *Kirkus*—the toughest of all the review publications. It was also a finalist for the MacAvity Award, given by Mystery Readers International.

Rhys has also contributed short stories to several anthologies. Her short story "The Seal of the Confessional" was nominated for both the Anthony and the Agatha awards in 2001. Her story "Doppelganger" was an Agatha nominee and won the Anthony Award at the world mystery convention for best short story. It was selected for the World's Best Crime and Mystery fiction anthology.

Her story "Voodoo" was the lead story in the October *Alfred Hitchcock Mystery Magazine* and nominated for an Anthony award.

Rhys is a former president of Mystery Writers of America, Northern California Chapter. She is a frequent speaker at conventions, bookstores and libraries. When not writing she still loves to sing, play her Celtic harp and travel. She can be reached at rhys@rhysbowen.com.

Don Bruns is a mystery writer and songwriter, dividing his time between Ohio and Florida. Bruns writes from experience about the gritty underworld of the entertainment industry, having traveled as a road musician for eight years. His books, *Jamaica Blue, Barbados Heat,* and *South Beach Shakedown,* reflect his travels, and Don travels "whenever I get the chance"—to the Caribbean, Europe, all over the United States and an especially memorable trip to Havana, Cuba. He also enjoys oil painting, and his artwork hangs (he claims) in a lot of people's basement closets. "They only bring it out when I visit."

Under pressure, Don admits that he's been fortunate in his reviews, "so far!"

Here are a few:

"Hot off the presses. *Barbados Heat* delivers exactly that… heat. Bruns' read won't let you down. It's a good look at another of the voices of rock and roll.…" —*Deadly Pleasures Mystery Magazine*

"In *Jamacia Blue*, Don Bruns has carved out his turf; sex, drugs, and rock and roll and murder. What more could you want?"—Sue Grafton

"A bright fresh dead-on debut from a great new voice. Buy it now and get in on the ground floor.…"—Lee Child.

Tom Corcoran's fifth Key West-based Alex Rutledge mystery, *Air Dance Iguana*, was published by St. Martin's Minotaur/Thomas Dunne Books in November 2005. Tom first moved to Florida in 1970. He has been a disc jockey, bartender, AAA travel counselor, Navy officer, freelance photographer, and automotive magazine editor. Tom's author photos have appeared on numerous book jackets, including those of Thomas McGuane (*An Outside Chance*), Winston Groom (*Forrest Gump*), and Florida novelists Les Standiford (*Black Mountain* and *Last Train to Paradise*) and James W. Hall (*Hot Damn*). His photographs also have appeared on seven Jimmy Buffett album covers and on numerous promotional and sheet music items (plus the annual Jimmy Buffett Calendar). Tom co-wrote the Buffett hits "Cuban Crime of Passion" and "Fins."

Jeffery Deaver is a former journalist, folksinger and attorney. Jeffery's novels have appeared on a number of best seller lists around the world, including *The New York Times*, the *Times of London* and *The Los Angeles Times*. The author of twenty-one novels, he's been nominated for six Edgar Awards from the Mystery Writers of America, a Steel Dagger and a Short Story Dagger from the British Crime Writers' Association, an Anthony Award, and a Gumshoe Award. He is a three-time recipient of the Ellery Queen Reader's Award for Best Short Story of the Year and is a winner of the British Thumping Good Read Award.

His book *A Maiden's Grave* was made into an HBO movie staring James Garner and Marlee Matlin, and his novel *The Bone Collector* was a feature release from Universal Pictures, starring Denzel Washington and Angelina Jolie. His most recent books are *The Twelfth Card, Garden of Beasts,* and *Twisted: Collected Stories.* And, yes, the rumors are true, he did appear as a corrupt reporter on his favorite soap opera, *As the World Turns.*

The song Jeff wrote for the short story "The Fan" is a down-home, heartland country-western song about love and longing. He wrote the lyrics first, then plucked out the melody on his old Martin D-35. Although he didn't perform in the country-western genre when he was a professional musician, he "likes the passion, raw emotion and cleverness of the best CW music," and thought it would make a good motif for a dark, twisted crime story, set in the Nashville world.

Readers can visit his website at www.jefferydeaver.com.

Mary Anna Evans is a lifelong music lover and, after 18 years, considers herself an adopted Floridian. Her first novel, *Artifacts,* received the Benjamin Franklin Award for best small press mystery, as well as the Patrick D. Smith Florida Literature Award.

Publishers Weekly said of *Artifacts* and its protagonist Faye Longchamp, "Few corners of Florida remain un-mined for crime fiction and now, happily, there's one less...Readers should welcome this strong new sleuth."

Relics, second in the Faye Longchamp archaeological mystery series, was an IMBA bestseller, and it has been nominated for the SIBA book award, given by independent booksellers in the southeast. *Publishers Weekly* said of *Relics,* "Evans' second archeological mystery is every bit as good as her debut, *Artifacts.*"

Mary Anna's short fiction has appeared in *A Kudzuchristmas, Plots With Guns,* and *North Florida Noir.* Her next novel, *Effigies,* will be published by Poisoned Pen Press in February 2007.

Mary Anna and David Evans live in Florida with their three children, approximately 20 musical instruments, and a cat. Her song for "Land of the Flowers" came in second place in the Florida 2006 Best Folk Song contest.

Jim Fusilli is the author of the award-winning Terry Orr series, which includes his current novel *Hard, Hard City*, named Best Novel of 2004 by *Mystery Ink* magazine. He's also the author of *Closing Time, A Well-Known Secret*, and *Tribeca Blues*, which feature New York City-based private investigator Terry Orr and his daughter Bella. In 2005, his book on Brian Wilson and the Beach Boys' album *Pet Sounds* was published by Continuum.

Jim also writes for *The Wall Street Journal*, for which he has served as a rock and pop critic since 1983, and is a contributor to National Public Radio's "All Things Considered." His book reviews have appeared in the *Los Angeles Times* and the *Boston Globe*.

Jim's crime series has enjoyed glowing reviews from readers and critics. "A wonderful new voice," reported *The Providence Journal*. "Superior," said *The Boston Globe*, which called Jim a "courageous and original writer who works against the grain of expectations."

"Fusilli is simply incredible," said Bookreporter.com. "(He) is that rare writer who both created and fulfilled the promise of greatness of his first novel...the ongoing creation of a new legend."

Jim has been praised for his vivid prose, particularly his depiction of his beloved New York City. Said *The New York Times*, "Jim Fusilli's noir novels are like cobblestones—smooth and hard and deeply embedded in the streets of New York." According to *Kirkus Reviews*, Jim's "noir prose is peerless, as is his darkly romantic portrait of the Big Apple."

And *The Washington Post* said, "If you've ever been in love with New York City—even for an instant—this book is for you."

Of *Closing Time*, the debut novel in the series, Robert B. Parker said, "Jim Fusilli paints a dead-perfect picture of contemporary New York City. It is a lovely story, full of tension and heartbreak, and, in the relationship between Terry Orr and his 12-year-old daughter, renders the intricacies of parenthood as few novels have."

Jim lives in New York City with his wife, Diane, a public relations executive. Their daughter, Cara, attends college in New York.

Rupert Holmes

Two-time Tony and two-time Edgar award winner Rupert Holmes has spent much of his career creating innovative works that frequently fuse mystery and music. As a singer-songwriter, his recording of *Brass Knuckles* became the first pop tune to be reviewed in *Ellery Queen's Mystery Magazine*, and his lyrics have since been reprinted in several *EQMM* anthologies. In 1986, he became the first person in theatrical history to singly win Tony awards for both Best Book and Best Score, for his Broadway musical *The Mystery of Edwin Drood* (which also won the Tony for Best Musical). He was given identical honors by the New York Drama Desk and yet another award in their additional category of Best Orchestration. His Broadway comedy-thrillers include the Edgar award-winning *Accomplice* and the Kennedy Center's record-breaking *Solitary Confinement*. Other plays of comedy and suspense seen on regional stages include *Thumbs* and his theatrical adaptation of R.L. Stine's internationally best-selling *Goosebumps* books.

His first novel, *Where the Truth Lies*, about the dark side of a music and comedy duo, was deemed one of Booklist's Top Ten debut crime novels, received a Nero Wolfe award nomination for Best American Mystery Novel, and was recently made into a motion picture written and directed by Atom Egoyan and starring Kevin Bacon and Colin Firth. (*Newsweek* called Holmes' novel "a delectable, wonderfully witty novel that will have you tossing and turning pages all night!" while the *Chicago Sun-Times* enthused, "Every debut should be so good!") His current mystery novel for Random House, *Swing*, is set in the 1940s and includes an original Big Band score (released on CD with the hardcover edition, now downloadable at www.RupertHolmes. com) containing additional musical clues to the book's solution. (Janet Maslin of *The New York Times* called it "Imaginative, smart and impressively elaborate, a sophisticated foray into musical mystery plotting!" while *The Pittsburgh Post-Gazette* declared, "It may be the best historical thriller of the year—certainly it is the most creative!"

Holmes is also the creator and writer of the Emmy award-winning television series *Remember WENN*, which featured several mystery episodes series songs, and he also provided the musical underscore. His non-mysteries include the recent Broadway hit *Say Goodnight, Gracie,* about the life of George Burns—for which Holmes received the 2003 National Broadway Theatre Award for Best Play and yet another Tony nomination in the same category. His latest mix of melody and murder is the musical comedy *Curtains,* which makes its pre-Broadway debut in 2006 at the Ahmanson Theatre in Los Angeles, featuring a book by Holmes and a score by Broadway legends John Kander and Fred Ebb (*Cabaret, Chicago*).

Rupert Holmes began his career as a pop singer-songwriter whose work has been recorded by many of the outstanding vocalists of our time, from opera star Renee Fleming to pop star Britney Spears, from jazz vocalist Cleo Laine to rap artist Wyclef, and most notably and frequently by Barbra Streisand, for whom he has written, arranged and conducted several multi-platinum recordings, including the album *Lazy Afternoon* as well as his original songs for the Golden Globe-winning score of *A Star is Born.* Holmes himself has had several top ten gold records as a recording artist and has charted in Billboard's #1 position in the United States, Canada, Australia and Japan.

To learn more about this author-composer whom *Newsweek* calls "a Renaissance man" and the *L.A. Times* deemed "an American treasure," visit www.RupertHolmes.com.

John Lescroart is a *New York Times* bestselling author of seventeen novels, including most recently *The Hunt Club.* He has also written thirteen books in the San Francisco based Dismas Hardy/Abe Glitsky series, and a couple of Sherlock Holmes pastiches: *Son of Holmes* and its sequel, *Rasputin's Revenge.* His books have been translated into fifteen languages in more than seventy-five countries, and his short stories have been included in several anthologies.

His first novel, *Sunburn*, won the San Francisco Foundation's Joseph Henry Jackson Award for best novel by a California author, and both *Dead Irish* and *The 13th Juror* were, respectively, nominees for the Shamus and Anthony Best Mystery Novel. *Guilt* was a Readers Digest Select Edition choice. A short story, "The Giant Rat of Sumatra," was included among the Best American Mystery Stories of 1998. The last several of John's books have been Main Selections of one or more of the Literary Guild, Mystery Guild, and Book of the Month Club. All of John's books, except *Sunburn*, are still in print.

In 2000, he founded CrowArt Records to facilitate releasing his music and that of his friends. Under the CrowArt label, *Date Night* is a CD of John's original music performed as solos by master pianist Antonio Castillo de la Gala, and *As the Crow Flies* is a ten-song geographic journey, with John singing his own tunes, accompanied by some terrifically accomplished musical acquaintances. Currently John is finishing work on another CD entitled *Whiskey and Roses*, featuring many of his original country & western songs. Finally, "Django Latino" features David Grisman Quintet alumnus and multi-instrumentalist Joe Craven interpreting the music of the great gypsy musician Django Reinhardt to the authentic rhythms and instruments of various Latin American cultures.

His song "Something Out There," from this collection, shows a new side of John as he delves for the first time into the genre of scary power pop. John and his musical guru and producer Richard Montgomery spent a night of careless drinking working out the arrangement, arguing as usual about arcane musical topics such as the inclusion of a 1-4-5 structure, the unusual instrumental figure between the first and second verses, and a weird F# that John wanted coming out of nowhere, but eventually peace and consensus prevailed. The next day, the session was at Soundfarm Studios in Vacaville, California, with Doug

Chancellor as engineer (and scary whisperer). Doug's brother Dave Chancellor, a monster in his own right, was there to play electric and ebo-lead guitar and sing background vocals. That's Chris Amato on the very-hot drum tracks and Odell Robenson cooking on bass. Frank Seidl, now a wine executive extraordinare but at one time John's college roommate and singing partner in the Two Alone, drove down from Sonoma for some nice harmonic vocal licks. And finally, Rick Montgomery chipped in again with the closing "creaking door." The pros had the basic track down, soup to nuts, in about three hours, after which Doug premixed the levels and EQs. Two more hours on the final mix the next day, and the song was complete.

Outside of the book and music world, John loves to cook. His original recipes have appeared in *Gourmet* magazine and in the cookbook *A Taste of Murder.* (He also wrote the Foreword to Francine Brevetti's paean to the famous San Francisco eatery Fior d'Italia entitled *The Fabulous Fior: 100 Years in an Italian Kitchen.*)

John and his wife, Lisa Sawyer, have two children and live in Northern California. He is working—perennially—on his next novel.

Val McDermid

Crime writer Val McDermid grew up in Kirkcaldy, Scotland, and studied English at Oxford University. She trained as a journalist and worked on various national newspapers for 14 years before becoming a writer. Her first published book was *Report for Murder* (1987), and since then, she has written a large number of crime novels. These include three different series of books: The Lindsay Gordon mystery series which comprises *Report for Murder* (1987), *Common Murder* (1989), *Final Edition* (1991), *Union Jack* (1993), *Booked for Murder* (1996), and *Hostage to Murder* (2003); the Kate Branningan mystery series which comprises *Dead Beat* (1992), *Kick Back* (1993), *Crack Down* (1994), *Clean Break* (1995), *Blue Genes* (1996), and *Star Struck* (1998); and the Dr. Tony Hill and Carol Jordan mystery series which comprises *The Mermaids Singing* (1995), *The Wire in the Blood* (1997), *The Last Temptation* (2002), and *The Torment of Others* (2004).

The Wire in the Blood has been made into a successful television series. Her latest book is *Stranded* (2005), her second collection of short stories. The first collection, *The Writing on the Wall and Other Stories* was published in 1997. She is also the author of a book of non-fiction, *A Suitable Job for a Woman: Inside the World of Women Private Eyes* (1995). Her next crime novel, *The Grave Tattoo*, is due in 2006.

Val McDermid was a crime reviewer for the *Manchester Evening News* for four years, still writes occasional journalism, and broadcasts regularly on BBC Radio 4 and Radio Scotland. Her work has been translated into more than 30 languages.

Bill Moody was born in Webb City, Missouri, and grew up in Santa Monica, California. A professional jazz drummer, Bill has played and/or recorded with Jr. Mance, Maynard Ferguson, Jon Hendricks, Annie Ross, and Lou Rawls. He lived in Las Vegas for many years as a musician on the Las Vegas Strip, hosted a weekly radio show at KUNV-FM, and taught in the UNLV English Department. He now lives in northern California, where he teaches creative writing at Sonoma State University and continues to be active in the Bay Area jazz scene with the Terry Henry Trio and Dick Conte's trio and quartet. He is the author of five Evan Horne novels: *Looking for Chet Baker, Bird Lives!, Sound of the Trumpet, Death of a Tenor Man*, and *Solo Hand*. His new novel, *Boplicity,* will appear later this year.

About his work Bill says: "The connection between playing jazz and writing crime fiction is a strong one for me. A jazz musician begins with the framework or the song—the chords, the structure, the form—but during a solo, he doesn't know what he's going to play or how until he reaches that part of the song. Writing crime fiction for me is a similar process. Working from the basic structure of the crime novel, I then improvise on a premise or motif, if you will, and I'm a fervent advocate of the 'what if' game during the writing process."

Peter Robinson is the author of sixteen Inspector Banks novels. The fifteenth, *Strange Affair,* was chosen as one of the best books of 2005 by the *Globe and Mail,* the *South Florida Sun-Sentinel* and *January Magazine.* He has also published two non-series novels, *The First Cut* and *No Cure for Love,* and a collection of short stories called *Not Safe After Dark.* His novels and short stories have been translated into more than sixteen languages, and he has won a number of international awards, including the MWA Edgar, the CWA Dagger in the Library, the Martin Beck Award from Sweden, the Danish Crime Academy's Novel of the Year Award, and the French Grand Prix de Littérature Policière. He has also won five Crime Writers of Canada Arthur Ellis Awards. The sixteenth Inspector Banks novel is *Piece of My Heart.*

Nathan Walpow writes the Joe Portugal mystery series. The most recent entry is *The Manipulated.* Nathan was born and raised in New York City, arrived in Los Angeles in 1979, and squandered the 1980s trying to make it as an actor. His fifteen minutes of fame came in 1985, when he was a five-times-undefeated champion on *Jeopardy!* In 1992, on a whim, he took a short story class and began kicking out stories, most of them science fiction or fantasy. Reading the complete works of Raymond Chandler prompted a switch to crime fiction.

In the third Joe Portugal adventure, the rock-and-roll-midlife-crisis-crime-novel *One Last Hit,* Joe picks up his electric guitar after a decades-long hiatus and tries to put his teenage band back together. Life imitates art: soon after the book was published, Nathan restrung his 1968 Fender Coronado II and began rocking once more, soon appearing at B.B. King's Blues Club with a Procol Harum cover band. He now owns twelve guitars and innumerable other musical gadgets.

Other Joe Portugal mysteries include *Death of an Orchid Lover* and *The Cactus Club Killings.* Nathan's short story "Push Comes to Shove" appeared in *The Best American Mystery Stories 2001*. He recently co-edited the anthology *Landmarked for Murder*. He is a former president of the Southern California chapter of Mystery Writers of America. His website is at www.walpow.com.

To receive a free catalog of Poisoned Pen Press titles, please contact us in one of the following ways:

Phone: 1-800-421-3976
Facsimile: 1-480-949-1707
Email: info@poisonedpenpress.com
Website: www.poisonedpenpress.com

Poisoned Pen Press
6962 E. First Ave. Ste. 103
Scottsdale, AZ 85251